Praise for Robert Asprin's M.Y.T.H. series

"Stuffed with rowdy fun."   —*The Philadelphia Inquirer*

"Give yourself the pleasure of working through the series. But not all at once; you'll wear out your funny bone."
                                        —*The Washington Times*

"Hysterically funny."   —*Analog*

"Breezy, pun-filled fantasy in the vein of Piers Anthony's Xanth series . . . a hilarious bit of froth and frolic."
                                        —*Library Journal*

"Asprin's major achievement as a writer—brisk pacing, wit, and a keen satirical eye."   —*Booklist*

"An excellent, lighthearted fantasy series."   —*Epic Illustrated*

"Tension getting to you? Take an Asprin! . . . His humor is broad and grows out of the fantasy world or dimensions in which his characters operate."   —*Fantasy Review*

continued . . .

ROBERT ASPRIN'S
MYTH-QUOTED

JODY LYNN NYE

ACE BOOKS, NEW YORK

THE BERKLEY PUBLISHING GROUP
Published by the Penguin Group
Penguin Group (USA) Inc.
375 Hudson Street, New York, New York 10014, USA

Penguin Group (Canada), 90 Eglinton Avenue East, Suite 700, Toronto, Ontario M4P 2Y3, Canada (a division of Pearson Penguin Canada Inc.) • Penguin Books Ltd., 80 Strand, London WC2R 0RL, England • Penguin Ireland, 25 St. Stephen's Green, Dublin 2, Ireland (a division of Penguin Books Ltd.) • Penguin Group (Australia), 707 Collins Street, Melbourne, Victoria 3008, Australia (a division of Pearson Australia Group Pty. Ltd.) • Penguin Books India Pvt. Ltd., 11 Community Centre, Panchsheel Park, New Delhi—110 017, India • Penguin Group (NZ), 67 Apollo Drive, Rosedale, Auckland 0632, New Zealand (a division of Pearson New Zealand Ltd.) • Penguin Books, Rosebank Office Park, 181 Jan Smuts Avenue, Parktown North 2193, South Africa • Penguin China, B7 Jaiming Center, 27 East Third Ring Road North, Chaoyang District, Beijing 100020, China

Penguin Books Ltd., Registered Offices: 80 Strand, London WC2R 0RL, England

This is an original publication of The Berkley Publishing Group.

This is a work of fiction. Names, characters, places, and incidents either are the product of the author's imagination or are used fictitiously, and any resemblance to actual persons, living or dead, business establishments, events, or locales is entirely coincidental. The publisher does not have any control over and does not assume any responsibility for author or third-party websites or their content.

PUBLISHING HISTORY
Ace trade paperback edition / December 2012

Library of Congress Cataloging-in-Publication Data

Nye, Jody Lynn, 1957–
Robert Asprin's Myth-quoted / Jody Lynn Nye. — Ace trade paperback ed.
p. cm.
ISBN 978-0-425-25701-2 (alk. paper)
I. Title. II. Title: Myth-quoted.
PS3564.Y415R63 2012
813'.54—dc23
2012026173

PRINTED IN THE UNITED STATES OF AMERICA

10 9 8 7 6 5 4 3 2 1

To the loving memory of Anne McCaffrey, great writer, friend, and mentor. We already miss you, missus.

CHAPTER ONE

*"No, there's no extra penalty for
wrong answers."*

—M. DE TORQUEMADA

They all came at me at once, eyes gleaming, teeth bared.
I braced myself, one lone, tall, young, skinny Klahd
with blond hair and blue eyes surrounded by hostile
beings of many colors, shapes, and sizes, bearing weapons of
extreme discomfort, all bent on taking me apart.

"Mr. Skeeve, Mr. Skeeve!" the first one cried. She was a
fuchsia-faced Imp woman dressed in an eye-piercing yellow jumpsuit. She shoved a stick with a metal mesh folded over its top
into my face. It smelled of perfume. "What do you think of the
Magik Reform Legislation? Don't you think it unfairly favors
M.Y.T.H., Inc., over other practitioners?"

"Uh, no comment," I rejoined.

"Is it true you sleep with a teddy bear?" a huge, pale-faced
Ghoul with a heavy jaw demanded, leaning eagerly over his
notepad. "How about underwear? Boxers, briefs, or loincloth?"

"The teddy bear doesn't wear any," I said, thankful for a

question I could answer. "But I'm just taking care of him for a friend. He has his own bed."

I had more to deal with than just questions. Foot-high bipeds with pale green skin and dressed in wisps of black silk bounded around me, smacking me in the legs with the hard edge of their tiny hands. Ouch! I danced in pain. The Injas shrieked triumph. I winced. The reporters moved in again. A Werewolf with glowing red eyes aimed a pencil at me.

"What's the source of your magik? Is it true you stole it from the treasury in Possiltum?"

The very absurdity of the question threw me off. I backed away. A huge hand landed on my shoulder and spun me half-way around. I gawked up at a stone-faced Gargoyle hefting a hammer in his free claw. He swung it at my head—where my head might have been if I had hesitated an instant. The wind from it whistled past my nose. Summoning magik from a force line beneath the floor, I pushed off from the ground with my mind and fled up toward the ceiling—where five giant spiders had woven an immense web in the shape of a pentacle. The glowing, sticky fibers seemed to reach for me. At my approach, the spiders scuttled along the incredibly narrow threads in my direction. I recoiled. My skin crawled faster than the webspinners. I hate spiders.

I did a back flip and fled down to the floor, where the reporters converged on me again. The Injas did another number on my legs. A shapely female Whelf with long golden hair framing her pointed ears loomed over me.

"What about the upcoming audit of the M.Y.T.H., Inc., ledgers?" she demanded. "What are you trying to cover up? What about this Bunny person? Is it true she is connected to Don Bruce?"

"What audit?" I squeaked, flinching. My voice tends to reach into the upper registers when I'm caught off guard. The Injas unsheathed twin blades crossed on their backs with over-hand strokes and came at me, shrilling sharp war cries.

I kicked them away. They tumbled in a heap, but were on their feet again in a moment.

The Gargoyle waded in among the reporters, swinging the war hammer. I ducked. My hair stirred as the metal block just missed me. The Gargoyle panted, his eyes red with fury.

"Don't deny it, Mr. Skeeve," the Whelf woman said severely, pursuing me even as I scrambled backward away from my giant attacker. The Injas kicked me in the shins. "All that gold had to go somewhere."

"No comment!" I bellowed.

Suddenly one of the huge spiders dropped down between us on a strand of glowing blue. The beast's body was at least as long as I was tall. Well-trained reflexes took over. I struck a pose and held up my palm. Flames licked up from my fingers. I thrust them toward the dangling monster. It flinched but didn't retreat.

Instead, the spider stretched out its two front legs to me. I gagged and recoiled at the sight of the bow-shaped claws. Then I noticed that between the claws was a bundle of pink the size of my fist. A baby spider looked up at me with its multiple-faceted eyes glowing with innocence. One small claw held a knitted toy fly. I glanced at the adult spider's face. Its own eyes wore an expression of fear, not hostility. I gawked. The flames in my hand died away.

"You want me to protect her?" I asked. The big spider nodded. My stomach turned.

"I can't . . ."

The urgency in the creature's face turned to desperation. I'm not sure how I could distinguish that on such an un-Klahd-like face, but I did.

". . . think of anything else I'd rather do," I finished. I gulped. Beating down the revulsion I felt in every muscle of my body, I put out a hand for the small arachnid.

Ugh! It felt just as horrible as I thought it would. The pointy little feet trailed strands of silk across my palm. It reminded me of nightmares I had had of being trapped in a giant web. The mother zipped up the line into the rafters, leaving me with the baby. The reporters crowded close, some holding up cameras so the Shutterbugs inside could draw pictures of us.

WHAM! Something heavy struck me in the back, sending me flying into the nearest wall. I had forgotten about the Gargoyle! It hefted its hammer again and came toward me. My back felt like one big bruise, but I pushed myself up off the ground.

Intently aware that I must not close my hand on the infant spider and crush her, I regathered my handful of flame. The Gargoyle swung. I threw a fireball at it. The Gargoyle batted it into the crowd of journalists. The Ghoul reached up and caught the ball in his bony hand. He closed his fingers, and the fire snuffed out. The Gargoyle started swinging at me again. I cradled my unwanted charge against my chest and flung myself backward, ducking every blow. I threw more firepower at my opponent, but he countered every measure. Gargoyles might have been primitive as far as dress and choice of weapons went, but they could handle magik far better than a Klahd like me. The press crowded around the two of us, clamoring for an exclusive interview with us.

Or with the Gargoyle, anyhow. As the mass of bodies engulfed us, I ducked down and crawled on my three free limbs along the floor and darted beneath the Gargoyle's stony legs. By the time the puzzled Gargoyle noticed I was missing, I was sitting on top of a rafter, hands behind my head, letting the baby spider take a walk along the rim of the iron chandelier.

The reporters looked around, then up.

"Mr. Skeeve, you don't get away from us this easy!" the Imp woman shouted. "Give us at least one good reason why you shouldn't be prosecuted for stealing an entire army."

"Sorry, no comment," I called down to her.

"But the audit . . . ?" She tried to levitate to my level. I put out a hand and pressed down. The magik force knocked her to the floor.

"No comment," I repeated. She scrambled up and tried to climb the air again.

"Awright, you slackers," Aahz growled, seeming to materialize out of nowhere. At least one of the "reporters" jumped with surprise. You would, too, if a Pervect with green-scaled skin, yellow eyes, bat-winged ears, and a mouthful of four-inch fangs popped into the room. Aahz is several inches shorter than I am, and a dozen times more impressive. "You blew it. Take a walk."

"Awww, Aahz," the Whelf moaned. Her fine head drooped. I felt sorry for her.

"C'mon, Aahz, just one more round," the Gargoyle said, resting his mace on his shoulder, his doglike face creased with disappointment. "I was gaining on him!"

"Harvey, that was the most pathetic onslaught I ever saw!" Aahz said. "You only connected with him once. Collect your fee from Guido before I change my mind about paying you."

"You try a decent melee with Injas bouncing around your feet," Harvey grumbled, but he headed for the door. The little creatures filed out behind him, calling insulting gibes at the large beast. The "reporters," all actors from various dimensions, put their gear away. The Imp woman smiled up at me.

"You sure know how to avoid a question," she said. "I might ask you for some pointers some time. For when I do interviews after a play."

"Sure, Babe," I said, "but Aahz is the one who taught me how to deal with the press."

She looked at Aahz hopefully, but he shook his head.

"Another time, Babe," he said. "We've got a meeting."

Something touched my arm. I turned. A pair of enormous, faceted eyes were inches from my own.

"Aagh!" I jumped away from the giant spider, who was hanging upside down beside me. "What do you want?"

"You gonna give Katinka back to Rosalie, or do you plan to keep her?" Aahz said. He grinned. "You gotta get over that thing of yours with spiders."

"I'm okay," I said, scowling. "She just startled me. My mind was somewhere else."

"It was in Arachnophobialand," Aahz said. "Move it. Bunny wants us to meet her three o'clock client."

I thought about using magik to pluck the small creature from her romps on the lamp fixture, but the gigantic mother might get upset. I crawled out on the rafter. Katinka decided this must mean I wanted to play. I had to chase her around the lamp twice before cornering her inside a glass chimney. I scooped up the pink spiderlet. She danced enthusiastically all over my hand. Trying not to shudder, I crept back and handed her over to the hovering Rosalie. Katinka descended a tiny pink line to her mother's waiting grasp. When she did, I noticed that she had left a heart-shaped web on my palm.

"See, they're not so bad," Aahz said, grinning.

I ignored him and led the way out of the room.

CHAPTER TWO

*"You can judge a man by the company
he keeps."*

—F. SINATRA

Bunny smiled up at us from behind the desk. Her office, formerly mine, as the president of M.Y.T.H., Inc.,[1] had been redecorated until no one would doubt to whom it belonged. Everything was tidy and so clean that a dust mote would look out of place. Stylish knickknacks were placed here and there on tabletops and desktops. I had no idea what some of them were, but they were pretty spiffy and absolutely nothing that I would ever in a thousand years lay out money to buy. Bunny had had the walls moved outward so that there was space for armchairs for every partner when we had meetings, which was at least once a week when everyone was in the Bazaar there in Deva.

The expansion itself didn't cause any hard feelings among

---

1. For details on this bloodless coup, see the fine volume *Myth-Chief*, available from your better booksellers.

the rest of us. It didn't rob anyone of office or living space. We had plenty of room to spare.

If you had come upon our headquarters on the loud, hot and crowded street of the Bazaar, you would be unimpressed by the humble, narrow tent with artistically distressed patching on the flap, jammed into the gap between two larger and more impressive pavilions full of showy merchandise, but once inside, you'd have gasped out loud. Our headquarters has only a door in Deva. The rest of the facility extends into another dimension, where we own enough property to expand to suit our needs. That dimension is Limbo, whose denizens are vampires, werewolves, and other beings that I associate with night and horror, though they are pretty peaceful neighbors overall. I had been out the rear door into Limbo only a few times since we had moved in. Aahz would not go near it unless forced; they had tried to execute him once, so he bore a grudge. A Pervish grudge was a lot more difficult to live with than vampires and werewolves, so we kept contact to a minimum.

Since I had rejoined M.Y.T.H., Inc., we had undergone a change of management. When we had founded it, I was its president. Now Bunny, niece of Don Bruce, Fairy Godfather of the Mob, was our leader. Her style was far different from mine. I had been involved but casual in terms of organization and oversight. I trusted my partners and expected them to come through on their assignments without a lot of oversight by me. Bunny trusted us, too, but she liked to hold meetings at least once a week, to keep track of progress and let the rest of us know where things stood. For all the underlying rivalry that still existed between Aahz and me, we were united in our belief that all those meetings were overkill, though we had to admit it seemed to be working. Nothing had fallen into the cracks since Bunny took over. As Aahz often said, if it works, don't fix it.

Almost all of my partners were present. Tananda, a shapely, green-haired Trollop from the dimension of Trollia, lounged delectably in a silken cushion. Her brother Chumley, a Troll, as the males were known, was between seven and eight feet tall and covered with shaggy purple hair, and his moon-shaped eyes were two different sizes. He sat upright on a wooden ladder-back chair that groaned under his weight, taking notes on a jotting pad in handwriting so neat it could have come off a printing press. Guido and Nunzio, a pair of big, muscular Klahds, lately of Don Bruce's service but seconded to M.Y.T.H., Inc., for years now, lurked in a corner, their backs to the wall and their eyes on the door. The former enforcers were good friends of ours. Pookie, another Pervect and Aahz's cousin, and Spyder, her Klahdish cohort, were dressed in elaborate purple robes with hoods that reached up over their heads and nearly touched their noses. They were on long-term assignment in another dimension.

A visitor but occasional contractor perched in a doll-sized rocker beside Bunny's desk. Markie was a former enemy who looked like a very young Klahd girl but was actually an adult from her home dimension of Cupy. She was a very useful operative, since no one would suspect her on sight. She, too, was on assignment, as the small daughter of a very wealthy king in Bandero who had been the victim of an attempted kidnapping plot by Fairies. Instead of her usual casual attire, she wore a pink velvet dress with full lace petticoats, and her blond hair, in corkscrew curls, was adorned with a sparkling tiara. A doll in matching clothing lay underneath the rocker. I was looking forward to hearing her update. Her description of life in the Bandero court was lively, and her one encounter so far with her would-be abductors left my ribs aching from laughter.

The last member of the company present was Gleep. He is my dragon. For his own species he is very young, but he is as smart as a whip. He can talk, but I'm the only one who knows it. The rest of my friends think all he can say is "Gleep!" We haven't let them in on the secret.

I sprawled in my personal armchair. A fresh fruit juice waited in the padded holder just a few inches from my hand. I like a glass of wine once a day—more than that and I regress to a state of my life I am ashamed of—but the lack of it meant Bunny wanted no chance of my mind being fuzzy. That had happened only once, when I drank some Pervish wine Aahz brought back from his home dimension. I should have known that would be trouble, since the wine hadn't stopped moving yet.

Have I described Bunny yet? She's well worth a close look. Small of stature but voluptuous of figure, especially on top, Bunny had caused plenty of our clients to forget about their purpose in coming when they saw her. She has deep-red hair cut short. It curls forward to frame small, perfect ears and high cheekbones in a heart-shaped face. Her wide eyes are flower blue. She has a turned-up nose, a rosebud mouth, and a decided chin. It has decided to be pointed and pert, and no one I know would disagree with it. That day she had on a tight-fitting, two-piece suit of leaf green. The skirt was short enough to cause my pulse to race, though I had long ago promised myself to regard Bunny as a trusted friend and associate only. Visitors who saw only a pretty, vacuous-seeming face, as I had when I first met her, were thrown off guard by the incisive brain behind it. She had a degree in accounting and a firm grounding in her uncle's business. She never failed to collect the fees we negotiated. Clients found it hard to say no to her. I know I did. If I had to surrender the presidency to anyone, she was the best choice.

"How'd he do?" Bunny asked, turning the wide blue eyes on Aahz.

My partner slid into his own custom-made recliner. The scalp massager moved forward to get to work on the scales between his ears.

"Not so great," Aahz said. "He's got to get used to dodging nosy questions under any circumstances. Sometimes reporters bring in their own muscle to beat answers out of interviewees."

"I thought I did okay," I protested, hurt. "You think you could have done better?"

"In my sleep," Aahz said, firmly. "On a bed of nails with sumo wrestlers playing tennis on my back."

I opened my mouth to ask what a *sumo* was, then shut it. "I didn't answer any questions I didn't want to."

"But you gave them information. Your expressions, the tone of your voice, all that tells them something that you didn't want them to know. You lost control of the situation. They saw your loss of confidence. That interview would have made every evening news broadcast on Perv, and you'd have looked like a fool. But nice save on the spider. You figured out they were good guys just in time. Rosalie said Katinka had fun." He leered playfully at me. "You want to sit for her Friday evening?"

"I'll be busy," I said firmly. "No matter when it is."

"You probably will," Bunny said with a cheerful grin. She sensibly refused to get involved in our ongoing rivalry. "I have assignments for both of you. And I want you present when I talk to this next caller."

"Miss Bunny?" a resonant tenor voice inquired from the door.

"Come in, Mr. Weavil," she said, gesturing the newcomer forward. By the look on her face, Bunny was uneasy with our potential client.

I was used to all kinds coming in to get M.Y.T.H., Inc.'s help. When the visitor entered, I suddenly understood why Bunny had all the partners and Markie on hand instead of seeing him alone. His aura felt creepy.

"Good afternoon, my friends," he said, turning to beam at us with a broad set of gleaming white teeth. He came around to grasp each of our hands and shake them vigorously, meeting our eyes with his large, sincere brown orbs. He was slim, with pale, shiny brown fur; a long snout; sharp, square teeth; furry ears that stood up on each side of his head; and narrow paws on his short arms and legs. "Emo Weavil. Proud to make your acquaintance! What a fine-looking bunch you are! Miss Bunny, I can't tell you how gratified I am that you are allowing me to meet so many of your associates today."

Gleep rose to a crouch. A growl erupted in his throat. A dragon's growl isn't like a dog's that warns you that you're under surveillance and you had better behave or leave. It's more like a reminder that you are in the presence of a really dangerous being who is sparing you from violent death only because at the moment it isn't worth his while to kill you. Weavil's eyes widened for an almost imperceptible moment, then eased. The smile increased in intensity.

"And what a fine dragon! Look at those scales! They are so shiny I can see my face in them."

Gleep was not placated by the compliment.

I distrusted Emo Weavil on sight as much as my dragon did, but I wasn't sure why. He seemed oily and dishonest—living in the Bazaar, you learned to size people up on sight—but that wasn't unusual. It was the depth of dislike I felt that surprised me. Even Tanda, who felt that showing off her pulchritude was the most natural thing in the world, pulled the lapels of her bodice closer together and moved a hand nearer to the dagger in her boot.

Bunny's voice was just above ice cold. "Please sit down, Mr. Weavil."

"Sure, sure, if you like!" He settled himself in the seat Bunny pointed to with the aplomb of a king. I noticed it was one of the uncomfortable iron chairs we kept when we didn't want a visitor to stay for long. "This certainly is an amazing place! It matches everything I've ever heard about your company."

"State your case, Mr. Weavil."

The abruptness of Bunny's tone didn't faze our visitor at all. He opened his huge brown eyes in a show of sincerity. "I would just love to! I want all of you on my side. I need the kind of help that only M.Y.T.H., Inc., can provide. I don't think I can get fair play unless you come and help me—help all of us. You see," he added, hooking his thumb into the lapel of his jacket, "I'm running for the office of governor of the fine island of Bokromi in the dimension of Tipicanoo."

I groaned quietly to myself. No wonder we distrusted him! He was a *politician*.

"Oh, I say," Chumley burst out. Astonished, Emo Weavil turned to stare at him. Trolls generally communicated with denizens of other dimensions in monosyllabic grunts. "Me mean, I say twist head off!" In emphasis, he threw his notebook into his mouth and chewed on it.

"No, no!" Emo protested. "I am trying to run an *honest* race! That's why I am here. I am under siege! My efforts to keep things all aboveboard and open are being attacked! The Friendship Party has entrusted me with its candidacy. I must not fail it. M.Y.T.H., Inc., is my last hope!"

Bunny rose.

"I'm sorry, Mr. Weavil. I don't think there's anything we can do for you."

Weavil remained seated. "But, dear lady, why not?"

"I don't think we want to get involved in something as dirty as politics. It's such a . . . *filthy* occupation." Bunny shuddered, a gesture that made her flesh quiver interestingly.

Emo regarded her with hurt astonishment, an expression that looked natural on his pleasant, almost innocent face.

"But aren't you Don Bruce's niece? The boss of an, er, organization? And you won't help me?"

"I'm sorry," Bunny said, with a bright, friendly smile that I knew meant trouble. "I may come from a Mob family, but there are some depths to which even we won't stoop. Have a nice day."

Evidently, Emo Weavil had run into plenty of falsely cheerful expressions in his time.

"I see. Well, thank you all for your time," he said, giving the rest of us a sorrowful look. His shoulders sank and his head drooped forward. The resonant voice choked with unshed tears. "I had to try—I believe in the effort of the underdog. And I had raised a substantial war chest for my campaign, too."

He was the picture of dejection as he rose from his seat and shuffled sadly toward the door. I felt my heart turn over with sympathy.

Then I shook myself. What a master manipulator! We were better off not having anything to do with him.

But before he reached the door, Aahz lifted a finger.

"Wait a minute. What's the rush?"

"Why shouldn't he leave, Aahz?" Bunny asked.

Aahz's eyes gleamed. "I think we could be of assistance to an honest servant of the people."

Emo bounced back into the room. "Well, well! I knew a Pervert couldn't resist jumping in to a fascinating situation!"

"That's Per-vect!" Aahz snarled. Emo reversed two paces, then recovered.

"That is just what I said," he declared. "Please, friend Per-vect, put in a good word with your lovely and discerning employer here."

"Why not?" Aahz shrugged, just a little too casually. "There's no reason we shouldn't hear him out, when he came this far to talk to us, is there, Bunny?"

"Aahz, he's a politician!"

"Unelected," Aahz pointed out. "Doesn't make him a dishonest, slime-eating crook *yet*."

Bunny let her shoulders drop. "True. All right, go ahead."

"With pleasure." Aahz turned to our visitor. "So, Emo—I can call you Emo, can't I?—How much is *in* this war chest? In the interest of honest financial disclosure, of course."

"Aahz!"

"It's a fair question," Aahz said. "Well, Emo?"

Emo could not have missed the implication, not if he knew *anything* about Pervects. He ran a finger around the inside of his collar. "But, my scaly friend, these funds are to promote my case with the people, to publicize the direction in which I want to take the administration. I am an amateur. This is my first try for elected office. I'm an outsider."

"Naturally we'd like to help you," Aahz purred, "but we don't work for free. Can you pay us?"

"Of course I can! Whatever you ask . . ." He looked at the avid expression on Aahz's face. ". . . Er, within reason."

"Then maybe we can help you . . . under certain conditions."

Emo began to look hopeful. "That would be fantastic, friend Pervect!"

I immediately detected a flaw in Aahz's suggestion.

"Now, wait just a minute, Aahz," I said. "If we threw our efforts behind Mr. Weavil, we'd overbalance the election in his favor. He'd win!"

Aahz lifted an eyebrow. "And what's wrong with that?"

"He said he wants a fair election!"

"There's no such thing," Aahz insisted.

"Why not?" I asked.

"Because it's impossible!"

"Isn't the impossible our specialty?" Tananda asked, with a raised eyebrow. She was baiting Aahz, and all of us knew it, but he winked at her.

"I want to win," Emo said, "though my intention is to win fairly. You can help me to do that, my dear friends."

Aahz grinned. "Now I know you're a politician. You are trying to talk out of both sides of your mouth at the same time."

I looked at our visitor. His mouth looked ordinary to me. "How could he talk any other way?"

"It means he t'inks he can be on both sides of the argument at the same time," Guido translated.

"No! I mean, you can make sure that my election will be a fair one. In our dimension, polling cannot go ahead unless all candidates agree. I absolutely cannot unless I am sure that it will be an honest and evenhanded fight. But my opponent spikes me at every turn. It has caused the election to be delayed five years!"

"Who is your opponent?" Pookie asked.

"My cousin, Wilmer Weavil-Scuttil. He knows every trick in the book."

"I doubt that," Markie said, making a face. "Tipicanoo isn't even on the main drag as far as ingrained corruption goes. He probably doesn't even know all the tricks in Volume One."

"Well, he knows enough!" Emo said. "He used some kind of magik on my nominating petitions so every one of the

twelve thousand signatures was the same—mine! I had to get
them all over again! And every reporter in my last press briefing fell asleep! The only way to wake them up was to kiss
them—and, well, one does what one must for one's country—
but that's typical of his perfidy and arrogance. Pernicious
rumors about me have spread throughout the press. My wife
is embarrassed every time she opens the morning paper. And
the mudslinging!"

Aahz waved a hand. "That's nothing. Name-calling is part
of the cost of doing business. What fun is an election without
mudslinging?"

"Not that kind of mudslinging. Real mud! Sticky, gooey,
swamp mud, sometimes with frogs and snails still in it!
Wilmer has no morals. That is why I *must* win. For the good
of Tipicanoo."

"And I suppose you're totally innocent of wrongdoing,"
Nunzio said, in a surprisingly high voice for a man of his size.

"I am!" Emo protested, with a hand flattened on his chest.
"You will never find a single person who can tie me to any
antisocial or illegal act, even with regard to my outrageous
cousin. What about it, friends? Can I count on you? Work
with me."

Bunny put a thoughtful finger to her chin.

"I can see that the only answer is for us to moderate this
election," she said.

"Wonderful!" Emo exclaimed.

". . . And that means we have to be paid by both sides,
not just you. The same amount from you and your cousin."

"Oh, no!" Emo looked horrified. "I mean . . . That's not
what . . . I'm not sure he'll go along with that."

Aahz shrugged. "Sounds like he should."

"He'll have to," I said firmly. "If he hears that we're coming
in as your consultants, the only way that *he* can ensure a fair
competition is if he hires us, too."

"Well, I don't want to have an unfair advantage . . ." Emo
began weakly.

"Baloney," Aahz said. "You wouldn't be much of a politician if you didn't take advantage."

"But what if I don't win?"

"That's the meaning of a fair election," Bunny said. "You said that's what you want. Those are our terms. Still want to hire us?"

Emo's head drooped. I could tell he wanted us only for his own purpose, but for appearances' sake if nothing else, he had to give in. "I have little choice. This campaign has gone on for five years! We have to settle it soon, or the electorate is going to revolt. The deadlock has to be broken. Very well!" He smashed a fist into his palm. "I will be the one to break it!"

Bunny stood up. "That's settled, then. We need to talk to your cousin."

CHAPTER THREE

"And the winner is . . . none of the above!"

—THE VOTING PUBLIC

Wilmer Weavil-Scuttil, the candidate for the Wisdom Party, looked at us from underneath shaggy white brows. They and the bouffant white wig on his head were as false as the long brown lashes that Emo wore. I had the same uncomfortable feeling about him that I had had about his cousin.

"I'm an old servant of the people," Wilmer drawled, putting a thumb behind the shoulder of the vertical straps that held his trousers up over his potbelly. He looked as if he had been an athlete in his youth, but his body had gone soft since. Not his mind. His eyes followed me and Bunny with shrewd intelligence. "Long time. Don't see that it's necessary for us to indulge ourselves in expensive consultants." He said the word *consultants* in the same tone I would use for *poisoners.* "But if you take the question to the people, I might consider calling the election soon. I want to represent their government; therefore, it is their money I'd be spending on you and your company. They have the final say! Otherwise, not a penny wasted! Did you get that, my dear?" he asked a slender, pretty Tipp with fair, golden-brown fur seated on a stool at the side of the large, sunny office. She was jotting rapidly in a small, blue-bound notebook. A rakish hat sat aslant on her fluffy hair. A small white card was stuck in its band.

"Yes, Mr. Weavil-Scuttil," she said, without looking up.

"According to your opponent," I said, "it's your, uh, subterfuges that have caused the delay in the first place. We just want to ensure a fair election so it can go ahead."

"That's a vile lie!" Wilmer thundered. "My opponent is causing all the difficulty. If he wants a fair election, then he has to stop his infernal tricks and come out fighting fair and square!"

"You know, he told us the same thing about you," I said, with an innocently bland expression on my face. Wilmer lowered his false brows fiercely.

"If I were guilty of half the ruses, subterfuges, and downright dirty trouble that he has engineered against me and my campaign, then I deserve to go to prison, not the governor's mansion! What makes you think that my opponent will give over and allow a fair election?"

"Because he came to us," I said, spreading my hands. "If he wasn't serious, then he's foolish to involve M.Y.T.H., Inc. We'd find out soon enough if he were the one stalling the election."

"Well, I'm doing no more than is necessary to get my message out unobstructed to the electorate!" Wilmer declared, one finger in the air. "I want the people to know that I am the best candidate, bar none!"

"Our job is to make sure the election goes smoothly," I said. "We'll get to the bottom of the tricks."

"See that you do!" Wilmer said, shaking a majestic finger at me. "I should have been governor years ago! I can't wait forever . . . a Tipp of my, er, maturity, you understand."

"Of course. So, if we get a consensus, you will pay half of

our fee?" Bunny asked, fluttering her eyelashes at him. "And expenses?"

A male of any species would have to be dead not to respond to Bunny's flirting. Wilmer's fierce expression melted into benevolence.

"Why, certainly, my dear! If the people speak, then I as a faithful servant will have to answer. Did you get that?" he asked the reporter.

"*Yes*, Mr. Weavil-Scuttil."

"Make sure it hits the front page, if you would be so kind," he said, with a slight inclination of his head that was meant to be a bow but came off as patronizing. "Thumb position, of course."

"That's up to my editor, Mr. Weavil-Scuttil." The reporter sounded slightly peeved but kept a pleasant smile on her face. I guessed he always asked for preferential treatment, and she always had to remind him it wasn't her job to offer it. Wilmer was unperturbed. He turned back to us.

"Best of luck to you!" he wished us. "I look forward to facing a fair fight. That's the only kind worth fighting. Did you get that?" he asked the reporter.

"*Yes*, Mr. Weavil-Scuttil."

We shook hands with the candidate and set out into the sunshine. I was about to ask Bunny where she thought we should start, when the reporter circled around to get in front of us.

"Just a few questions," the young female said. She grabbed our hands and shook them vigorously. "Ecstra Talkweather, *Morning Gossip*. Do you really think you can break the deadlock that has kept Bokromi from holding an election for five years?"

"That's what we're here to do," Bunny said evenly.

"The money's the reason you came, isn't it?" Ecstra asked, a skeptical eyebrow raised.

"No! Our reputation for fairness is worth more than mere money," I said.

"But who is going to believe that?" Ecstra asked. "This is

just another ploy by Emo Weavil to get the voting going so he can stuff the ballot boxes, isn't it?"

"*Another* ploy?" I asked, and wished I hadn't. I bit my tongue. Never let a reporter think he, or in this case she, knows more than you. If Aahz had been there, he would have slapped his forehead in disgust. Or mine. Ecstra's eyes narrowed craftily.

"So you are being scammed as well? Wow. Maybe you had better pull out now before your *reputation* gets dragged through the mud, and I mean mud!"

"We've heard about the mud," Bunny said, her own eyes narrowing. "Sounds like you're working for Wilmer. Isn't that a violation of journalistic integrity?"

Ecstra's brows drew down over her petite nose. "Who said I was?"

Bunny raised a chestnut eyebrow. "I infer it from the fact that you believe what he tells you about Emo Weavil."

I watched in admiration. Bunny was much better at being interviewed than I was.

Ecstra waved her arm. "I don't have to believe him! I've seen the dirty tricks myself! We all have. I hardly have to work to find stories for the *Morning Gossip*. There's a new prank every single day, no matter what you heard. Some of them are really rotten," she added with glee.

Bunny and I looked at one another. I raised a brow meaningfully. There seemed to be a lot that Emo hadn't told us. Bunny's eyes told me that she would find out what at the earliest opportunity.

Ecstra shook her head. "I should tell you, I'm fluent in Glance. And Innuendo."

"Would you care to bring us up to date on the Weavil cousins?" I asked, hastily breaking off my silent conversation.

"In exchange for what?" Ecstra countered. "The free press runs on information."

"We'll answer questions related to our business here," Bunny said. "Reserving the right to refuse to discuss anything proprietary."

"Okay," Ecstra said, cheerfully. "Sounds good. Come on back with me to the newspaper. The editor will want to meet you!" She set off at a brisk trot down the cobblestoned street, dodging carts and foot traffic.

I had never seen a town like this one. Instead of houses and shops, it had big glass windows and doors set into the wall of a high, steep, raked cliff and the lines of uneven foothills facing it. Magik was strong here. Some of the carts were beast-drawn, but just as many ran with nothing between the traces or hooked to the yoke pulling them. I saw several force lines both overhead and underground, a white-hot line running right up the middle of the street, a jagged red line. Beneath us was a wavy blue line, crossing the red line near Wilmer Weavil-Scuttil's office and another point in the distance that I couldn't see yet. Ecstra seemed as unaware of them as Bunny, so I didn't mention them. I filled up my internal batteries with magik, just in case.

However, we couldn't miss the colorful posters and pictures that were plastered on most vertical surfaces throughout the town. They were campaign posters for both Wilmer and Emo, featuring poses of both men in heroic, sage, or exaggeratedly friendly expressions. At least some of the images were colorful. Others had faded in the sun or fallen victim to vandalism, in some cases pretty creative vandalism. A mustache drew itself over and over again on a picture of Emo Weavil, making him look sinister and foolish at the same time. The largest image of Wilmer had been similarly defaced. His eyes crossed and uncrossed, and his tongue protruded off the surface of the poster. Passersby didn't notice or even look up. I could tell the broadsheets had been there a long while, possibly the entire five years that this campaign had been going on. Shiny, translucent purple and green dots the size of my palm decorated walls everywhere.

In the gutter were the scraps of more posters and pamphlets, some torn to shreds. The Tipps around us seemed to be divided among three groups: those wearing Emo's green campaign rosette attached to their clothes or fur, those sporting Wilmer's purple ribbon, and the last and largest with no insignia at all. I stopped a mature male Tipp in the third category.

"Excuse me, sir," I said. "I notice that you don't seem to be affiliated to either of the candidates running for governor. May I ask why?"

"Because I can't stand this fliffing-floffing election one more day!" the Tipp said with a fierce expression. "Are you tied up with either one of those fools running for office?"

"I'm with M.Y.T.H., Inc.," I said. "We're an independent concern from Deva trying to facilitate getting the voting under way."

"You are?" the man said, seizing my arm. "Bless you, stranger!" He grabbed me around the neck and kissed both my cheeks. He bestowed the same salute on Bunny, who blushed prettily. Then he hurried away whistling, a spring in his step.

"Wow," I said.

At my side, Ecstra had taken out her notepad and was scribbling avidly.

"If everyone wants the election to be over with, then why are Emo and Wilmer holding back on setting the date for Voting Day?" Bunny asked.

"They don't want to take a chance on losing. The job's for life if you can get it," Ecstra explained, putting the notepad back into the pouch hanging at her side. "Incumbents tend to get reelected over and over again. And there are all kinds of perks, like plenty of patronage jobs to hand out to friends and relatives, like unrestricted access to the treasury—Bokromi's wealthy, if you can believe it."

I scanned the littered streets and ill-maintained walkways. Piles of stinking garbage and animal dung were heaped in the gutter. Passersby had to veer to avoid them. Even the beasts of burden stayed clear of the debris.

"You couldn't tell to look at it."

Ecstra shrugged.

"Well, with no one in charge of government, no one's handing out city contracts. Even the maintenance wizards weren't getting reimbursed for their time, so they quit en masse a couple of years ago. Tipps who can do it fix their own sidewalks, but the rest of us fall in potholes all the time. It's the press's editorial conclusion that neither Emo nor Wilmer wants to declare a date unless he's absolutely sure of winning. *I* wouldn't. Come on. I want you to meet my boss." Ecstra beckoned us to follow her.

CHAPTER FOUR

*"The police are not here to create disorder;
they're here to preserve disorder."*

—R. J. DALEY (THIS IS A *REAL* QUOTE)

On the corner outside the newspaper office on the street at the foot of the cliff was the first activity I'd seen in town. Two large groups of Tipps faced off against one another, shouting slogans and brandishing signs. One group waved green *Vote for Emo* banners in the faces of purple-streamer-carrying *Elect Wilmer* devotees. They clearly disliked one another, but the animus had a weariness about it, like relatives who never got along but were forced to deal with each other for decades at family parties. After five years, I couldn't blame them. I wondered if our other associates polling in other parts of the town were running up against the same attitude.

"Emo, no! Emo, no! Emo, no!" one group chanted. "Weavil-Scuttil's the only way to go!"

"Wilmer Scuttil's out-of-date! Vote for Emo! Now! Don't wait!"

A heavyset and prosperous-looking male Tipp in a chalk-striped charcoal-gray jacket and a bow tie sat on a wooden chair propped up on its back legs in the doorway of the glass-fronted office. He grinned at the crowd through a haze of cigar smoke. Ecstra brought us over and introduced us.

"Skeeve, Bunny, this is my boss, Tolomi Papirus, editor in chief of the *Morning Gossip*." He shook our hands and gestured us to a couple of empty chairs.

"What are they doing here?" I asked, nodding toward the crowd. "Why aren't they rallying near the candidates' offices?"

"Who'd see them there?" Tolomi asked, with a casual wave. "This is where they get covered by the press."

I glanced behind him. Other Tipps were hard at work in the office, but none of them were standing by with pencil and paper. "I don't see any reporters."

Tolomi waved a hand.

"Oh, my people are already writing up the story. We know what's going to happen. There's the copy of the speeches they're giving." He gestured to the cluttered table behind him. I picked one of them up. The parchment was dog-eared and creased. The date at the top right of the page had been crossed out and rewritten several times.

"This looks like they've used it before," I said.

"There's not much new to say about the election," Tolomi said. "This has got to be some kind of record, for the time between declaration and voting."

"You don't seem upset about that," I said.

"It sells papers, my boy! History in the making!" he said, leaning back. He pointed at the middle of the crowd. "Wait, here comes some action."

Two Tipps hauled an upturned wooden box onto the pavement, and a middle-aged female dressed in green clutching a large handbag stood up on it.

"My friends, I want to ask for your support for my friend and colleague, Emo Weavil! You can trust him with your vote. He will make an excellent governor. I have listened to everything he has said about his plans, and they will be good for all of us!"

"You're his mother!" one of the purple-wearing Tipps yelled. "Of course you believe him! But why should we?"

"Because my son is a good, decent boy!" Mrs. Weavil shrilled, shaking a forefinger at the sky. "You all do such terrible things to him! Especially that Wilmer! Setting fire to his lectern while he's speaking the other day! That's just plain dangerous!"

"That's a lie!"

The voice came from the midst of the Weavil-Scuttil contingent. A bulky male got up on another soapbox. He wore a white suit and a bow tie.

"That's my daddy you're maligning!" he said, puffing out his cheeks. "He never did any such thing!"

"Well, one of his friends, then," Mrs. Weavil said, not backing down an inch. "Every single time Emo tries to get up and tell the public what he plans to do, something awful happens to him!"

Almost at the moment she said the word *awful*, a gray glob came hurtling out of the crowd and splattered in the female Tipp's face.

"Why, you wretches! How dare you do that to a lady!" Mrs. Weavil gasped in horror and dove for her purse. From it she took a cloth and a round mirror and tried to wipe off the dirt. To my astonishment, it refused to budge. It formed a gluey mask on her face. Weavil-Scuttil Junior laughed. Mrs. Weavil looked furious. She reached into the air and came up with a handful of mire. She hurled it at her opponent. Alarmed, Weavil-Scuttil tried to duck, but the missile followed him. It hit him square in the mouth. He goggled and sputtered, dribbling globules down the front of his immaculate white suit. I raised an eyebrow. Mrs. Weavil had used magik. Beside me, Tolomi nodded. I frowned. He had expected that to happen. Was this all being staged?

The Weavil party cheered their leader, but the Weavil-Scuttils weren't beaten yet. Out of buckets, purses, pockets, or knapsacks came a barrage of mudballs and rotten vegetables, which they hurtled at the opposing party. The Weavils responded by reaching into their own reticules for ammunition. Battle was joined. Missiles flew messily in every direction, splashing people, streetlights, and buildings with adhesive gray ooze and reeking streaks of color. One rotten tomato hit the doorway right beside us and exploded into orange slime. Alarmed, Bunny jumped out of her chair and hid behind it.

"Don't worry, Bunny," Ecstra said easily. "They'd never attack the press."

"But I'm not the press!" she said.

As if to prove that the journalistic shield did not extend to us, a dripping missile came arcing toward me. I reached into my internal batteries and set up a shield of magik. The first mud-ball splattered across empty air like an overripe melon. I braced myself as a barrage hammered after it. I held the magik firmly in place as blow after blow rained on it. A wall of gray concealed my view of the crowd. I let the goo drip to the ground so I could see what was going on.

PLOP! In that instant, a stinking handful of cold, wet mire hit me in the left ear. It dribbled into my collar and down inside my shirt, in cold, wet rivulets. Hoots of laughter erupted from the crowd. More missiles followed, decorating me in shades of gray.

I saw red.

My hands started to move, gathering power from the force lines above and below me.

"Skeeve . . ." Bunny's voice was a warning in my ear.

"Don't worry, Bunny," I said, my own voice tight. "I'm just returning the property that these fine people dropped."

Amusement turned to alarm as I used magik to peel the gobs of sticky mess off my skin and round each into a ball that floated lightly around my head. I couldn't swear to each individual who had launched mud in our direction, but I could spot furtive expressions. I chose the guiltiest-looking Tipps, aimed, and fired.

WHIFF! WHIFF! WHIFF!

One after another, the mudballs sped toward the crowd. My first target was a burly young male Tipp who saw it coming and tried to run away. He fell to the ground bellowing.

"My back! I'm hit!"

Ecstra leaped up, notepad in hand, scribbling away, tongue sticking out of the corner of her mouth.

"What a baby!" hooted a female with purple-dyed hair. Coincidentally, she was my second target. The words were barely out of her mouth before she got a faceful of muck. I grinned at her indignant glare as the mud dripped down. The last, and I hated to attack a lady, was Mrs. Weavil herself. I wound up and pushed the power back toward her, carrying what part of the sticky mud I could detach from my clothes and skin.

Her eyes widened, and she threw up her hands to ward it off. She was pretty good, I had to admit. The dirt hit an invisible shield, similar to the way I had protected myself, and exploded off in all directions but toward her. Well, if this had been going on for five years, the combatants had to have developed some quick moves, both defensive and offensive.

The latter came into play immediately. Mrs. Weavil hauled a substantial handful of power out of the force line above her and wove it into a blob of mud the size of a bucket. It hurtled in my direction. I ducked. The mud stopped short before it sailed over my head into the office.

As I had surmised, the newspaper was protected from attack. Mrs. Weavil's missile had vanished without a dribble. I started to gather more to make my own blob, then hesitated. I'd made my point. I let my hands drop.

"Okay, folks," I called out, smiling. "That's enough. Go on with your rally."

Letting my guard down was a mistake. The crowd wasn't ready to let the fight die. Before I could think of resurrecting my defense, I was pounded not only by the assailants on whom I had returned fire, but half of the remaining crowd as well. My clothes, hair, and face were covered with cold, wet, gray goo.

I recycled the mud that had been thrown at me and flung it back. I wished, like Mrs. Weavil, I could create brand-new slime, conjured from the plentiful magikal force above and below me, but that was still beyond my half-trained abilities. Still, there was no shortage of material. I scooped and threw, scooped and threw. I intended only to return fire at those who had attacked me, but constantly having to wipe my eyes meant I wasn't sure where the mud that hit me was coming from.

"Get him!"

I cleared my vision in time to realize that I had moved out of the shelter of the newspaper office. Some of the Tipps I targeted banded together and rushed toward me. I dodged back and forth, not wanting to get trapped in the office or against the cliff wall. With my long legs, I could outdistance them easily if I ran—but why run?

Pushing off against the ground with my mind, I soared into the air. The crowd squawked its protest. I grinned. I was soon out of range of all their mudballs and jeers. Mrs. Weavil shook her fist at me. All of the Tipps on the ground were as thoroughly splashed with adhesive gray and smears of vegetable matter as I was. In fact, I noticed, I smelled terrible, as if I had gone more than a week without a bath. Bunny would understand if I just popped back to Deva and got cleaned up.

WHIFF!

The sound of something rushing through the air was my only clue that someone was in the air near me before I found myself struggling against tangles of rope. I had been netted!

"Awright, mister," a stern-looking Tipp in a dark brown uniform growled at me. He floated in the air about twenty feet off the edge of the nearest street cut into the cliff face. The fur on his face was heavy around his muzzle and chin, giving him the look of a heavy beard. He pushed the cap on his head back between his ears and fixed me with a couple of stern brown eyes under thick brows. "And what do you think you are doing?"

"Well, officer," I said, "I got involved with a little altercation down there on the ground." I gave him a sheepish grin, but the officer didn't return it. "I tried to calm everyone down, but no one would listen to me, so I thought it would be a good idea to get out of the way."

"You were participating in that mayhem down there?" the officer asked, aiming a thumb at the crowd, which had melded into one chaotic group. Some of the green supporters and purple fans were wrestling on the ground. Mrs. Weavil, still recognizable in spite of the mud, was pounding one of them on the back with her handbag.

"Well, not exactly participating," I began. It was hard to look harmless and convincing while I was wrapped in a net. "It was kind of accidental. Well, not really. A few of them threw things at me, so I . . . sent them back again."

"So you were slinging mud and vegetables?" the officer pressed.

"Just a little mud," I said. "Those people did it first. I just returned it."

"And shouting? You were shouting slogans?"

"Not slogans," I said. "I was trying to get everyone to stop yelling."

"What for?"

"So they could have a peaceful rally," I said. "I assume that's why they gathered."

"So, let me get this straight," the officer said, peering more closely at me. "You were shouting and throwing things. Were you calling names?"

"Uh, no. I don't know anyone there. Er, except two members of the press," I added hopefully. He remained stern.

"Are you a registered member of either political party?"

"No. I'm an independent contractor. I come from Deva."

"Uh-huh," the officer said. "You are under arrest. Malarkey!"

An eager-faced young Tipp zipped over and saluted.

"Yes, Sergeant Boxty!"

"Take him in and book him!"

"Yes, sergeant!" Malarkey said. He grabbed hold of me.

"Wait a minute!" I shouted. "Why? Because I'm from Deva?"

"No, sir. We in Tipicanoo never discriminate on the basis of dimensional origin."

"Then why?" I demanded. "What did I do? Everyone else was throwing dirtballs and shouting."

Sergeant Boxty shook his head seriously. "Sir, the activities in which you confess you were involved are reserved for card-carrying political agitators only. If you'd only troubled to peruse the island bylaws, you would have found that out. Take him away!"

In spite of my protests, I was hauled toward the street, where a beast-drawn wagon waited. Officer Malarkey threw me into the rear. I had the presence of mind to soften my landing with a little magik, but I didn't have to worry. The wagon was well padded.

I had to get out of there. I thrust against the bed of the paddy wagon with all the force I could summon up, but I couldn't move. They were used to dealing with magikal miscreants. I let myself go limp and hoped that Bunny or Ecstra had seen what had happened to me and would come bail me out.

CHAPTER FIVE

"But that was off the record!"

—J. BIDEN

"**S**keeve!"

I looked up. The jailer's voice cut through the mood of gloom in which I had sat on the bench in my cell all night and the following morning. I didn't get up for a moment. I was immured in a mire of regret, embarrassment, and shame. The heavy steel door creaked open in the stone wall of the cell. I found myself blinking in the feeble light of a square glass lantern. My fellow prisoners, hearing a release in progress, started banging on their own doors and shouting. I had gotten to know all of their voices during the night. Three drunks were in the cell to my left. They had gotten into a brawl at a local tavern and had been hauled in during the night. In the cell across from me was a very angry female who had apparently attacked her husband with a flower vase. He had had her arrested, and she yelled threats against him all night long. The weeping from the cell immediately to my right was a traveling preacher who had attempted to bilk his ad hoc congregation out of their hard-earned gold. Along with the usual muggers, thieves, prostitutes, and other scum of the earth, there was me. I was in for rioting and causing an affray.

My arrest was my own fault. I had lost my temper. I got involved in a local dispute that I should only have observed. I had made a fool of myself in front of hundreds of people and caused trouble that would impact negatively on our clients. Besides, I was keenly aware that the other witnesses included members of the press. I had publicly disgraced M.Y.T.H., Inc. It hadn't been that long since the others had let me rejoin the company that I had founded. I did not feel I was entitled to any special ego trips or temper tantrums. I was ashamed of myself. All night long those images had raced through my mind. I could feel the mud in my hands. I had let irritation wipe out my common sense.

The dirt wasn't there anymore, of course. When I had arrived at the jail, the officer on duty, staying at a reasonable distance, threw me a tiny packet. I had examined it dubiously, since my clothes and skin were encrusted an inch deep with stiffened grime. To my surprise, the little square unfolded into a gigantic, damp white cloth. I tried it on my arm. The dirt vanished into it without a trace. I applied it to the rest of my body. The cloth sucked all the mud but stayed pristine white.

My impromptu bath replaced the stench of mud and rotten vegetation with an aggressively perky perfume halfway between pine and a wildflower meadow. It wiped away all traces of my misadventure, except the memory. What an idiot I had been. It was lucky nothing worse had happened to me, or Bunny.

I hadn't forgotten about Bunny, whom I had left taking cover behind a table. I was sure she was furious with me. Why else would I have had to spend the night in jail? She was good at working systems. The delay had to be to teach me a lesson, and boy, had I learned one. I vowed to keep a closer watch on my reactions. It wouldn't be easy; I had always had a volatile temper. I thought I had learned to keep it in check, but events had just proved it could be triggered under provocation as easily as it always could. I knew better. I just hadn't acted better.

The smell of the white-cloth disinfectant made the people in the waiting room shy away from me. I wished I could turn off my own nose.

"Skeeve?" inquired the uniformed female Tipp. She was stocky with a jaw you could have used as a doorstop. On the battered table before her was a small pile of gold coins next to a small document with a fancy red seal affixed to its bottom.

"Yes, ma'am," I said.

"Your bail's been paid. Out that way." She pointed the feather end of a quill pen toward the door through which I had entered many hours before.

I made my way out with alacrity, in case the police changed their minds. That had happened before. But I digress.

In the waiting room, among a crowd of crying Tipp mothers and irate Tipp attorneys, was Aahz. When he saw me, his lips drew back from his gigantic pointed teeth in a grin. He gestured to me.

"C'mon, kid," he said. He turned and walked out.

I ran to catch up with him. He strode along the street. Aahz is shorter than I am, but he can move faster than I can. We walked in silence, dodging the crowds of Tipps going about their daily business. A beast-drawn cart got between us at a corner. When it moved, Aahz was on the opposite side still waiting for me. He gave me a chance to catch up and kept walking. I thought from the direction, we must be going toward the newspaper office.

After a while, my nerves were shredded raw. I couldn't stand the silence any longer.

"Aren't you going to rub it in?" I blurted out.

Aahz gave me a wink and a grin.

"Nope," he said. "You've probably obsessed over everything that happened and berated yourself plenty. I doubt anything I say is going to sound new after that. Do you need something to eat?"

"No, they gave me breakfast," I said. "The food was pretty good." I had had much worse in jail—during the times of incarceration that I *had* been fed. In fact, I couldn't complain about my treatment, except for the unfairness of being jailed in the first place.

"Good. Hurry up. We've got a meeting."

Our destination was the *Morning Gossip.* The office was bustling with activity. Tipps hurried back and forth with purposeful expressions, carrying stacks of papers, writing on pads, or talking into devices of every size and shape that I assumed were magikal analogues to Bunny's Perfectly Darling Assistant, Bytina. Stacks of newspapers bound with string flew out the door past me like bats on the wing and zipped off in all directions. I tried to get a glimpse at the headlines, but they were moving too fast. Aahz grabbed me by the shoulder and marched me inside.

I had barely gone through the glass doors when Bunny flew into my arms and enveloped me in a rib-cracking hug.

"Are you all right?" she asked.

"I'm fine," I assured her.

"Good." She let me go and handed me a clipboard from a nearby table. "We have a meeting with the campaign organizers from both sides in an hour. We need to go over our strategy. Tolomi is letting us go through the archives for information on the issues we need to cover and what we need to look out for. Mich is getting them for us." She pointed toward a high wall of file cabinets. Drawers flew open and files came swirling out of them to form a stack on the desk of a skinny bored-looking male with patchy fur on his face. If he had been a Klahd, I would have said he had acne. He checked off another entry on a list before him, then flicked a finger up toward another cabinet. "Start reading through them. I want to have all the objections covered before we meet with them."

No lecture from her, either. I was surprised. No one was going to berate or scold me.

Well, I reasoned, as Aahz had said, I had already done that.

None of my colleagues was going to treat me like a child, in spite of my childish behavior. They knew my behavior was temporary and I knew better. All of them had to deal with their own issues. I felt a rush of affection for them. They trusted me to know what was right even when I didn't do it. I would give my life for any of them. I had never felt like that about anyone, even my family. Now they were my family, my primary social group, my support, and my teachers. How did I ever think I was worthy to lead them? It was much better to have Bunny in charge. I had more to learn by working for her. Everything was going to be all right.

Then I got a good look at a copy of that day's paper.

Klahd in Disorderly Conduct Scandal! A close-up picture of me hanging in the police net was below, between two columns of type in all capital letters. I grabbed the news sheet off the table and scanned the article. It made me sound like a complete idiot.

"Skeeve!" Ecstra's voice made me jump. She appeared at my side, with pencil poised above pad and an expression of intent interest. "Tell me, how does it feel to be arrested on your first day in Tipicanoo?"

The astonishment on my face probably mirrored the one in the article, but I remembered Aahz's instructions.

"No comment," I said.

"I want to know for the sake of our readers who have never run afoul of the law," she said. "And for my own information. I've never spent the night in jail. What was it like?"

"No comment," I said. "We've got a lot of work to do right now."

"I can help with that," Ecstra offered promptly. "I was an eyewitness to plenty of the candidates' antics. Most of what you folks are reading is from news reports I wrote. I could give you details that didn't make it into the paper."

"Great!" I said. "Thanks, Ecstra! That would save us a lot of time. When did the mudslinging start?"

". . . But first you have to give me an exclusive interview

on your experiences in the Bokromi lockup," Ecstra finished. I groaned. She went down a checklist on the page. "How about the booking? Would you say you were treated unfairly by the police? Deprived of your rights? Humiliated in any way?" She looked up at me, her pencil poised.

I glanced at Aahz for a suggestion. He raised his eyebrows, telling me that I had better be careful.

I recited the bare events of my incarceration, careful not to make personal comments or identify anyone whose name I had heard. I could see my colleagues stifling smiles. Ecstra looked disappointed. She frowned and pointed the quill end of her pen at me.

"So you are not ashamed of your actions yesterday, Skeeve?"

That caught me off guard. There was no good way to answer *that* question. "I . . . of course I am! I mean, I am ashamed of my actions. But I don't understand why I was the only one arrested!"

"The police checked everyone's cards once they took you in. They were all paid-up political party members. Mrs. Weavil gave me a personal statement. She thought you were a natural. She'd love to have you join Emo's party." She flipped back through her notebook a couple of pages and read, " '. . . if only to keep him from targeting a helpless old woman who just wants to defend her son from malicious slander.' "

I groaned. Mich stifled a snort in a thick file folder.

"Don't feel bad about *her*," Ecstra said. "Mrs. Weavil's tough. I've seen her take on the whole Weavil-Scuttil faction by herself when a late ferry delayed her supporters from showing up to a rally on time. You ought to be proud. An endorsement like that doesn't come along every day."

"Why didn't you tell me it was against the law for outsiders to riot?" I asked, knowing how foolish I sounded even asking the question. "You could have stopped me from getting in trouble."

Ecstra shrugged. "We only report the news. We don't make it. We aren't supposed to get involved. The only reason Tolomi said to help you in your fact-finding mission is that you're impartial contractors. As long as you stay that way, we're glad to assist." She took her notebook to the editor. Tolomi had his feet on his desk and a cigar clenched in the corner of his mouth. He went over the notes and chortled.

"This is gonna make a *great* article tomorrow," he crowed. "I could run a dozen follow-ups. Great personal-interest story."

"That is just what we didn't want to have happen," Bunny said in a small voice that I thought only I could hear, but I'd forgotten Ecstra's talent at reading expressions.

"Sorry," she said. "No hard feelings, but that's our job, and that's news. In fact, this is going to be the best new story we've had in years."

"There's no such thing as bad publicity," Aahz said, waving away our objections with a sweep of his hand. "We could cause a hundred riots. It would just improve our standing in this backwater." He brandished a handful of articles at us. "Tolomi, I gotta give your people credit. You have found a thousand different ways to say that nothing's happening on this island and make it sound interesting. I'd be bored to death if I lived here. I can see why you had to jump on my friend's unfortunate propensity for getting involved in civic activities."

Tolomi grasped Aahz's hand and shook it. "Glad to meet a fellow philosopher," he said. "My daddy ran the paper before me. He used to say, 'Just spell the names right, and people will make up the facts to suit themselves.' "

Aahz grinned. "Any Pervects in your history?"

Tolomi grinned back. "Not that I know of, but your teeth look familiar. Come on and see us set up the front page for tomorrow."

We followed him to the back of the office.

The press, which filled most of the available room, was tended by a dozen or so young Tipps. I had never seen anything like it. The roaring machine rose to the ceiling. Steel traps on every side clattered like a hundred dragons' jaws demanding food. The Tipps ran around the device with armfuls of paper or rolled-up scrolls. Series of wheels and cogs spun faster than my eye could follow. Huge rolls of paper suspended from brackets above our heads unspooled down into a rectangular maw that sucked them into the bowels of the machine. The constant din of ratcheting noises was loud enough to make me wince, but before long it became a hypnotic drone. Jeweled lights flickered on and off on one face of the monster machine—it did resemble a malevolent face with red eyes and long, glowing yellow teeth. I sensed a tremendous amount of magik running to it from the force lines, enough to power the workings of a dozen or more master magicians. The reporters and press-Tipps didn't seem worried by the presence of so much magik. In fact, I observed that they had little to worry about. The power was being channeled neatly through bronze pipes bent at right angles that led in and out of the sides of the machine. At a desk that was attached to the right side of the huge contraption, a slightly built female Tipp in a square hat folded from parchment stood with a box of small bronze cubes at her fingertips. She was placing them into a rectangular frame. As she set each one down, it nudged the other pieces on each side until it was comfortable. I saw that the lines of squares formed words. The words formed sentences that grew into paragraphs that spread out and grew until they crowded against the framework. Pictures blossomed in empty spaces like square flowers, filling in with detail in shining bronze.

"Don't you use Shutterbugs to supply your illustrations?" I asked.

"No," the typesetter said, her fingers moving faster than I thought fingers could go. Magik filled the room. I felt it surging in from the force lines above and below me. "One picture's worth a thousand words. For every thousand in the column, the picture draws itself. See?"

As she worked, I saw a tiny square pop up on the form. As she added words, the square grew and took on shape. Before long, I could recognize the figures pictured. One of them was me with mud on my gawking face, occupying a third of the page.

"Do you have to put that?" I asked, sourly.

"It's all part of the story," she said, slapping letters into the form. "We can't let personal feelings get in the way of the facts."

"Is there anything I can do to persuade you not to put that on page one?"

She shook her head. "Only if a bigger story comes up. Gotta doubt that. This place has been stuck in a rut for years."

I was annoyed, but there was nothing I could do. As printed papers flew out of the press, they sailed out of the door by themselves. I could have chased down each bundle, but I'd probably get arrested again. Instead, I concentrated on my task and opened the files Mich shoved in front of me.

I found myself grinning over the details of the practical jokes and other ruses the candidates had played on one another. I'd played some tricks on people in my day, but the briefcase that exploded in a bubble of adhesive purple goo, the babble charm that made every word out of their mouths abusive nonsense, and the crowd of simulacra that no one could tell from the actual candidate on the podium all shouting different speeches at once were my favorites. Those took real imagination. It seemed that every time one candidate, Emo or Wilmer, announced he was going to go through with it at last and call for an election, the opposition would commit some form of sabotage. It had never worked out so that both of them had their hands clean at the same time. We had to think five steps ahead of their objections. The island, as I read from the editorials, was on the edge of a revolt against the government.

"It's time," Bunny said, standing up. She gathered all the documents together and tapped them neatly on the desk to square them off, then took Bytina out of her shoulder bag. She opened the small red case, rolled up the papers, and held them over it. Bytina swallowed them up and produced a flurry of words on her little round screen. Bunny now had a dossier that no one could read without her permission.

Once we left the newspaper office, people gave me amused and knowing looks. It was embarrassing. Every time I stopped at a street corner, someone would lean over and ask me the same thing.

"Weren't you the Klahd we saw in the paper?"

I had to bite off my retort. If I didn't smile and keep walking, Aahz would grab me by the shoulder.

"Just smile and nod," he said.

I should have flown.

CHAPTER SIX

*"With careful preparation, nothing can
ever go wrong."*

—M. STEWART

"Down with corruption! Up with Emo!"

"Wilmer and honesty! We need both!"

The shouting from both sides bombarded our
ears as we shoved our way toward the imposing doors of the
Hotel Tippmore.

We had rented a small office in the middle of town, half-
way between the two campaign headquarters, but we thought
it was better to hold a meeting between the candidates and their
staffs in completely neutral ground, far from all three locations.
Nunzio found the private meeting room in the Tippmore and
made detailed arrangements with the management.

Guido stood guard at the main door of the hotel, preventing
anyone from entering. Word of the conference had obviously
slipped out, probably leaked by both groups to the press, so the
hotel was surrounded by a mob. By the banners and signs, the
crowd consisted of supporters and protesters from both sides,

but Guido looked blank-faced and serene. No one had attempted to pass him, but they might try once the door opened for us.

Nunzio looked grim. "It took a long time to persuade the managers to let us hold the meeting here. They are concerned that the crowd might cause an affray. We're liable for all damages."

"This is calm compared with last night," I said. Having been in a Tipicanoo political exhibition and reading about dozens more, I considered myself a connoisseur of local civil disobedience.

As I said that, I spied a rotten grapefruit at eleven o'clock high. I flicked a thread of magik at it. It collided with the off-yellow globe, causing it to explode in a shower of sour juice. The Tipps who got rained on wailed a protest. They surged toward us, waving their signs.

"Me lead!" Chumley exclaimed. He put himself in front of our small group, rounded both huge purple-furred hands into fists, and showed his teeth. "Grrr!"

The protesters backpedaled hastily. The ones at the front windmilled backward into the faces of the onrushers behind them. A forest of arms and legs stuck out of the mass. The rest of the crowd started tossing mudballs and rotten fruit.

Chumley made way for us by throwing anyone who stepped in his way over his shoulder into the crowd. Making liberal use of the force lines, I ran interference against the hail of gooey missiles. I spotted Mrs. Weavil near the wall with a bucket of dung. She heaved handfuls at us, but I was ready for her this time. I fielded every shot so that not a drop hit any of us. Her final throw smacked into the invisible barrier at my back. It slid onto the pavement with a SQUELCH! I grinned back at her. She looked disappointed.

The door closed behind us, and the elegantly dressed hotel staff rushed to bar and lock it. The last thing I saw before daylight was shut out was Ecstra struggling through the crowd trying to get inside. I threw a handful of magik in her way. The door slammed. She was still outside. I was relieved. I didn't want to have to watch every word in case it made it into print. Once was enough.

The manager, a tall male Tipp in a starched white collar that stood up nearly to his ears, led us down a dim corridor paneled in dark brown wood and with a thick carpet so deep I sank to my ankles at every step. It smelled of oil polish and lemons. He stopped before a set of double doors and clapped his hands. Two of his flunkies hurried to pull the doors open. The manager gestured us in with a flourish. We stepped inside. Aahz looked around.

"Not bad," Aahz said, with a disdainful curl of his lip. The manager looked crestfallen. "I mean, if it was what you could whip together on short notice."

"Sir, this is our finest parlor!"

Aahz continued to look unimpressed. "Oh, well. I guess it'll have to do."

"I think it looks pretty nice, Aahz," I said.

Aahz shot me a look and returned to the manager. "Ignore my partner. He's nearsighted. What's with the walnut veneer? A place with claims as high as you make them should have nothing but solid wood panels."

That evidently hit home with the manager. "Our decorating costs increase all the time, sir. I think you will find that our service is what sets us apart. May I offer a complimentary beverage while you wait? A bottle of our best champagne?"

There was nothing Aahz liked more than a free drink. "Certainly, my good man," he said, beaming. "And bring a bottle for my friends, too."

In spite of Aahz's scorn, the hotel had gone all out for us. The chamber was elegantly furnished and set up to accommodate both camps. Identical sets of liquor bottles and glasses were arranged at either end of the room. Hors d'oeuvres on trays had been placed in easy reach of both groups so neither would have to approach the wrong side of the room. We would moderate the meeting from the buffer zone in the center.

There was one more feature the room had that no other

chamber in the dimensions possessed: my dragon. Gleep
yanked his leash loose from Nunzio's grip and came hurtling
toward me as soon as the hotel staff had left. He slimed me
with his long, agile tongue.

"Ugh! Gleep, get down!"

"Gleep!" he said brightly.

"Anyone get in here? No surprise installations or listening
devices?" Aahz asked Nunzio.

"The place is clean, Aahz," the enforcer said. His high voice
was always surprising in a man of his size. "Gleep found an
Earwig under the liquor table over there and two Shutterbugs
behind peepholes in the woodwork."

"Where are they? I want to question them, find out who
planted them."

"Gleep!" my pet said, running his tongue over his chops.

"Sorry, that's not going to be possible. Gleep ate them,"
Nunzio said.

"Figures," Aahz said, disgustedly. "Stupid dragon."

I glanced at Gleep. He winked one of his large blue eyes
at me.

I stood near the door and closed my eyes. The key to good
magik, as Aahz always told me, is visualization. You can do
almost anything with strong force lines handy, as long as you
remember that magik is not intelligent in and of itself. You
have to be very thorough in picturing what you need and
intend to have happen. That was one of the reasons that Garkin and other magicians used pentacles and other physical
objects, not to mention chanted spells, to perform their feats.
They were mnemonics, aids to help one remember what details
were needed to accomplish the spell. In this case, the job was
pretty straightforward: an uninterrupted meeting among hostile peers. I needed to prevent anything that wasn't air, elec-
tricity, or light from coming into the room. I pictured a very
fine mesh of unbreakable energy lining the walls, ceiling and
floor.

A-ha, I thought, feeling a slight disturbance in the force line. *Someone is trying to get in right now!*

I felt toward the intrusion with my mind, but the probing withdrew almost as quickly as it had begun. A subtle spy. Well, whoever it was was destined to be disappointed. I introduced a second layer of force, a fluffy, thick one that would prevent sounds from the room from being heard outside, even if someone had his or her ear to the door. Once I had completed the lining, I drew a door in it to correspond with the way we had come in. I would close the spell as soon as everyone had arrived. There would be no trouble maintaining the spell; the hotel stood over a bright green line of force as thick as my wrist.

Bunny sat in a high-backed chair in the center of the long, oval table and propped Bytina in front of her on its polished surface. I slid into a chair opposite her. Aahz plunked down beside me. He emptied the newly arrived champagne into the bucket and swigged a quarter of it in one gulp. I ran a thread of magik through my glass and was pleased to see it come up bright and clear. The wine was clean: no philters or potions had been introduced. I nodded to the others.

Bunny looked across at us. "Are we ready?" she asked.

I glanced around the room. Guido and Nunzio flanked the door, their arms folded, but with their miniature crossbows handy in their inside breast pockets. Chumley hulked behind Bunny like an overprotective purple mammoth. Gleep lay curled at my feet under the table.

"If you ask me, this is overkill. We have enough muscle here to take over a medium-sized dimension."

"I want to take control of this situation as early as possible," Bunny said. "My conversations with the campaign managers last night were . . . unproductive."

The little disk rang, clattering on the table. Bunny opened it. She lifted it to her ear and talked in a quiet voice. Her feathery brows drew down over her little nose, and a line of concern drew itself across her smooth forehead.

"What's the matter?" I asked, when she set Bytina down again.

She seemed a little distracted. "Oh, nothing. Family matters. It's not important. Mother wants me to come and see her on Klah later on when we're done here."

"Oh," I said. "Do you need any of us to come with you?"

She smiled at me, though she still looked worried. "No, it'll be all right. But thanks for offering."

CHAPTER SEVEN

"Politics makes strange bedfellows."

—J. EDWARDS

W e heard a commotion in the hallway. I stood up as the door swung open. The candidates had arrived, their entourages rushing side by side up the hallway. Emo and Wilmer rushed to enter the room first, but they tied, jamming their shoulders in the doorway. With a hard tug from Nunzio, they popped loose. The candidates glared at one another, brushing at their clothes and fur as if the other had some kind of communicable parasite.

"I'm gonna need a shower when we get through here," Aahz muttered.

"Me, too." The feeling of oily dislike that I had experienced when I first met Emo and Wilmer was more than doubled with both present. It seemed to wrap them like a miasma.

Naturally, they had not come alone. Besides their campaign managers, each of them had more than a dozen clerks, secretaries and gofers tagging along behind carrying clipboards, briefcases, or arcane gear and trying to look important. Guido stopped them with a meaty hand in the chest of the first one in line.

"Three henchmen each, no more," he said. "Dere's enough of a crowd in here."

"Three? But what if *they* get disruptive?" Emo asked, pointing at Wilmer's entourage.

"You're a fine one to suggest that we might cause trouble," Wilmer sputtered. "I need at least six of my staff present! My dignity and"—he coughed delicately—"my advanced years demand the courtesy."

"Well, I need all of mine! And I might need more!"

Emo and Wilmer each narrowed an eye at one another.

"Enough!" Bunny held up her hands. "Gentlemen, please. We want this to go as smoothly as possible. Three each. No more. Decide now, or my partners will have to decide for you."

Guido and Nunzio loomed over the candidates. Chumley, behind Bunny, let out a low growl of warning. Wilmer gulped and ran a finger around his collar. Wilmer took an older female and a young, pretty Tipp, then nodded to a couple of middle-aged males, who followed him toward the table.

"That's four. Choose one more to send home," Bunny said.

"But, Miss Bunny," he said, with a gallant little bow, "they are my trusted advisors."

Bunny tilted her head to Guido. He flip-flopped his hand rhythmically between the two males.

"Hasty-tasty-chipolata, veeraswami-bottisatva, eeny-meeny-chili-beenie, you-are-out!" Guido's finger ended up pointing to the male on the left. He grabbed the Tipp by the shoulders and shoved him toward the door. Nunzio opened it and slammed it in the male's face.

"That was childish!" Wilmer complained when Guido returned, dusting his hands together.

"Ain't as childish as pretendin' you can't count to three," Guido said. He folded his arms. He turned to Emo. "How 'bout you?"

Emo beamed at him. "Three's fine, my dear sir!" He jabbed

a forefinger at a tall, skinny female, a stocky, older male, and a younger male with protruding incisors. "The rest of you go on back to the office. We'll have a strategy meeting later."

"Yes, Mr. Weavil," they chorused, except for one male, a dark-furred Tipp going strategically gray at the temples and in the middle of his deep chest. He broke out of the group and walked to Emo's side. Guido started for him, hands out. Bunny waved him back.

"He's all right," she said. "Orlow Suposi is Mr. Weavil's campaign manager."

A senior female who had dyed her head-fur scarlet and wearing a stole of luxurious, long-haired rodents stepped forward and presented a long-nailed hand to Bunny. "How nice to see you again," she said. The rodents around her neck chirped a greeting. The female turned to the rest of us. "I'm Carnelia Vole. I chair Mr. Weavil-Scuttle's election committee for the Wisdom Party."

"Won't you sit down?" Bunny invited her. Wilmer ostentatiously assisted Carnelia into a seat and tossed the stole onto a chair. The rodents let go of one another and curled up in individual balls on the cushion to go to sleep. I closed the seclusion spell.

Emo stood at his end of the table and gave us all one of his wide smiles. "I would like to thank all of you for coming. This has been a long and puzzling road. I hope that we can come to an agreement and bring our journey to a fair and considered end. I now call this meeting to order." He tapped the wood with the base of his glass. His assistants scribbled busily in their notebooks.

Wilmer leaped up from his chair. "You aren't chairing this meeting, you scoundrel! If anyone is, it should be me!"

Bunny turned her most authoritative glance on both of them. I had been on the receiving end of it more than once. They both reacted exactly the same way I would have: They cringed. "*I* am running it, on behalf of M.Y.T.H., Inc. *I* declare this meeting open."

"Death to Weavil-Scuttils!"

A loud, female shriek burst upon our eardrums. The speaker materialized standing on the table. She was a Tipp with green-dyed fur, artistically ripped leggings, and a loose smock. She ran toward Wilmer and upended a metal pail.

"Don't you dare!" Wilmer protested, but too late. Soggy ooze cascaded down over his head.

"Skeeve!" Aahz yelled.

I was already on it. I clapped my hands.

The mud halted in midair. Well, most of it. About a cupful hit Wilmer square in the mouth.

"Confound it!" he bellowed, spitting out gray matter. "Farsnarit! Megrabolindo!"

"Watch your language, pal," Guido snapped. "Dere are ladies present."

Wilmer shut his mouth and wiped peevishly at his face with a handkerchief.

I reversed the flow. The mud sucked upward into its container. The intruder looked stunned. She turned the bucket upward to see what had happened. I let the mud go. It exploded up into her face. Momentarily blinded, she sneezed liquid sand.

By the time she came up for air, Guido and Nunzio had hauled her off the board. They marched her unceremoniously to the door and tossed her out into the empty hallway. Her pail went tumbling after, clattering on the floor. Aahz glared at me.

"You're gonna have to lock the place up, kid," he said.

"I *did* lock it up," I said, peevishly. "Someone broke my spell."

I reached into my reserves and started to rebuild the invisible walls, but not before more protesters burst into the room. A young Tipp in purple charged out of the air waving a banner that proclaimed *Weavil-Scuttil forever!* Chumley grabbed him and tossed him out the door before he could drape it on Emo. The banner fluttered out after him. Chumley slammed the door. He had to open it again a second later to eject a pair of screaming Emo fans and a very hefty Wilmer supporter who were already fighting among themselves when they appeared. Aahz took all three of them by their collars and heaved them out. I sucked up as much magik as I could and rebuilt the screens tighter than a Pervect's wallet.

"You did that!" Emo and Wilmer shouted at one another, pointing accusing fingers. They turned to Bunny in unison. "I had nothing to do with that!"

"Sit *down*," Bunny commanded.

The candidates glanced at their campaign managers. Orlow and Carnelia nodded slightly. Emo and Wilmer sat down.

"Now, if there are no more interruptions," Bunny said, pausing to see if there were any, "thank you all for coming. Please help yourselves to refreshments. I am sure you need a stiff drink after all that."

One underling on each side leaped up and made for the beverage tables. They served the candidates and their managers before they brought anything for themselves or the other underlings. I also noticed that the managers got served first. That told me something about the chain of command. I saw by the slight narrowing in her eyes that Bunny hadn't missed it. Neither had Aahz. He finished his bucket of champagne and cracked the neck off another bottle with his teeth. Carnelia cringed. He grinned at her.

"Let's cut right to the chase, shall we?" Bunny asked. "At the request of both Mr. Weavil and Mr. Weavil-Scuttil, we polled the citizens of Tipicanoo regarding this election, and they want—"

"Which one of us do they want?" Emo burst out. "It has to be me!"

"In your dreams, youngster!" Wilmer said. "It's me the good people of this island deserve."

"—and the absolute consensus among the citizens is that they want this election over with as soon as possible!" Bunny raised her voice over theirs. "You agreed that you would *both* sponsor M.Y.T.H., Inc., to oversee an election if it was found to be the will of the people, and I promise you, it is. So, what's the hangup? Why can't you two agree on a date and settle this already?"

Carnelia cleared her throat. "I speak for Mr. Weavil-Scuttil when I say that I'm happy to have your fine company offering its assistance. We have been uncertain of the fairness of such an operation. We had to wait until we were sure that there were no tricks involved in the vote count. If it took a long time to gain that assurance, then so be it. We just don't trust those people over there to keep their word."

"You . . . *people* are the reason nothing has happened," Orlow said, jabbing a finger into the tabletop. "Miserable tricksters! Rumormongers! Every time we offer the olive branch, you batter us over the head with it!"

"Who dropped what on whose head?" Carnelia demanded. "How about that ten-ton weight that came out of nowhere during Wilmer's speech on the environment last month?"

"It didn't hit him, did it?" Orlow countered. "Your campaign magicians caught it before it hurt anyone. And let me say again we had nothing to do with that!"

"Just like you had nothing to do with that mudslinger who broke in here just a minute ago? That's why we don't want to set the date. We don't want you setting traps for us on election day!"

"Well, you can hold your breath waiting!" Emo snarled. "I was all ready to let it happen last fall when you came to that private little breakfast meeting with us. I thought you all had agreed on the terms. It was all settled and set. Then the next morning there was an article in the paper saying that there was collusion between the parties and the voters were going to be disenfranchised! Violently! You must have leaked a false rumor to the press. I felt betrayed. Betrayed!" He slapped a dramatic hand to his chest. "I can never take part in a farce with you purple poltroons!"

"We didn't leak anything to the press! We told you that at the time!" Wilmer said.

"Pardon me for not believing you," Emo said.

"Well, it's not as if your word is any better!"

"Are you waiting for one of you to drop dead?" Aahz asked. "Letting it drag on for five years would be punishable by death in some dimensions." He eyed Emo and Wilmer with a speculative yellow eye. They recoiled and fell silent. I grinned. Bunny rapped Bytina on the table.

"We have gone over the records," she said. "I'd say that the dirty tricks have been pretty well divided between both sides. So, whoever was responsible, since both of you are claiming total innocence, was an equal opportunity annoyer."

"Whoever it was," Carnelia said, with a saintly expression.

"Exactly," Orlow agreed.

Bunny went on. "We will give you our professional guarantee that only registered voters will vote, no one will be coerced to choose a candidate that he or she doesn't want, and the count will be certified by Hass and Gotz of Zoorik." Chumley shuffled forward, in full Stupid-Troll mode, and handed each manager a crumpled parchment with the well-known gold seal of the Gnomes on it.

"Well . . . that *sounds* pretty nice," Orlow said, after straightening out the document and perusing it twice. He aimed an accusing finger at the opposition. "But we have to get our issues before the people before they go to the polls! What's going to stop those scalawags over there from sabotaging our speeches?"

"Debates," I said. "We'll oversee a number of public debates. You'll have a chance to put your case before the voters on topics agreed on beforehand. We'll referee them so that each of you has exactly the same amount of time to talk . . ."

". . . Tell all your lies," Aahz added. "Make all your campaign promises that you won't keep . . ."

"Aahz!" Bunny said.

"It's an election, Bunny!" Aahz said, turning up a palm. "If it were science they'd be proposing a theorem, then proving it. As it is, all they can do is tell the people what they think they want to hear. The most convincing one wins. Politics is a game in which plausible people who want the job come out and tell outrageous lies to the constituents, who buy one story or the other, and then when they get elected to office, they do whatever they want, regardless of the promises they made."

"That's stupid," I said.

"That's politics," said Aahz, with a shrug. He leered at the candidates. "I can't wait to judge your speeches. Which one of you saps is going to lose the most debates?"

"Mr. Aahz!"

"Just Aahz." He leaned back and put his hands behind his head.

Bunny went on, reading from a paper she had prepared. "We will oversee a fair, calm, and rational campaign. With that in mind, you will have to follow certain rules. You all must agree that there will be no attempt to buy votes. No gifts may be given to anyone over one copper piece in value. You'll stick to a schedule agreed upon beforehand by all parties. All events will be handled with dignity and respect for your opponent and his colleagues. And, at the end of the month, the voters will go to the polls," she concluded.

"One month!" Emo said.

"That's hardly enough time to tell my constituents all my plans for them!" Wilmer said.

"One month," Bunny said firmly. "Aahz is right. If five years hasn't been long enough to persuade people to vote for you, then you should step aside and let a better-prepared candidate take office. Well? Decide now. You have"—she opened Bytina and consulted the clock face that popped up on the little round screen—"five minutes to decide." Bytina began to play a perky little tune with a ticktock beat.

Emo and Wilmer eyed one another.

"Dear lady, may I have a word with you?" Orlow rose from his seat and made his way around the table. He put an arm around Carnelia's shoulders and led her smoothly to one side of the room. The two of them put their heads together. Their mouths moved, but from where I sat I could hear only a faint hiss. Aahz tilted one ear in their direction. I sent a small thread of magik snaking through the air to eavesdrop.

BZZZP!

A loud burst of static exploded in my ears. I jumped. From the look on Aahz's face, he got the same treatment. I glanced at the campaign managers. They had surrounded themselves with a silence spell overlaid with a masking noise. I tried to penetrate it with a little more magik. All I got was louder static. I thought it was a pretty good spell. I'd have to try out something similar for future use when I needed confidentiality.

Orlow and Carnelia came up for air and went to whisper in their employers' ears. Emo and Wilmer looked surprised, then suspicious, then resigned. They nodded. Bytina finished her song and erupted with a cheery DING!

Orlow turned to us. "My guy says yes."

"So does mine," Carnelia said.

"Good," Bunny said. She looked as relieved as I felt.

"And no one will know the terms of our agreement here?" Orlow asked.

"You have our word that no one in *our* company will let the details drop," Bunny promised.

"Even though you have established a *very cushy* relationship with the *Morning Gossip?*" Carnelia asked.

"So cushy they published an embarrassing story about me on the front page this morning?" I asked pointedly.

Carnelia looked surprised. "Well, perhaps my sources were incorrect," she said apologetically.

I frowned. "What sources?" I asked.

"Well, you don't think the *Morning Gossip* is the only paper in town, do you?" she asked.

"Of course not," Bunny said, smoothly. "But they were the first ones to open their archives for us. That gives them first crack at an exclusive. When we decide to give it to them."

"And what exclusive would that be?" Orlow asked.

"Well, how about our decision here?" Bunny asked. "That would be a scoop anywhere. The rest of the papers would rush to interview both of the candidates. Front-page headlines!"

The candidates perked up. "Of course we would have to prepare statements," Emo said.

"And prepare press kits."

"Then we won't make the announcement until tomorrow morning," Bunny said. "Don't leak it until we give Tolomi the heads-up. Do you promise to keep it under wraps until then? Cross your hearts and hope to die?"

"Of course!" Emo and Wilmer chorused. The assistants all hastily jotted down notes. I wondered how long that promise would last.

"Good! That's all settled."

"There's one more *teeny-weeny* little thing," Carnelia said.

"Of course," Bunny said, smiling. "We'll do whatever we can to help."

Carnelia pointed at Aahz. "I don't want that Pervert involved."

Aahz snarled. "That's Per-*vect*."

"Not from where I'm standing, Scaly," she snapped back. "I'm not used to having my intelligence insulted."

"You work in politics. I thought that was a given," Aahz said.

"Aahz!"

"It goes for our side, too," Orlow said firmly. "We're willing to work with you, Miss Bunny, and the rest of your staff, but that Per . . . that guy's got to go. Otherwise, we'll just have to muddle through the way we've been going on. We don't need M.Y.T.H., Inc., that badly."

Bunny bit her lip. "All right. If that's the way you want it."

"We do," the managers said in unison.

She turned to Aahz. "We'll meet you back at the office in a little while, Aahz."

Aahz's ears drooped. "You're kidding! You're going to let them shove me out of here like an unwanted puppy?" He pointed at me. "What about Skeeve? He's the one who had to be bailed out of the hoosegow."

Bunny gave him a look of heartbreaking appeal.

"You heard the clients, Aahz. Please? We'll talk later."

I was appalled, but torn at the same time. Bunny couldn't be sacrificing one of our partners for the convenience of a client, could she? She was throwing out Aahz, my best friend, so we could take on a job? "Bunny, you can't do that."

Her wide blue eyes appealed to me. "Skeeve, I have to. The customer is always right. You know that."

The customers in question couldn't hide their smug satisfaction.

"All right," Aahz said, kicking back his chair in disgust. "I'm done with this situation. I wouldn't come back to this dimension if you begged me."

BAMF!

He disappeared in a swirl of papers. The room had gone very silent.

"Very well," Bunny said, in a small voice. She cleared her throat, and her voice regained strength. "I want both candidates and your managers to sign this agreement. It sets out the conditions we've been discussing and binds you to them. We're going to hold an election next month. Everything has to be in order."

She pushed the stack of documents to me but wouldn't meet my eyes. I floated the papers to both parties, nearly overshooting the ends of the table because I was so distracted. I knew Bunny could be ruthless; it ran in her Family. I had simply never seen her do anything like that before.

The candidates and their managers signed on the dotted lines. Bunny had bought the forms from the same suppliers in the Bazaar who furnished paperwork to the Mob, so as each Tipp set pen to paper, the sharp corner of the contract turned up and ran itself against the palm of the signer.

"Ow!" Wilmer bellowed. "That thing drew blood! Look! It's all over the bottom of the page!"

Bunny smiled sweetly. "Just to make sure you don't dispute whose signature is on it later, Mr. Weavil-Scuttil."

"You act like you don't trust us, Miss Bunny," Carnelia protested.

"Just being a careful businesswoman, Miss Vole."

"Not used to signing in *blood*," Wilmer muttered, finishing his name with a flourish.

"*I* am," Orlow said. He didn't wince as the contract did the same to him. A drop fell to the parchment.

With another wisp of magik I retrieved the documents. I shoved the stack over to Bunny, who squared up the stack and handed them to Chumley.

She put on a bright smile and beamed at Emo and Wilmer.

"That's it, then! We're going to have an election!"

"May the best Tipp win," I said.

CHAPTER EIGHT

"Life is a matter of give and take."

—U.S. "UNCONDITIONAL SURRENDER" GRANT

We escorted the two parties out into the hallway, now vacant. They hustled out, the managers in deep conversation with their candidates. The underlings trailed behind, scribbling in their notebooks.

I sniffed the air. It smelled of flowers and oil, as it had before, but there was a hint of still-warm cigar smoke close to the door. None of the campaign staffs had been smoking. I took Gleep up and down the corridors. No one else was in this part of the building. Where had it come from? Had someone been listening to us?

Bunny came up and tapped me on the shoulder.

"We're all clear. Let's go back to the Bazaar."

I spun to face her, bitter words pushing at my lips, but I held them in.

"Right," I said tightly. When everyone was close enough, I set my D-hopper and pushed the button for home.

BAMF!

Holding on to my temper, I moved everyone back to our tent in the Bazaar. As soon as the familiar wave of hot, dry air hit me in the face, I turned to confront Bunny.

"How could you do that to Aahz?" I demanded. The others backed out of the room quietly. Even Gleep slunk out of sight.

Bunny didn't pretend not to know what I was talking about. Suddenly, she looked very tired.

"I had no choice, Skeeve," she said. She slumped into the chair at the front desk, which was usually empty, since we didn't have a receptionist. I stood over her with my hands on my hips. "As you ought to know, sometimes a leader has to make on-the-spot decisions for the good of the group. That's why I was chosen as president."

"*I* didn't choose you," I said. I had wanted to be president again.[2]

"But the others wanted me," she said. "All of them but you and Aahz. Both of you had lost sight of the goal of this business, which is to help other people. And I thought you had come to like having me as president. Do you think I failed Aahz in the conference room?"

I exploded. "Yes! You didn't stand up for him!"

Bunny raised her eyebrows. "Did he deserve it? He was taunting the customers. He insulted them to their faces when we were trying to secure their cooperation. That's unprofessional. If an associate behaved that badly in front of someone outside the Family, my uncle Bruce would have someone like Guido take him outside and deal with him."

"I might have insulted them, too," I said. I knew I was sulking, but I didn't care. "Emo and Wilmer were maneuvering every way they could to get the best advantage for themselves."

"Of course they were!" Bunny said. "If they weren't, one of

---

2. For details of this epic struggle, read *Myth-Chief*, a gripping volume available from your local purveyor of literature.

them would have ceded the office of governor to the other long
ago. I had to give them something they could win at, so they
would feel good about going along with the rest of our plans."

"Why would we care if they felt good?" I asked. "Emo came
to us, remember? He asked for *our* help. You don't even like him."

"It doesn't matter if I like him. He's the client. One of them.
We agreed to take the job, and that means handling all the
factors involved. That includes the people." She tilted her head
and studied me. "You've been sheltered from the worst of
everything in your life. There are consequences you have never
even dreamed of that could happen to people."

"Worse than imprisonment, torture, or death?" I taunted her.

"Well, yes," she said, surprised by my question. "Having
to live with humiliation every day of your life. Having your
self-worth called into question. Never being able to redeem
yourself or hold your head high. That's why the Ax was so effective. As a Character Assassin, the Ax destroys people without
killing them. Having been on the receiving end of that yourself,
can't you have a little sympathy for two silly men who have
spent five years avoiding asking for the truth?"

I hated lectures, especially if I deserved them. But she was
right. I accepted what she said. I was determined not to revert
to the stubborn apprentice I had been in Garkin's house or the
brooding hermit I had been during my self-imposed exile in
my own inn. I pulled back on my temper and sat down on one
of our guest chairs opposite her. "I see your point, but we're a
team!"

"You think Aahz is off the team because he's not working
on one assignment?" Bunny countered. "We don't all go around
in lockstep. Do you want to join Pookie undercover in that
monastery?"

I was taken aback. "No . . ."

"Then see it my way." She smiled at me, her big blue eyes
turned up to mine. Bunny was a very beautiful woman. I found
myself falling into her gaze. I could smell her perfume. She
wore the scent of the lilacs, like those that had grown around

my mother's garden. "I would never do anything that deliberately harmed Aahz. I did consider the ramifications before I
asked him to leave. There are upsides to having him out of the
picture, too. It might come in handy later on when we're too
deeply mired to see what our next move should be. We can lean
on Aahz's perspective. You know how he loves giving advice."

"That's for sure," I said. You could set Aahz off on a daylong
lecture with one simple question.

"It's only a month, plus an extra day or two for arguing over
the ballot count, and not anywhere close to the last job we'll
take as a group. Besides, wasn't his exit just a little *too* dramatic?"

"Well . . ." I looked around. "Then where is he? If he's not
mad, he should be back here."

"Think for a second, Skeeve," Bunny said, with a grin. "This
is Aahz we're talking about. Where do you think he went,
after a session like that?"

"An inn," I said at once. "I'll go find him."

"Why?"

"Well, just to see how he's doing."

"Don't do it. Why chase him down? Aahz is a big boy. If
he wanted company, he would have left word where he went.
I bet he's telling the bartender and everyone else in earshot
that he got the situation just where he wanted it. And he'd be
right, too. There's no one single way to handle a client."

I grinned back.

"Right," I said. "Then what do we do next?"

"Chumley's got the files. I want him to formulate questions
for the debates."

I nodded. He had by far the most analytical mind among us.

"Guido and Nunzio?"

"I hope they won't be needed over the next few days. They're
putting together a team to oversee the polling places. Nunzio
thinks that Gleep will be able to sniff out any spells or devices
that either side sets. Tanda is sitting this one out. She liked
Emo even less than you did."

"What do you want me to do?"

"Nothing," she said.

"Is it because of what I said a minute ago?" I asked. I got up and took her hand. I felt terrible. "I just have to tell you that what I said is true. I didn't want you as president." Bunny looked crestfallen. "Not then. I mean, only for that single moment, when I was disappointed that the rest of our friends didn't want me back. I do now. I really do. You've been a great president. I'm sorry. I had no business saying that."

"It's all right, Skeeve," she said. "I understand. I felt like blowing off steam myself. I know you really do support me. It's not what you say that counts. It's what you do."

"Then why don't you have a job for me?"

"Oh, I do! But you can have the night off. You're going to be busier than anyone else besides me. Besides providing our backup magikal firepower, I need you to help me judge the debates. I was going to include Aahz on the panel, but he talked himself out of the job." Her eyes twinkled. "I really think he did it on purpose. Ooh, I hate politics!"

"May I buy you a milk shake?" I asked solicitously. "It will cheer you up. Gus makes a terrific strawberry shake."

She kissed me on the cheek. It was a sisterly gesture, but it still made my blood tingle. "Thanks, but I can't. I have to get home to Mother! She hates it when I'm late for dinner." She stood up.

"Do you need a lift?"

"No, thanks. One of Uncle Bruce's magicians is coming for me any minute."

"There you are!"

A brassy trumpet of a voice burst out in the quiet of the tent. A female Klahd about Bunny's age and height pushed through the front flap. She had black hair, a firm chin, round cheeks and dark blue eyes. Her low-cut, electric-blue dress drew attention to her rounded décolletage, even more impressive than Bunny's. It was also cut short enough that I could see most of her shapely legs. It reminded me of the kind of outfit Bunny had worn until she felt comfortable enough to dress the way she really liked, in tailored suits that hugged but didn't reveal her figure. This one didn't mind letting everyone glimpse ninety percent of the goods. The magician from the Mob was a Moll?

"You were supposed to meet me near Crazy Ichor's perfume tent!"

"Sorry, Sylvia," Bunny said.

Sylvia eyed me up and down. Her brows rose in approval. "Say, who's this?"

"Sylvia, this is Skeeve. Skeeve, this is my cousin Sylvia." Bunny performed the introductions hastily. "We ought to get going, Sylvia."

"Skeeve? Really? Skeeve the Magnificent? Say, he's cute! I like them tall and lean and blond. C'mere, Handsome." Sylvia sidled up to me and began to run her hands where her eyes had just traveled. I squirmed aside. She followed me.

"Sylvia!"

The newcomer stopped, but she looked perturbed. "Uncle Bruce said you weren't going to put dibs on him, so he's fair game."

"No, he's not!" Bunny exclaimed.

Sylvia put her hand on her hips. "Well, make up your mind, already! Forget it. We don't have time. Everyone's already waiting for us. Come on. Gascon!"

A Deveel stuck his head inside. "Miss Sylvia? Hello, Miss Bunny."

"Hi, Gascon."

"Three to beam out," Sylvia commanded.

"Yes, Miss Sylvia," he said.

"Move it, Bunny!"

"Yes, sorry, I'm coming." Bunny picked up Bytina from the desk and stuck her into a shoulder bag. "See you later, Skeeve."

"Right. Have a good dinner, Bunny."

She gave me an enigmatic look. I couldn't translate it, and with company present, I couldn't ask.

Gascon came in, rubbing his hands together nervously. I don't know what he'd been told about M.Y.T.H., Inc., but he looked impressed at our domicile. I didn't know why. Even though we took up plenty of interdimensional space, our office was small and underadorned by the standards of Deveel architects, who liked to act poor and live rich. Behind the rear flap of a humble shoemaker's hut might be a pleasure palace with solid-gold fountains and a zoo filled with exotic animals from a hundred dimensions. Gascon drew a circle in the air around him and the two women. The lines that followed his fingertips were bright blue. They grew into a cylinder that surrounded the three of them. It flashed brightly, then disappeared.

BAMF!

"Wait a minute, Bunny!" I called.

I was left by myself, trying to make sense out of what had just happened. Dibs? Fair game? The contract to provide a foothold for the Mob in the Bazaar had ended, but I knew Don Bruce still considered me a powerful ally. I thought he had stopped matchmaking between me and one of his female associates. Maybe he hadn't. Bunny would know. I wished that I could ask her then.

And I hadn't had a chance to tell her that my containment spell at the hotel had been broken from the *inside*.

CHAPTER NINE

"Good politics is cleaning up the town."

—W. EARP

Aahz had not returned by the time Bunny and I left for Tipicanoo the next day. I kept looking for him as we prepared to go.

"Don't worry about him," Bunny insisted.

She was right. Aahz had a solid ego. I ought to have been more worried about what we had to deal with in Tipicanoo. I had had a good night's sleep, but Bunny had circles under her eyes.

"What about you?" I asked. "You look tired."

"Too much family, and too much food," she said. She brightened up and straightened her suit, a businesslike pale-blue coat, though the skirt was still enticingly short. "Let's go!"

BAMF!

I brought us directly into the offices of the *Morning Gossip*. The press was rolling full blast as always. Bales of paper flew overhead, ready to keep their appointment with corner news-stands. I glanced at the clock: a few minutes before ten. We were on time for our planned announcement. Bunny had the press release Chumley had written for us ready in her hand.

Ecstra saw us appear and hurdled her desk. She ran toward us, notebook in hand.

"Skeeve! Bunny! What have you got to say about the report that you have engineered a fixed election date by the two candidates?"

We looked at each other.

"How do you know about that?" I asked.

Ecstra beamed. "So it's true! Tell me everything! Who agreed first? How did you decide on a month from now? Does it have anything to do with favorable conditions in the stars? What sign are you? Give me your impressions of the two candidates! Who has the best chance of winning?"

"Hold it," I said. "Where did you get the impression that there was an agreement?"

Ecstra wrinkled her nose at me. "Don't try to deny it. It's all over town!"

"Who told *you*?"

"Skeeve! I can't reveal my sources. That would be unethical. Now, give me details! We'll put the follow-up in tomorrow's paper!"

"What do you mean, tomorrow's paper?" Bunny asked.

I reached up and snagged a stack of papers flying overhead toward the door. The headline read, *M.Y.T.H., Inc., Maneuvers!* The subhead went on to say, *Backroom confab yields a crop in one month!*

I scanned the article. Bunny read over my shoulder. It contained almost an entire transcript of our meeting. There were no pictures, fortunately. The images on either side of the front page must have been official portraits of Emo and Wilmer.

"I really didn't expect them to stick to their promise," Bunny said, with a shrug. "I suppose that's what the assistants were writing down." She handed the paper to Ecstra. "We wanted you to have an exclusive."

The young reporter scanned the sheet. "Yes, I've seen this stuff already," she said.

"How?"

"Every paper in town has it! Now, give me something juicy. What did you have to promise them to get them to agree? Did Skeeve here have to wrestle them? Was it bribery? How much?"

"We just showed them it was in their best interests," Bunny said.

"Very quotable!" Ecstra said, pleased. "Well, come on, or we'll be late!"

"For what?" I asked.

"For the baby-kissing contest. It's scheduled for ten o'clock."

We followed Ecstra to the town square, where an enormous crowd had already gathered. A white-painted gazebo in the center gave it the air of a quaint country town, except for the campaign decorations all over. Dozens of fresh posters had been plastered on every available wall. *Go Emo!* and *Why Not Wilmer?* were printed on signs stuck every few feet next to pathways and sidewalks. Vehicles bore gaudy slogans on their sides and buckboards and even hanging around the cart animals' necks. The purple and green motif was so strong it took me a minute to realize that all the garbage was gone. The fences and light posts were freshly painted. Every piece of metal in sight had been polished. The grass had been clipped and huge beds of flowers planted. Butterfly birds flew and sang as if they had been especially imported to make the city look festive. I suspected they had. The air smelled of roses and popcorn.

"When did all this happen?" Bunny said.

"About sunset last evening," Ecstra said. "Hordes of campaign workers canvassed the city. And swept and cleaned and painted. It was impressive."

"Uh-huh," I said. "It all started about the time we left. They cleaned the place up pretty well."

Badges in swarms surrounded visitors and pinned themselves onto any available inch. We fought them off, managing to go without being inadvertently adorned. A stack of brochures floating in the air by itself made for us. Three of the pamphlets dealt themselves from the top.

"No, thanks," I said, holding up a hand. The flyer tried to stick itself between my fingers. I shook it loose. It dropped a few inches, then retreated to the main group.

"Aggressive, aren't they?" Bunny observed.

Printed material was not the only voter enticement available. Attractive young Tipps of both genders offered toys, candy, and drinks from trays slung around their necks. As soon as a newcomer entered the town square, he or she was descended upon by a host of eager Emo or Wilmer supporters. Few children went without a toy or balloon in green or purple.

And there were a lot of children. I had never seen so many youngsters in one place outside a school or an amusement park: big ones, little ones, but especially babies in arms. A horde of mothers with infants that extended all around the center and out of the square was being lined up four abreast by more cheerful campaign workers wearing straw hats with purple or green ribbons. Dozens of the babies were crying.

"I hear they have brought in about five thousand babies," Ecstra said. "Good turnout! I wonder if it's going to be a straight count or double elimination."

"Where are the candidates?" Bunny asked.

We looked around. I spotted Wilmer, Emo, and their campaign managers bustling around in the gazebo.

"There they are," I said, pointing over the heads of the crowd.

"Take us over there," Bunny said. Her auburn brows folded downward. "I need to have a word with them."

I put an arm around her waist and pushed off against the ground with my mind.

"Wait for me!" Ecstra called.

She jumped up and grabbed onto my ankle. With her

additional weight, we sank fast. I was afraid of dropping Bunny. I shook my foot, but Ecstra hung on firmly.

"Let go!" I said.

"The press has the right to observe!"

"You're pulling my leg off!"

"Let her come along," Bunny said. "You can do it, Skeeve. I know you can!"

Well, if she believed in me, I couldn't let her down. Grimly, I drew in additional magik from the force lines. Pushing hard, I managed to get all three of us airborne.

CHAPTER TEN

"Some jobs just require lip service."

—M. JAGGER

We sailed over the throng until we came to a barrier at the foot of the gazebo steps with a dozen police patrolling behind it. Three of the officers rose to intercept us. One was my old nemesis, Sergeant Boxty. The other two spread out a dragnet. Sergeant Boxty sat back in the air as if he were in a comfortable chair and patted his belly with both hands.

"Well, well, well, Mr. Skeeve, isn't it? And where do you think you're going?"

"We need to get through. We're overseeing this election."

"A likely story. Let's see your identification!"

"I don't *have* any identification. You already know who I am!"

"It's all right, Nert," Orlow called to him. "They're official staff!"

"Whatever you say, Orlow," Sergeant Boxty. I could tell he was disappointed. He and his men flew off to harass a couple of teenage Tipps who were daring each other to vault the barricade. I found a patch of floor that wasn't occupied at that moment and set us down.

"Welcome, Miss Bunny!" Orlow said, coming over to pump our hands. Carnelia sailed through a crowd of workers hanging up bunting to grab our hands immediately afterward. Her rodent stole chittered happily.

"How do you like the decorations?" she asked, waving a hand behind her. "Aren't they exciting?"

The enormous images of Emo and Wilmer made them look friendly and sage, respectively. Streamers and bunting in their signature colors adorned the railings of the gazebo. Tiny Pixies shot green and purple glitter out of small bronze cannons up on the roof. The bright sparkles rained down on the crowds in drifts. I coughed as a cloud of it floated in my face. Shutterbugs flew everywhere, collecting images in their multilayered wings.

"What is all this?" Bunny asked. "We had a dignified announcement to the press scheduled for this morning, and the first debate this evening!"

"Well, you see, we talked it over, and that just won't do," Carnelia said, her mouth pursed. "Your schedule doesn't allow our candidates to *shine*. The way they deserve, you understand."

Orlow nodded eagerly. "We went over your schedule, and found it a bit . . . lackluster. We wanted to bring out the electorate, really get them excited about the upcoming vote. So we decided to add a few items to the agenda."

Bunny and I looked at each other. I shrugged. "Why not, as long as it's fair. Both candidates must get equal time in front of the public."

"Of course!" both protested.

"May I see the new agenda?" Bunny asked.

"Naturally, ma'am," Orlow said, producing ribbon-tied scrolls. He handed one to each of us, including Ecstra. We unrolled them.

Bunny read down the list, her eyebrows rising higher the further she went on. "Baby kissing, posing with family, debate.

Speeches, shaking hands with constituents, breakfast with the mayor, debate. Press club luncheon, factory visit, debate, pig lifting, opening parks, debate . . . There's eighty-five items here!"

"Yes!" Carnelia said. "And there would have been more, but you've only given us one month to fit it all in! Now, we're just about to begin. Would you care to keep score for us? We want this all to be fair and aboveboard. Since you are the chosen arbiter of this election, you're the logical choice."

"Of course," Orlow agreed. "We would really appreciate it."

"All right," Bunny said, reluctantly. Orlow escorted her to a massive scoreboard furnished with several colors of chalk. Ecstra took up a post at her elbow, notebook in hand. "What do I look for?"

"You have to grade them on kissing style, efficiency, and lack of crying," Orlow said.

"The babies or the candidates?" I asked pointedly.

"Both. And if the candidates get a baby to laugh or smile, they get extra points."

"I understand," Bunny said. She chose a piece of blue chalk. "Ready."

"Let 'er rip!" Carnelia called out.

Emo and Wilmer took their places on either side of the platform. Mothers had formed two lines leading up the white wooden stairs of the gazebo. A stout and prosperous Tipp in a ridiculously tall, conical hat stepped forward. He held up his hands to the crowd. The hubbub fell slightly. His voice boomed out over the thousands of heads.

"Ladies and gentlemen! As your mayor, I am proud to present your candidates for governor of this fair island, Mr. Emo Weavil and Mr. Wilmer Weavil-Scuttil! Let the smooching begin!" He stepped back, clapping his hands. The audience joined in the applause.

Grinning, Emo came forward. He plucked the first infant, a tiny female in a red ruffled dress, out of her mother's hands and bestowed a resounding kiss on the little one's cheek. She made a face but did not burst into tears. The crowd cheered. Emo handed her back to her mother with an expression of relief. Bunny etched a line on his side of the scoreboard. Wilmer went next, bussing a boy on the top of the head between his furry little ears. The child ducked but grinned. Bunny scored Wilmer a point.

"That's one, plus a half for style," Carnelia said. "You can see that it was a clever twist on the standard kiss."

"Well, all right," Bunny said, adding a half mark to the board.

"Thank you for seeing my obvious superiority, ma'am," Wilmer said, graciously, seizing a green-clad tot from a carriage. Emo, not to be outdone, tossed the next baby into the air and got it giggling before he kissed it on the cheek. Bunny gave him two points. Chagrined, Wilmer danced with the next baby in line. I could see him glancing out of the corner of his eye to see if Bunny was impressed. She was.

As time went by, though, she began to pick up on the finer points of the event. A flourish that had caught her attention the first time didn't earn a reward on the fifth or tenth repeat.

"Look at that," she whispered to me. "Wilmer is tickling them with his whiskers! He's making more of them laugh."

"But Emo has a more soothing voice," I noted. "He's got fewer crybabies."

Wilmer bowed to the mother and swept another infant out of his stroller high in the air.

"Incoming!" an aide warned.

Too late.

"Uuurp!"

The boy spat his breakfast all over Wilmer's coat. The Shutterbugs zipped in to take a close exposure.

"A fine child," Wilmer said, never breaking his smile. He handed the lad off hastily. One of his other aides leaped forward to clean Wilmer up as the next mother came forward. "And what's your name, you little sweetie?" The little girl poked him in the eye with her rattle. Wilmer didn't even blink. "Smoochy

smoochy smoochy!" He kissed her and went on to the next baby. He was knocking off five children per minute.

Emo was a little slower, averaging about four, but he showed better scores for style. A very sturdy boy child smacked Emo in the nose with his bottle and kicked wildly. Emo held on to him long enough to give him a peck and passed him back to his mother. The boy didn't start crying until the mother was half-way down the stairs.

I had to give the candidates credit. Baby kissing was a task I wouldn't undertake for anything less than ten gold pieces.

"Waaaaaahhhh!"

A pink-dressed infant burst out crying as soon as Emo picked her up. He looked aghast.

"I didn't do anything yet!" he said. "That's not fair."

"We have a weeper!" Carnelia said. "No points for you."

"It's not his fault," Bunny said. "She was already crying."

"You're siding with him!" Carnelia protested. "I appeal the point!"

"I am not siding with him!" Bunny said. "Fair is fair. He still has to kiss her. Then I can score him."

"I call partisanship!" Carnelia said.

"You haven't seen a challenge you don't like," Orlow complained. "Miss Bunny, I agree with your ruling."

"I want you to mark that one as disputed," Carnelia said.

I began to see why the campaign managers wanted a referee: so they could have someone to blame if their candidate lost the contest. Bunny looked upset.

"Don't pick on her," I said. "*I'll* keep track of disputes. We'll discuss them when this is all over."

I reached for another piece of chalk. Just as I did, Emo let out a strange noise. I turned in time to see pale-blue tentacles reaching up from the baby blanket in his arms. They wound around his neck and started to squeeze. His eyes bugged out and his tongue protruded from his open mouth.

"Gack!" he choked.

"No fair!" Orlow protested.

I dropped the chalk and reached down for a big double handful of magik. "Hang in there, Emo," I said.

Carnelia rushed at me and knocked my hands down. "No!" she said. "You can't interfere with the contest."

I looked at the armful of writhing snakes. "But it's going to kill him!"

"He still has to kiss it," she said. "It's part of the rules."

"No one said you could bring in a squid-snake," Orlow snarled.

Carnelia looked smug. "It's a baby. There's nothing in the rules that you and I agreed on says it has to be a baby Tipp."

"Missed that," Orlow grunted, but he backed away. "Dang."

"He's got to kiss it, or die trying." Carnelia watched the spectacle with pleasure. Bunny and I were aghast. Wilmer, still pecking away at his file of babies, peered out of the corner of his eye.

Emo's eyes had turned red, but he gamely tried to force his mouth close to the huge-eyed face in the midst of the tentacles.

Smack!

As soon as Emo delivered the kiss, the tentacles let go. A beaklike mouth under the enormous eyes opened.

"Gah!" the baby cooed happily. The female who had brought it gathered it back. Emo backed off, gasping.

"That was a dirty trick," I said.

"Not at all," Carnelia said. "It goes by the rules."

"It could have killed him!"

"Isn't the high office he is trying to attain worth the sacrifice?" she asked.

I didn't have an answer for that.

Wilmer let out a howl. The baby in his arms waved six skinny black legs. It was an insect the size of a dog.

"Coochy-coo," he warbled. He leaned in to kiss it, but it grabbed his nose with its mandibles. Wilmer was game, though. "Dice baby. Hode still, dow."

"Why, you stinker," Carnelia said, admiringly.

"Who, me, dear?" Orlow asked, looking pleased. "Nothing to do with us. It must be adopted! Oops, that's a demerit."

The blood spurting from Wilmer's nose scared the next baby in line to tears. Carnelia protested. I chalked it down. I had to add the lemon-skunk disguised as a girl Tipplet that came up about five babies later, not to mention the Tipp quadruplets who all screamed to be kissed first. The candidates certainly had their work cut out for them, but they pressed on. Emo backed away, panting, to apply lip balm. Wilmer changed his immaculate white coats often, as babies seemed to possess dead aim for vomiting, urinating, or defecating on the nice white target.

The contest was long, but the crowd grew instead of shrinking. Baby Tipps began to blur into one another. I know I lost count. Bunny hung on with determination, her forehead wrinkled with concentration. It was hard to keep my attention focused. Five thousand babies was proving to be a contest for me, too. I drew some fresh power out of the force lines to help me stay awake. I used two spikes of magik to hold my eyelids open. I yawned. If I propped my chin on my palm, I could keep my head up.

"Hold it, that's an adult, not a baby!" Orlow protested. He pulled open the blanket in Wilmer's arms. "You're disqualified, sir!"

"Sorry," the blue-skinned Gremlin said, hopping down to the floor and straightening his onesie. "Just a joke, you know."

"Kissing candidates not in your district! I've a good mind to report you."

"Report who?" Carnelia asked, innocently, as the Gremlin disappeared. They had a way of doing that.

Orlow was indignant. His immaculate hair stood up on end.

"Well, I want to make sure that one doesn't get a point!"

"There's a rule against adults posing as babies?" I asked.

"Yes!" Orlow said. "The candidates are supposed to be clever enough to detect them. They get points off for being fooled!"

"I had no idea there were so many rules involved," I said.

"This is nothing," Ecstra said. She patted a yawn. "They are using the beginner's rules. It can get really cutthroat. They're probably saving that for later in the month."

I scanned the scroll. Yes, there was an advanced baby-kissing tournament a few days before the election, no holds barred. I was impressed. Orlow was still upset.

"It's a clear violation of the rules as agreed to substitute adults for the infants, no matter what race! Miss Bunny, as judge, you agree with me, don't you?"

We all turned to her.

"What?" Bunny asked. She raised her head from her folded arms and blinked several times. Her eyelids looked heavy. "I'm sorry, I didn't hear the question."

Orlow sputtered.

"I call for the contest to be voided!" he said. "The judge was asleep!"

"I wasn't . . . !" Bunny said, but she looked uncertain.

"How many babies did you miss?" Carnelia demanded.

"I don't think I missed any," Bunny said. "At least . . . I don't think so." She yawned. Her eyes tried to close again. So did mine.

I realized it wasn't a natural drowsiness. We had been sandbagged by magik. I reached inside for some more power to counteract it, but even my batteries were reacting sluggishly.

"Whichever one of you spelled us, stop it," I said. My voice slurred. I could hardly keep my eyes open. "Otherwise, I'm going to declare this contest invalid, and you'll have to start all over again!"

"No!" Emo and Wilmer shouted. They looked out at the line of babies still to be kissed, and shuddered.

"We want a recount!" Orlow turned to Carnelia. "I put up with a lot of tricks today, but this is the worst! Kayoing the judges!"

Carnelia looked outraged. "I . . . we had nothing to do with this! We're not interfering! We signed a contract."

"As if that means anything to you!"

"Well, how about you?" she countered. "I've seen you put on plenty of good shows while you were lying through your teeth!"

"No! I didn't do it!"

I raised my hands, though it took an effort. "Hold it!" I said. "I don't care who's responsible. Just stop it! Take the spell off. Now."

"We can't," Carnelia said. "We don't know who's doing it."

I yawned.

Yawns are as catching as colds. When I yawned, so did all the Tipps near me. Then the people near them began. The wave of gaping mouths spread outward like a ripple. It reached the edge of the crowd, then started inward once more. I knew that if it hit me again I'd probably fall asleep where I stood. Babies, hit with the weariness spell, started to fuss. I'd been around enough children to know that when one cried, the rest of them would start up in sympathy. With their inborn magical abilities they would wreak their own brand of havoc. Onlookers without their own children started to clear the square. The rally was falling apart. Carnelia and Orlow saw it coming. They decided what to do. They rounded on Bunny.

"This is your fault! You should have kept this from happening! We counted on you!" Orlow said. Carnelia nodded vigorously.

"You insisted on total control. Now, exercise it!"

Bunny's nose was bright red and her eyes shiny with unshed tears of frustration, but she was too strong to break down in front of the clients.

"How can I control a spectacle that I didn't know about?" she asked. "You gave me no time to prepare."

Orlow shook a finger at her. "That doesn't matter. Emo wanted to hire M.Y.T.H., Inc., because he heard you were quick to react, spectacle or no spectacle."

"Of course we can!" Bunny protested.

Spectacle, that was it!

"Don't worry," I said. "We can handle it."

Fighting hard against the lethargy that enveloped my limbs as well as my eyelids, I kicked off against the floor and scrambled up on the roof of the gazebo. The Pixies drooped in webs of sunlight strung between the eaves. They'd been hit by the sleep spell, too.

"Fire off all the glitter cannons!" I ordered. "Do you know any fireworks spells?"

"Sure," the lead Pixie said, stretching her tiny arms. She was dressed in red with a fluffy skirt. "But they were for the grand finale."

"It's the finale now," I said. I glanced down. The wave of yawns was making a second ripple. Babies were starting to kick and cry.

The Pixies swung leisurely from their makeshift hammocks, stretching and scratching. They fluttered together and began to braid one another's hair and shine each other's wings.

"Hurry," I said.

"You can't hurry perfection!" the lead Pixie squeaked.

"WAAAAAAAAHHHHHHH!!!"

It was too late. The first toys went sailing across the square. With the force of the combined magik behind them, they struck hard.

Wailing rose from the babies hit by flying rattles and dolls. They unleashed their own missiles. More than infants fell casualty to the onslaught. Innocent adults took baby bottles to the head. They burst into tears, too. Many of them sat down on the cobblestones, refusing to move even when their companions urged them. Few forces in the universe were stronger than an unhappy infant. They had a way of spreading their miserable mood to those nearby, and the problem here was multiplied by five thousand. The smell of hundreds of dirty diapers rose to the skies. Adults and babies snatched toys away from one another. Hair-pulling and scratching incidents multiplied.

"Can I help?" I asked.

"Don't rush us!" a Pixie in green complained.

"Pixies, together!" the leader said. "Pixie power!"

They took their places behind the ornate bronze cannons. Balls of colored light bloomed in their palms. They applied the light to the base of each cannon. Brilliant sparkles erupted over the heads of the crowd.

"Babies!" I shouted. "Up here!"

Suddenly, the faces of hundreds of babies were upturned, as particles of glittering amethyst and emerald twinkled down on them. The green Pixie zipped upward and began to draw huge clusters of light in the sky. They exploded into starbursts with booms and whistles.

"Ooh!" the children exclaimed happily, pointing with tiny fingers. "Pretty!" "Want!" "Goodie!"

Once the display was well underway, I swooped down to rejoin Bunny. Whatever the source of the drowsiness spell, it had abated. No doubt neither Orlow or Carnelia could maintain it while arguing with one another.

"You ruined this whole event," Carnelia said.

"I ruined it? How? By not surrendering the first time you brought in a nonstandard baby? Or by not going to sleep on the job?"

"That's enough!" Bunny said. "I declare a tie."

"You can't do that!" Carnelia and Orlow said in unison.

Bunny smiled sweetly. "Sure I can. You put me in charge of this contest, as well as this election. I am invoking paragraph three point one eight of the contract. Mr. Mayor, would you like to make the announcement? We'd be honored to have you do it."

The mayor blinked at her. "Why, yes, little lady, I would consider it a privilege!"

She turned to the campaign managers. "Both of you go back to your headquarters. I don't want either of you or your candidates out doing anything until the debate starts this evening. I don't care who's to blame for what just happened."

"My goodness, you're strict," Carnelia said.

"I don't like it, but we'll go along with it. Emo Weavil is known for sticking to the rules! He stands for fairness and justice!"

"That's why I hate being involved with politics," Bunny whispered to me as the mayor held up his hands for silence. "I can't tell which one of them is lying!"

CHAPTER ELEVEN

"Be careful not to step in the katunga."

—B. HILL

BAMF!

I had never been so glad to get back to M.Y.T.H., Inc., headquarters. The smells of dust, dung, perfume, and hot sun drifting through the tent door were a welcome change from the overwhelming odors of sickly perfume and unchanged baby in the Bokromi town square. I felt like a wrung-out rag.

"Excuse me, Skeeve," Bunny said. "I need a little time to myself."

"Would you like a cup of wine first?" I asked. "I could sure use one."

She smiled at me. "Not at the moment, Skeeve. Thanks."

She went into her room and locked the door. I poured myself a welcome goblet from the pitcher on the table by the wall and settled into one of the comfortable couches in the atrium. The fountain played gently, and the pale gray glow that passed for sunlight in Limbo slanted through the skylight. Gleep bounded into the room and put his head in my lap.

"Hey, boy," I said, scratching his ears.

"Skeeve . . . okay?"

"I'm fine." I sighed. "That was exhausting! And we're not finished for the day."

"So, how is it going?" Aahz appeared at my side, holding a bucket-sized stein. He took a swig from it.

"Aahz! You're here!"

He winked at me. "Where else would I be? I was just letting someone out."

Suddenly I noticed that there was a second cup on the table between the couches. It was considerably smaller than the one he was holding. I smelled a flowery, nutty fragrance—perfume—and looked around with a guilty start.

"Did I interrupt something?" I asked.

Aahz shook his head.

"No. She was ready to leave anyhow."

"Oh." Aahz didn't offer any more details, and I didn't ask. His personal life was none of my business. I looked Aahz straight in the eye.

"I thought you were pretty upset yesterday when Bunny threw you out of the meeting."

"You fell for the act, too?" Aahz asked, nonchalantly. "Pretty good, wasn't it?"

I stared at him. "That was all an act?"

He put a hand to his chest. "Of course! Do you think I care if I am involved in a penny-ante local election? Those two are so small-time they could duke it out in a matchbox."

"Bunny shouldn't have made you leave."

"No, she was right, kid. The customer is always right. What's the difference? You've got my wisdom to draw on, no matter where I am. I'd rather be the power behind the throne than Target Number One any time. You think I stomped out of there because my feelings were hurt?"

"Well, I . . ."

Aahz cut off my speculation with a gesture. "Of course not! They wanted to win something, so I let them. It's good strategy. It made them more inclined to say yes to whatever else Bunny wanted. It worked!"

That was pretty much what Bunny had said.

"So you goaded them on purpose?"

"Not especially. I did it because it was fun. Also, I wanted to see just how thick their skins were. Pretty solid, not a surprise, but every bit of information gives you insight into how they'll behave. Not that I'm that interested in it. I've got some other business to take care of." He finished with an expression that caused me to doubt his words.

"Are you really all right?" I asked. He waved the question away.

"Ha! I'm fine. Are you? You look like the last man standing in a jitterbug contest."

"*What* kind of bug?" I asked.

"Forget it," Aahz said. "How are our clients doing?"

"Well, they lie. And they cheat," I said. "On everything. We were supposed to make the statement about the scheduled vote, but they spread the word right after we left last night. And they have arranged all kinds of events that they never discussed with us."

I handed Aahz the scroll. His scaly eyebrows rose almost to the top of his head as he read. He grinned as he handed it back.

"That's some creative time-wasting," he said. "They don't want to talk about the real issues. This way they get lots of attention without discussing anything substantial."

"Well, they won't get away with it," I said, resolutely. "We want to run this like a real election."

"Kid, I have some bad news—this is stuff that they do in real elections."

"You're joking!"

"Were you old enough to vote before you left home?" Aahz asked. "No? Well, you never saw any real action. People running for office will do anything to gain an advantage, even if it's temporary."

I felt my temper heating up. "They made Bunny cry."

"That just means she's mad, not sad. I would worry more about you than her."

"Well, you don't have to worry about me."

"I know that." Aahz swigged his beer. "So, what's next on the agenda?"

"The first debate," I said. "I gave them Chumley's questions so they could prepare their answers."

"They won't bother."

"Sure they will! We're making the rules. They said they would follow them."

"Kid, I will bet you a hundred gold pieces that they do not answer one single question substantively at any time," Aahz said.

Aahz never made any kind of wager that he considered had even a minute chance of him having to pay out. I eyed him. "So why are they going through with it?"

"To give the electorate the illusion that they are choosing the best candidate in the field. Don't worry about it. Enjoy it. It's theater. You might pick up a few pointers in how to lie effectively. You could use the help."

"Thanks a lot," I said.

Bunny's door opened. We looked up. She emerged in a bright red suit that had been ironed to a low sheen.

"Oh, hi, Aahz."

"Hey, Bunny. Nice power suit."

"Thank you, Aahz." She smiled at him. "You want to come along and hear the fairy tales?"

"No, thanks. I'd rather stay here and pound myself on the foot with a jackhammer."

"Me, too," Bunny said with a sigh. "But it's part of the job. Are you ready, Skeeve?"

"Gleep!"

I glanced down at my dragon. His large blue eyes were beseeching. I saw something else in his gaze.

"I want to bring him with us, Bunny."

"I don't think that's a good idea, Skeeve."

"I do," Aahz said suddenly. "That pesky dragon might be useful."

"Gleep!" my pet exclaimed. He leaped up on Aahz, trying to slime him with his long, agile tongue.

"Down!" Aahz bellowed. "When are you going to teach him some manners?"

"He's just showing he likes you, Aahz," I said, pulling Gleep's long neck back so he dropped to all fours on the floor. "You're one of his favorite people."

"I think I could live a few more centuries before hearing that I was number one on a dragon's hit parade," Aahz grumbled.

"He didn't hit you!" I said, in defense of my pet. Gleep put his head against my legs and looked guilty. Aahz waved a hand.

"That's not . . . never mind. Go on, or you'll be late for the show."

CHAPTER TWELVE

"Lies, damned lies, and statistics."

—THE AGENDA IN ANY POLITICAL DEBATE

And a show it proved to be. As we didn't want any accusations of favoritism, the debates were to be held in the open air, in a field miles from either campaign headquarters. We hired a local carriage from our point of arrival in Bokromi to take us there. It took about half an hour through the gathering twilight. We discussed strategy on the way.

"I arranged for a stage ten feet high, with lecterns for each candidate and a desk for us, the moderators, in the middle," Bunny said. "I also wanted about ten Echoes to repeat our voices all the way to the back of the crowd. The contractor said he could get it all here on time."

As I got out of the enclosed carriage, I saw a small wooden stage. A small table lined with green and purple bunting stood on it alone.

"The desk is there," I said, "but where are the lecterns?"

"And what are those flagpoles on either side?" Bunny asked.

The standards stood at least two hundred feet high. I squinted into the dark sky.

"I can't tell."

As we watched, the poles grew taller, first on one side, then the other. I could feel erratic surges of magik. It came from a narrow white force line running about a hundred feet away.

"What is going on there?" Bunny asked. A small crowd had gathered in front of the stage. We joined it. Ecstra was already there. I guessed from their hats, sharp-brimmed fedoras with a card in the brim, that they were fellow reporters. They all had notebooks. Shutterbugs fluttered overhead, snapping exposures with the filmy wings under their hard shells.

"Miss Bunny!" Orlow greeted us. "And Mr. Skeeve." He grabbed my hand, pulled me close, and turned his head to smile for the Shutterbug.

"Well, hello, there," Carnelia added, throwing a companionable arm over Bunny's shoulder. "We are just making a few little bitty changes to the arrangement here." The reporters scribbled busily in their notebooks.

"What happened to the speakers' tables?" Bunny asked. "Where is Thorwald?"

A Tipp with silvery gray fur raised a forefinger. "Right here, ma'am."

"You said you could have everything ready for this evening."

"And I did, ma'am, until these folks got here." He shot an accusing look at Orlow and Carnelia. "Everything's gotten a little out of hand."

"What has?" Bunny asked, planting her hands on her hips. "Where are the speakers' platforms?"

Thorwald pointed. "Up there." I craned my head back to look. The narrow staffs were surmounted by a tiny square.

"Why are they so high up?"

"It was him," Carnelia said, sneering at Orlow. "He started it."

Orlow huffed, expanding his cheeks.

"Well, as the leading candidate, I felt that Emo should have

a slightly higher stage. So I had my magician, Riginald, lift
it a bit." One of the campaign workers, a paunchy middle-aged
male, raised a hand and wiggled his fingers at us. "Not very
much, you understand. Purely symbolic."

"Well, that little symbol was an insult to Wilmer as the
senior candidate," Carnelia said. "So Morton had to raise ours."

"We want Emo to be outstanding in this field, as he is in
all others," Orlow said, pitching his voice so the gang of reporters behind me could hear him clearly. "So that meant bringing
him up just a little more. Then they jacked theirs up!"

"Then he did it again!"

"Then she did!"

I turned to Carnelia. "What about Wilmer?" I asked. "Why
did his have to go higher?"

"Well, he wants to show that Wilmer rises above any and
all petty issues," Carnelia said. "Especially those brought up by
his opponent."

"But they're too high," I said, reasonably. "How can we see
how they stand on their platforms if they're above anyone's eye
level?"

The assembled reporters leaned over their notebooks so as
not to miss a word.

"We'll reduce the height temporarily," Carnelia said, aware
that she was being overheard. "But we want credit for wanting
to meet the people on their level first. Before the opposition."

"We were already willing to bring our stage down!" Orlow
complained.

"So bring them down," Bunny said. "Pronto. We've only
got a couple of minutes before the debate starts."

"He has to do it first," Carnelia said, pointing at Orlow. "As
a gesture of good faith."

"I want assurances first that if we move on this point, she
will respond in kind," Orlow said. "It's the ladylike thing
to do."

Bunny groaned with frustration. She turned to me.
"Skeeve?"

Reducing the size of platforms wasn't in my skill set, and Bunny knew that, but she trusted me. I kicked off from the ground and flew up to the top of the teetering platforms. It took a good deal of magik, but I lifted both lecterns off their perches and brought them down with me to the ground. Thorvald's grips took them from me and arranged them on the dais.

"There," Bunny said brightly. "They can be on the stage with us, on either side of our table. Let's get started."

Bunny and I took our places in straight-backed chairs behind the bunting-covered table. We had a pitcher of water and glasses, the list of questions, and an hourglass and a little silver bell that we were supposed to ring if either candidate went over time in his answers. Gleep lay on the stage behind us, curled up in case we needed him. I had spread the word that he would personally eat anyone who physically attacked any of us on stage. In reality, I knew Gleep wouldn't do such a thing. For a dragon he was very gentle.

The candidates came out. They shook hands and sauntered to their lecterns as the crowd went wild cheering. The bands played rival fight songs, and the air filled with confetti.

"My dear friends! Thank you for your attention!" Wilmer bellowed.

"Welcome, all!" Emo shouted.

The debate was meant to give both candidates a chance to show off for their adoring fans. Thousands of them had gathered, along with two marching bands and confetti cannons. Emo was at his adorable best. I kind of liked the gaudy green coat and tie he had on, though Bunny had rolled her eyes at his clothes. I admit I wasn't much of a judge of fashion. His eyelashes had been augmented even more outrageously. He looked as if he had a brush over each eye. His eyes, too, seemed larger and more luminously brown than usual. Whenever Wilmer was answering a question, Emo took the time to flirt with the audience, smiling and pointing at individuals.

Wilmer, too, found opportunities to look dignified and grandfatherly. His wig was freshly styled and bleached to blinding whiteness. When Emo went off on high-flying prose jaunts, Wilmer shook his head gravely in disapproval. He clutched the lapels of his white flannel coat and bowed from the waist whenever one of his supporters called out his name.

I suspected both campaign managers had orchestrated at least some of the outpourings of approval. On the other hand, ordinary townsfolk, those without an obvious Wilmer or Emo badge or colored button, were showing a lot more interest in the proceedings than before. I wondered if they were waiting for another disaster to strike as it had at the baby-kissing contest. I kept my eyes open for any obvious attempts at sabotage, though I had no idea what those would be.

Apart from the obvious, that was. Mrs. Weavil was in the front row, clutching her handbag close. When she heard answers she didn't like, which was almost every time Wilmer spoke, she dipped into her inexhaustible supply of gooey ammunition hidden within. So did the rest of the green-wearing crew, as well as the purple-banner wearers. Bunny and I were untouched so far because of a magikal shield I had erected, not to mention a rumor I had let get around that Gleep would personally eat anyone who threw something at one of us.

"In answer to your question on the economy, little miss," Wilmer said, his voice deep and ponderous, "I can't say that my opponent is an unscrupulous scalawag, as I have heard others say, but I can't disprove it, either. However"—he ducked just in time to avoid a handful of sticky goo that sailed past his head—"I can add that his announced plans give me no confidence. And you should feel the same. Thank you."

A rain of sodden vegetables hit the stage in front of him, spattering his immaculate white trousers. Gleep bounded over and began to eat the missiles with relish. He even liked the mud.

"Mr. Weavil-Scuttil," Bunny said, pitching her voice so the Echoes, huge-eared, sunset-hued cliff dwellers from Desybell, would hear it and repeat it to the enormous crowd, "you haven't answered me. What will you do to improve the economy on Bokromi? What are your specific plans?"

"Why, little miss," Wilmer began, not realizing how much his continued use of the phrase was trying Bunny's temper, "I promise you that I rely upon trusted advisors who have their finger, their very finger, on the pulse of the local merchants!"

"All that proves is that you know they're not dead," Emo quipped. It earned him laughter from most of the crowd and a bunch of rotten onions from a burly Wilmer supporter. He dodged them neatly. Gleep slithered around behind his feet to retrieve them. The sound of my dragon noisily munching could be heard to the last row of the audience.

One point for Emo. I made a note on the slate in front of me. That had to have been improvised on the spot. Most of their answers, especially the lengthy ones, suggested the employment of professional scriptwriters. I doubted that either Emo or Wilmer was capable of such verbal pyrotechnics. It *was* entertaining, since I had given up during the first half hour any hope that this would be a discussion of the issues. Bunny had not. She persisted in trying to get them to answer her questions.

"Mr. Weavil, one for you, then," Bunny said, patiently.

"Yes, dear lady?" Emo fluttered his eyelashes at her.

"If elected governor, how will you root out corruption in the administration?"

"Well, since none of my opponent's friends or colleagues will be in office with me, I assume that the problem will be moot," Emo said. Everyone laughed. He smiled and waved. Wilmer emitted a squawk of outrage. Bunny gestured him to silence and leaned forward with a follow-up.

"Does that mean you are replacing the entire government when you take office? Police, firefighters, magicians, file clerks, gardeners—everyone?"

Emo put on a deeply sincere expression. "Well, Miss Bunny, I believe that deep down most people are good and honest. I always seek to surround myself with those who believe as I do."

"Hurray for Emo!" Mrs. Weavil led the cheering.

"In that case, we are all doomed," Wilmer barked out. "Anyone who is as deluded as that should be nowhere near

government of the people, by the people, and for the people!"
He held his hand in the air.

"Mr. Weavil-Scuttil." Bunny tried to make herself heard
over the cheering from his side. "It's not your turn to speak."

"Well, he interrupted me!"

"Only because you have no self-control," Emo said. "Think
what you'll be like in office. Dancing in the streets! Fiscal
irresponsibility!"

"Better than your cowardly refusal to take steps to combat
problems!"

"Gentlemen!" Bunny shouted. "Mr. Weavil, would you like
to conclude your statement?"

Emo bowed to her. "I certainly would, dear lady. I promise
that in my first term, I will investigate all questions as they
are put to me, and I put to you wow bubbuh dim bootah wuh!"
The audience tittered nervously. He stopped talking and glared
at Wilmer. "Duh bah nin toom vip skap lo!"

"Well, that's an improvement," Wilmer said, grinning.

"What did you do to him, Mr. Weavil-Scuttil?" Bunny
asked, fury coloring her pretty face the same red as her hair.
He turned to her with his eyes nearly as wide as Emo's.

"Me? I didn't do a darn thing. I'm no magician. I am just
a humble servant of the people." He made a courtly little bow.
Bunny was not amused.

"You have magicians working for you. If you don't take the
spell off him before I count to three, I will declare the debate
Emo's by default!"

"You can't do that!"

"Stop telling me what I can't do!" Bunny snapped. She held
up a finger. "One . . . TWO . . ."

Wilmer thrust out his hands to forestall Bunny's wrath. "I
swear, I didn't tell anyone to make him talk nonsense. You have
got me all wrong, Miss Bunny!" His voice rose in pitch until
he sounded like a mosquito. As we watched, Wilmer shrank.
His head got smaller and smaller until he disappeared inside

his pristine suit. The suit collapsed to the floor. A tiny hand reached out and grabbed the tie. Wilmer emerged from the collar wearing the cravat around his waist like a bath towel.

In spite of his momentary lack of vocal skills, Emo started braying with laughter. All his supporters howled and pointed.

"This is outrageous!" Wilmer squeaked. "This is no position for a man of my years and dignity!"

"Bunny." I reached over and touched her on the arm. She nearly bit my head off as she turned. "This isn't going to get better. We should call it a day."

She went very still, then nodded. "You're right." She picked up the tiny bell and tinkled it. The sound carried amazingly well through the Echo sound system. "Ladies and gentlemen, this concludes tonight's debate. Thank you all for coming."

"But who won?" Mrs. Weavil shouted from the lip of the stage. "My baby was the better debater!"

"No! Wilmer was!" shouted one of the Weavil-Scuttils. The crowd all shouted for their favorites.

Bunny cleared her throat, and the voices fell silent. "I declare that this debate was . . . a tie. Each of the candidates answered questions with the same level of . . . clarity and dignity."

Emo raised his hands over his head in a victory sign. Carnelia rescued the miniature Wilmer and held him up to receive acclaim from his fans.

"We'll be back to normal in the morning," she told us as the crowd cleared out. "Don't you believe for a moment that a little setback like this will stop Wilmer. And, fine job, all of you." She smiled. "Didn't think you all would last through the evening, but you did."

She left the stage. I could hear Wilmer squeaking indignantly in her grasp.

Orlow came to shake our hands. "Emo wants you to know that he's grateful for your firm hand on tonight's debate. We can't let those Weavil-Scuttils cast this election into a pool of nonsense. See you tomorrow."

Bunny leaned on my shoulder. "Politics isn't for sissies," she said.

"Hey, Skeeve!"

I glanced at the edge of the stage. Ecstra grinned up at me.

"This is going to make terrific copy! Thanks!"

"At least someone is happy," Bunny said.

CHAPTER THIRTEEN

*"Never let the facts get in the way of
a good story."*

—R. MURDOCH

When we popped into Tipicanoo the next morning, Ecstra was waiting for us. She was more neatly attired than usual, every hair in place, her hat at an extra rakish angle. I glanced around at the street corner where we had arrived.

"How do you know where and when we were going to be here?" I asked. "Sometimes I don't even know."

Ecstra held her nose in the air. "Inside sources," she said.

I leaned toward her conspiratorially. "I'd sure like to talk to those sources," I said. "In the interest of making my magik more effective."

"Sorry," she said coldly. She backed away from me. "I can't possibly trust you with any of my confidential informants."

I was taken aback by the unfriendliness of her tone.

"Why not?" I asked. "What's happened?" She had been so friendly the night before.

"I thought you folks were going to be nonpartisan!"

"Of course we are," Bunny said. "Why?"

She thrust a newspaper at us. I opened it. In the center of the front page of the *Sunrise Tipp-Off* was a picture of Bunny and me. In my hand was a purse bulging with coins. I was dropping it into the outstretched hand of a male Tipp bathed in shadow. It was impossible to tell who it was. The headline read, *Corruption in our Midst!*

"Then how do you explain this?" she demanded. "Last night? Midnight? In the alley next to the garbage dump?"

The article cited "one of the candidates," speaking under condition of anonymity. "'It's a sure thing,' he said to our reporter. 'I can't lose this election. My opponent is perpetrating a number of underhanded schemes to sway the voters. He has even arranged for the judges to be biased toward him at upcoming events. But the truth will come out! The truth always does! Once the extent of his perfidy is known, he will be disqualified, he and all his co-conspirators!'"

Growing more outraged with every line, I read down the columns.

"And it says that last night's debate was rigged because the other side had gotten the questions in advance," Ecstra added, pointing at a paragraph.

"*Both* candidates got them in advance!" I said.

Ecstra raised her eyebrows. "So one line of this interview is true. What about the rest? What about the picture?"

"That never happened," I said. "We went home after the debate. I fell asleep before I took my shoes off."

"I talked to the Shutterbug who took it last night," Ecstra insisted. "Pola was adamant that it was the two of you, offering a bribe to one of the Weavils. How many Klahds are there in Tipicanoo? It seems pretty straightforward."

"If you're so certain, then who were we supposed to have given it to?" I asked. "And according to the article, the bribes were going from one of the candidates to us! If your Shutterbug was right there, she should know who took the money.

I can't tell who's in the picture. It might not be Emo or Wilmer at all."

Ecstra hesitated. "She said he couldn't see him clearly. But there was no doubt about you or the bag of money!"

"That's ridiculous," Bunny said. "Any magician worth his salt can put an illusion on two people and make them look like anyone else. You can't prove it was us. Who told the Shutterbug to be in the alley at midnight?"

"Uh . . ."

"More confidential sources?" I asked.

Ecstra nearly bit my nose off.

"My boss told me to talk to her! Pola is very reliable. She wouldn't lie to a fellow reporter!"

"Was someone lying to *her*?" I asked.

"She's not easy to fool," Ecstra said. "Images are her profession. She's good at seeing the truth."

"The article is very confusing. The picture says one thing, the words say another, and neither one is true," I insisted.

"It had to be something that Carnelia or Orlow set up to discredit the other side," Bunny said.

Ecstra pushed her hat up in the back so it settled at a more rakish angle over her nose. "Then I will find out which," she said. "The public deserves to know the truth!"

She turned and stomped away from us.

"She's heading for Emo," I said. "Let's go check with Wilmer first."

The white-haired solon had been restored overnight to his normal height. He was outraged at the article in the *Tipp-Off*. Copies of it were strewn all around his office. Carnelia sat on a desktop. Her rodents romped around her, tearing up pieces of newsprint and rolling in them. They seemed to be the only creatures having a good time. Wilmer was quick to avow his innocence.

"I tell you, good people, I did not do this! I did not give an interview to the *Tipp-Off*, and I most certainly did not receive a purse of money from anyone last night. Not that it wouldn't be welcome, but aboveboard and in the light of day, on behalf of the people of Bokromi, you understand. I wouldn't accept a donation in a dark alley. You never know what kind of people congregate there. But slander! That is something up with which I will not put!"

"That was another thing," I said. "The grammar quoted from the 'candidate speaking on condition of anonymity' was perfect. My mother was a schoolteacher. She hammered the rules into me. I'm not saying they all took, but she did the best she could with me."

"And your point, young sir?"

"Neither of you speaks that way," I pointed out. "Nor do your campaign managers. Now I haven't spoken to all of your workers, but is there one who is unusually fussy about grammar?"

Wilmer exchanged frowns with Carnelia. She shook her head. "Can't say that I've noticed someone who corrects my whys and wherefores, son. But I'll keep an ear open."

"In the meantime," Bunny added sweetly, "I'd appreciate it if you would make copies for us of any interviews you give the press. Or if anyone approaches you with an offer to provide . . . unusual help?"

Wilmer bowed over her hand. "Why, of course, little lady. Anything to be fair."

Emo, also restored to his usual loquaciousness, insisted that no one from his office was involved in the alleged bribery scheme.

"I don't do subterfuge," he said, blinking his long false lashes at us. "It's counterproductive. The public doesn't like it. That is what I told Miss Ecstra a short while ago. She said she would quote me. I hope you believe me. No one who works for me would have done such a thing, not even Orlow. As I have told you from the beginning, I don't want an unfair advantage."

He gave us both a soulful look. The workers in his office sighed with pleasure. They all had signed portraits of him on their desks. "I did not give that interview. Nor would I take part in either side of a buy-off. The money is never worth it. That's one of my mottos. Do you have a copy of my memoirs? There's an index to my sayings in the back." He held out his hand, and one of the young Tipps came running with a leather-bound book. He pressed it into Bunny's hands. She gave it back.

"No, thanks," Bunny said. "We can't accept gifts from either one of you. Remember the rules? No gifts over a copper piece in value?"

Emo smacked himself in the forehead. The office workers let out whimpers of sympathy. "Oh, why didn't I think of that! I am sorry! I had no intention of causing any impropriety! You know I have been straightforward through this whole process!"

I wasn't going to get into a circular argument. "Do you have any reason to believe that someone masqueraded as you to the reporter for the *Sunrise Tipp-Off?*"

"I can imagine," Emo said. "It had to be Wilmer! He would tell any kind of falsehood to get elected. I stand above that kind of thing. Absolutely! May I count on your support at the family picture event at two o'clock?"

"For both you *and* Wilmer," I said firmly.

"Of course," Emo said, with a winning smile. "But my family is more appealing than his."

We left the office and went out. It was starting to drizzle. Foot traffic had grown heavy since we were inside. Shoppers, pulling unwilling toddlers or wheeling babies along the walkway, browsed in and out of the storefronts. They flew up and back between the street levels. Carts carrying enormous loads under canvas passed by, throwing water up out of the gutters. Those remained clear of garbage. I wondered how many of Emo's and Wilmer's people had been out all night cleaning them up. It all looked so ordinary, but I felt uneasy.

"One of them is lying," Bunny said, putting her arm through mine. "But which one?"

I dragged my attention back to her and considered the question. "I can't tell. They both seem like they're telling the truth."

"Why do you keep looking over your shoulder?" Bunny asked, as I glanced back again.

"I think someone is following us," I said. "I can feel it."

A Tipp in a high collar and a cap pulled low over his eyes broke through the crowd behind us.

"Hey!" a mother shouted. Her toddler had been knocked to the ground. "I said, hey!"

She threw a handful of magik at the male. It bounced off him and hit us instead. My head rang as a slap knocked me sideways. Bunny gasped with outrage. Her cheek turned pink, too.

"That wasn't nice!" she said to the woman.

The female gasped. "I didn't mean to . . ."

By then, the male had reached us. He grabbed my hand and pressed a thick brown envelope into it. I tried to hand it back. He dodged me and shot upward.

I kicked off the ground and went off after him.

"Who are you? Who is this from?"

He swooped in between floating lanterns, lines of laundry, and other Tipps taking the airborne shortcut. I did my best to follow him, but he knew the layout of the city much better than I did. He ducked into a market on the third level up from the ground. I came up after him and found myself looking down a solid row of fruit and vegetable stands, with hundreds of customers shopping.

"Come on, getcha nice fresh pompom melons here!" called one lushly built female, holding up a couple of round, red fruits. "Deeeeee-licious!"

"Purple berries! Ripe this morning! Purple berries! Put hair on your chest!" A Tipp with a large ruff of fur showing between the lapels of his striped jacket thrust boxes of fruit at me as I went past. "Hey, Klahd! Eat some! Make up for what nature didn't do for you! Only two coppers!"

"No, thanks," I said. I scanned the row of carts. There!

Underneath a wagon full of orange finger-fruit was the Tipp in the cap. I upset a woman's market basket. Green pippins cascaded down over both of us. She screamed abuse at me. I apologized and dove underneath the fruit cart. The Tipp squeezed out onto the sidewalk and started running.

I flew up above the canopies, doing my best to follow him, but lines of washing hung down from windows overhead. I dodged a load of diapers, but a pair of long underwear swung up in the breeze. It hit me in the face. I brushed the wet cloth out of my eyes and looked down. The Tipp was gone. I was left with the envelope and no answers to where it came from or who had sent it.

I returned to Bunny. A crowd had gathered around her and the female who had struck us. She regarded us wide-eyed.

"So you're the bribe-taking Klahds I read about in the paper!" she said with delight. Her hand flew to the side of her head. "Oh my, and I came out of the house without fixing myself up! My hair is a mess! And I don't have a lick of makeup on. I wasn't ready for the Shutterbugs! It's an honor to meet you!" She grasped my hand and pumped it. "Oh, how exciting! I actually saw it happen! And that reporter asked my name, and everything! He said I'll be in the papers tomorrow! Wait until I tell my husband!" She scooped up her toddler and hurried away, burbling to the child.

"Reporter?" I asked Bunny, as the crowd melted away.

"We were set up," she said grimly. "A Shutterbug caught you taking the envelope from that Tipp. A reporter took statements from a bunch of witnesses, including that woman."

I examined the envelope. It was old but unmarked, giving no clue as to where it had come from.

"Be careful!" Bunny cautioned me. "It could be a bomb!"

Picturing the sequence of events I wished to happen in my mind, I sent the envelope about twenty feet in the air. My action attracted more attention to us, but I thought it better to err on the side of safety. Bunny stuck her fingers in her ears. I made the flap of the flying envelope open.

Nothing happened.

I beckoned it down to me and looked inside.

"What's in it?" Bunny asked.

"Nothing," I said, displaying the contents. "Cut-up newspapers. From several different papers." Droplets of rain made a pattern on the gray sheets. The whole bundle sagged in my hands.

"Who would do that?" Bunny asked in dismay. "Someone is going to a lot of trouble to ruin our credibility."

"Whichever candidate is lying to us the most," I said. "It'll be page one tomorrow."

Bunny took my wrist. "Then we're going to set a backfire," she said. "We're going to give Ecstra an exclusive. We'll start our own rumors."

CHAPTER FOURTEEN

"Not all of one's offspring are presentable."

—HER MAJESTY, E. R. II

Ecstra was tickled to be taken into our confidence. We sat across from her, leaning over her desk. No one could hear us anyhow over the noise of the press, but I tried to construct a shield as Orlow and Carnelia had done in our meeting. Anyone listening in would hear boring, tinny music from a wind-up music box I had bought at the Bazaar.

"And none of this is true?" she asked, jotting down note after note.

"Not a word of it," Bunny said.

"Zow! So, you set up the bribe in the main street this morning yourself?"

"Absolutely," Bunny said, crossing her fingers on her lap. "We wanted to let the Tipicanoo public know how easy it is to destroy a reputation. And how easily a rumor can get started."

"Wow," Ecstra said, her eyes huge. "It's been the talk of every newspaper in town, how you took an envelope full of money from a guy in broad daylight!"

"Now, isn't that just a little too obvious?" Bunny said, with a broad wink. "You know all about my background. I would be laughed out of our next Family reunion if I ever arranged for a dropoff in public. But I might later on, just for effect. Only you and we will know it's a phony." Bunny let her long eyelashes droop in an exaggerated wink.

"That's fantastic," Ecstra said. "Can I see the envelope?"

I handed it to her. She wrote a full description of it, noting the contents in detail, and how we said it had come into our possession. When she took it to the typesetter, the image appeared right in the center of the column. Bunny and I smiled.

Whereas the baby-kissing and the debate had been held in the open air, the family portraits were going to be taken at an address on a side street.

"How cute!" Bunny exclaimed, as we caught sight of the cozy little blue-painted cottage. "But that's not big enough for everyone."

"It's bigger on the inside than it is on the outside," Ecstra assured us.

I whistled as we entered.

In spite of its outward appearance, the house had been expanded extradimensionally inside so there was more than enough room for the candidates, their managers, a host of campaign workers in both green and purple, Shutterbugs, and hundreds of reporters. Not only that, members of the public stood pushing against a barrier nearby, holding gifts for their favorite. I looked around cautiously.

"I don't see any protesters here yet," I said.

"They won't come in here," Ecstra said, gleefully. "They wouldn't dare."

In spite of her confidence, I felt around the room with my mind. I didn't feel anything out of the ordinary. I ran threads of force around the walls to give me a warning in case there was a magikal invasion, though I knew that trying to prevent one would be futile. The place had too many doors, not to mention the skylight in the ceiling open to let the sun in. All I could do was keep an eye on things and stop trouble when it started.

Bunny looked at her list of events. "The campaign managers have us scheduled to moderate which candidate shows the most family appeal."

"What does that mean?" I asked.

"Carnelia said we would know it when we saw it."

"Which candidate are you here for?" a young female in a white jersey with a clipboard asked us.

"Press," Ecstra said, presenting her notebook.

The girl turned to Bunny and me. "How about you? Purple or green? I gotta know what line to put you in."

"Uh, we're not with either party," I said. "We're election officials."

She beamed at me. "Oh, sorry! You're *those* Klahds. Please go in. If you do want to have your image taken, please come back to me and get a number."

"I don't like the way she said *those* Klahds," Bunny said.

"Don't let it bother you," I said.

"Mr. Weavil, please!" the Shutterbug on the right called. The orange-and-blue beetle about the size of my fist was perched on a high stool surrounded by lightning bugs fluttering and flashing their tails. He beckoned with a tiny forearm. "I'm ready for you."

Emo collected a female Tipp and a group of little ones and hurried over. The Shutterbug launched himself off the stool and fluttered around their heads, arranging the group in front of a handsome stone fireplace. A small, bright fire danced in the grate. The mantel had been strewn with a wheelbarrowful of sentimental-looking junk, probably straight out of the nearest bazaar. Emo put an arm around the shoulders of the female. He was garbed in his usual bright clothing, but she wore a subdued tan smock. The Shutterbug fussed around them. They had produced a trio of photogenic tots: a gap-toothed toddler, a slightly older girl with bows on her ears, and a sturdy young lad who held a ball and bat. The Shutterbug moved the toddler in between his elder brother and sister and pushed the parents close to make an attractive family ensemble.

Ecstra made a note with great excitement. "That's Anselmo!" she said. "One of the greatest Shutterbug portrait artists in the whole dimension of Olympia! Oh, look! That's the other one! Leabawits, here! I have to get an interview with her."

A yellow and red beetle, slightly larger than Anselmo, made Wilmer and his wife sit down on an overstuffed sofa. A number of other Tipps stood behind him, looking proud or embarrassed. She fluffed up Wilmer's wig, and then, licking her finger, she rubbed a spot of blue eye shadow off the fur on his wife's cheek.

From the look of the group, Wilmer's family was much older than Emo's. He had a healthy and athletic son who wore an athletic jersey, and a married daughter who held a small baby in her arms. The baby was so adorable that even I found him enchanting. Her husband put his arms around her shoulder and looked heroic.

All the Weavil-Scuttils were old pros at having their portraits done. The children turned their shoulders toward the Shutterbug and moved close together. On her signal, they smiled. The lightning bugs flashed again and again. I saw pink spots before my eyes.

"Great!" Leabawits shouted. "Awright, we're done with the individual family pictures! Who else is getting in on dis?"

"Eggar!" Wilmer said, holding out a welcoming hand. A male Tipp about his own age accompanied by a female and two youths came into the scene. Leabawits pushed them around until she had arranged them to her satisfaction with the Weavil-Scuttils. The lightning bugs let loose. Blinking, Eggar and his family retired to make room for another group.

"Who are those people?" I asked, as the statuesque female and her stout husband plastered on big fake smiles for Leabawits.

"Constituents, family friends, campaign contributors," Ecstra said. "Anyone who wants a Shutterbug picture with the candidates. This is one expensive event!"

"Who's paying for it?"

"Oh, they budget for this," she said. "What they don't collect today, they'll make up in the fund-raising events later in the week."

"I had better remind Orlow and Carnelia that I want a strict accounting of any contributions they take in today," Bunny said. She marched off toward Carnelia, who was standing with the Tipps waiting in line for their turn.

"Doubt you'll get that," Ecstra called after her. "They're always 'forgetting' some donation or other."

I watched Wilmer and Emo posturing, offering handshakes and huge smiles for the Shutterbugs. Ecstra gave me a funny look.

"What's the matter? Isn't this fascinating?"

"I guess I don't get the point of all these events. Why would anyone pay to pose with one of these guys?"

"The whole perception is that taking a picture with the candidate will give them exclusive access. People want to feel special. Even if it isn't real. Or for very long."

"And this is popular?" I asked, trying to make sense of it.

"People *love* it."

"They want this more than the candidates talking about the issues?"

"Bores them silly," Ecstra assured me. "That's how the mud fights got started, in my opinion. I can't prove it, of course, but people really started coming out for the rallies when news of the battles got out. Without public interest, the campaigns would have just died. They need the cash to keep going."

I frowned. "If they need money from people, why don't they just ask for it? Charge admission to these events, or sell tickets outright?"

"Because then it would sound like they're begging. In spite of the title, public servants act more like public *masters*. It would be beneath their dignity. So, they make it sound like they're doing people a favor by shaking their hands. This is a personal, hands-on connection. An election is the only time that the voters have the candidates at their mercy."

"So I've noticed," I said. "It's the same everywhere I have been. It just seems so roundabout, with everyone pretending they are getting something for nothing, when in the end everyone on both sides pays."

Ecstra laughed. "You're too straightforward for politics."

"That's what one of my partners said," I replied. "He says you can't stop someone from being a sucker if he really wants to be one."

"That'd be the Pervert?" Ecstra asked. "I noticed he hasn't been back."

"That's Per-*vect*," I corrected her. "He's got another assignment. We can handle this job ourselves."

Privately, I hoped that was true. So far, not a single rotten potato or handful of mud had appeared, but something told me the peaceful mood couldn't last.

And it didn't. I felt the tingling as one of my threads broke. I turned automatically in the direction of the disturbance. A protester dyed deep purple sprang into the tableau where Emo sat. He had a bucket with him.

"Down with Weavils!"

I ran to intercept him. I surrounded the pail with a bag of magik. Nothing would come out of it. He still might hit Emo.

"What—I ask, what are you doing interrupting *my work*?" Anselmo shrieked. The fist-sized beetle flew into the protester's face. "You hairy barbarian! You never interfere with art! Bzzz! Get out of here! Flies! Take him away! Bzzz!"

The purple Tipp waved his free hand to shoo the Shutterbug away. I reached out and grabbed for the protester's bucket arm. I missed. He swung the bucket at me. I wasn't concerned because I had sealed it with magik.

He had unsealed it. The protest movement had learned after our conference in the hotel. A wave of purple sloshed out. It hit me in the face. I gasped. The Tipp turned to take care of his original target. Blinking to clear my eyes, I dove for him. He yelled as I landed on his back. We fell to the ground together. The bucket went scooting across the floor. We both crawled for it, me trailing purple paint behind me like a slime-slug. He got to it first. He struggled to his feet. I scrambled to my knees on the slippery floor. I wanted to hang on to his elbow so he couldn't throw. I missed again.

The arm was no longer there. I stared up. The protester was dangling in the air, yelling and kicking. The entire host of lightning bugs had attached themselves to his clothes, hair, and paws. They hummed angrily as they carried him out through the skylight.

The Shutterbug described a figure-eight turn in midair and ended up nose to nose with me. "You, young Klahd, get out of my light! I give you credit for trying, but go away. Take your mess with you. I am working here!"

Grumbling, I pulled myself to my feet and brushed at my clothes. Orlow strode to my side.

"No need to thank me," I said, looking up. "I was just doing my job."

That turned out not to be his intention at all. The campaign manager eyed my tunic and trousers, now mostly dyed purple, with annoyance. "Are you going to wear the opponent's colors for the rest of the day?" he asked me.

"It wasn't exactly my idea!" I said. "I just saved Emo from being splattered!"

"That's no excuse! You have damaged your nonpartisan standing!"

Arguing with him was futile. Instead, I pictured my clothes as they had been before, blue trousers and tan tunic, neatly pressed, with a snappy belt pouch in russet leather attached to my brown belt. Applying magik to my vision, I laid a disguise spell over myself. When I looked down, I still saw my clothes as they were, disheveled and dripping with paint, but everyone else would see the illusion of neatness.

"Better?" I asked, sarcastically.

"Well, yes," Orlow said, with a look of admiration. "Forgot you were a magician. Nice work."

I stomped back to Ecstra's side.

"See," she said. "That's why I told you not to worry. The Shutterbugs are very territorial. They bite, too."

"You could have told me," I said.

"Are you kidding? I wouldn't have missed that for anything! Page one, tomorrow!"

I groaned.

"Miss Ecstra!" Wilmer said, waving to us as the last of his donors left the spotlight. "Come on over! Great to have you here! And Mr. Skeeve!" He beckoned us over. Ecstra grinned.

"Great! Now, come and see how a real pro behaves."

"You mean you?" I asked.

"No! Mrs. Weavil-Scuttil. You can't dent her aplomb with a battering ram. Come on."

Ecstra drew herself up and headed into the fray, pencil out. I trailed along behind.

She shook hands heartily with the candidate and his wife. "Mr. Weavil-Scuttil! And Mrs. Weavil-Scuttil. How nice to see you here. Let me get your take on just how you feel the race is going for your husband."

"Very well," the lady said. She had soft, light-brown fur gently shot with gray. Her dress was light blue, and she wore a string of iridescent shells around her neck. "He is showing his electability in every way." She looked up adoringly at Wilmer and squeezed his arm. He smiled down at her.

"You don't feel that the outburst at last night's debate made him look like a fool?"

The light-brown eyes regarded Ecstra reprovingly. "I think any foolishness belongs to that young man over there." She tilted her head very slightly in Emo's direction. "Do you suppose he took some bad fashion advice? He does rather stand out, doesn't he? And not in a good way. I am afraid that people won't take him seriously dressed like that. Now, Wilmer is always sartorially splendid."

"If you don't mind my saying so, your hair is a little wild today," Ecstra said. I eyed the older lady. To me she looked as perfect as a store mannequin.

Mrs. Weavil-Scuttil primped her hair with a hand. Her expression never changed. "Do you like it? I wanted to appeal to the younger generation. The youth of Bokromi are our future, you know. Wilmer is always telling me to remember that."

I was impressed at how well she managed to turn all of Ecstra's questions, however provocative, to Wilmer's advantage. She was a real asset to his campaign.

"I see that you have a grandson now," Ecstra said. "Saving your big guns for the important events?"

"Well, we are very proud of little Barnby," Mrs. Weavil-Scuttil said. "Come and meet the little darling." She took the infant out of her daughter's arms and cradled him for us and the Shutterbug who flew up just behind my shoulder. Barnby stirred in his grandmother's arms and started to fuss. She waved a hand, and his eyes closed. I felt the magik surge as she sent him to sleep. She held him up close to my face. "Isn't he beautiful?"

"Yes. Mina must be very proud."

"Oh, I am," Mina said. She wasn't quite as good as her mother at disguising her annoyance. She retrieved her child and clicked her fingers over his face. He woke up with a start and began to cry.

"And you, Gibbly," Ecstra said, turning to the tall young male. "I haven't seen you since you graduated from secondary school. You're looking good. How's the foozball?"

"Just great, Ecstra!" the youth said. His voice was deep and musical.

"Are you doing well at Tipicanoo Executive University?"

"Yes, ma'am!" he said. "Gotta love old Tip Ex U."

Ecstra studied his face closely.

"Wait a moment. You're *not* Gibbly."

The boy recoiled. "Sure I am. I grew up a lot since you saw me last."

"And changed the shape of your head? You had a broad forehead. And you didn't have a split between your front teeth." She turned to Wilmer. "You brought in an impostor! Isn't the real Gibbly good-looking enough for the Shutterbugs?"

"Now, this may seem like a publicity stunt, Miss Ecstra, but I assure you, it's entirely permissible."

"Under what rules?" Ecstra asked.

"Why, their rules," Wilmer said, nodding to me.

"Ours?" I squawked. "We'd never allow you to bring in a ringer to substitute for your own son."

Wilmer lowered his snowy brows. "Well, you most certainly did, young man. And I must tell you what a relief it was, not having to trot him out, since Gibbly turned out to look like my late father-in-law, may he rest in peace, the big lumpish brute, like an ox with an overbite. And he's only interested in games and books, not sports. I mean, we still love Gibbly, but you have to admit that Prager here is a much better-looking boy . . ."

"Wilmer!" Mrs. Weavil-Scuttil protested.

"I read the contract over before we presented it at our conference," I said. "There's nothing in it about using substitutes for family members."

"There most certainly is."

"No, there wasn't!"

Over on the Weavil side of the room, a similar argument was taking place.

"Everyone knows we only have two children," Emo shouted, raising his voice above the crowd. "We brought in the girl to bridge the gap between our older and younger sons. Doesn't she look pretty?"

"That's not the point!" Bunny's voice overpowered his with authority. "Tell me exactly when we agreed that you could defraud the public and not be disqualified from this election!"

"Well, I thought you would never ask," Orlow said, coming over with a sheaf of paper in his hand. I broke away from the Weavil-Scuttils to see what he had. Carnelia and Wilmer followed me. "I have to admit, it sounded rather seedy to me, but I figured, you're M.Y.T.H., Inc., you know what you're doing."

"Who are you calling seedy?" Bunny asked, rounding on Orlow.

"No offense intended, ma'am."

He backed up a pace. She glared. He stretched out his arm as far as it would go and tendered the contract to her on tippy-toe. Bunny snatched it out of his fingers. He stayed at a safe distance and pointed.

"Page four, clause thirty-eight point three. I assure you, we went over everything very carefully."

Bunny flipped over through pages and found the indicated paragraph. I read over her shoulder.

". . . 'Such substitution will not be construed to be fraud, in that it adds to the perceived status of the candidate.' What?"

"Do you see?" Orlow asked. "We followed it to the letter."

"Of your own interpretation," Carnelia said, triumphantly, bringing out her own copy of the contract. "It does not say a single thing about *adding* to the number of your family members! Miss Bunny, I want you to declare this event a win for Wilmer."

"It doesn't say we can't! My family is much cuter than his. I claim the victory!" Emo said.

Bunny scanned the paper. "We didn't include these clauses. This is a forgery!"

"No, ma'am," Orlow said. He flipped to the last page. "There are our signatures, in blood. These are the papers that we signed, all right."

I ran a hand over the seal on the bottom. The bubble of magik that ensured its cohesion was intact. It was a Deveel tactic to ensure that the wording couldn't be altered by either side after signing.

"He's right," I said.

"But that means that the contracts I brought to the conference were tainted while we were there," Bunny said. "These are unbreakable contract forms. My uncle uses them all the time.

Once you've made a deal, you can't refuse to honor it. Something has gone wrong here. The original doesn't contain any of these clauses!"

"I'd surely like to see that," Orlow said. "We have planned out our whole campaign according to your rules, and now you are saying that we have been operating under false pretenses? That is not what we expected of you and M.Y.T.H., Inc."

"I agree," Carnelia said. "Are you trying to make fun of us? Changing things on us in the middle of a very tense time?"

Bunny was horrified at the inference. "No! I can prove that these have been altered. We have the original draft under lock and key at our headquarters."

"Well, I for one want to see it!" Carnelia said. Orlow nodded vigorously.

"So do I! Emo is not used to being trifled with!"

"I'll go back to the office and get our copy," I offered. Bunny, her lips pressed tightly together, nodded.

I fired up the D-hopper and bounced back into Deva.

BAMF!

CHAPTER FIFTEEN

"It looked good on paper."

—B. MADOFF

By the time I got back, the candidates' families and fans had been pushed to the periphery of the big room. The candidates themselves were in the middle, shouting at one another and at Bunny. I hurried to her side.

". . . How dare you make such an accusation!" Carnelia said furiously. Orlow looked self-righteous.

"Well, what else can I assume? M.Y.T.H., Inc., says it didn't put in those clauses. So who did? It had to be you!"

Carnelia drew herself up. "What about you? You had the opportunity as well. We were all alone in that room. It certainly wasn't one of *my* people."

Orlow was equally outraged. He leaned toward Carnelia. "Well, it wasn't one of mine! They're loyal to Emo!"

"Wilmer's workers would rather die than do something to jeopardize his campaign! He deserves to be governor!"

"Over Emo's dead body!"

Carnelia narrowed her eyes. She opened her palm, and green light danced upon it. "That can be arranged."

"Hold on there!" Emo said, opening his large eyes as wide as they would go. "I ask you to calm down, my friends. People are watching. *Voters* are watching."

"Yes," Wilmer said, waving to the people who were straining at the ropes holding them back and the reporters nearby who were listening with their tongues out and pencils flying. The two campaign managers backed away from one another. "Let us see what is in the draft that Mr. Skeeve here has brought for us. I am sure that will clear everything up. May we see it?"

"Sure," I said. I handed the bound pages to Bunny with a flourish.

"This will clear everything up," she said. "This hasn't been out of our office since it was written." She flipped over the first page.

Suddenly, a wind began swirling around our feet. It picked up Mrs. Weavil-Scuttil's skirt and flapped Baby Weavil's blankets.

"Stop that!" Wilmer said to Emo.

"I'm not doing it!"

"Well, one of your people is!"

"You just say that to cover up *your* people's magikal pranks!"

"Page four," Bunny said, pointing to the clause in question. "It says here very clearly that . . . Stop that contract!"

The wind yanked the paper out of her hands. She made a grab for it and missed.

With my longer reach, I jumped to get it. I tried to catch it by magik, but a force stronger than mine had it. I looked around, but I couldn't tell who was causing it. I didn't have time to think about that. I needed to get the contract back, then deal with the prankster.

"I'll help you, Mr. Skeeve!" Riginald said. He lumbered forward as I leaped toward the paper. We collided. The contract skipped upward. Morton, Wilmer's magician, jumped up. I stood up just as he threw a spell to capture it. I was dragged backward into his embrace. He let me go with intense embarrassment on his face.

"Oh, sorry, Mr. Skeeve!"

"No problem," I assured him. I hurried out in front of him and flew after the contract.

The sheaf of paper reached a wall and rustled back and forth as if undecided which way to go. Gathering force, I pictured a hand closing in on it but barked up against a solid invisible wall. I sent a shock back through the spell to get whoever it was to let go. My fellow magicians leaped backward, shaking their hands in pain. They seemed to have had the same idea I had. In the confusion, the paper slipped away. I pushed Riginald and Morton aside. The only certain way to catch it was to get it in my own hands. I opened my stride and pursued it.

The contract danced ahead of me, daring me to get it. I chased it around the room. It nipped up and down, just out of my grasp. I leaped for it and landed belly first on the couch in the Weavil-Scuttil tableau. The contract swirled upward, as if it were laughing at me. Before I could pick myself up, it swooped up and out of the skylight.

"Don't let it get away!" Bunny shouted.

I had no intention of letting that happen. I levitated upward and flew after it with every erg of magik I could gather. Several of the reporters took to the air on my heels, following me out of the propped glass panel.

I halted in midair above the roof of the little blue cottage, scanning the open sky for my quarry. I spotted a square of white on the chimney of the building next door. The contract had settled there. I pushed off to retrieve it.

As if sensing my pursuit, the sheaf of papers picked itself up and whisked away. I followed it with grim determination. An updraft took it high into the air in a rapid series of spirals.

That wind had not been an accident. Someone in one of the camps had altered the wording of the copies Wilmer and Emo had in their possession, and they didn't want the truth known.

This paper was the only proof we had of that perfidy. The reporters joined in the chase, pushing me out of the way any chance they got. Any of them would consider it a scoop to get his or her hands on it first. I was determined not to let them take it. I put on a burst of speed and pulled ahead of the pack. A bird squawked as I leapfrogged its nest to stay on the trail of my quarry.

Then I thought for a moment. If the press got it, they would print the whole thing in the paper, and the true details of our agreement with the two parties would be known. No one could accuse us of hiding the truth. That wasn't all bad. Instead of putting an elbow in the eye of the next reporter to sweep past me, a pale golden Tipp with a side parting in his head fur, I flew side by side with him. He gave me a wink.

The contract, or rather the magician controlling it, didn't want either one of us to get it. It climbed high, swished around us just out of reach, then dove down through the skylight again.

Like hawks chasing a pigeon, we pursued it. I landed on the slick floor of the cottage, just in time to see the contract skip lightly over the tiles and land in the merry fire burning in the brass grate behind Emo Weavil's family.

"No!" Bunny cried.

I reached out with magik to pull the papers out of the fire. I had them secure, and then the white sheets burst and crackled into black ash. I stopped just short of the hearth, aghast. Our original, destroyed! I used force to try to drag them toward me. The black fragments sifted out of the grasp of my spell.

I threw myself on my knees before the fireplace, trying to see if there was anything left to retrieve. Whoever had snared the document from me had left nothing to chance. The contract was crushed into powder. I glanced up at Bunny. She looked horrified. The room went completely silent.

Wilmer broke the hush by clearing his throat.

"Well, then," he said, putting his thumbs behind his lapels. "That leaves only one question. Who won this contest today?"

"What?" Bunny asked. She turned to him with disbelief on her face. "How could you ask that now?"

"Well, ma'am," Wilmer said, with a courtly bow, "since you say that was the only copy of the contract that said different from what we knew, we are bound by the documents that remain intact, such as that held by my lovely campaign manager here." Carnelia held it up. "So, the question arises: Based upon the rules that we have been going by, who has the more photogenic family? I believe that since I followed more of the regulations than my distinguished colleague, you must declare me the winner."

"Never," Emo said, raising a forefinger to heaven. "My family is the more adorable. Why, look at them!"

Wilmer lifted his lip in a sneer.

"*All* of them? Including the extra daughter?"

"Of course! If you include the boy who isn't your son, I am justified."

"You went beyond the spirit of the rules. You shouldn't be given any consideration by the judges."

"Well, if you disqualify my family, I will withdraw from the voting at the end of the month," Emo said, throwing up his hands. "I will await an apology before I consent to reschedule."

"There's no need for that," Bunny said, taking his arm. She favored him with a beseeching look. Emo was not in a mood to be melted. He detached her hand and drew himself up.

"I have been brought into disrepute by false allegations by my opponent! I refuse to be made a fool."

"Too late for that," Wilmer said.

"And what about you?" Emo demanded, spinning and putting an accusing forefinger in his opponent's face. "Just because your son is a lump of gristle is no reason to bring in a pinch sitter."

Wilmer bowed gallantly to Bunny. He was enjoying being the cooler head. "To the best of my knowledge, it was within the wheelhouse of the rules. I defer to the judges of this contest and ask them to be fair."

"We've been hoodwinked," Bunny murmured to me. "There was no clause thirty-eight point three."

"What do you want to do?" I whispered back. "I'll back anything you decide."

The entire crowd was watching our every move with anticipation. She shrugged. "We'll have to allow it. In the end, I suppose it hardly matters." She raised her voice and addressed the candidates. "All right, then. We go by the portraits?"

"That's right," Emo said.

The Shutterbugs flew forward with a great show of ceremony. Tipp helpers from both sides set high wooden stools in front of Bunny for each of them to land upon. One at a time they unfolded the tiny films from their underwings and displayed them to us.

"Ya gotta like that one, honey," Leabawits said, pointing a tiny claw at a group shot showing Wilmer holding his grandson and beaming. "Look at the halo lighting. Makes the family look like they just came from heaven."

"If you like *representational art*," Anselmo said, with a tiny snort. "I prefer the symbolism in my work."

I squinted at the little images from his collection. I was always impressed by the art of Shutterbuggery. On Klah, pictures were usually made by artists or unusually talented wizards. The bugs had captured such lifelike pictures that I almost expected them to speak. I looked from one set of images to another, trying to find anything that caught my eye more than the other. Bunny looked as perplexed as I felt.

"Well?" Orlow asked, peering over my shoulder. "Who wins this contest? I think it's clear that Emo's family is by far the most attractive and appealing. You can't look at that wholesome group and not see the next governor!"

Carnelia stuck a finger in my face. "Well, you'll forgive me for disagreeing. Wilmer has shepherded his family into the third generation! Can Emo boast a grandson?"

Orlow rocked on his heels with a jovial laugh. "Hope not, since his eldest son's only eight!"

With Anselmo and Leabawits watching us closely, we scanned the tiny films, comparing them side by side by the light of a candle. I had to admit I couldn't see any difference between the two family groups. Both of them looked wholesome and loving. None of the backbiting or double dealing came through in a still image.

I looked at Bunny and shook my head.

"Very well," she said. "I declare this contest . . ."

The entire crowd held its breath in anticipation.

". . . a draw."

"Oooooh." The mood of the room deflated.

"Miss Bunny, I most strenuously protest!" Wilmer said.

"So do I!" Emo added.

"Well, how can you?" Bunny said brightly. "Your families are so adorable that I can't help but love both of them! Now, isn't that nice?"

The reporters wrote it down. The candidates watched them out of the corner of their eyes and pasted on big smiles.

"Both of you are winners," I said. "I'd settle for that. If you want us to go over the collections *again* . . . ?" I could tell neither side wanted that.

"Oh, all right," Wilmer said. With a wary expression, he put out a hand. Emo took it as though he expected it to break his off. They shook. Wilmer broke away immediately. He raised both hands over his head and turned to the audience. "Thank you to all my friends who came here today! I am grateful to the judges for their intelligent conclusion!"

"I was about to say the same thing," Emo said. "I am grateful to all of you for visiting my little family. Your pictures will be available at my campaign headquarters in the morning. And now, I will take questions from the press!"

"Mr. Weavil! Mr. Weavil!" "Mr. Weavil-Scuttil!"

Bunny and I backed away as the reporters closed in. Once we were clear of the crowd, I swept us home to Deva.

CHAPTER SIXTEEN

*"One little peek behind the curtain, and my
cushy lifestyle is over."*

—OZ THE GREAT AND TERRIBLE

"Another draw," Bunny said, kicking off her shoes and throwing herself onto her desk chair. "This election is going to go down to a tiebreaker, I can just tell. And then I will scream. Who stole the contract out of my hands? That took a lot of nerve."

"I couldn't tell," I said. I had never felt so tired in my life, and the purple paint had caked hard on my clothes. I scattered flakes everywhere I walked. Gleep followed me, licking them up off the floor. "I tried to see who looked like they were concentrating on a spell, but everyone seemed to be watching us. Whoever it was had to be in the room so they could keep the paper away from me. And I lost it."

"You did your best," Bunny said. The assurance didn't make me feel any better. I brushed at my clothes. The tunic was probably ruined, but I would give Sansabeld a crack at it. He ran the best laundry in the Bazaar.

Guido and Nunzio emerged from the corridor where they had a small suite of rooms.

"Hey, you look wrecked," Guido said.

"You don't have to rub it in," I said, making a face. I felt like a bag of rags next to the Mob enforcers' usual dapper attire.

"No offense, boss, and boss," Guido said, with a nod to Bunny. He and Nunzio couldn't seem to break the habit of giving me that title, even though I hadn't had it for a while now. "But you guys look like you got run over by a parade. Wanna come out and get a drink? First round's on me."

"I can't face any more people today," Bunny said. She looked so pale and drawn that I wanted to hold her in my arms. Guido looked as if the same impulse had hit him, but the expression vanished in a twinkling. He never tried to buck the chain of command. If she wanted a hug, she wasn't shy about asking for one.

"No problem." He aimed a thumb over his shoulder at the hallway. "Nunzio and I had a good day pickin' up receipts for Don Bruce. We was just gonna pay a visit to obtain comestibles from the Yellow Crescent Inn. We had intended to dine in, but it would be my extreme pleasure to increase the order and enjoy my repast here wit' youse. I am sure my cousin here would concur dat your company would be better'n any hoi polloi, no offense to Gus and his clientele."

"You bet," Nunzio agreed.

"Thanks, Guido," I said. "That would be great."

I must have fallen asleep in my chair, because the next thing I remembered was the smell of hot food. A tray had been placed across my lap. Paper-wrapped sandwiches, cut-up fried vegetables, and a tall strawberry milk shake were arrayed on it. Everyone else was already eating. I reached for the cup and took a long swig through the straw.

"Aaah," I said, sighing with satisfaction.

I could tell that I had also missed a lot of the conversation, but I guessed from the context that they had been discussing the events of the day.

"Do you need more personnel on the ground, boss?" Guido asked.

"No!" Bunny said. "We handled it."

"We have to find out where the leak is coming from," I said. "There's collusion going on between the two parties. I told you all on the day of the conference that there was something going on. Someone broke my security spell from the inside."

Bunny nodded. "And someone substituted false documents for ours before the signatures went on. Who could have done that?"

"Either the managers or the candidates," Nunzio said. "Both of them had plenty of time while they were examining the contracts."

Bunny frowned. She took off her shoes and rubbed the soles of her feet. "But they insist they are following the rules that we set out."

"Who else could it have been?"

Guido pointed with half a sandwich. "The assistants. Dat means dere is a mole in each camp."

"But who are *they* working for?"

"Who else?" Aahz asked, appearing in the doorway. He ambled over to my tray and helped himself to a handful of fried vegetable sticks. He chased it down with a generous swig from my milk shake. "Who benefits from making this election chaotic? Who could possibly want this to keep going on forever?"

"No one," Bunny said. "The island's a wreck. The people are sick to pieces of the whole election process."

Aahz never asked rhetorical questions. There was an answer, and he wanted us to guess. I wasn't in the mood.

"Who?" I asked.

Aahz grinned. "Ask yourself who is making money even though the island is running without a government? Maybe you're too close to the situation to have perspective. Who can't lose? Even *you* should have figured it out by now."

"Who is it?" I asked, peeved. Aahz always thought that I

couldn't put two and two together without help. In this case, he might have been right. "Just tell us."

"I shouldn't have to. If it were any more obvious, you'd have bite marks on your behind! Is this job getting to be too much for you? You can always back out."

"No!" Bunny said. "Is this a sneaky way to get the company to reopen the question of who's the head of M.Y.T.H., Inc.?"

"I'm shocked," Aahz said, putting on an innocent expression. "Shocked that you would even *think* I would use a lever like this on you."

"Aahz," I said warningly.

Aahz dropped the joking and became serious. "No. This is not a referendum on your leadership, which has been excellent. Anyone can make a good decision that turns out to be the wrong one when the rest of the facts come out. We've gotten stiffed before. There's always something that they don't tell you. It's lucky this time that it probably won't be fatal."

"Excepting for the minute point that we'll hafta return the deposit we collected in advance," Guido added.

"No problem," I said. "We have been keeping a full list of expenses."

"No! We started the job," Aahz said, with a jab at his own palm. "We're going to keep it."

"We can't," I said. "It wouldn't be fair."

"This whole situation is a waste of our time and talent!"

"You were the one who insisted we take it in the beginning," I pointed out.

Aahz had to drag the admission out from behind his teeth. "I was wrong! Tell them to draw straws. Short straw takes the governorship. We should have done that from the beginning. They should have gotten it over with a long time ago. It's not worthy of M.Y.T.H., Inc."

"No!" I said. "It's not up to us to tell them how they want their election to progress. We said we'd help. We have a reputation to protect. We're going to see this through according to their laws and customs."

"Uh-huh. Either of them showing a lead in the polls?"

"No," I said thoughtfully. I took a bite of my sandwich. "They are running almost exactly equal. And neither one will give the other an inch. And they keep coming up with new events to add to the roster. Each of them thinks he's going to be show-cased, but it always comes out a tie. There's really no difference between them. No wonder it's gone on so long. If you took away Wilmer's wig and Emo's eyelashes, they might be twins."

Aahz raised an eyebrow. "So there's no lesser of two Weavils." He laughed heartily at his own joke. I didn't get it.

"Not really, I guess."

"You can admit it if this is all getting to be too much for you," Aahz said. "Politics really isn't a game for amateurs, even talented ones."

"No!" I said. "We can handle it."

"We're doing all right," Bunny said, with determination.

"Okay," Aahz said. "I will be happy to come back in if you need me."

"Thanks, Aahz," I said. "But we won't."

CHAPTER SEVENTEEN

"The medium is the message."

—T. TURNER

I held the copy of the *Morning Gossip* in my hands and read the headline again.

Whose Island Is This Anyway? it read. The subhead went on to insinuate, *Handing over the deed to Bokromi?* In the center of the page, taking up three columns, was a picture of me offering Bunny the contract. The contract that had gotten burned up.

Ecstra had met us on a street corner a few blocks away from her office with her usual astonishing foreknowledge, and handed us the paper.

"I wanted you to see it before you talked to anyone else," she said. "I didn't write it; Tolomi did. He said he got an exclusive from both candidates. I'm sorry. It sounds bad." She took her notebook out of her purse. "Would you two like to comment on it? For the record?"

"I want to read it first," Bunny said, holding up her hand.

"So do I," I added.

Ecstra had stood back to let us go over it.

The article was worse than the header. According to both camps, we had done our best to make the candidates appear unattractive during the portrait event of the day before. My hijinks, during which I had "severely injured" one or both of the campaign magicians, were nothing more than a screen to cover our perfidy and incompetence. We had forced the candidates to participate in a number of exploits that did nothing to display their intelligence and fitness for office. Instead, we had subjected them to a media circus that wasted both taxpayer money and hard-earned contributions from loving supporters of either Emo or Wilmer. Moreover, we had asked for, and received, bribes from each party so neither one would be left behind in the polls, which we were manipulating in a masterful fashion. Though the "interviews" ran in two columns, they were almost identical in content. The entire election was corrupt, the candidates insisted, and it was all down to M.Y.T.H., Inc. We had brought down evil on their fair island community, evil and fear and suffering.

"They don't know what real evil is like," I commented.

The article concluded that if we were permitted to hold the election in two weeks' time, the outcome would almost certainly be to the candidate who donated the most illicit money to the Klahds from Outside. The crooked candidate would win, and the honest one would be left out in the cold, along with the entire electorate. By the time I finished reading, I could hardly see the print for the rage I felt. Then I remembered we were not alone. I made myself calm down and handed the paper back to Ecstra.

"What do you think?" she asked.

"I don't think this came from Emo or Wilmer. This doesn't sound like their scriptwriters," Bunny commented.

"No," I mused. "It's that flawless grammar again."

Bunny knew what I was thinking. "We have to talk to Orlow and Carnelia."

"Excuse us," I said to Ecstra. I took Bunny's arm and started

to walk in the direction of Emo Weavil's campaign headquarters.

"Wait," she said, running after us. "What about my
interview!"

"Not now," Bunny said.

Ecstra doubled around in front of us.

"Is there some kind of conspiracy going on?" she asked,
licking the point of her pencil.

"No comment," I said.

"Who's involved? You say you want to speak to the managers. Do you suspect them of talking to the press behind your
back?"

"No comment," I said.

"Do you know your shoe is untied?" she asked.

I stopped and looked down. She grabbed hold of my other
arm and hung on. "I'm coming with you. There's something
going on, and the press has the right to know!"

I could have shaken her off, but I was in too much of a hurry.
Summoning up magikal force, I pictured the ground passing
by in a blur under my feet. Suddenly, we were running faster
than I had ever moved before. I had to dodge wagons and trash
carts, mothers with their babies, and messenger boys on two-
wheeled conveyances who shot me looks of admiration as I wove
in and out of the traffic.

Luckily, the streets weren't that busy so early in the morning. I arrived at the door of the Weavil headquarters. Bunny's
cheeks were pink, but Ecstra was panting. She let go of me. I
slipped past her, pulled Bunny inside, and locked the door
behind me.

"No fair!" Ecstra shouted, pounding on the glass. "The
press has a right to hear!"

Orlow looked up at us and glared. "So you're helping the
opposition! I should have known that Emo was too good and
innocent to know what he was doing when he brought you in!
This bodes poorly for a fair election! Bribes! I'm surprised at
you! And not cutting us in!"

"We have not taken a single bribe," I said.

"Multiple bribes, then!"

"Uh, no."

Bunny took over. She pushed past me and confronted Orlow face to face. "I have it on good authority that this slander came from both these offices, so it's time you did some talking."

Orlow favored her with a stern expression. "What about, Miss Bunny? It seems that it doesn't matter what I tell you, or do for you, you're going to cut us down in the end."

"That is, if you're not the 'unnamed source,'" Bunny said.

"Of course I'm not! None of us are!"

"I want to get to the bottom of this right now. We need to talk to both sides, immediately. I'm going to get Carnelia. You and Skeeve meet me at the hotel conference room in one hour. Be on time and alone. Got it?" She poked him in the chest with her forefinger. Orlow unconsciously rubbed the spot.

"Well, yes, ma'am." He turned to me as Bunny stormed off. "She has a powerful way of expressing herself, doesn't she?"

"Yes, she does," I said. Ecstra followed Bunny away. I could hear her yapping out questions. I knew Bunny was too angry to answer.

Orlow and I reached the meeting with plenty of time to spare. I surrounded the conference room with a triple layer of magikal silence. You'd have thought I had done the same thing inside, for all the communication going on between the others in there with me. The two campaign managers glared at us and one another.

Finally, Carnelia broke the silence.

"You have a fat lot of nerve, dragging us away from the legitimate pursuit of running for office," she said. "We trusted you, and we spent a lot of time on you, and what do we get? Defeated before the first vote is cast!"

"Now, hold on, they're cheating us, not you!" Orlow said. "Your candidate is paying bribes, not mine."

Carnelia looked outraged. "*We're* not responsible for this. *You* are. We're going to call this all off, and it's your fault!"

"Our reputation is at stake, and you're to blame!"

The more the two of them argued, the more certain I was that they were telling the truth. I'd heard some good liars in my life, but Orlow and Carnelia didn't even make the top hundred. But I could hear Aahz's voice in the back of my mind, and I knew what he had been trying to get us to understand. It was as clear as crystal to me now.

I stopped the bickering with an upturned hand.

"Please, just listen for a moment."

"Well?" Orlow demanded. "And what have you got to say, as if it matters now?"

"Do you know why you can't ever get all the way to an election day?" I asked them.

"Why not?"

"Because it's too profitable to have both sides continue the endless campaign. It's become a cottage industry here on Bokromi. You're probably employing hundreds, if not thousands of people. You're a percentage of the economy!"

"Well, that's true," Carnelia said, thoughtfully. "About two percent, maybe, over the last five years."

"And do you know who profits the most? Who has an interest in prolonging this into infinity?"

"The suppliers, I suppose," Orlow said. "They make a pretty decent buck out of us, what with the posters, balloons, hats, buttons, favors—and those rush orders! Whew!"

"You don't have to tell *me* about rush orders," Carnelia said, adjusting her stole. The rodents rearranged themselves fetchingly. "We had to send out for emergency donations to cover the last rally!" She frowned at me. "But how are they keeping us from holding the election?"

Bunny slapped herself in the forehead.

"We are so stupid," she said. "The newspapers! We've been consorting with the enemy, telling them our every move!"

"The newspapers?" Orlow asked.

I nodded. "Every time it looks like the two sides agree and are going to go through with the vote, there's an article, or an editorial, or an interview from 'undisclosed sources' revealing some secret information or a crooked trick. Just like trained pets, one or the other of you backs off and cancels the election."

"But they have transcripts of interviews," Carnelia said.

"Yes," I said. "Who said these interviews took place?"

"Well, it's in the papers!" Orlow replied.

Carnelia nodded, horrified. "And if *you* didn't put it there, and *we* didn't put it there . . ."

Orlow finished her sentence as enlightenment dawned on them both. ". . . *They* put it in."

"He's right, you know," Carnelia said, shaking her head. "Every time. We figure we can't trust you, and it all starts over again."

"We should have known better," Orlow said. "But how could we have known?"

"You couldn't," I said. "You didn't believe anything the other side said, so the printed transcript was the only source."

"Newspapers aren't supposed to make the news by themselves!" Carnelia declared. Both managers were as outraged as I was.

"No, they're not," Bunny said. "And from now on, they will get what we want them to, and only in front of enough witnesses that we will have credibility."

"How are we going to do that?"

"Press releases," Bunny said. "From now on, they get printed press releases that will be distributed in public, identical ones to every paper in town. No interviews, private or public. The only input they get from either side goes through us. You can't have an interview if we're not present. Is that clear?"

"Clear as crystal," Orlow said.

"And by the way, both of you have leaks in your offices," I put in. "Someone let eavesdroppers overhear that first conference. And I suspect all of our plans have been passed along to the newspapers."

Orlow looked grim. "I've got a file folder with teeth. I should have been using it all along."

"And from now on I will keep all sensitive information on my person," Carnelia said. "No one can get past my stole. They bite anyone who gets too close."

"Do you suppose anyone can bribe them?" I asked.

"Hah!" Carnelia snorted. She petted the little animals, but her expression was feral. "They know which side their kibble is buttered on."

"Mr. Skeeve!" Ecstra called to me. She had been waiting in the corridor outside our room. She followed us out of the hotel and down the street. "What was the subject of this emergency conference with the rival campaign managers? The public has a right to know!"

"You're absolutely right," I said. I reached into my belt pouch and came up with a rolled-up scroll. The building manager had a copy-elf on duty, and I had hired his services. I had thirty identical papers beside the one I handed Ecstra. "Here's your briefing."

Ecstra scanned it. She read faster than anyone else I had ever seen. "All this says is that you're issuing press releases from now until the election! Will you comment on that? For me?" She gave me a winning smile.

"No, I can't," I said firmly. "That's all you will get."

"Are you giving exclusives to another reporter?" she asked.

"No," I said. "The candidates will now communicate with the press solely through press releases that we have gone over and verified. All of you will get the same information at the same time. We have to keep it fair."

"But what about personal-interest stories?" she asked, desperately. "What about that individual touch? How can I set mine apart from all the other articles that will be based on this information?"

"How you write it is up to you," Bunny said.

The young reporter looked stricken. Even her jaunty hat seemed to droop.

"Did I, personally, do something wrong to you?" Ecstra asked.

"No, honey," Bunny said, sympathetically. "You didn't. Really. But we have to protect the process. It's gotten . . . out of control. I'm really sorry."

"What would it take to get back on the inside with you?"

I halted and glanced around the open street to make sure no one was close to us. "Tell me who leaked information about the first conference that we held with the candidates."

Ecstra shook her head. "I can't do that! I was told it in confidence."

I lifted my hands. "Then we can't be sure what you're hearing where, and how much truth there is. Our credibility is suffering. So, everyone has to get the same information from us at the same time, so we can be sure that the message is getting out the way we intend it to."

"I think I understand," Ecstra said. "But you're interfering with the power of the press! It's there to protect public interest."

"It hasn't exactly helped us. Why should we help you make us look stupid?"

Ecstra thought for a moment. "Well . . . can I ask you about other things?"

"Certainly," Bunny said. "As long as they don't have to do with the election."

"All right." She held up her pad and pencil and looked me square in the eye. "What about the rumors that your company has purchased a building in the middle of town?"

"Completely false," I said, at once. "We're working out of the same office space we were when we first met you. And on Deva in our own headquarters."

"So you don't know of any purchase?" she pressed.

I glanced at Bunny. "No. What should we know?"

She shook her head. "Can't let anything slip. It was a lead I got . . ."

I rolled my eyes. "I know: from confidential sources."

Ecstra looked hopeful. "If you trusted me a little, I could trust you."

"But everything we say to you ends up in the paper."

"That's my job!"

"Well, this is our job," I said, unhappily. "We have to go."

"No hard feelings, I hope?" Ecstra asked, sadly.

"None," I said. "I would be happy to buy us all dinner after the election."

"I'd like that," Ecstra said. "Once you're not bound to be impartial, we can have a *lot* of fun. I have plenty of stories that can't be printed. See you later." She ran a finger down the side of her fedora and walked off. I felt my heart sink.

"Bye," Bunny called after her. Her large blue eyes were full of woe. "Skeeve, this is one of the parts of this job that I hate."

"Me, too," I said.

CHAPTER EIGHTEEN

"The press will settle for what I tell them."

—R. M. NIXON

Keeping the press on a need-to-know basis worked better than I hoped it would. Every paper printed slightly different versions of the same information, and there were no more "anonymous interviews." Over the following week, Emo and Wilmer began to relax. Their platforms began to mature and stand apart from one another. Now that they weren't going to be thrown off by false statements purportedly given by their opponent, they started to enjoy themselves. It must have been a long time since they were able to concentrate on the business of getting elected.

I needed to make certain that to avoid claims of favoritism every newspaper got the briefings at the same time. I hired a Deveel process server, who guaranteed that he would get the scrolls into the hands of the managing editors every morning within five seconds of one another. Other than making every newspaper in town smell like brimstone, it worked like a charm. I felt it was well worth the cost to the clients.

Not that the editors were happy with us. Following our strict instructions, neither the candidates nor their campaign managers spoke in private with any of them, even to ones who were old friends. I had to field complaints from Emo and Wilmer as well as the editors. However, what the candidates did and said appeared accurately in every paper. When one was inaccurate for one reason or another, the remaining papers lampooned it.

I also hired a town crier, an old friend, Sid the She from Ban She, to read the releases in public in the gazebo every day at noon, in between the morning and afternoon political events. She was a dynamite performer. I had met her in Vaygus on a vacation not long before. Her readings swiftly became a regular spectacle. People gathered from all corners of Bokromi to listen. I just checked to make sure that Sid showed up, then vacated the area as quickly as I could. Her shrill voice hurt my ears, but I guarantee she could be heard for blocks. The crowds grew bigger every day. Again, the newspapers complained, this time because that we were undercutting them.

"All they have to do to hear the latest developments on the election is to show up and listen!" the editor of the *Tipp Sheet*, a middle-aged female with pale-gray fur artfully arranged, told me before Sid the She got started on the day of the pig-lifting contest. "They don't have to buy a paper!"

"Is that all you have in it?" I asked her.

She hesitated. "Well, no, but it's the big story of the day! Pig lifting isn't something that happens very often. And now they know about it without having to read all about it."

"All they know is where and when," I said. I made certain to pitch my voice loudly so anyone nearby could hear me. "They don't know who lifted which pig or anything else. You'll be able to cover that."

The *Tipp Sheet* editor went away, shaking her head.

I noticed Ecstra in the crowd. I saw her sad little face almost every day at the political gatherings. She covered the speeches, made notes during all the events, and left without ever trying to talk to me. Some of the reporters respected the no-interviews policy. Others just considered it a barrier to be overcome by persistence. Bunny and I had gotten very good at saying no. All events were covered that week, or not covered, depending on whether a paper was angry with us on a particular day for not cooperating with them.

The morning debate had gone off without a hitch, though also without a clear winner. The pig-lifting contest was just as dull as it sounded. We traveled there in a caravan of carriages with banners flying from the roofs and streamers woven into the harnesses of the pack animals. The huge farmstead on which it took place was a few miles outside the main city. The eye-watering stench reminded me of the feedlot next door to my home in Klah, though usually the farmers who came to heft piglets were there to buy them. I didn't understand the logic of why political candidates had to hoist swine, but both Orlow and Carnelia assured me that it was customary and expected. At least there was no need for Bunny or me to judge the event. The name, weight, and temperament of each pig were posted on a large board next to the pen. A grand total would determine the winner.

During round six of the pig lifting, we were approached by a merchant who was opening a new store and wanted to have a grand ribbon cutting featuring both candidates fitted into the schedule for the next day. Since it would take less than half an hour, Bunny and I agreed to put it in and tell Orlow and Carnelia when this event was finished.

I made a note on a scrap of parchment. A shadow fell across it. Automatically, I covered what I was writing. I looked up to see Ecstra.

She smiled at me with hope in her large brown eyes. "Tolomi is pushing me for a scoop. Do you have anything for me? Even a small item?" She held up her thumb and forefinger a tiny distance apart. I shook my head.

"No, sorry. Don't you have copies of the speeches? I know they were handed out this morning."

She wrinkled her nose. "Canned speeches. They were stale last year! I mean, something new."

"A favor for a favor," I said.

She knew what I meant. Her face fell.

"I can't. It would go against the Journalists' Creed!"

"I'm sorry," I said. "I really shouldn't push you. I know you believe in what you're doing. But so do I."

"No, *I'm* sorry," she said. She walked away, her head drooping. Bunny squeezed my arm. She looked as rueful as I felt.

"*I'll* help you," a voice said.

"What?" I turned around.

A tall, very attractive, deep-brown Tipp female stood in the doorway of one of the farmyard buildings. She beckoned to me. I glanced at Bunny. She shrugged. I followed the Tipp into the dim building, careful to keep my eye on the open door. She wore a gray suit and a matching gray fedora with a black card in the band. The card identified her as a reporter for the *Evening Screed*, one of the *Gossip*'s rival papers.

"What can I do for you?" I asked. "I'm not giving any interviews. I hope you understand that."

"I'm not buying," she said, with a smile at my astonished face. "I'm selling. I saw you talking to Ecstra. She won't let you talk to the people who gave her the scoop from the planning meeting. I will."

"Great," I said. I looked around. I was pretty sure we were alone. "Who was it?"

Her large eyes widened with alarm.

"I can't tell you here," she said. "We can be overheard. I don't think I should let myself be seen with you. Not if you want to continue the impression that you're treating all of the papers the same."

I saw her point.

"Uh, yeah. All right. Where should we go?"

She shook her head. "Not now! Tomorrow." She took a card out of her pocket and scribbled a note on it. "Be here at five in the morning, before I have to clock in at the *Screed*. Come alone, please."

"All right," I said.

I rejoined Bunny, who gave me a curious look. I was excited to tell her, but I waited until we were home again.

"I've got a lead," I said, as soon as we reached the office. I was pleased to see that several of my partners were there to hear my good news. I held up the card. "That reporter told me she'd give me the name of the person who leaked the information about our meeting."

"Who was she?" asked Bunny.

I looked at the card. "Her name is Pattikin Lockheart, from the *Evening Screed*. She wants me to meet her tomorrow, alone."

Bunny gave me a pitying look. I glanced around at the faces of the others in the office. Something told me I should feel more cautious about that amazing stroke of luck.

"I shouldn't go alone, should I?" I asked.

"Absolutely not," Aahz said, emphatically. "I'll go with you."

"*I* will," Tananda insisted. "It would be better if another woman were there. I didn't want to get involved in this job, but for Skeeve I'll swallow my disgust." She melted up against me and ran her fingers down my chest. "No offense, tiger, but even you admit that you don't know a lot about the way women think."

"I guess not," I said. It was impossible to feel offended when she did that. My whole body tingled at her touch. "She wants me there by five in the morning."

"No problem," she said, smiling at me. She raised her brows lazily. "We'll just . . . stay up."

My pulse went into double taps. Tananda was almost like a sister to me, but Trollops were sexy by nature. Unbelievably sexy. I had to remind myself we were just friends.

"Don't bother, Tanda," Pookie said, her voice like a rumbling avalanche after Tananda's silken murmur. She nodded to her partner. "Spyder and I aren't due back at the monastery until after noon prayers. *I'll* go with him."

I glanced between them, concerned that Tananda's feelings would be hurt, but she was smiling broadly. She and Pookie slapped palms.

"That would be even better," she said.

CHAPTER NINETEEN

*"Pardon me while I slip into something a
little more comfortable."*

—J. E. HOOVER

My friends' concern was borne out as soon as we arrived at the location that Pattikin had written down for me, the Happy Sleeper. It was a hotel, but nothing like the Hotel Tippmore. The paint on the cliff face that made up the front wall was worn to a suggestion of color, and the reinforced wooden door hung at an angle, letting light out in two wedges, one at the top and one at the bottom. I put a disguise spell on Pookie to look like a hangerful of tunics and trousers. We were both wrapped in heavy cloaks with the hoods pulled down low to conceal our faces. She stayed close to my back.

A Tipp with a squint in his filmy eyes peered at us as we entered the foyer, which was lit by one feeble torch. He eyed my "wardrobe," then looked me up and down.

"How long ya stayin'?" he asked. "Up to four hours's three silver pieces."

"I'm meeting someone," I said.

"Figured that one out by meself. How long?"

"Uh, an hour?"

"Quick worker, huh?"

"I just need to talk to her!" I blurted. He grinned at me. Pookie poked me in the back. I handed over my three silver pieces and was given a huge iron key.

"Down the hall on the left," the old Tipp said.

"About what I thought," Pookie said, throwing off the cloak as soon as we were in the room. Underneath it she was wearing a smooth, body-hugging, midnight-blue leather jumpsuit. Unlike her cousin, she was slender, even shapely. She surveyed the room with evident distaste. It had a bed that I would have considered too narrow for two people and a washbasin with a cracked pitcher against one wall, and a battered wooden table and two chairs against the other. The floor was cut out of the native stone, but it probably hadn't been cleaned since it was excavated. "What a dump. I would estimate that the six- and eight-legged inhabitants outnumber the two- or four-legged guests here by a factor of a million or so."

She pointed a finger around the perimeter of the floor. I heard tiny high-pitched screeches and smelled burning. Unlike Aahz, Pookie had all her magikal powers. I winced, but it was better than scratching flea bites. She opened her belt pouch and shook out two passengers, an Earwig and a Shutterbug. The Earwig, a multilegged gray insect about a foot long, scuttled underneath the bed. The Shutterbug opened his shell and fluttered up to hide behind the lantern next to the door.

I pulled the table into the middle of the room and arranged a chair on each side. I sat down in one, facing the door.

A soft tap came at the door. Pookie stepped into the shadow and vanished. It was a neat trick. I'd have to get her to show me how she did it.

"Come in," I called.

The door opened, and Pattikin peered in. I beckoned to her. To my surprise, my hand shook. I guess I was more nervous than I had anticipated. I folded my hands on the tabletop.

"Hi, there," she said. She slipped inside. Like us, she had worn a heavy cloak with a hood. She stopped and peered out into the corridor before closing the door behind her. "I wasn't sure you'd come."

"You have information I need," I said. "It's really important. I guess you know that."

She smiled. "Oh, I do." She moved toward me, her eyelids half lowered. "But it's a big secret. I didn't want anyone else to overhear us."

"No one will," I assured her. "Tell me."

"Just like that?" she asked, looking disappointed.

"Well, that's why I came here so early in the morning," I said. "I could be back in bed."

She raised her eyebrows. "There's a bed right here."

"I think I'll just stay in my chair," I said. "Why don't you sit down?"

"Sure," she said. She threw off the cloak and came toward me. My partners had been more than right. Underneath the cloak she was wearing the briefest of panties and a filmy blue lace tube that squeezed her top upward. It looked amazingly uncomfortable to wear. She pushed the table aside and came to stand over me. I squirmed backward in my seat. "Why don't I just sit down on your lap?"

"How about not?"

Pookie's voice was harsh at the best of times, and coming out of nowhere in a small hotel room brought out all its worst qualities. Pattikin almost jumped out of her thin garments. Pookie stepped forward and put her hands on her hips.

Pattikin looked shocked. "Who are you?"

Pookie polished her hand talons on her jumpsuit.

"I'm Mr. Skeeve's bodyguard."

"He looks like he can take care of himself," Pattikin said, wiggling her fingers at me.

"He *can* take care of himself," Pookie agreed. "I'm here to take care of *you*. Now, if you have an interview to conduct with Mr. Skeeve, you can do that. From there." She pointed to the empty chair. "On that side of the table. There will be no physical contact. No coming closer, no handshakes, no touching. I don't want there to be any misunderstanding later on."

"But there already will be," Pattikin said, tossing her head back. "Both of us were seen coming in here. Everyone is going to know. Unless you want to make a deal with me."

"No deal," Pookie said. She crossed her arms and moved toward Pattikin until the Tipp was forced to step backward, away from me.

"It'll just be his word against mine, and you know what they say about Klahds!"

"That they're loyal but gullible?" Pookie suggested.

"Hey!" I protested.

Pattikin smiled. "No, that's not the description I had in mind. When I leave here, I'll tell my side of the story to my paper. I can say anything I want. And my Shutterbug will back me up. He's been hidden in this room for hours."

Pookie grinned, showing all her teeth. "I have some very bad news about your cameraman," she said. "I did a little pest-control when I came in. Collateral damage. Sorry."

Pattikin looked dismayed, but kept on. "You have no witnesses to tell your side. It's going to look . . . very compromising."

"Not really," Pookie said. "We have our own witnesses. Guys?"

The Earwig poked his head out from underneath the bed and waved a leg. Earwigs had the facility to hear and then repeat hours of verbatim conversations accurately. They were invaluable at court trials. The Shutterbug peeked out from behind the lantern. Pattikin looked at them and her face fell. Pookie went on.

"Now, I have proof that you came in here under false pretenses, to try to catch Mr. Skeeve in a show of depravity and corruption. Maybe you even have a bag of coins in that hold-all of yours. I'm going to put together quite a little photo album, containing our side of everything that has happened in here this morning. I'm going to make two copies, one for our office and one extra. What happens to that second copy is up to you. It could get incorporated into the next daily briefing, or it can disappear forever."

Pattikin gathered up her cloak and wrapped herself in it. "What do you want?"

"Who sent you here?" I asked. "What do they want? Why do they want to smear me? Are they behind the other attack articles that I've seen?"

The Tipp shook her head. "Publish and be damned," she said. "You can't do to me anything worse than what would happen to me if I told you what you want to know."

I regarded her with regret. "You never were going to tell me who was eavesdropping on us, were you?"

Pattikin smiled at me pityingly. "So it *is* true what they say about Klahds."

"And what they say about Pervects," Pookie said, her voice dropping to a dangerous purr. Her yellow eyes seemed to glint with their own light. "Maybe you had better get out of here while you still have feet to walk on."

Pattikin took her advice. With one eye on Pookie, she backed toward the door, felt behind her for the latch, and slipped out into the corridor.

When she had gone, I found that my muscles were tensed rock solid. I did my best to relax.

"Thanks, Pookie," I said.

"Don't mention it," she said gruffly. "I owe you and Cousin Aahz plenty, though this wipes out a bunch of favors. I have lied, stolen, killed, hijacked, and taken the last string of beads from a crippled, blind old woman. I've done a lot of things on Perv you couldn't get me to tell you about even under torture, but I have two firm rules: I never babysit, and I never get involved in politics. This is why."

CHAPTER TWENTY

"How could you possibly think I'm lying?"

—PINOCCHIO

Pookie went home with the Earwig and Shutterbug safely stowed in her satchel. I marched out into the pale sunrise and headed for the *Evening Screed*.

As Pattikin had said, the news-gathering business didn't wait for daylight to begin its operations. The *Screed* office looked just like the *Morning Gossip* except for the faces of the reporters, typesetters, and editors. I asked for the managing editor.

"Romses Beleeger," said the tall Tipp who came out of a private room to shake my hand. "How may I help you?"

"You can stop trying to slander me or my people," I said conversationally.

"I beg your pardon? Are you sure it is I whom you seek?"

The way he phrased his sentences told me I had found my perfect grammarian.

"Only if you're the person who runs this rag."

Romses drew himself up. "I beg your pardon?"

I looked down my nose at him. "No need to beg. I will grant it freely, if you don't print details of the phony attempt at seduction perpetrated on me by one of your reporters a short while ago."

"One of my reporters tried to seduce you? Which one?"

"Pattikin Lockheart."

Romses shook his head. "I regret to contradict you, sir, but no one by that name is employed here."

"What?" I asked. I felt in my belt pouch for the card she had given me. I fished it out and handed it to Romses. He took it as if it were a fin from a week-dead fish.

"This is a forgery, sir," Romses said, handing it back. "I promise you, I have no one by that name in my office."

"But she said . . ." I realized I had been gullible, in more ways than one. "Someone sent her to me. We set up a private meeting . . ."

"Is that so?" Romses asked, the light of battle illuminating his light-brown eyes. "Tell me all about it."

"No!" I said, not wishing to dig myself in deeper trouble than I already had. I should have led *him* to admit he had instructed her to set it up. "So she didn't bring you material for an article about me?"

"Oh, yes, we received one from someone by that name. My people are setting it up now for today's paper." He gestured at the press running in the rear of the shop.

"You can't print it!" I said.

"I refuse to allow our paper to be the only digest in town that didn't," Romses told me sternly. "The story is already in circulation."

"Already?" I asked. "How? Where?"

Romses lifted an eyebrow toward one of the clerks slitting open envelopes at a desk near the door.

"Dag, send me today's *Morning Gossip*."

The young Tipp lifted a rolled-up newspaper and sent it flying toward us. It landed in Romses's hands with a SMACK! He folded the front page outward and showed it to me.

I read the page with my temper flaring into a volcanic blaze. It was an account of the first few moments of my meeting with Pattikin, but after the point when she dropped her cloak it became a nauseatingly coy but vivid description of a tryst, with me as a willing participant if not instigator. It had not been written by Pattikin herself, but was billed "as told to" Milligan Stemplemeier, staff reporter. At least there were no images.

"None of this is true!" I protested. "This is complete fantasy!"

"Scandals sell papers, Mr. Skeeve, don't they? And that's our business—to sell papers."

"But I just left Pattikin a few moments ago," I said. "How did it get into print so quickly?" Then I realized the truth. "It must have been planted even before she met me at that hotel. This was all a setup!"

"I am certain that I have no idea of what you speak," Romses said. "I am terribly sorry, but I have a great deal to get done. Thank you for stopping by."

He carefully maneuvered me to the glass doors and out onto the street.

I stood on the public footpath, feeling like a complete idiot. In spite of the precautions I had taken, I had still been made to look not only corrupt, but depraved.

I thought about going to the *Morning Gossip* but realized an indignant denial would just confirm in their minds that I was guilty of something. A relationship between two adult beings was not illegal. It would be an issue only if I made something of it. I had a choice between calling further attention to the story or letting it die. If it would.

Bunny met me at our temporary office. The early papers were in a stack in front of her. She raised her eyebrows at me.

"We were prepared," I said, "but not for everything."

"Aahz thought something like that might happen," she said.

"He told you? When?"

"This morning," she said. "The papers are getting even with

us for cutting them out of the circuit. They don't want to give up control of the situation."

"They're not getting it back," I said. "I don't care what they say about me. I haven't done anything wrong!"

"Who's going to believe that?" Bunny asked. "They make it sound like you did. Everything in the papers could be phony, including the horoscopes, and the average Tipp on the street would never know."

I frowned. "The horoscopes are false?" On Klah, magicians wrote the fortunes.

"Yes. Ecstra told me. They're written for entertainment value. Otherwise they might have to tell bad news some days, and that wouldn't sell papers. The truth can be a dangerous thing."

"I know," I said. I remembered a famous psychic in the kingdom where I grew up who had been hauled away by an angry baron and never seen again. "We'd better take precautions. Come back with me. I'm going to get some of the others."

"No!" Bunny said. "We can handle this."

"Well . . ." I thought for a moment. "At least let me bring Gleep back. This could turn physical, and I want to make sure you're protected. The papers' magicians are stronger than I am, but I doubt they can do much with a dragon. Besides, he's a better judge of character than I am."

Bunny touched my cheek. "No, he's not."

CHAPTER TWENTY-ONE

"I'm telling you the naked truth."

—LADY GODIVA

I could tell my effectiveness was being hampered by the rumors in the papers. When we went out to a square on the second terrace above the main street to oversee the candidates offering speeches on behalf of Parents' Day, reporters and onlookers alike kept glancing over their shoulders at us instead of keeping their eyes on the candidates up on the platform.

". . . And I say that everyone who has had a parent, or who has ever been a parent, should appreciate the contributions that they have provided to society!" Wilmer thundered. He held a finger in the air and struck a pose.

No one clapped or cheered.

"I say, you should appreciate the contributions of parents!" Wilmer shouted. The Echoes picked up his voice and sent it around. The audience, aware that they were being addressed, turned and gave him a faint smattering of applause. "Thank you. As a parent and a grandparent myself, I am grateful for my fellow parents. I want all of you fine children to keep in mind all you owe to your parents. Without them, where would you be?"

"Nonexistent?" I muttered to myself, then realized I was surrounded by reporters. Gleep kept them at a distance, but they were still close enough to have heard what I said. They all wrote in their notebooks. My cheeks grew hot. I didn't want to attract more attention.

Emo went next. He put a companionable arm around the statues of a mother and father Tipp cradling a baby. Somewhere, a melody struck up, and Emo burst into song.

"P is for progenitors of people. A is for affection in their eyes. R, responsibility they teach us, E, to emulate their ways so wise. N, wiping our runny little nooooo-ses, TS, telling stories nightly tooooo us. All of this together this spells out Parents! I love my parents. And you should love yours, too!"

The reporters turned openly to see if I was going to comment. I stayed steadfastly silent. It didn't help. They wrote something down anyhow.

"Well?" Carnelia said, descending upon us when the speeches were done.

"I thought Wilmer did a fine job," I said. "And Emo, too," I added to Orlow. "That was quite a song."

"As if anyone could tell," Orlow said, sourly. "He gave the performance of a lifetime, and no one paid any attention, thanks to *you*."

"I'm sorry," I said. "I didn't mean to."

"No offense," Carnelia said, "but I am beginning to wonder if you folks are not taking away more from the process than you are contributing to it."

"That story was phony," I said. "We told you the papers are making things up now. They don't want either of your candidates elected."

"They made it up?" Orlow asked. "So it's all a lie? You never met with that woman in a seedy hotel room?"

I hated to lie. "Well, I *did* . . ."

"So it was true!"

"I met her, but none of that happened! I have three witnesses!"

"It doesn't matter," Carnelia said. "Public perception counts! You're getting to be an embarrassment to the candidates."

"Well, I'm not," Bunny said, pushing in front of me. "You can deal with me in the future. Skeeve will just help me a little more behind the scenes."

Orlow and Carnelia exchanged glances.

"Well, all right," Orlow agreed. "We'll keep our agreement with you for now, but no more surprises!"

"None," Bunny promised.

We went back to our office, feeling chastened. Gleep circled around us as we walked, growling in low tones at anyone who came close to us. Mothers with children retreated to the far side of the street. They were afraid of Gleep, but at that moment *I* was probably more dangerous to them. I felt angry and embarrassed.

"Who would ever have thought we'd be told to clean up our behavior by politicians?" I blurted as soon as our door closed behind us.

"I'll never live this down at home," Bunny said.

"None of our partners would ever tease you about it," I said. "Not even Aahz. He's on our side."

"I don't mean on Deva," Bunny said. Someone started pounding on the door. "I don't care who it is, tell them to go away. I need five minutes to pull myself together."

I put on the guise of a Tipp in a white jacket and leaned out the door. It was Ecstra.

"I'm sorry, but the office is closed just now."

"Skeeve, I need to talk to you!"

I frowned. "How do you know it's me?" I asked.

"You may look like a Tipp, but you smell the same," she said. "Kind of like coffee and dust."

Since those were two scents prevalent in our home on Deva, I had to admit she had me there. "Sorry, you still can't come in."

"Gleep!"

My dragon shot around my legs, cut around Ecstra, and herded her inside. When I tried to protest, he turned his long neck and slurped me in the face with his tongue. I went sprawling. His tail hit the door and shut it.

"He knows I want to help you, even if you don't," Ecstra said.

"How?" I asked.

"I want to get the truth out there," she said. "I know you're not the type to get involved with strange women. Both of you have been very honest and straightforward since you got here. It's been a nice change. And now I understand why you're keeping all the journalists at a distance. Something *is* going on."

"So you can understand why we have to ask you to leave."

"Gleep!" my dragon said, warningly. Ecstra put her arm around his neck and appealed to us.

"No, I want to help! I've been steered this way and that by people I trusted. I know I can believe what you say. I want to get to the bottom of it."

Gleep was there to help protect us. When he let her get close to us, I realized he must know something I didn't. I had to relent.

"All right. You can stay. For a few moments." I pulled out a chair and helped Ecstra to sit down in it. She smiled up at me as she whipped out her notebook.

"Thanks. I'm working on a special report. I have to investigate this. I hope you'll cooperate with me. It's really important. It is not about the polls, I promise."

Bunny and I exchanged glances that turned from reluctant to resigned.

"I guess," I said.

"I appreciate it," Ecstra said. She turned to Bunny. "It's an exposé about you."

"Me?" Bunny asked. "What about me?"

"Uh, well, it's kind of hard to explain," Ecstra began, clearly embarrassed.

"Try."

"Well, I have received information from an unnamed source—"

"Naturally," I said.

"—who says he has proof that the only reason you have gotten the candidates to cooperate is by your feminine wiles." Ecstra was almost hiding her face by the time she finished the sentence.

"What?" Bunny asked, dumbfounded. "I mean, I am proud of my feminine wiles, but let me assure you that I have never used them and will never use them on any Tipp, particularly not our two clients. Of all the stupid things to imply!"

Ecstra glanced at me uncomfortably.

"Well, my source had some specifics, how you interested the gentlemen with . . ." She leaned forward and whispered in Bunny's ear. ". . . And absolutely *hypnotized* them by . . . and then, you took your . . ." I watched Bunny's eyes and open mouth grow wider and wider with every word. I expected her to explode in fury and throw Ecstra out of the room. Instead, she burst out laughing. Ecstra and I watched her with growing bemusement. Bunny wiped her eyes.

She took the reporter's hand. "Come on," she said. She pulled her toward the bathroom. I started after them. She shook a finger at me. "Not you, Skeeve. Ladies only."

The door closed firmly behind them.

Ecstra's voice echoed hollowly in the tiled room. "I'm not sure if you have to . . ."

"C'mon, we're just girls here," Bunny said. "I'll show you mine if you show me yours. Never mind, you don't have to. Look." I heard the sound of rustling cloth swishing to the floor.

Ecstra gasped.

I became very interested in what was going on in there. I took a step toward the door. Gleep zipped around in front of me. He snaked his long neck up so we were eye to eye and gave me a severe stare.

"Gleep!"

"I just want to check to see if they're all right," I said.

"Gleep!" he told me, reproachfully.

"Oh, fine," I said. I sighed. I stared at the door, wishing I could see through it.

Ecstra's voice was filled with wonder. "You mean there aren't any . . . ?"

"Nope," Bunny said.

"And what about the spikes on the . . . ?"

"No," Bunny said.

"And the line of extra . . . ?"

"No, not there, either."

"Wow," Ecstra said, admiringly. "And you do all that without needing . . . ?"

"I've *never* needed anything like that."

I was agog by the time Bunny and Ecstra emerged. Rather than seeming embarrassed by the private display, Bunny looked confident and in control. Ecstra scribbled madly in her notebook. She was very excited.

"This is going to be a great article!" she gushed. "An exposé on the exposure exposé that was supposed to expose you! Thanks!" She shook both of our hands and rushed out of the door.

"I hope that helps with the corruption accusations," I said.

"I doubt it," Bunny said thoughtfully.

She was right. The article never appeared. I checked the *Morning Gossip* and all the other papers. I asked Ecstra about it the next day at the morning debate. She looked depressed.

"My boss killed it," she said. "He even took my notes. It was good journalism!"

CHAPTER TWENTY-TWO

"The truth never hurt anybody."

—O. WILDE

I wasn't going to let the newspapers control the truth. I had other ways of getting the word out. We were going to regain control of the situation one way or another.

Bunny and I wrote up everything we could recall about the attempts at bribery, seduction, and slander, not getting too graphic about the show-and-tell I had not witnessed, but making it clear we were being victimized to draw attention away from the election.

I caught Sid before the She went on for her noon recitation in the main square. She was a tall, bony female with gray skin and flowing green hair, dressed in a robe of thin, moss-green cloth that fluttered when she walked. The She smiled, which pulled the sparse skin of her face away from her snaggled teeth.

"Hi, Bunny. Hi, Skeeve. What can I do for you?" she asked. Her high-pitched voice made me shudder, but there was no doubt that she was an effective speaker. She knew that my difficulty tolerating the sound was nothing personal.

"I've got a special addition for you," I said. I gave her the script. She glanced through it.

"This will make them open their eyes! I'll give it my best play," she promised. The town clock in the nearby tower struck midday with a friendly tenor chime. "You'd better get going if you're not going to listen to my performance."

Bunny and I looked at each other. "We'd better stay," I said. "I want to make sure it gets out."

I had already found a spot as far away from the gazebo as possible, with no buildings behind us to echo the sound. Bunny reassured Sid.

"We'll stay."

"All right," Sid the She said. "By the way, thanks for the gig. I've been between jobs for a while. This has helped me pay off some of my outstanding bills."

"No problem," I said. "I have discovered elections can be good for the economy."

With our ears stuffed with wax, Bunny and I sat down on a park bench under a flowering tree. A large blue butterfly flapped around our heads and settled on the nearest colorful blossom. The crowd started filling in around us. Some even unpacked picnic baskets. The largest part of the audience seemed to be young Tipps who must have just been old enough to vote in their first election. I felt a measure of pride for getting them interested in civic responsibility. The day was fine and sunny. I prepared to enjoy myself.

Sid the She took her place in the center of the gazebo. A real professional at her craft, she never needed cue cards or an accompanist. She struck a pose, waiting until every eye was on her. Then she placed her hand upon her midsection to monitor her breathing, and opened her mouth.

"Hail, citizens of Bokromi!" she sang. "These are the tidings of the day, and woe upon those who pay no heed!"

The butterfly fled. It had good sense. I wish I could have done the same. I gritted my teeth.

Sid's voice wailed up and down the scales, filling the square and echoing off every building, tree, and fence. If it hadn't been for the wax in my ears, I would have been writhing in pain. Bunny's face twisted with discomfort.

". . . The names of Skeeve and Bunny, good citizens who have been friends to Tipicanoo, must not suffer the torment of slander!"

She went down the list I had given her of the many attempts to make us out to be crooks and asserted that they were all untrue. The adults listened, nodding their heads in time with the cadence of her words. I searched their faces for signs that they understood, but it was the young people who seemed the most moved by the She's performance. Literally, in fact. They got up and danced, gyrating to the sound of the wailing voice. I was amazed. The She had them in the palm of her hand.

"I'm surprised she doesn't get more work," I whispered to Bunny.

"What?" Bunny asked.

I had forgotten about the wax.

"I said," raising my voice, "I'm sorry she doesn't get more work!"

Bunny gestured at her ears. "I can't hear you!"

"Shhh!" Some of the listeners said, turning around with their fingers to their lips. I settled down to listen. Sid was good, no doubt about it. She lifted her arms up to the sky and hit her big crescendo.

". . . This has been a pai-aaaii—aaaiiid political announcement!"

The entire audience sprang to its feet and burst into applause. Bunny and I rose and joined them. I clapped wildly as Sid took an encore.

"Do not forget to voooo-ooo-oote! It is your ri-iii-iiight!"

The She hit a final high note that went straight through my head, and all the lights went out.

CHAPTER TWENTY-THREE

"Trust us, things are just fine as they are."

—WALL STREET

I woke up in pitch-darkness. A faint echo told me I was in a stone room. A thrumming like a heartbeat vibrated up through the soles of my shoes. I tried to get up, but my hands were tied to the arms of the chair in which I was seated. So were my ankles. The wax was no longer in my ears.

"Bunny?" I whispered.

"Skeeve?" her voice came from beside me. She sounded shaken. I wasn't surprised. "Are you all right?"

"I'm fine. Are you hurt?"

"No. Can you get us loose?"

I closed my eyes and felt around for force lines. Two were close by: a spiky white line that ran below our feet, and a wide yellow line overhead. I was not familiar with either of them, but they didn't fight me as I gathered magikal force from them. I pictured the ropes at my wrists unknotting. The magik got to work on my bonds. I felt the pressure around my left arm lessening. Then it increased again. The ropes secured themselves more firmly. I went to gather up more magik. A stronger force prevented me from reaching the force lines.

"Not so fast."

A deep male voice boomed in the darkness. I realized that we were not alone. Using magik I struck a spark of light that was quickly extinguished. Before it was, I saw the outlines of several people seated in chairs. They were all looking at us.

"Who are you?" I asked the blackness. "Why have you kidnapped us?"

"*Kidnap* is such a harsh word," the deep voice said. "Say, perhaps, that we have invited you for an ad hoc mandatory private meeting."

"No, thanks, I'll stick with *kidnap*," I said.

"As you wish."

"Why are we here?"

A new voice spoke, a thin tenor. "You are interfering with us. We cannot permit that."

Enlightenment filled in the features in my memory that were attached to that style of speaking.

"You're Romses Beleeger," I said. "And Tolomi Papirus. You're both editors. Are you all editors?"

"We knew you were intelligent," a female voice said, approvingly. I knew without a doubt that she was the editor of the *Tipp Sheet*. "We were simply hoping you were intelligent enough not to push hard where you weren't allowed."

I raised my eyebrows, though no one knew it but me. "Not allowed to do what?"

Romses answered for the group. "Restrict our future income. We have a sinecure here. You must not try to continue in this enterprise."

"This enterprise? The election? Is that why you're working so hard to make us look bad?" I asked. "You don't want there to be an election. You really want Bokromi to go on with this endless campaign so you can *sell newspapers*?"

Tolomi cleared his throat. "Yes. We knew you would catch on. We hoped that after a little pressure you would understand the way things are here. The way things need to be. It's in our best interests."

"For you, maybe," Bunny said. "This island is falling apart without decent management. Until last week no one was fixing broken lamps or cleaning the streets. The city streets were full of trash. No one could be proud of that."

"That's not important to the Syndication," Tolomi said, sounding amused. "We profit whether there's garbage pickup or not." I heard murmurs of agreement.

I shook my head. "So it's not just one or a couple of papers involved in this conspiracy—it's all of you!"

"Even more impressive," the *Tipp Sheet* editor said. "Though rather late in coming. And does that realization show you how futile it would be to continue your efforts?"

"We're not going to quit," Bunny said in a tight voice. I could tell that she was furious.

"How can you go on? You've lost your credibility. Your clients are beginning to find you an embarrassment. They want themselves in the headlines, not their handpicked organizers. If you were removed from the scene, everything could go back to the way it was before. Everyone would have a job, and there would be no more questions about ending such a nice way of life."

I felt ice forming in my belly. I struggled against my bonds, trying to find a gap in the magik holding me.

"You have to let us go," I said. "Too many people would ask questions if we didn't come back. We have friends who would find out who is responsible, and they believe in vengeance."

"Vengeance?" the *Tipp Sheet* editor asked. "For what?"

"If you . . . disposed of us. That's what's going to happen, isn't it?"

"You fear we would *kill* you?" Romses asked incredulously. "When you have provided us with the most impressive increase in circulation in years? Certainly not! My stockholders would never forgive me!"

"But you know when we leave we're going to tell everyone what happened here," I said.

"It won't matter what you tell anyone," Tolomi said, clearly amused. "Who are they going to believe, you or what they read in the papers?"

"We can get the message to the electorate," I said. "We're watching out for your dirty tricks now."

"Said the Klahd tied to a chair," Romses said. "Clea, set them free."

"All right," said the *Tipp Sheet* editor.

The bonds on my wrists and ankles fell to the floor. I reached out for Bunny. Her hand met mine and twined in it.

"I just want you to know you'll never get away with it," I said.

"It doesn't matter what you think," Tolomi said. "No exposé you write will ever get into a single paper. Your town crier will come down with a bad case of laryngitis, and no one will hear it. We have a long reach. Information travels faster than the fleetest foot or the most powerful magik."

I fumed. These Tipps were accustomed to being despots in their own domains. They worked together to make sure they all did well, no matter who else it hurt.

"Why are you doing this?" I asked. "Why can't you just let the election continue? There will be other great stories in the future. You just have to let them happen!"

"Not as good as this one," Clea said. "We've kept it going for five years. I don't see why we can't keep it up for another five. Or maybe ten. We'll keep this going on as long as we want."

"The candidates will quit," I said.

"Then new ones will take their place. Bokromi needs a governor."

"But you won't let one be elected!"

Tolomi laughed, and the entire Syndication joined in. The sound was chilling in the hollow cave. "*They* don't know that."

"Then we have a lot of work to do to prove you wrong,"

I said, rising to my feet. I put an arm around Bunny. "Now, are you going to let us out, or do I have to show you what I can do when I'm really angry?"

"I am certain it is futile to propose it again," Romses said, "but if you choose to cooperate with us, you may receive part of our profit. A small emolument for your time and trouble."

"Forget it," I snarled.

"As you wish," the voice in the dark said. "A pity. We could have used your brains."

I steeled myself. If they were going to attack again, this was the moment. I gathered all the magik I could and stood ready.

"Forty," Clea said. The word seemed full of portent.

Silence filled my ears.

When I woke up, Bunny and I were back on the park bench. We were alone. The square had cleared out, except for two street sweepers, one wearing green and one in purple, gathering up banners and confetti. Sergeant Boxty looked down at us.

"Loitering!" he said. "And I can add vagrancy to disturbing the peace!"

"Now, just a minute," I sputtered. "We were just sitting here for a moment."

"Snoring!" Sergeant Boxty said. "If you can't sing like your skinny friend, then you shouldn't make noise in public! I should run you in."

Bunny rose and smiled at him. "Oh, you aren't going to do that, are you? Not on such a beautiful day?"

As if on cue, some of the hired birds burst into song. A scarlet butterfly danced on the breeze. Sergeant Boxty started to relent.

"Well, just this once," he said. "I'm a fan of Sid the She. If you can get me an autograph, I'll forget what I just saw."

"I will," I promised. Sergeant Boxty touched his hat with his nightstick and flew up the face of the cliff to the next terrace.

"That was close," I said to Bunny. She had an odd expression on her face. I couldn't tell if she was upset, angry, or in despair.

"Do you want to give up?" I asked her.

"Not a chance," Bunny said, firmly. She was angry but not at me. "Not now, after they threatened us. Not if you pulled out my nails with pliers."

"Good," I said. "Neither do I. We'll just have to take more precautions."

"And play as dirty as they do, if we have to."

I smiled at her. "But it would be so much more satisfying to win playing by the rules."

CHAPTER TWENTY-FOUR

"Old habits are hard to break."

—C. SHEEN

"This is totally against the contract you signed," Bunny said, holding up a sheaf of receipts to Orlow. The Friendship Party manager had been backed up against a wall in the Hotel Tippmore conference room. "Tickets to the zoo for a thousand children? They're marked at seven copper pieces each!"

"Er, volume discount?" Orlow suggested hopefully.

Bunny wasn't buying it. "You agreed not to give gifts over a copper piece in value."

"We had to! The Wisdom Party set up a carnival outside of town and gave free Pegasus rides!"

"I have already dealt with them," Bunny said. "We sent the Pegasus home after he gave me his bill for five copper pieces a ride!"

"An honest mistake," Carnelia said, placatingly. "We misunderstood his fee. It was a trifle more than we thought it was going to be."

Bunny was unimpressed. "What is the matter with both of you? You know the terms. You are not allowed to buy votes! It's illegal!"

"Er, the kiddies can't vote, you know . . ."

"But their parents can, and I suppose they were admitted to the zoo as well? I certainly saw adults on the Pegasus's back!"

I couldn't blame her for being upset. We were fighting a war on two fronts now. The Syndication continued to print whatever it felt like. No longer did newspapers bother to tell the truth about the campaign events. In fact, they departed from fact so drastically that it was hard to reconcile the events of real life with what I read in the papers. I was struck by the masterful fantasy of trained writers putting together fictional accounts of what had happened. Newspaper circulation shot up, but attendance at the debates, speeches, and other functions went down.

What was worse, word of more "anonymous interviews" was hinted in the gossip columns. The Syndication redoubled its allegations that we were to blame for all the delays in the past, notwithstanding the fact that we had been in Bokromi for only two weeks.

Not surprisingly, with our reputation getting muddied, the campaign managers began to feel as though they were free to behave any way they wanted to. They started to leak things to the press on their own. And give out large gifts to influential people, such as big-business owners. And make open promotions during speeches and other appearances, such as tickets to the zoo and Pegasus rides. Such things couldn't go on too long before Bunny got wind of them, and she descended upon both candidates, or rather their managers, like an avalanche.

When we had paid visits to both party headquarters, you would have thought we were the most welcome visitors possible, short of the Gnomish Clearing House Reward Squad bringing them sacks full of gold coins.

"Why, Miss Bunny, Mr. Skeeve," Carnelia had said, embracing us like long-lost rich relatives. "I was just about to call upon you! How would you like to join me for lunch? I have engaged that nice room at the Hotel Tippmore."

"By an outstanding coincidence, Orlow invited us there for lunch just a few minutes ago," Bunny said. "I think that it would be a very good idea. We need to talk, and I think you will want us to have that conversation in *private*."

Carnelia hastily donned her fur stole and accompanied us to the hotel.

I was beginning to think of the conference room as a home away from home. Carnelia fussed over us, making sure we each had enough delicate little sandwiches and pouring tea for us from the trays she had ordered. Orlow offered us cigars, candy, liquor, each more expensive than the last, from the trays that *he* had ordered. I recognized a buttering-up when I saw it.

"I must admit I am a little surprised to find him here," Carnelia said.

"And I reserved this room for a private chat with you! I didn't know *she* was coming."

"Well, I reserved it yesterday morning!"

Bunny stretched out her hands and cracked her knuckles. "I'm glad both of you are here. We have a few things to discuss."

Both campaign managers were sitting hunched over in their chairs like chastened schoolchildren by the time Bunny had finished with them.

". . . Then there's the general negative campaigning. Carnelia. It has come to my attention that you have been planting fake posters of Emo that say insulting things to people as they pass by."

"Yes!" Orlow said, pointing at her. "One of them told his mother she was ugly. Unconscionable!"

"And you!" Bunny said, turning to him. "Handing out gray wigs to Emo's supporters in the crowd. That's so insulting I'm surprised you even considered it."

"It's not exactly against the *rules* . . ."

"It's unsportsmanlike. I thought we were going to have an election that was above all that pettiness and bad behavior."

Orlow pouted. "Well, by the sound of it, you're no stranger to bad behavior. You ought to embrace some good, *clean* fun!"

"You can't believe what you read!" I said. "I told you the papers were stepping up their smear campaign. It's a ploy."

"An effective one! Everyone believes those stories. I mean, I don't. But it's making us look bad to have you working for us. It's tough on Emo. He's very sensitive."

"I understand that," Bunny said, relenting. "But we're so close now. You've been campaigning for five years. A couple of weeks is all that is left."

"Too little," Carnelia said abruptly. "Wilmer wants more time now. He has to separate himself from the downright corruption that is coming to the fore. You know what I mean."

"I certainly don't," Bunny said coldly.

"Oh, not that trash about Mr. Skeeve. It was in the *Evening Screed*. Wilmer learned that Emo's candidacy is based on fraud! He doesn't own the house he lives in as he claimed! He lives out of town!"

"Well, Emo wants the vote moved up!" Orlow exclaimed. "We're tired of waiting around. No sense postponing it. We want it sooner! We read the report in the *Tipp Sheet*. Wilmer is running on fraudulent terms, not Emo. Who fudged his birth date so as not to seem ancient and out of touch? We'd better have it sooner, or Wilmer might die on you! Who knows if he's physically fit to run?"

"We're not afraid of a little delay! That's why we want a postponement!"

"And we want the election at the end of this week!"

"You signed a contract setting the date!"

Both of them looked at us. "So what?" they asked in unison.

Bunny shook her head. "You're challenging your opponents' legitimacy after all this time? But didn't you check everything before?"

"I stand by my assertion," Orlow said. "It's a matter of public record that Wilmer filed false documents."

"Me, too," Carnelia said. "This is my last word on the subject. We refuse to go through with it if Emo is the candidate."

"But aren't you both saying the same thing?"

"He lies!"

"She prevaricates!"

"The Syndication is behind this," I said. "Look, since both challenge one another's candidate, then you *both* have to bring out your proof that you are legitimate candidates. Do not show them to anyone else, but we will have a public rally instead of a debate. Everyone will be satisfied. You can have legal counsel standing by to verify your birth certificates, proof of residence, nominating petitions, donation accounting, and whatever else you used to put yourself up as a candidate for governor. It will be a completely public process, and everyone will be satisfied. All right?"

"I hate to cede anything to that scoundrel," Carnelia said. Her rodents chirped agreement.

"You don't have to," Bunny said. "We are going to take it directly to the people without the interference of a middleman, and it will be fair. I will personally go over every single document you present, and I will certify whether any fakes have been presented. From now on, we won't have any more surprises."

CHAPTER TWENTY-FIVE

"This will go on your permanent record."

—M. SUPERIOR

The next debate was scheduled in the middle of the field where it had been before. Gleep and I were there early to make sure that neither side altered the stage in any way. The Echoes were perched on their poles all the way to the back of what looked like the entire population of the island. I spotted a number of non-Tipps. Like Deva, Tipicanoo welcomed denizens of other dimensions. I had seen Deveel merchants, Imp tailors, Troll construction workers, and a host of other immigrants I couldn't identify who had set up shop in the towns. They had not shown a lot of interest in the election to date. It didn't surprise me, since little new had happened in five long years, but we were going to bring this one to a close within two weeks, or die trying. I was so tired of the endless seesawing that I was going to take a vacation when it was all over. Bunny needed to take one, too. She looked tired, and it wasn't just this situation that was weighing on her mind. When we returned to Deva each evening I offered to talk, but she put me off, insisting it was nothing. But we had been seeing a lot more of her cousin Sylvia. Something was going on in her Family. I just didn't know what.

The press corps had been bottled up inside a cordon guarded by Guido and Nunzio. The quiet air of authority they wielded, not to mention the miniature crossbows that I knew Guido had allowed to be seen just once, had put them on reasonably good behavior. I had no faith that the peace would last beyond the beginning of the rally, but at least we'd start well. Ecstra, in the midst of the band, had shot me a couple of rueful looks. I felt bad about that, but whether she had intended it or not, she had been the conduit to the Syndication of a lot of our plans. Her attempt to make up for it had failed. It wasn't her fault, but I couldn't let her get close again.

"Skeeve . . . worried?" Gleep asked. I wiped the frown off my face.

"Not this time," I said. "I think we have everything under control. At least I hope so. Bunny and I have gone over everything we can think of that might go wrong. All the paperwork is in order. Copies have been made of everything and hidden in six different dimensions so they can't be altered without detection. Once the—"

"Gleep!" my pet said. He reared up and planted an affectionate, if disgustingly slimy, kiss on my face.

The campaign workers made their way through the crowd, offering pennants and buttons to the supporters. Children cheered and laughed at the acrobats and fire eaters that each side had hired for the day. I had the word of both candidates and their managers that they had made no mention of the actual character of the event to anyone else, even though it had meant doing a lot of paperwork on their own.

As moderator, Bunny sat alone at the little table, glass of water and silver bell at hand. Gleep and I stood ready to intervene if she needed us, but I doubted she would. Bunny was much better at handling a crowd than I was.

The mayor of Bokromi came forward, his tall hat perched

on the back of his head. "My friends, welcome to the next in the series of debates between our great candidates, your friends and neighbors, you know them, you love them: Wilmer Weavil-Scuttil and Emo Weavil!"

The crowd screamed and yelled. The mayor lifted his hands. The shouting died away. "I want to welcome the contenders! Come on out, boys! Let's hear it for them!"

On either side of the stage erupted clouds of smoke, green on the right and purple on the left.

BAMF! BAMF!

Emo and Wilmer emerged from the puffs, hands up to acknowledge the joyful acclaim of their public. They went to their respective lecterns. Aides in purple or green jackets followed, carrying briefcases that had been bespelled so they could not put them down and sealed with magikal locks. The need for security was at an end. Under the curious gaze of the crowd, Emo and Wilmer unlocked the boxes. Each took therefrom a stack of official papers bristling with ribbons and seals.

Bunny smiled out at them. "Friends and voters, by popular demand, we are deviating just a little bit from the usual format."

The reporters in the audience murmured loudly among themselves. They loved anything new, and for once, they had no advance notice of our intention. I hoped the Syndication had not done anything to interfere.

"What's the scoop?" Ecstra shouted.

"There has been some question lately, I won't say from whom, that one or the other of the good gentlemen up here does not have the qualifications to serve as governor of this island. So, today we are going to go down the list of every requirement from the written statutes concerning candidacy." She held up a large, flat lens attached to a black handle. "I have here an Inspector-Detector that will tell me whether a document is real or forged. Is everyone ready?"

"Yes, ma'am!" Emo said, winking and pointing at the reporters in the front row.

"I most certainly am!" Wilmer added.

The reporters beamed. Every paper in town had run competing features on the subject. They were eager to get the follow-up.

"First, gentlemen, where were you born?"

Emo scrabbled through his collection of papers, but Wilmer had his in order. He held up a yellowed rectangle of parchment and waved it in the air.

"Right here, on the island of Bokromi!" he said. "I have been here all my life!"

Emo came up with his within a few seconds. "Me, too! And my mother is here if you need to ask her. Hi, Mom!" He waved to Mrs. Weavil, who was seated on a flowered armchair at the side of the stage. Smiling indulgently, she waved back. The reporters scribbled down notes. I predicted that a picture of Mrs. Weavil would appear in the next edition of every paper in town. I had confiscated her handbag so she couldn't throw anything at Wilmer.

Bunny took the documents and looked them over with the Detector. I had borrowed it from the treasury in Possiltum, where it had been used to prove the worth of letters of credit for two centuries. Queen Hemlock had exacted the promise of a favor for its use, as well as vowing that I would be sorry if I didn't return it intact. I couldn't see any problem with getting it back to her within a couple of hours. Bunny nodded and set down the two birth certificates. She looked up at the candidates.

"The next item on the list concerns residency. Are you presently residents of this island? Where do you live?"

With a bow, Wilmer handed Bunny a rolled parchment and several envelopes. "This is the deed to my house in town, plus recently delivered mail. I can produce the Snail Carrier as a witness." Bunny took the envelopes, then had to wipe viscous threads of slime off her hands with her handkerchief. Emo presented his deed and an album of pictures of his home with his family posing in the garden.

Bunny looked them over carefully. "These pass the test, too."

The audience broke into applause.

"I told you before, there was nothing underhanded about my campaign!" Wilmer said to Emo over Bunny's head.

Emo looked at him wide-eyed. "I never said there was! I said you were an unfit, out-of-touch sack of fur. I never said you were underhanded!"

"Next," Bunny said, raising her voice. The Echoes repeated her peeved tones for the assembly. "Your nominating petitions. You have to have two thousand signatures each of voters who are registered with the Bokromi government."

"I have ten thousand," Wilmer declared.

"I have twelve thousand!"

"Well, you can't count the eight thousand that were just you practicing your penmanship," Wilmer said, with a humorous wink at the audience. His supporters guffawed. "They have to be real people."

Emo opened up large eyes at him. "Are you maligning the voters of this great island?" he asked. "Because they all signed my petitions in good faith."

"Ooooh," the audience crooned. One point for Emo. They had been scoring off one another since the beginning. That put the green team one point ahead.

Bunny went over each page with the glass lens. On almost every page, the lens burst into blue light, indicating that the name it was magnifying was a phony. Bunny marked it off. Emo and Wilmer got more and more nervous as she proceeded. I lost count of how many she disqualified. The audience was on tiptoe with excitement.

At last, Bunny came to the final page of each petition and smacked them down on the table. "Each candidate has exactly eight thousand, two hundred and four legal signatures," she said. "The last thing on the list is a proper accounting of campaign donations with donor names and relationship to the candidate."

"Can we get copies of those documents?" a male reporter called.

"I believe these are public records," Bunny said. Orlow and Carnelia, on their respective sides of the stage, mimed *No!* "According to advice given to me by the Government Records Office, they are supposed to be."

"Very well," Carnelia said. Even her stole furs looked depressed. "They will be put on display."

"Yay!" shouted the reporters.

Very slowly, Wilmer and Emo brought out ledgers. They didn't set them down. Instead, they held on to them, while taking a long, careful look at the opposition.

"Sometime today," Bunny said, impatiently. "These good people have other places to be, and so do I." She patted the desk. Reluctantly, the two candidates put their books down at opposite edges of the table and backed away, each never letting the other one out of his sight. Wilmer took a step toward Bunny with his finger raised to say something. In a flash, Emo closed the distance.

"I was only going to say I will answer any questions you have, Miss Bunny," Wilmer said.

Another point for Wilmer. They were tied again.

Bunny put on a blue eyeshade that went well with her red hair and began to page through the ledgers. For this task she did not need magik or anyone else's aid. She had a university degree in accounting and plenty of experience handling the Mob's books. Her pencil ticked off entries. The two candidates couldn't help but notice that her lips were pressed tightly together.

"Mm-hm," she murmured to herself. "Mm-mm. Mm-hm."

The campaign managers came out to bolster their candidates. Orlow kept his arm over Emo's shoulders as Emo bit his nails. Wilmer paced up and back at his end of the stage. Carnelia stopped him every so often to mop his brow with a handkerchief. I wondered what they all had to hide. Bunny was not going to be hurried by any of them or the audience. At last, she put down her pencil and took off her eyeshade.

"According to my calculations, all donations are accounted for to date. I'll be going over the books weekly until the election."

"Does that mean you didn't find any irregularities?" Ecstra called out.

Bunny smiled at her, her blue eyes crinkling at the corners. "Well, there are a *lot* of entries near the end that look like they were entered in a big hurry, but it all balanced out." Everyone laughed except the campaign managers.

"Well, Miss Bunny?" Orlow asked.

"I'm getting to it!" she said. "There's a procedure to follow in the laws. So, therefore, I am pleased to declare these two Tipps the sole and well-qualified candidates for the high office of gov—"

"Not so fast!"

A squeaky voice burst out from the center of the audience. The crowd parted suddenly to allow the passage of a creature who would have stood no higher than my breastbone. She—I believed the newcomer was female—had large, round dark eyes; a small, black, upturned nose; plushy gray-and-white fur; round white ears; and mean little claws on her hands and feet. She wore a long, lightweight, very colorful silk robe with big shoulders and wide sleeves belted around her waist with a wide sash. The little creature bustled straight for the stage.

Gleep broke away from my side and glided to confront the intruder. He hunkered down and let out a fearsome growl. His eyes, normally bright blue like Bunny's, glowed fearsome red. Everyone in the audience recoiled. Except the newcomer. She reached over and rapped Gleep on the nose. He was so astonished that he backed up. The female shook a finger at him.

"Don't interfere!" she said in a high, harsh voice. "I'm not here to hurt anyone, except the chances of those two losers up there!" She pointed at the stage.

Bunny was on her feet. "What is the meaning of this?" she demanded. "Who are you?"

"The meaning, missy, is that you are wrong! There are more than two sole and well-qualified candidates for governor! You can't certify them without inspecting the documents of my client!"

"And who is your client?" Bunny asked.

"I am."

Five steps behind the little gray-furred female walked a figure in black tunic and trousers edged with wavy lines. His eyes were bright yellow, his skin covered in rough green scales. He had ears like bat wings. When he smiled, two rows of gleaming, four-inch pointed teeth showed.

It was Aahz.

CHAPTER TWENTY-SIX

"Give the people a third choice, and they'll always go for it."

—H. R. PEROT

The outcry over Aahz's appearance was immediate. Both candidates and their entire campaign staff converged on Bunny, shouting and waving their arms.

"He's a Pervert! He can't run for governor!"

"He's an outsider—he works for you!"

"This is a conflict of interest!"

"We don't want a Pervert in this race!"

"Stand aside, all of you," the little female said, pushing her way into their midst. Aahz and I followed her onto the stage. "My client has a right to present his credentials for certification."

"Aahz, what are you doing?" I asked. I grabbed Gleep around the muzzle in case he went after Aahz's—agent?—and held on to him.

"Running for office, kid. Watch me." He slapped me on the back.

Bunny looked at Aahz. "What's going on here?"

"Didn't you hear my campaign manager? I am here to run."

"Campaign manager?"

"Yes. Didn't I introduce you? Bunny, this is Shomitamoni. Shomi, this is Bunny, and that's Skeeve, two of my partners."

"Gleep!" my pet interjected with reproof in his large blue eyes.

"Yeah," Aahz added, exasperatedly, "and that's Skeeve's dragon."

"Gleep!" Gleep looked satisfied and settled down at my side.

"Nice to meet you," Shomitamoni said. She tucked her hands into her sleeves. "So, all right, then, let's get down to business. What do you need to see first?"

"Miss Bunny, this is outrageous!" Orlow said. "I thought we agreed that this Pervert would have nothing to do with this election!"

"That's Per-*vect*!" Aahz bellowed.

"Pervert, Pervect, call him what you like," Shomi said, with a dismissive toss of her head. "Very soon you will be calling him Governor."

"We'll see about that!" Carnelia said. "Miss Bunny, have him and this . . . *powder puff* removed from these proceedings!"

Shomi drew herself up to her not-very-impressive height. "Powder puff! You watch it, madam, or I'll organize your fur stole into the Interdimensional Ladies' Working Garments Union!"

Carnelia drew her rodents close to her bosom. "There's no need to take that tack with me! I am just saying that that Pervert should not be here! Send him away!"

"I can't do that," Bunny said. "If he qualifies, then he is entitled to run. Your statutes say so."

"What?" Orlow demanded. "Let me see them!"

Bunny shrugged and beckoned to a pair of hefty Tipp assistants at the foot of the stage. Sighing, they bent and picked up each end of a large trunk. They trundled it up the stairs and dropped it with a BANG. One flipped open the lid to reveal dozens of dusty, leather-bound books.

"Help yourself," she said.

Wilmer drew himself up. "I believe that I am sufficiently familiar with the relevant laws."

"And . . . ?" I prompted him.

"I would sooner you didn't entertain them."

"But you promised he would have nothing to do with this election!" Emo said.

"We guaranteed that he wouldn't be involved in running the election," Bunny said. "I couldn't promise he wouldn't run for office."

Aahz smiled. "So, let's get this show on the road!"

"All right," Bunny said, holding out her palm. "Birth certificate."

Shomi reached into her sleeve and came out with a translucent sheet of green glass. I could see words etched into it. She slapped it into Bunny's hand. "Birth certificate. Official copy."

"And where was this distinguished gentleman born, as if I didn't know?" Emo asked.

"Perv," Shomi replied. She whisked a sheet of blue paper from the other sleeve and smacked it onto the desk. "Translation into Tipp and Klahdish."

Bunny turned over the shining green square with interest. "I've never seen one of these before. It's pretty!"

"But he wasn't born in Tipicanoo!" Orlow sputtered.

"Doesn't have to be," Shomi said. She pointed at the trunk. "Volume nine of the statutes for elective office, page eleven oh four, column two, lines forty-six to forty-eight: a candidate is not required to be born a native of Tipicanoo to run for office. It is merely required that he or she or it will have been born. No Golems, Robots, or Figments of Imagination allowed."

"Really?" I asked.

"Really," Shomi replied. "Can we get on? My client is eager to participate in the election!"

"I need proof of residence," Bunny said.

Shomi produced a scroll tied with a black ribbon and sealed in gold. "Residence."

"Now I know you can't fulfill that requirement," Emo said.

"A candidate has to be resident in Bokromi to be governor. You live in Deva."

"I did," Aahz said. "But I picked up a nice little property right here in town. Nothing fancy, just seven bedrooms, a swimming pool, billiards room with wet bar. Just a little pied-à-terre. It was a real steal. The owner was motivated to sell."

"When did you buy it?" I asked, then I realized I knew. "Ecstra told me that someone from our company had bought a piece of property in Bokromi. I thought she was making a mistake."

"No mistake," Shomi said. "This is the plat of survey." She held out a small globe. She shook it, and the particles of sand inside settled into a small blueprint, complete with arrows and a transparent image of a house, or rather mansion, superimposed above it.

"You've been planning this for a while, Aahz," Bunny said, with a look that said *We'll talk about this later.*

Aahz brushed it away and grinned. "I have always prided myself on making a plan come together. This little place just fell into my lap."

"I'll bet it did," I said. I was torn between admiration and annoyance that he had been doing all this behind our backs.

"And why not?" Shomi asked. She didn't wait for an answer. "Next, please?"

"Nominating petitions," Bunny said. The thick ream of paper that landed in front of her made the desk shake. She looked up at Aahz. "What did you tell people to get them to sign this?"

"I told them I represented the A Plague on Both Your Houses Party," Aahz said, with a grin. "They couldn't wait to sign up."

Bunny donned her visor and went to work with her lens. You could have heard grass growing as she thumbed through page after page. To my astonishment, not a single name lit up. When she came to an end, Bunny squared the papers off and set them down. "Aahz has over twenty thousand signatures here. They're all valid."

"Twenty thousand?" Emo echoed. The two Tipp candidates were dumbfounded. Aahz's outnumbered their totals put together. By contrast, the managers looked admiring, even envious.

"Nothing but the best," Aahz said. "I have some pretty motivated campaign workers."

"And donations," Bunny said.

Shomitamoni handed over a ledger. Bunny went through it. Emo and Wilmer peered curiously at it, then edged closer and closer to see, until they were looking over Bunny's shoulders.

"Do you mind?" she asked.

They looked sheepish, but retreated only one pace.

"Say, wait a minute!" Wilmer said, squinting to read. "Frimple, Deva, five gold coins . . . Trlngn, Ymryg, three gold coins? These are all from outside Tipicanoo?"

"Nothing in the rules says all donations have to come from here," Shomi said, dismissively. "Or any, for that matter."

"But . . . donations are usually given by people who want to support a candidate where they live or work," Emo said.

"In other words, what's in it for them?" Shomi asked. She didn't seem to be a big fan of dancing around a topic. "Access! Aahz is the next governor. If they are interested in trade with this sad little backwater, and I don't know why they should be, he has promised to look at their proposals favorably in exchange for donations."

"That's unethical!" Wilmer stated.

"Is it?" Shomi asked, peering up at him with her bright black eyes. "And what do your constituents get for helping elect you to office?"

Wilmer leaned back and grasped his lapels. "The thanks of a grateful governor, that's what."

"Pah! You can't take that to the bank." She turned to Bunny. "Well, missy? Is everything in order?"

Aahz had a way of taking over a room, but his associate

carried assertiveness to a much higher standard. To my surprise, it didn't seem to offend Bunny.

"It is." She cleared her throat. The Echoes picked up the noise and carried it all the way to the back of the crowd, though it was so silent that she could have whispered it unamplified and everyone on the island would have known in a minute. "Aahz is qualified to run. I am pleased to declare that these three gentlemen are the sole and well-qualified candidates for the high office of governor of the island of Bokromi in the dimension of Tipicanoo."

The audience went crazy with joy. Aahz grinned out at the sea of Tipps. At his side, Shomi tucked her little hands into her sleeves.

"But . . . but . . ." Emo Weavil sputtered. "This is making a mockery of the election system!"

Aahz shrugged. "Sounds like politics to me."

Shomi turned to the crowd, which was watching this whole proceeding agog. "Aahz is hosting a small party tonight at his townhouse. Drinks and hors d'oeuvres. You are all invited."

"Yay!" the audience cheered.

"But that's not on our schedule," Carnelia said.

Orlow looked horrified. "We haven't had time to plan *parties*."

"Does that sound like *my* problem?" Shomi asked. "Come on. We have a fleet of luxury carriages waiting for all you nice members of the press corps. Aahz!" Shomi didn't wait to see if he followed her. She bustled off the stage.

"Aahz, wait a minute!" I called.

He tipped me a wink and strode down the steps of the stage in her wake. The gang of reporters at the foot of the stairs surrounded him, shouting questions. The crowd closed around them.

"Wait for us!" Emo shouted. He hurried off, followed by Wilmer and the rest of their staffs. Bunny came up to stand beside me and Gleep. We watched the crowd hurry away.

"What is he up to?" Bunny asked.

CHAPTER TWENTY-SEVEN

"I like starting off with a big splash."

—M. PHELPS

"Hey, how ya doing? Vote for Aahz!" Aahz shook hands with an astonished Tipp in a checked cap and tweed jacket on the third tier on the cliff above the main square. "Morning. A vote for Aahz is a vote for sanity, if you know what that means." A grasped hand and a big grin, and he strode on to a group of mothers. "Cute kids. You know they'd do better under my administration than those other two clowns, right? Vote for me. Only two weeks left until the big day!" He pinched a pretty girl's cheek. "Hey, gorgeous, vote Pervect! You know you want to."

Aahz's legs were shorter than mine, but I had to run to keep up with him. Behind us a cadre of reporters all armed with notepads pursued us along the pathway, shouting questions. New posters had joined Wilmer's and Emo's on walls and signposts. Aahz's face leered at me from every side. I ducked under an ornamental hanging flowerpot and hurried up to his side. I lowered my voice.

"Aahz, what's going on? What are you *doing* here?"

"Looks like you needed some help, kid," he said. He thrust his way into the crowded vegetable market and stopped to pick up a huge green melon. He took a huge bite out of it. Juice ran down the sides of his mouth. "That's great! When I'm governor, this will be the official fruit of Bokromi!" He handed the half-chewed fruit to the nearest reporter. "Here, hang on to this for me." The others gathered around to look at it. Aahz moved on, shaking hands and kissing women.

"Aahz, you can't do that!"

He raised his eyebrows at me. "Name an official fruit? Why not? Some places even have official bacteria."

I had no idea what a bacteria was, and at that moment didn't care.

"No, I mean run for governor. They already have two candidates."

"Had two. Now they have three. Hey, how ya doing? I'm running for governor. The only viable candidate. Vote Aahz. I'll make sure you have job security." This last was addressed to a street sweeper who was picking up fruit peels and rotten vegetables.

"Aahz, what would you get out of taking office in Tipicanoo?"

Aahz kept his grin in place as he shook hands and picked up babies to kiss. To my surprise, the infants cooed and laughed at him instead of the way their parents reacted, which was to recoil in disgust. "Skeeve, this is the biggest power vacuum I've seen in a long time. It wouldn't take much to waltz in and take over. Maybe I want a cushy office job for a change. Without my magikal powers, I've been stunted. I like the sound of 'Governor Aahz.' Looks good on the résumé. Got to fund my retirement."

"But aren't you spending a lot of money on this campaign?" I asked. "A house, posters, hats and parties and everything?"

Aahz turned to me in shock. "Kid, haven't you absorbed a single thing I've taught you? Never, never, *never* use your own money. Everything I've spent has come from donations and contributions. Which reminds me, we're going to have a major fund-raiser tomorrow. Come on down and see the event. It'll be a blockbuster. I hired a couple of musical acts and a tumbling team that'll knock your eyes out!"

"That's the same day as the next debate," I said.

"So?"

"Don't you want to participate in the scheduled events?"

"I'm a leader, not a follower," Aahz said dismissively. "Shomi will inform the other guys of what I'm doing. They can decide if they want to go through with their debate or join me shaking the can." He glanced ahead and pointed to a painted sign swinging from a horizontal standard. It said *The Tipp o' the Hat*. "There's a tavern. Let's go inside. I want to get to know the locals and find out what's on their minds. Bartender!" He pushed through the door and shouted to a round-bellied Tipp who was indeed wearing a distinctive hat. "A round for the house!"

". . . And that's what's wrong with the government today," said an elderly Tipp with prominent front incisors, pointing a finger at Aahz's nose. "No respect for the working Tipp. Everyone pays in, but nothing comes out."

"Aye," his cronies intoned, like a theatrical chorus. "Not like it used to be."

"Things are gonna be better," Aahz said, firmly, pounding a fist on the bar. "I promise when I'm governor, people will get out of government what they put into it."

"About time someone understood that," another gray Tipp said. "Bartender, another one for my friend. Beer okay with you, Mr. Aahz?"

"Beer, wine, liquor, whatever you're having," Aahz said expansively.

I had to admire Aahz's tactics. There had been a dozen old males in the inn when we had arrived. I knew how much he hated to part with money, so I was a little shocked to see him buy a round of drinks, but it had paid off handsomely. Presenting himself as a willing listener, and a generous one at that, had gotten him an earful of complaints but tray after tray of free drinks. He quaffed beer out of a half keg while his new friends hoisted pewter tankards. And of course, you couldn't drink without something to eat. At the request of the regulars, the bartender had put out baskets of crispy snacks. I tried one and found it greasy and salty—in other words, perfect tavern food. Aahz downed them by the handful, offering his wisdom in between bites. The crowd grew, supplemented by the noontime crowd and the host of reporters who had followed us there. Everyone wanted to tell the new candidate what they thought, and he was such a good listener! Inexorably, I was shoved away from his side until he was surrounded by Tipps talking and waving their arms.

"Now, if you really want to know what I think, I'll tell you," Aahz said. "When it comes to money, nothing works like having a lot of it."

He held forth at length on something that sounded like economics, but I couldn't follow all the jargon. To me it sounded like nonsense, but the crowd filling the room nodded knowingly as if he were letting them in on valuable secrets. My mind started to wander. I yawned. Aahz making a long speech was nothing new to me. When he stopped to take a breath, an ocher-furred male Tipp I recognized as a reporter for the *Daily Tipp-Word* held up a pencil.

"Sir, may I ask you a question?"

Aahz turned a big smile on him.

"The gentleman from the press?"

"Yes, Mr. Aahz. You're new on the scene. What do you think you can bring to the electoral process that's been missing the last five years?"

"Fresh perspective," Aahz said promptly, as if he had been waiting for someone to ask him just exactly that question—and I suspected that he had set it up to be asked. "You've been listening to the same guff for a long time now. And what have they told you? The same old thing. Now, I have experience ranging across a hundred dimensions about how to bring prosperity, order, and safety to Tipicanoo, starting from right here in Bokromi. I want every one of you to join me on that journey."

"Mr. Aahz! Mr. Aahz!"

"Yes, the pretty girl in the blue lighting up the room." Aahz pointed. "Hey, babe."

She simpered with pleasure. "Mr. Aahz, do you have plans to expand government or reduce it?"

"You can bet on it, sweetie," he said. "Next question?"

"Mr. Aahz! Mr. Aahz!"

Aahz sat back with a big grin and a newly refilled beer, offering his opinion to anyone who asked for it. He posed for Shutterbug images, signed autographs, and shook hands. I could see Tipps crowding in the door trying to catch sight of him.

"Mr. Aahz!" a broad-chested Tipp called to him. "What about the debate tomorrow?"

Aahz waved a hand. "You want to be bored? Go ahead! If you want to hear *interesting* ideas about your future, come and listen to me the day after tomorrow! I'll be speaking in the gazebo in the town square at two o'clock sharp. But I'm not greedy. I invite my opponents to take their place on the stage with me and offer their own suggestions! Tomorrow, I'm holding a fund-raiser. If you can spare a coin or two for the sake of your government, bring it tomorrow. Even copper pieces will be welcome. Every little bit will help build the road to your future!"

It would have made a great personal-interest story in the paper, except nothing favorable about the campaign was being published. The Syndication would find a way to skew the story of Aahz's candidacy to push the election as far into the future as possible. I thought I should warn him, but I was interrupted by a fanfare of horns from outside the building.

Oom-pa-paa! Oom-pa-paa!

Aahz's ears pricked upward. "What could that be?" he

asked, pitching his voice to the darkest corners of the inn. "I'd better go take a look."

He rose from the bar stool and shoved his way through the crowd. I wormed my way between people to follow. I was just in time to look over his shoulder as he threw open the door.

TA-DAAAAA!

Brass horns blared right in our faces. Drums boomed, making my chest echo. I blinked to clear my eyes.

Filling the narrow street was a parade. Not a small parade, a huge one. At its head was a Whelf drum major in tan livery and striped with gold frogging, wearing a tall white hat on his handsome head and holding a huge baton up to the sky. Behind him, Deveel women wearing very short yellow skirts threw somersaults and cartwheels.

"Aahz! Aahz! Aahz!" they chanted.

Filling the rest of the street was at least one marching band, possibly two or three. Teams of Acrobats from Acrobe in skimpy gold tights flew overhead, tumbling over one another in the sky, their scalloped black wings intersecting at dangerous angles. They flew together in a mass, then spread out to spell *Aahz for Governor!* The same message was repeated on signs and banners held by uniformed Tipps in lines that reached out of sight. Working Tipps had poured out of shops, banks, and buildings to see what was going on. They lined the sidewalk, poking one another and pointing. Aahz waved to them.

The drum major swung his baton, and the bands struck up a discordant fanfare. I recognized the Pervish national anthem.

"All this, for me?" Aahz asked, a hand held modestly to his chest. The reporters surged forward to see. Their pencils whisked across their notepads, leaving behind excited trails of black print.

The drum major blew a whistle. The bands parted to allow a carriage to emerge. Not only had the beasts' harness been adorned with shining gold, which Aahz seemed to have chosen as his campaign color, but their hides had been dyed the same hue. On each side of the carriage was a golden banner that read *Vote for Aahz!* The Tipp driver waved him forward.

"Come on, Skeeve," Aahz said, grabbing my arm. "Ride with me."

"Aahz, what is all this?"

He grinned. "Bread and circuses, Skeeve. I've told you. Give 'em bread and circuses, and they won't be able to resist. Come on!"

I glanced at the reporters.

"I don't think so, Aahz. I have to maintain neutrality."

"Suit yourself," Aahz said. He swung up to stand in the rear of the carriage and waved to the crowd. The marchers waved back, cheering. A little more uncertainly, the crowd joined in.

The drum major blew a whistle, and the parade moved forward. I watched the wagon carrying Aahz disappear down the street. Tipps surged behind him, waving and yelling.

I went back to our small office through strangely empty streets. I could hear the music from the parade receding in the distance. When Aahz did something, he did it thoroughly.

"Papah! Sah, come and get yer papah!" A peaky-faced Tipp lad in a flat cap brandished the *Morning Gossip* at me. "Papah, mistah?"

I caught a glimpse of the word *Perv*— in the headline, and fished in my belt pouch for a copper piece. The boy grinned at me as he handed over a copy. I spread out the front page and groaned.

Dangerous Pervert on the Loose! Beside it in a black frame was Aahz holding up his hand to block the Shutterbug from taking his picture. The article didn't name him, but the details made it clear who it meant. The Syndication was wasting no time in debasing Aahz's credibility as a candidate.

It wasn't that I wanted Aahz to win this election. If he stayed here to govern and quit M.Y.T.H., Inc., I would miss him. But this wasn't the first time he had talked about retirement or moving on to other careers. Pervects lived a long time. Our partnership was the best thing that had ever happened to me.

It had taken my losing perspective and gaining it back to appreciate that. I didn't want it to end, but I couldn't hold Aahz back if this was something he really wanted to try.

I made up my mind that I would do everything I could to ensure it was a fair election. If Aahz really wanted to be governor of a Tipp island, then I would see he was elected. After all he had done for me it was the least I could do.

I stuffed the newspaper into my belt pouch and marched back to the office.

CHAPTER TWENTY-EIGHT

"Three's a crowd."

—S. SOMERS

"Nothing, I say, nothing in this agreement allows you to introduce a third candidate into this election!" Orlow fumed, smacking the copy of our contract that lay on the desk in front of Bunny.

He and Carnelia loomed over her. Bunny sat bolt upright with her hands folded in front of her on the tabletop. In the corner, Bunny's cousin Sylvia sat in a chair with her arms folded, kicking one foot impatiently. When Sylvia saw me, her face brightened and she got up to undulate toward me.

"No!" Bunny made a curt, shushing gesture with one hand. Sylvia sat back down and looked sulky. "I'm sorry, Orlow. What were you saying?"

"He's a brute and a bully!"

"Only on occasion. What's the specific complaint?"

"It's humiliating! Have you heard the things that Aahz says about Wilmer?" Carnelia said. She sniffed back tears, and one of her rodents handed her a handkerchief. "Thank you, dear. I cannot believe that he kisses his mother with that mouth!"

"I know Aahz's mother," I said. "The Duchess actually said worse things." And, if I knew Aahz, he was holding back.

"His mother's a duchess?" Orlow asked, impressed.

"Uh, no, that's just what she's called."

Bunny's nose was pink, which meant she was on the edge of angry tears. This tirade must have been going on for a while. I was sorry I hadn't been there to help her.

"There is nothing in the contract that says I can prevent another candidate from joining the race! Your laws allow anyone with the right qualifications to stand for office. The fact that your two clients have gone uncontested for so long doesn't allow them to change that! If the winner wants to introduce legislation *after* the election, that's fine! In the meantime, what do you want me to do about it?"

"I would have thought that was obvious," Orlow said. "Send him back to Deva."

"He doesn't work for me. He's my partner. I'm only the administrative head of M.Y.T.H., Inc. I can't affect what he does on his own time, and I can't fire him. Next problem?"

"He doesn't belong here!"

"We've already swum that moat," Bunny said flatly. "He qualifies. He can run if he wants. He does want to. Next problem?"

"*Well*," Carnelia said, "we sent his *campaign manager* a copy of our upcoming events, and that Shomi sent it back in pieces! She is ignoring what we've already scheduled. She made up her own list!"

"Have you tried discussing coordinating events with her?"

"That little puffball said she is *not interested*."

"And what do you want me to do about it?"

"Talk to her!" Orlow pleaded. "We don't want to end up splitting the crowd. We've cooperated fully with one another before this. Please, Miss Bunny. If, uh, if I haven't said lately how much we appreciate your calming influence over these last weeks, please allow me to rectify the situation." He gave her his most charming smile.

Bunny returned a wan scowl. "All right," she said. "I'll talk to Shomi and see if we can't work out a schedule that works for everyone."

"Then there's no more to be said at the moment except thank you for trying," Carnelia said.

"You're welcome," Bunny said. "And if you'll excuse us, we have work to do, and so do you."

"Of course," Orlow said. He turned to Carnelia and made a little bow.

"Miss Vole, would you care to share a carriage back to your headquarters?"

Carnelia looked surprised but pleased. "Thank you, Mr. Suposi, I'd appreciate it."

Orlow put out an elbow and Carnelia took it. A few of her rodents even ventured out onto his sleeve. I watched them go.

"There's nothing like a common foe to push enemies into alliances," Bunny said.

"Like the Bogile Family joining up with us to clear out the Von Podrasts three years ago?" Sylvia asked.

My ears perked up, but no story was forthcoming.

Bunny stood up and took a deep breath. "I don't think I'll have any more influence over Aahz's campaign manager than they did, but I promised I'd try. Coming, Skeeve?"

CHAPTER TWENTY-NINE

"You always get what you pay for."

—R. BLAGOJEVICH

"**Form an orderly line!**" **Shomi bellowed. Small as she** was, she didn't need the Echoes to make herself heard. "Donors to the right, volunteers to the left!" Dressed in a bright yellow robe that was actually kind of becoming on her light-gray fur, she pointed arriving Tipps into the correct file.

Supporters of the Plague Party lined up five and six deep all the way around the park. The donors crowded toward a line of volunteers holding enormous hats. *Pass the Hat!* was emblazoned on posters and banners plastered on every vertical surface. As each person reached the front of the line, they threw coins into the hats. Bright-eyed young people in yellow blazers thanked them profusely and handed them yellow straw hats with Aahz's name and picture embossed on them. Children got balloons shaped like Aahz's head. Infants received soft, green rubber toys in the same shape that made a rude noise when the babies chewed on them.

The candidate himself made a point of greeting his new army

of supporters. Aahz walked among the crowd, shaking hands, waving, and talking to anyone who even looked at him for too long. He had a smile plastered on his face from ear to ear. In his wake, a campaign worker slapped a round of sticky paper on each supporter's chest. In spite of the reputation (largely earned) that Pervects had throughout the dimensions, people seemed genuinely thrilled to meet him. A dozen reporters circled him as closely as flies around a garbage heap. I kept my distance. I was officially in charge of this fund-raiser. Bunny had begged off for the day. After we had talked with Shomi, Bunny told me she had to return to Klah for a talk with Don Bruce. I hoped there was no problem. I promised her I could handle the event by myself. She and Sylvia had left before dinner.

Everything seemed to be going just fine this morning. I felt excitement in the air that had not been there before, at least not since I had become involved in the election. To my amazement, the people of Tipicanoo looked on the possibility of having Aahz as their governor as a good thing. It showed me how desperate they were for something different. It would be a big change for Aahz, too. I never thought of him as being an official officeholder before. Sure, I considered him a mentor and teacher, but he normally hated having to deal with ordinary people. He preferred to be an outside consultant, highly paid and not often bothered by his clients. I was dismayed how little I really knew about the way he thought.

Not every Tipp was glad at the change in the lineup. Emo Weavil arrived on the scene surrounded by a dozen campaign workers and supporters. He took one horrified look at the crowd Aahz had amassed and went into a huddle. A young male Tipp broke away and went running out of the square. Shortly, he arrived back with hundreds of Emo supporters behind him, most of them carrying suspiciously drippy packages. I groaned. I had hoped everyone had gotten over the mudslinging.

In contrast, Wilmer's people turned up in force. He must have gotten advance information, because Tipps in purple nearly outnumbered the yellow-ribboned army assembling around the gazebo. A large brass band marched in their wake, blaring away. Overhead, young Tipps with baskets in their arms flew from terrace to terrace, giving little purple favors to the onlookers in the upper streets. I knew it was all improvised, but not a bad effort for short notice. Aahz had shaken them up. I felt it was a good thing for the election.

Shomitamoni had absolutely refused to cooperate with the planned activities of their opponents. The others had no choice but to do things on Aahz's schedule. The debate that ought to have taken place that morning was pushed back to the afternoon three days from now. The lightning round of the baby-kissing contest would be the next afternoon. The Meet the Candidate's Family session would follow that evening. I had the new list in my belt pouch.

As the ten o'clock hour approached, the green and purple parties pushed their way up into the gazebo. Arguments broke out between the three groups. Shomi had taken up most of the space with easels holding posters of Aahz, a flagpole, and several small tables. After a heated exchange, Wilmer's and Emo's people marched down to me.

"Skeeve, we need your help," Carnelia said. "That little puffball won't let us up there!"

I had to grin, though at the same time it was my job to make certain everything was handled as fairly as possible. I squeezed in past the jingling hats.

"You have to move some of this stuff, Shomi," I said.

"Why?" she asked. "We were here first."

"Because this is a shared event."

Shomi crossed her arms. She glared at the Tipps behind me. "Not as far as I am concerned. This was set up for Aahz. If they care to participate, they get what is left."

"We're paying you to make this a fair election!" Orlow said.

"You don't have to remind me," I said, holding up a hand. I didn't want to referee a three-way argument. "Shomi, you get a third of this space."

The little female snorted at me. "Even though Aahz has more voters than both of them?"

"He can have the whole thing after the election," I said, "*if* he wins. Clear the way, please."

Shomi unfolded her arms and crossed them the other way. "Make me."

Orlow started to roll up his sleeves. "Why, I sure will!"

Alarmed, I put myself between them.

"Gee, Orlow, don't do it!"

I shouldn't have been afraid that Orlow would hit a creature smaller than he was. Instead, his ire was aimed at the trappings of the Plague Party. He scooped up a handful of magik from the line of force running underneath the main street and flung it hard. The posters collapsed together in a clatter, followed by the tables.

"You rude man!" Shomi screeched from under my arm.

She whipped an arm in a circle, and every green-suited Tipp on the podium went flying backward. I gawked. She packed a lot of magikal muscle.

"Why, how dare you do that to all those nice Friendship Party people!" Carnelia said. She crossed both hands in front of her. A powerful wind hit Shomi in the face, forcing her eyes closed and parting her fur in the middle all the way down her body. Shomi was forced back one step. She let out an angry grunt, and the wind died away. She turned toward Carnelia, eyes blazing. Her hands wove a busy pattern. I could feel her drawing heavily on the force lines. I imagined myself as a locked door, preventing her from getting any more magik. She thrust my efforts aside without trouble. A whirlwind danced out of her hands straight for Carnelia. It grew from a dust devil to a cyclone, sucking in chairs, posters, and an unwary campaign worker or two as it marched. Carnelia's rodents went flying off her shoulders.

"Hold on, dear lady!" Orlow bellowed. He rushed in to grasp Carnelia's hand. Together, they threw all their strength against the tornado. It towered over their heads, screaming, but they held it back. I think they were as surprised as any of the onlookers. Fighting the powerful wind, they moved to either side of it. With strained faces, they squeezed forward, compressing the twister until it shrank from a huge gray-black cone to a silver strand. Then it vanished, leaving a couple of confused Tipps with windblown pelts sitting on the ground. Carnelia and Orlow gave each other a brief, triumphant smile, then turned to face Shomi.

"All right, you made me," she said, and turned to shriek at her workers. "Clear off the gazebo!" The yellow-coated brigade hopped at her words and picked up all the fallen furniture. A Tipp with a broom followed them and carefully swept two-thirds of the round stage clean.

"Why didn't you just do that before?" Orlow asked.

"I had no reason to," Shomi said. She eyed them. "I heard you two had it too soft before. Where I come from, you wouldn't survive an election. I'll show you what real politics is all about!"

"Well! If you are any example, I don't want to learn what real politics is about," Carnelia said. Her rodents, shaken and disheveled, tottered out of the crowd and climbed up her body to her neck. Trembling, they reassembled themselves into a stole. Carnelia petted them. With a ladylike snort in Shomi's direction, she stalked up the painted white steps to Wilmer. Orlow gave Shomi one more severe look and marched to Emo's side.

The clock struck ten. The mayor, hat firmly in place, walked out to greet the crowd.

"Ladies and gentlemen! Welcome! I know you will all dig deep into your pockets to show your support for your candidates for governor! And remember, it's just one more week until Voting Day! So let me introduce the three fine folks we have running for the office! First, in the green corner, weighing in at about sixty kilos of love and kindness, the candidate for the Friendship Party, Emo Weavil!"

Emo came out and fluttered his eyelashes fetchingly at the crowd. Cheers rose from the audience, and green confetti rained down on everyone. Glitter filled the air. I spat out scraps of paper. Emo shook hands with the mayor and raised an arm to wave. Almost on cue, dozens of mudballs came hurtling through the air toward him. Emo cringed, throwing up his hands to protect his face.

He had nothing to fear. I was ready. With a healthy scoop of power from the force line I erected a magikal shield. The missiles smacked against it and slid down. Worms, snails, and chunks of grass and weeds exploded in every direction but toward the intended target. Emo straightened up and brushed an invisible speck of dust off his still spotless green-and-white-striped suit.

"Thank you, friends, thank you!" he shouted.

"In the purple corner, with the total acclaim of the Wisdom Party, weighing seventy-five kilos, dignity in every bone in his body, Wilmer Weavil-Scuttil!"

Wilmer strutted forward, hands grasping lapels and bowed gravely to each direction.

On cue, a rain of spoiled grapes and seeping tomatoes hurtled toward him. Wilmer stood his ground bravely, trusting me to protect him.

I didn't let him down. Not only did I manage to prevent a single fruity sphere from impacting on his pristine white suit, I made the magik rebound the missiles in the direction from which they had come. Like a rain of arrows from an army of greengrocers, the vegetation pelted down on the Friendship Party. They let out some pretty unfriendly-sounding gripes as they wiped verjuice and tomato paste out of their eyes. I grinned. I'd been practicing that move for days.

"And at a little over ninety kilos of muscle and, er, scales, the newcomer to our fair shores and a mighty contender in his own right, the favorite of the A Plague on Both Your Houses Party, Aahz!"

Aahz sprang forward with his fists pumping toward the sky. "Good morning, Bokromi!" he roared.

I braced myself. From all directions, vegetables that had probably been decaying for months came hurtling toward Aahz. I built a cylinder of power around him. The heaps of stinking onions, gourds, peaches, and limons hammered at it until he was almost waist-deep in them. Aahz looked supremely unconcerned. With a flick of his wrist, the rotten vegetables went flying outward.

I was astonished. I had not really had a chance to talk with Aahz in days. Maybe the joke powder that Garkin had used on him in our cottage on Klah had worn off at last. He looked as if he were back to the way he used to be, a master magician with full control of his power. Maybe that was why he didn't need us anymore.

Then I saw Shomi. She flicked her little claws very close to her wide sash, as if she were conducting an orchestra of ants. She was doing it, making it look as if Aahz had a Pervect's full complement of magikal control. I was relieved. It also impressed the onlookers. They kept on heaving mud and soggy fruit at Aahz and took it without rancor if it came hurtling back at them. In fact, they were all having a great time. Maybe Bunny and I had been wrong to deny them that part of their campaign.

I could have smacked myself in the forehead. What was I thinking? This was supposed to be a dignified process!

"Now, I hope you folks are gonna fight this election out fairly, with peace and mutual respect," the mayor said.

"What makes you think something like that?" Aahz asked. He slapped the astonished mayor on the back. "Absolutely! I plan to show my opponents every bit of respect they deserve. Right, folks?" He turned to the audience. His volunteers laughed uproariously. Wilmer and Emo didn't look that amused.

"Now, all three of you have a little presentation for us, don't you?" the mayor asked.

"Yes, indeed," Wilmer said. He took a card from his pocket. "I want the good people of Bokromi to know exactly where their donations have gone to date, and where they will go if they are generous enough to open their pocketbooks to us today. First, office rental. My manager, Orlow Suposi, managed to get us a good deal on an empty building at the most reasonable fee of nine silver pieces a day. Now, that may sound like a lot, but for a property that size, it's pretty good. Next, posters. Can't have a campaign if no one knows you're there. The copy-elves have been great, just great. Their fees to date ran . . ."

"Aaaa—oooo—*booo*—*rrringgg*—aaagh!" Aahz stretched his arms and yawned. Wilmer turned to glare at him.

"Sir! I beg your pardon!"

Aahz was the picture of innocence.

"What's your problem?" he asked.

"You . . . yawned."

"Excuse me, I didn't get too much sleep last night. Sorry to interrupt."

"Well, all right," Wilmer said. ". . . Posters and banners, twenty-four gold pieces. Meals and entertainment . . ."

"Eeeee—yah!" Aahz nearly yodeled, throwing back his head. His mouth opened wide, giving the crowd an excellent look at two rows of pointed, four-inch teeth, a purple tongue, and four tonsils. "Sorry. I fell asleep in accounting class in school, too. Go on. It's very interesting. Isn't it, folks?"

". . . Fourteen-gold-pieces-transportation-five-gold-pieces-rental-ninegoldpiecesbuttonshatsandothergiftstwenty-twogoldpieces!" Wilmer finished in a breathless rush. His eyes bulged out, and he panted. "Thank you all. I look forward to receiving your kind donations and good wishes!"

His supporters let out a ragged cheer. Emo took his place. He shot Aahz a cautious glance. Aahz appeared to be examining his nails. Emo fluttered his false lashes and smiled at the audience.

"Ladies and gentlemen and children, I've prepared a little song for you today." He beckoned, and a couple of musicians dressed in green climbed up to the podium carrying a guitar and a harp. They sat down on either side of Emo and struck up a gentle air. Emo burst out singing. "Bokromi needs a leader / someone who is good and true / who has your best interests in mind / so what's a candidate to do? Oh, run run run / like your life depended on it / Run run run / that's what I plan to do!"

He dropped to one knee and threw his arms imploringly to the people. "Run run run / straight to the gov'nor's *mansion*—"

Taaa-ran-taaa-raaaa!

The blare of horns exploded deafeningly in the square. Everyone clapped their hands to their ears. Around the corner from both ends of the street, two enormous groups of musicians strode, converging on the gazebo. From the east came the brass band that had led Aahz's parade. From the west a more diverse assemblage approached. It consisted of jazz musicians from Satchmo, a dimension that was famous for its music, led by a gray-haired Satch in a lemon-yellow suit and hat and carrying a matching umbrella over his head. Emo looked shocked, then furious. He leaped to his feet.

"Who is respo—" he bellowed.

Brrruuum! Brrruuum! Brrrum-tum-tum! Bid-biddidity-bop, biddy-bop! Ran-a-tang-tang-tang, bop-pity bop. Bop. Biddity-bop. Bop. Ba-daaaa! The Satches tootled, banged, bowed, strummed, and struck their instruments in such an exciting fanfare that almost no one could keep from moving to the rhythm.

"Silence!" Emo shouted. The music died away. "I wasn't finished with my song!"

"Sorry," Aahz said. "The entertainment I hired arrived a little early. Shame on you guys," he told them. The musicians bowed their heads. "Go on. I'm sure everyone wants to hear the rest of it."

"All right," Emo said, a little mollified. He turned to his accompanists. "From the chorus? Oh, run run run / like your life depended on it . . ."

Bippity-bop-bippity-bop, boop de boop!

"What are they doing? Make them stop!" Emo cried, jumping up and down. The Satch players looked up, askance.

"They're just joining in with your musicians," Aahz explained. "To give you more of a backup."

"I don't need them! I wanted to do it my way. You've *ruined* it."

Aahz shrugged. "A fellow tries to do you a favor, and this is the thanks I get."

"I didn't ask you for a favor," Emo said, pulling himself together. "It was very kind of you, but your help isn't needed. Ladies and gentlemen, I want to be your governor. I promise that I will do my best to see that your needs are met and that I can help Bokromi to prosper. You will always find a listening ear and an open heart in my office. Please give generously. Thank you."

With a final flirt of his eyelashes, he withdrew. His supporters cheered. The marching bands offered a smattering of applause, then struck up a loud chorus as Aahz strode up to the edge of the stage.

"Morning, everyone!" he said. "Nice of you to save the best for last! Now I'm sure my two opponents are worthy of taking office and doing great things with it—that is, if you want your governor to be a math teacher or a song-and-dance man." Emo and Wilmer looked shocked. A gasp rose from the crowd. Aahz kept going. "I believe that you all want your political leader to have a clue as to how to get a point across. I'm a successful businessman. I want to be your governor. I need your help and your money to get elected. Now, enjoy the show."

The Satch bandleader and the Whelf drum major beat out a four-count.

BIPPITY-DO-BOP BOP. BIP—

"Now, just hold on here!" a voice bellowed from above.

The music died away. I recognized the voice as my adversary, Sergeant Boxty, echoing in the stone canyon. From every direction, both on the ground and from the air, hordes of Tipicanoo police descended on the gazebo and formed a stern-faced ring around it, facing outward. Boxty himself flew in and landed right in front of us. He smacked his nightstick into his palm and walked around Aahz, looking him up and down.

"Disturbing the peace, are you?" he asked.

Aahz snarled at him. He had never been too fond of legal authorities. "Who says I am? A flying stoat?"

With a disapproving glare, Boxty flipped open his ticket book. "Well, I'll just add giving lip to a police officer as one of the charges against you!"

"Charges?" I asked, pushing up beside Aahz. "What charges?"

Boxty flicked his pencil point down a list on the page. "Running an unregistered campaign? Enrolling workers who don't have proper identification? Interfering in the functions of duly certified candidates for a lofty and dignified office?"

"Who says I am?" Aahz demanded.

The other two candidates and their managers watched this exchange with growing satisfaction. Their eyes gleamed with malice.

"We do!" Wilmer said.

"He's not unregistered, sergeant," I said, alarmed. "That was all settled last night!"

"What about all of these people here?" Boxty asked, aiming the eraser end of his pencil at the crowd.

"Well, I don't know . . ."

"Take him in, sergeant, so we can go on with this fundraiser!" Emo said. "These good people shouldn't be troubled by a *Pervert* who can't follow the law!"

"That's Per-*vect*," Aahz announced in a voice that shook the gazebo. "So, sergeant, what do you intend to charge me with?"

"I'm sure there's been some kind of misunderstanding," I said. I didn't want Aahz to go to jail as I had.

"You would know all about misunderstandings regarding campaign laws, *Mr. Skeeve*," Sergeant Boxty said.

"Well, I didn't, but I do now. Aahz hasn't done anything wrong! Can we talk about this?"

"And to what end would we be talking, Mr. Skeeve? It would be pointless. Officer Malarkey!"

"Yes, sergeant!" The burly Tipp landed beside his senior officer and saluted.

"I accuse this Pervect"—he glanced at the crowd and the other two candidates—"of being a very fine fellow who *will make a damned good governor!*"

"What?" I demanded.

"What are you saying?" Wilmer asked, running a finger around in his ear to clear it. "I'm not sure I understand what you mean!"

"Arrest him!" Emo exclaimed.

"Don't have to," Boxty said. He and Aahz gripped hands and laughed. "This fellow cares about the law! He's been working with me all along to be sure his supporters are registered properly, with cards and all. He's going to have my vote next week!"

"You can't do that! It's a violation of practice!" Orlow said.

"What practice is that?" Sergeant Boxty asked.

"Public servants aren't supposed to endorse candidates!" Wilmer said.

"Or take part in cheap charades!" Emo added.

"That wasn't a cheap charade," Aahz said. "It cost me plenty! One big contribution . . . to the Police Benevolent Fund. Naturally, Sergeant Boxty wouldn't take money for his own enrichment. That would be bribery of a public official!"

"But . . . but . . . this is against our agreement," Carnelia said.

Aahz stared her down.

"Did I sign a contract?"

"No! But you should!"

"Why?"

"Aahz!" I said. He grinned at me. I was too shaken to grin back. "Was this a setup all the time?"

"Sure! Good publicity. Sergeant Boxty was glad to go along. It got everyone's attention. It got yours."

"Aahz, I thought you were going to be arrested!" I said.

"Don't worry about me, kid," Aahz said, spreading out his hands. "I have this in the bag."

"Only if you finish in first place," I said, suddenly angry. "You could still get disqualified."

"On what grounds?" Aahz asked. He was miffed that I didn't see the joke.

"On the grounds of not following the rules of this election!"

"What rules?"

"There are books full of them! Bunny followed them to certify you so you could participate. There are codes of conduct. The others have agreed to follow them, and they're paying us to administer this election. Are you planning to chip in?"

The Aahz I knew hated to spend money, but he certainly had been spreading it around in Bokromi, and he knew how much work Bunny and I had been doing. He tilted his head, doing some internal calculations.

"Well . . ."

"Why should we?" Shomi asked, pushing up and poking me in the chest. "Since you are already doing it, are you planning to stop running things just because Aahz has joined the contest?"

"Well, no," I said. "But . . ."

She cut me off. "No? Then we decline. But thank you for your good service. I trust it will continue as smoothly it has been? When Aahz is governor I am sure that he will consider you for a trusted position."

At least Aahz looked a little embarrassed by Shomi's statement, but I felt my temper flare up.

"No, thanks!" I said. "When Aahz is governor, this is the last dimension where I'm going to spend any more time!"

I stormed away. So much for a dignified process!

"Come on, people!" I could hear Shomi call behind me. "Donations, please! Pass the hat!"

CHAPTER THIRTY

"Just a little something to remember me by."

—SHAH JEHAN

I scanned the *Morning Gossip* by the thin light filtering in the north-facing window of our little office. It had rained all morning, which suited my bleak mood.

To no one's surprise, the fund-raiser had not made the papers. Instead, they carried extensive coverage of a children's hopscotch tournament in the outlying suburbs. In a way I was glad. I was furious at Aahz. How could he fool me like that, for the sake of publicity?

He had warned me that politics corrupted people. I never thought that it could take someone like Aahz down. I would have expected him to tip me off beforehand that he was pulling a stunt.

I guess I was just sore that he had strung me along with the crowd. He wanted me to react with everyone else, as if he thought I might betray the joke with some word or gesture. I thought he trusted me more than that. I could keep a secret!

To be fair, though, I was an election official, and I was

supposed to remain neutral. I supposed I could see the point. I just hated being taken in.

"Are you coming with me to see Sid the She?" I asked Bunny. Gleep, excited at the prospect of a walk, romped and cavorted around my legs, his weight shaking the floor with every bounce.

She had her nose in a thick ledger filled with black and red ink. Startled, she glanced up when I spoke.

"No, thanks," she said, with a quick smile. "I'll meet you at the debate. Is that all right with you?"

"You're the boss," I said. I used the word playfully, but she seemed to wince at it. Did my cruel words of the week before still sting? A thought struck me. I looked down. "Gleep, stay here with Bunny."

"Gleep!" my pet said, his eyes huge with disappointment.

I knelt down beside him and looked deep into those blue orbs. "Make sure she gets there safely, all right?"

"Oh, Skeeve, I'll be fine," Bunny protested.

"Gleep," my dragon said, closing one eye in a wink. I nodded. I didn't trust the Syndication, or the two other parties, and at the moment, I didn't trust Aahz.

". . . Dooo-ooo-ooo-naaaa-tions were generous! The gods looook down favor-aaaably on those with oooopen hands!"

Sid held her arms out before her, her face glowing beatifically as if seeing a sacred vision. The square around the gazebo was packed with young people dancing and older people listening intently. There was no doubt about it: The crowds got larger every day. Sid was a hit. I was pleased. We had managed to work around the Syndication's obduracy.

". . . In gratitude, the candidates did give balloons and toys to the smallest and youngest! Those of age received the waters of life!"

I frowned. Elixirs? Potions? Who could afford to give away potions? I waited until Sid made an announcement about the upcoming debate and parties at all three campaign headquarters to follow and concluded her performance. As the crowd started to clear out, I skirted puddles and met her at the bottom of the stairs. The She swept down to me, her gray gown fluttering around her feet.

"How was that, Skeeve?" she asked.

"Uh, effective as always," I said. Her cheeks hollowed with pleasure. I had removed the wax from my ears so she wouldn't see the plugs. "What was that about gifts from the candidates? That wasn't in the briefing we gave you."

"It's true," she said. "I'm sorry to alter your report, but I remained after your departure. To the children, the three distributed small presents of a harmless nature. Then, Aahz gave the adults bottles of Whisky."

"He *did*?" I asked. "Real Whisky?"

"Not the true liquor from Whis, but the distillation served in most bars around the dimensions." She looked at me with concern. "Did I do something wrong? My understanding was that we are still the only true source of news in this place. I thought it best to inform people accurately as to the events. I didn't include my observations of the annoyance of the other two candidates, because I felt that would be editorializing, and I am only supposed to report."

"No, Sid, it's my fault for not staying," I said. I cursed my temper. I shouldn't have let Aahz and Shomitamoni get to me, especially when I knew they were baiting me on purpose. He probably wanted me out of the way before he bribed as many voters as possible. "Thanks for getting the facts out there. You're doing a great job."

The She smiled. "It's a great job. I'll miss it when it's over."

I sighed. "I wish I could say the same thing."

CHAPTER THIRTY-ONE

"You have to know how to handle children."

—R. PLANTAGENET

"**W**aaaaahhhhhhhh!!!!"

I felt like crying myself. The lightning round of the baby-kissing contest was not going as smoothly as the first one had. Bunny and I sat dejectedly at a table in front of the gazebo where we could see all three candidates. The files of mothers with infants reached well out of the square and into the nearby streets. We were required by legal precedent not to block our ears, so the full brunt of the blubbering babies couldn't be shut out. Bunny winced every time a new child started to cry.

"I thought I wanted to have children one day," she said, between gritted teeth. "Now I just want a flower garden."

Even Gleep hid under the table with his paws over his ears, crooning unhappily. I would have sent him home, but his presence helped keep the crowd in line. Not that the usual protesters would have endangered small children, but I had seen them cause disruption in countless other ways. Painful as it was for him, Gleep understood.

The rules of the lightning round were different than in the previous contest. The candidates were going for speed over accuracy. Not surprisingly, having Aahz lunge toward a Tipp infant sent both mother and baby into hysterical tears more than half the time. The chalk marks under his name on our slate mounted up steadily.

As fast as he was going, Aahz did his best not to upset the babies. I knew he was a father, and one of his pieces of advice I had never forgotten was, "The proof that a person learns from experience is that no one ever wakes a baby twice to see it smile." I began to suspect that not every outburst was from seeing a Pervish face full of fangs leaning close for a kiss.

I glanced toward Wilmer's team. The candidate himself was too busy to cause trouble, and Carnelia stood beside him, offering anxious encouragement. Instead, I watched Morton, the Wisdom Party magician. He seemed more intent on how Aahz was doing than on Wilmer. I felt power growing subtly and stood up so I could see what he was doing. As Aahz bent to smooch a little boy holding a silver rattle, a surge of magik hit me in the back. Then another hit me in the front, from the opposite direction. The baby and I both began to cry.

"Waah!" the little boy yelled.

"Boo-hoo-hoo!" I sobbed. I took a deep breath, trying to control myself. Bunny looked up in concern.

"Skeeve, what's wrong?"

"Illicit interference," I said, taking a deep breath, then burst into tears again. A very little girl in a pink dress nearby looked up sympathetically and offered me her lollipop. I was so unhappy I almost took it. "M-m-m-Morton did it! Boo-hoo-hoo!" Then I noticed that Riginald looked pleased with himself. A strong miasma of magik swirled around him. I pointed at the Friendship Party's magician. "And Riginald, too! Wah-hah-haaa!" I gasped for breath and sobbed again.

"Now, just a moment!" Carnelia said, bustling over to me. One of her rodents offered a handkerchief. She took it and dabbed my face with it in a motherly fashion. "You surely aren't accusing our magician of interfering with Mr. Aahz's efforts? Not when he has so many natural disadvantages of his own? I mean, that face and everything! You're just feeling hysterical. Crom knows the rest of us feel that way about now."

Orlow was right beside her. "You can't blame our fellow! Why, he can hardly see Aahz from where he's standing."

I took another deep breath.

"Ju-ust beca-*hic*-use I'm crying doesn't mean I am hysterical! I felt the spells hit me," I said, trying to catch my breath. I rubbed my eye with my fist. "I saw—I saw—I *saw* them! They've been making tho-ose babies cry!"

"Right," Bunny said. "That's ten points against Wilmer, and *twenty* against Emo!" She chalked firm lines on the board.

"What?" Orlow declared. "Why?"

"For cheating, then lying about it!" She turned back to the stage and clapped her hands. "Candidates, a fifteen-second break! I have an announcement to make!" Emo, Aahz, and Wilmer put down their current smoochees. "Cheating is not going to be tolerated while Skeeve or I am here! If anyone on your staff causes interference with another candidate's babies, you'll get a penalty. With every subsequent infraction, it will go up by ten more points. Do I make myself understood?"

"Yes, ma'am," Orlow said.

"All right." Carnelia let out a loud sigh.

Aahz's campaign manager didn't reply.

"Shomitamoni?" Bunny asked, warningly.

The little female waved a dismissive hand. "All right, whatever!"

"Good. Candidates! Pick up your next baby, aaa-and *kiss*!"

I sat down next to Bunny.

"Are you all right?" she asked.

I nodded, not trusting myself to speak. From the broad

white force line overhead, I pulled down as much energy as I could possibly hold. I enveloped myself in it, imagining that I was in a cloud, floating high in the sky. Soon, the deep unhappiness receded. I opened my eyes. Bunny was looking at me intently. I smiled at her and picked up the chalk.

Even with the threatened penalties keeping potential cheating at bay, Aahz was so far behind I didn't know how he could recover enough to win the contest. He was crooning obscenities, but in a nice, soothing voice so as not to upset the children.

"Ratzining framling heptapods should be boiled in lava sauce," he cooed, dandling a tiny baby girl. She poked him in the eye with a finger. He kissed her hastily and handed her back. "Yank their gizzards out with a slather-hook and feed them to a pack of wild landsharks, yes, I will." The next baby began to whimper as Aahz reached for him.

"What a shame that you can't charm the babies with illicit gifts, Mr. Aahz," Wilmer said, as he picked up a pair of twin girls from their carriage.

"What illicit gifts?" Aahz asked, giving a hasty peck to a young Gorillaard that tried to climb up his tunic and plant a long skinny tongue in his ear. "Cut it out, kid, or I'll tie a knot in that."

"Waaaah!" Sensing disapproval, the baby whimpered at him. Aahz looked sulky. I had to chalk a penalty against his name. Aahz thrust it back into the arms of the Tipp female who had brought it up.

"Seems like you just lack the knack, sir," Emo said, tickling a Deveel infant under the chin. It went to bite his finger, but to give him credit, it didn't cry. "What are you, a couple hundred points down already?"

Aahz shot a glance at the chalkboard and looked peeved. "If I thought there was any point in these stupid contests, I'd be worried," he said.

"Of course there's a point!" Wilmer said, shocked.

Aahz put down the child he was holding. "And that is?"

"To show the public we care about them!" Emo said. He hugged the little girl in his arms. She let out a squeak of protest.

Aahz raised an eyebrow. "By exposing yourself to the little plague-carriers' germs? I bet the public is *thrilled*, especially the moms who are number two thousand in line. How many colds are you giving the kids by passing along every virus that you pick up? Not to mention exposing yourselves. You'll probably have to govern the first two months of your term from a hospital bed. I'm going to go get a drink. If all these parents are smart, they'll join me!"

The females began to look uneasy. They started whispering among themselves. A few pulled out of the queue and strolled nonchalantly toward the edge of the square.

"No, ladies, come back," Emo pleaded. "I promise you we have your children's very best interests at heart."

"Aahz," I said, warningly. "You agreed to participate in this event. We're not here to judge how Tipicanoo structures its elections."

"And *you* started believing in the Prime Directive, when?" Aahz challenged me.

Since I had no idea what he was talking about, I let his gibe roll off my back. He was in a dangerously petty mood. I was familiar with the symptoms. All I could do was try to sweet-talk him back into cooperating.

"But, Aahz," I said, "you want to win a *Tipp* office. I know you could take on a slate of Pervects without even breaking a sweat."

Aahz considered the question. "Well, I've never been nominated . . ." he began, modestly.

"That's just because no one knew you might be interested," I went on, with all the sincerity I could muster. "Now, here in Tipicanoo, it's a fresh challenge. Hardly worth your talents, I know. *Of course* you could win doing things the Pervect way, but if you win honoring the Tipp customs, there will be no doubt that the voters elected you because they wanted you, not because you were a novelty candidate."

Beside me, Bunny held still, not daring to breathe. I watched Aahz's expression go from scornful to suspicious. I kept my face devoid of anything but concerned innocence. Then, he let out a loud laugh. He slapped his knee.

"Kid, you're right. I can beat anyone at their own game. Gimme that baby!"

The next mother in line, overwhelmed by the force of his demand, handed him her infant, a little boy wrapped in a yellow blanket. Aahz crooned at it before giving it a sound kiss that I thought might take off one of the baby's ears. He thrust it back at her and scooped up the next infant. I gave him an admiring look, then signaled to the other two to resume their osculations.

The fact remained that Aahz was probably too far behind to win this contest. Emo and Wilmer were far too experienced at the game to make easy mistakes, as Aahz was. It didn't help him that when a baby broke out in hysterics on seeing him, he couldn't calm it down. With a grim expression, he carried on.

Bunny looked at the clock in the square and tinkled her little bell.

"Candidates, we're down to the last fifteen minutes!"

I did a quick calculation on the chalkboard. No doubt about it, Aahz was going to lose by a huge margin. The other two were virtually neck and neck.

"Uuurp!"

Wilmer jumped back as the inevitable happened, for the fourth time that morning. The child who spat up on his white coat smiled up at him toothlessly. Wilmer pecked him on the top of his little head as aides rushed to help him change clothes. Emo couldn't help but laugh at him.

"How come they never do that to you?" Wilmer asked Emo. "Your clothes make adults sick."

"I charm them," Emo said, holding a little darling tenderly. I noticed Shomitamoni watching him. She raised an eyebrow. Suddenly, Emo held the baby away from him. An assistant moved in hastily to dab at his colorful waistcoat with a cloth.

"I see," Wilmer crowed. "They prefer to show their opinion in *other* ways!"

"That's not funny!" Emo said.

"Why, I think it is!"

"A little yellow looks good on you!" Shomi yelled.

"Did Shomi do that?" Bunny asked.

"I don't know," I said. "If she did, her magik is too subtle for me to detect."

Emo looked furious. He shot a meaningful look at Riginald. The bulky Tipp nodded acknowledgment. The very next child Wilmer took out of its stroller vomited spectacularly.

"That one I felt." I stood up. "Thirty points against Emo!"

"Why, you rogue!" Wilmer said.

The rate of accidental bladder voidings increased dramatically, as did upchucking, wailing, tantrums, and screams. Both the Friendship Party and Wisdom Party magicians threw spells freely. I had a hard time keeping up with the penalties earned by both sides. The candidates kept trying to kiss babies while avoiding their outbursts. Aahz put down the last child he was holding and watched with obvious glee.

The clock struck the hour. Bunny tinkled her little bell. The candidates stopped and stared at her in bemusement.

"The contest is over!" she announced. "Skeeve, what's the score?"

I turned to the chalkboard and my scrawled addition in the corner.

"Well, Aahz kissed six hundred and three babies. He lost three hundred and four points for crying. That means he has a total score of two hundred ninety-nine." The other two candidates looked smug. "Emo kissed six hundred twenty-five, but he lost three hundred thirty points . . ."

"What?" Emo said, horrified.

"I told you that the penalty increased every time your staff used magik against another contestant," Bunny said severely. "It added up! Your score is two hundred ninety-five."

Wilmer looked smug. "And me, Mr. Skeeve?"

"Six hundred thirty, minus three thirty-five. That's also two ninety-five." Bunny shook her head. "That means Aahz is the winner!"

"Gee, we haven't had a winner before," I said. "Congratulations, Aahz!"

Aahz held his hands over his head as the crowd cheered. Reporters converged on him, shouting questions. It was a shame that nothing Aahz said was going to appear in the papers.

Wilmer, Emo, and their managers approached our desk.

"I wish to contest this outcome, dear lady," Wilmer said.

"On what grounds?" Bunny asked.

"On account of that Pervert cheated! I just conferred with my magician here, and he swears that he did not start the, er, leaks that plagued the last round of the contest."

"Skeeve the Magnificent is a magician with repute across many dimensions," Bunny said. "He sensed Morton and Riginald breaking the rules, and after I warned all of you!"

"But Aahz cheated, too!"

"Can you prove it?" Bunny asked.

"Yes!" Emo said. "I felt magik coming from his direction just before one of the babies, er, expressed himself."

"That's impossible," I said.

"How can you say that?" Emo demanded. "He's a Pervert! They are powerful magicians. A tiny thread of magik like that! I wouldn't have noticed it at all except that I have had to learn to look out for such subterfuge in these contests." He looked at Wilmer, who nodded agreement.

"Well, because I know Aahz," I said. "He wouldn't cheat like that." I couldn't explain that Aahz didn't have any magik. No one in this dimension knew that except for me and Bunny. If anyone was to blame, it was Shomi, but I would never be able to get either of them to admit it.

"Perverts are Perverts!" Emo said. "If only Tipps were involved, I wouldn't have these concerns."

"Quite right!" Wilmer declared. The two of them exchanged emphatic nods.

"All right," Bunny said, with a deep sigh. "I'll declare the contest void, in that case—if you'll excuse the expression. One event more or less won't make any difference on Voting Day."

"Thank you, Miss Bunny," Wilmer said, bowing over her hand. "You are the soul of grace."

Emo took her hand and looked deeply into her eyes. "Until the evening, dear lady."

"Yes," Bunny said, retrieving her fingers and checking to see if they were still there. After all, they had just been handled by two politicians. "When we do this all over again."

CHAPTER THIRTY-TWO

"A good wife is hard to find."

—HENRY VIII

The Hotel Tippmore was the site of Meet the Candidate's Family event. With Bunny's help, I chose a formal outfit in the Bazaar's most exclusive boutique that catered to Klahds and other demons who didn't have tails. I came out dressed in a dark-blue silk shirt that Bunny said went well with my hair and eyes, smoke-gray suede vest and trousers, and a gleaming black leather boots and belt. She wore a plum-colored dress that dived low between her breasts and was open nearly all the way down her back. If it hadn't had a long skirt as well, I would have found it impossible to concentrate on anything else but her. I bought her a pair of long gold earrings with bronze-colored stones that she had admired. After all, what was the fun of having money if you couldn't buy things for your friends?

We did not attend alone. Guido wore a black suit with a black shirt and white tie that made him look like a solid wall with a white stripe on it. Gleep wore a new collar that I made him promise not to eat until after the event was over. I wanted to have something to hang on to if he decided to chase someone I didn't want him to chase.

The room was full of reporters and Shutterbugs, as well as several hundred members of the public browsing around and chatting quietly to one another. Ecstra caught my eye. She gave me a hopeful little wave. I waved back, then pointed toward the middle of the room as if I had something important to do. She looked sad but resigned. I was, too. The Syndication had been unusually quiet. We had been able to publicize our notices with the help of Sid the She and my process servers without interference for days. Call me paranoid, but I suspected a strike of some kind was imminent. I didn't want to end up in a dark cave again, but I wished that the papers were covering the election as they should have been. This event would have made for several great articles.

All three candidates had set up refreshment tables in three corners of the chandelier-draped ballroom. The fourth corner was occupied by an eight-piece orchestra in formal black coats or dresses, sawing away at something slow and classical.

"Mrs. Weavil-Scuttil, you look lovely," I said, bowing over her hand. Wilmer's wife wore a pale-blue dress. Bunny give her an admiring look, so it must have been very nice. My taste in clothes had been instilled in me by Bunny, but I would never in a hundred years know as much as she did about fashion.

"You are too kind, Mr. Skeeve," she said. "Wilmer bought the dress for me. The pin"—she indicated a cluster of pearls the size of grapes on her shoulder—"was also a present from Wilmer, on our twenty-fifth anniversary."

"Very nice," I said.

"Please excuse me," Mrs. Weavil-Scuttil said, with an imperious nod. "I must attend to something.

The whole family was present. As well as his married daughter and the handsome boy who had been in the Shutterbug portraits, there was a bulky youth with overly long brown fur and ill-fitting clothes. That had to be Prager. He stayed toward the back, playing with a crystal disk that looked like the inside of Bunny's Perfectly Darling Assistant. Beams of brilliant color shot out of it, to the evident annoyance of his mother. She swooped down on him and confiscated it. He stuffed his hands in his coat pockets and kicked at the carpet.

Emo's family, auxiliary daughter and all, arrived with a fanfare more suitable to the arrival of actors on stage. Emo bowed his wife into the room and gave each of his children an ostentatious cuddle. They squirmed loose and headed for the table with the green cloth.

Bunny and I went to meet them.

"Miss Bunny, you are enchanting," Emo said. "You remember my wife?"

Mrs. Weavil wiggled her fingers at us. Bunny returned the gesture, and they both giggled.

"I love your dress," Mrs. Weavil said.

"And I love yours," Bunny said. Instead of the drab clothes she had had on during the portrait event, the Tipp female wore something silky and slinky in deep red. "Where did you find it?"

The two of them began to talk fashion.

"May I offer you a drink?" Emo asked, indicating the Friendship Party table.

"I'd better not right now," I said. I was afraid to appear partisan by sampling refreshments from one and not the other two. After the judging, Bunny and I planned to have a quiet meal in the hotel restaurant.

Emo understood. "Well, I'd better greet my guests," he said. He collected his wife and went to shake hands with his supporters.

Bunny returned from her little chat. "She's very nice," Bunny said. "We're going to swap some dresses after the election is over."

"Sure," I said. This was some kind of female bonding I probably would never understand. I could never imagine trading clothes with one of my male friends. "I wonder where Aahz is?"

"I don't know," Bunny said. "I didn't think he had a family to bring to this event."

"I know he's been married at least once," I said. "He once mentioned grandchildren."

"Aahz? Really?"

BAMF!

Though the noise came from the foyer outside the ballroom, it was unmistakably that of a D-hopper spell displacing air. I went to meet Aahz.

He wasn't alone. I found myself gawking. Clinging to his arm was a slender Pervect female at least eight inches taller than he was. By Pervish standards, she was a knockout. I had no basis for judging the age of Aahz's people, but my guess was that she was decades younger than he was, though well above adolescence. She was clad, barely, in a slinky garment that made the other wives' clothing look like dishrags. The fabric was so fine that it shimmered when she moved. Aahz's other hand had a firm grip on the collars of two small Pervish boys. If they had been Klahds, I would have guessed them to be between six and nine years old. A much smaller boy sat on the ground, sucking his thumb and looking sulky. He had a solid-steel rattle in one hand that he used to pound on the floor. The fourth, a girl around eleven, stood on the outer edge of her feet so the soles pointed toward one another. She twisted back and forth to some internal rhythm.

"Hi, Skeeve," Aahz said, waving us over. "Come and meet the gang."

I thought my eyes would bulge out of my head. "I . . . you never told me . . . hey, pleased to meet you, Mrs. Aahz."

"Rodna," the female Pervect said, shaking my hand politely. "Aahz has told me so much about you."

"Uh, well, he hasn't told me *anything* about you," I said. I felt a sharp-toed foot kick me in the ankle. "Um, this is Bunny."

Rodna extended a hand with perfectly manicured three-inch nails to Bunny. "Pleased to meet you."

"Very happy to meet you," Bunny said. "Please, come in. The event is about to start."

"Children!" Rodna said, clapping her hands. "Move! That way. Now!"

The four children glanced up from what they were doing and fell in line immediately. I was impressed, but not surprised. Considering that Pervects were born with magikal abilities as well as intelligence and enormous physical strength, no parent with any sense of self-preservation would let them run wild. The children gathered behind Rodna and followed her obediently into the ballroom.

I hardly knew what to say. To the best of my recollection, Aahz rarely referred to his family connections. I knew he had a nephew, who had dropped by to cause us trouble once.[3] Pookie was his cousin. Beyond that, I knew very little about his family. There had never been reason to ask. Aahz didn't invite personal questions. To give him credit, he rarely asked them, either. Our relationship had always been in the here and now. But unless he had left Rodna to raise four children all by herself, though she looked perfectly capable of doing so, he must have been going off to Perv to visit them often during the time I had known him. I had never had a clue.

"Aahz, how long have you been with Rodna?" I asked, trying to make it sound natural.

"Long enough," Aahz said, with an outrageous wink. "Gorgeous, isn't she?"

"Well, yeah. I mean, I've never seen a more beautiful Pervect." I swallowed, trying to think of how to phrase the question. He wasn't making it easy. "Did you . . . I mean . . . when . . . ?"

"I need a drink. I hope that Shomi brought in enough booze. There she is!"

---

3. Regarding Rupert, see *Myth-Directions*, no doubt downloadable on your own Perfectly Darling Assistant.

Aahz shepherded his family to the Plague Party table, where Shomi was waiting.

"What do you think?" he asked her.

"Very nice," the campaign manager said, looking Rodna up and down. "Very first-ladyish."

"Thanks," Aahz said.

"Can she cook?"

"Naturally."

That struck me as a very strange thing for Shomi to ask, but she had almost as little tact as a Pervect herself.

Gallantly, Aahz served Rodna a generous tot of white wine in a glass the size of a flower vase. The children clamored for pastries, but Rodna made them take fruit instead. Very strict. Aahz helped himself to a gallon of beer and chugged half of it in a gulp.

"Aaah!" he said, with satisfaction. He let out a room-shaking belch. Everyone turned to look at him. "Well, we're here! Let's get this party started!"

I had no idea how the event was supposed to go. Fortunately, the locals took the lead.

Mrs. Weavil, Emo's wife, came over to us with a tray. On it were arranged square cookies sprinkled with blue and green sugar, fragrant with spice. She offered it to me. "Please, try one of these. I made them myself this afternoon."

"Thanks," I said. I handed one to Bunny. We each took a bite. They were still warm. I suspected Mrs. Weavil used a little magik to maintain that fresh-out-of-the-oven flavor, but I didn't mind. Ginger, nutmeg, and something slightly tart that I couldn't identify permeated the crispy wafer. I could have eaten dozens of them.

"They're delicious," I said.

"They are," Bunny said. "I want the recipe, Bolla."

Mrs. Weavil beamed. "I would be just delighted to share it with you, Bunny."

"*Ex*-cuse me," Mrs. Weavil-Scuttil said austerely to Bolla.

The younger female moved aside. Wilmer's wife swept in, carrying an embossed silver tray.

"How gorgeous," Bunny said.

Reposing—there was no other word for it—on a rectangular white lace doily were miniature cakes. I was stunned by the skill it must have taken to make them. There were tiny three-layer tiered cakes that would have been great for Shutterbug weddings, birthday cakes with hair-thin candles burning, and a dozen others that were so beautiful and fragile-looking I was afraid to touch them.

Mrs. Weavil-Scuttil took care of the problem for me. Somehow, she managed to produce a flat silver implement with a pierced paddle and scooped two pastries apiece onto little plates that were balanced on the edge of the tray. The paddle disappeared, and Mrs. Weavil-Scuttil handed Bunny and me each a plate.

"Please, enjoy them," she said. She watched us as I picked up a little wedding cake and bit it in half. Her eyebrows went down just a little in disapproval. I wondered if I should have put the whole thing in my mouth.

I chewed. To tell the truth, the little cakes were a bit dry and too sweet. If I hadn't tried Bolla's cookies first, I would have thought they tasted pretty good. I swallowed, and wished I had accepted Emo's offer of a drink.

"Uh, great!" I said. Mrs. Weavil-Scuttil relaxed just a hair. I realized she was as nervous as her rival, but she hid it better.

"I am so glad you like them," she said. "I serve them at all my parties."

"Your guests must be very impressed," Bunny said.

"Oh, they are!" Mrs. Weavil-Scuttil said, with a superior smile.

"I beg your pardon?"

Rodna shifted in between us so swiftly and gracefully that Mrs. Weavil-Scuttil *almost* jumped in surprise. She smiled down at the tray of mini-cakes.

"My goodness, how old-fashioned!" she said, with a musical laugh. "Oh, please forgive me. I'm sure you have been making them for years." She held out her hands. I felt power rise from the floor. A tray appeared balanced on her forearms. The aroma that rose from the little round pastries made my mouth water. I swallowed and reached for one, then hesitated.

"Try the ones on the edge near you," Rodna said. "They have a nut-paste filling that is out of this world!"

"They aren't made with any . . . living things . . . are they?" I asked, gingerly. My experience to date was that if Pervects didn't beat their food two falls out of three they felt they were losing something in the dining experience.

Rodna laughed again with a sound like tinkling bells. "Oh, no! I adapted the recipe from a Klahdish cookbook and two Tipp recipe collections."

"Very thorough," Mrs. Weavil-Scuttil said. "It sounds like scientific research. Now, *I* see cookery as an art, not a science."

"Then you probably have a lot of fallen cakes," Rodna replied, sweetly. "Baking is science."

Mrs. Weavil-Scuttil recoiled in high dudgeon.

"I beg your pardon! My pastries have been praised to the skies for decades now! I don't cobble together collections of ingredients from other people's kitchens!"

"What a shame. I like to learn from people who do things well," Rodna said. Mrs. Weavil-Scuttil's eyes blazed.

I ignored the genteel argument and bit into the cake. My eyes closed automatically in bliss. The dough was flaky and delicate, and inside it was a just-sweet-enough fruity-caramelly mass that melted into my mouth and took my tongue hostage. I opened my eyes to see Bunny with her eyes closed and a dreamy smile on her face.

"Wow," I said, when I could speak again. As good as Bolla's baking was, Rodna beat it ten times over. Bolla knew it. Mrs. Weavil-Scuttil had tasted one of the cakes, too. They both wore a look of dismay.

"I trust . . . you will be fair in your judgment?" she asked.

"Yes, ma'am," I promised her, but we both knew what that verdict would be.

SKREEK! SKROK! SKRREEK-EEEK!

I spun, ready to defend Bunny and the ladies against the attacking Felinodon.

There was no giant catlike monster holding the guests at bay. Instead, I saw Emo's elder boy standing all alone with a violin under his chin, sawing away at a melody that was clearly somewhat beyond him. Emo stood nearby, a proud expression on his face. He saw me watching and beckoned to me.

"Isn't he amazing?" Emo shouted over the music. "He's been taking lessons for two years!"

"Amazing," I agreed.

"Yes," said Wilmer, unimpressed. "It is amazing that two years of lessons had no effect on him whatsoever!"

Emo lifted an indignant chin. "And I suppose your kid will do better?"

"Why, yes, he will!"

Just when I thought my nerves couldn't take any more, the piece mercifully came to an end. The assembled guests clapped politely. The boy ducked his head nervously toward the audience and set his bow to his instrument to provide us with an encore.

"That's enough!" I said hastily, rushing in to prevent any further damage to my eardrums. "So, who's next?"

"My boy, Gibbly," Wilmer said, and waved to the bulky teenager sitting on a couch in a dark corner. Very reluctantly, Gibbly made his way onto the dance floor. His mother bustled over and gave him a brass horn with a U-shaped slide. As subtly as I could, I took the wax plugs I used to protect myself from Sid the She's shrill voice and stuffed them in my ears. Gibbly raised the horn to his lips.

To my surprise, the music that issued from it was fun and lively. Gibbly played a Satchish tune with a swinging rhythm that invited people to dance. Unlike the previous child, I was sorry when he finished, but I couldn't show favor. I clapped politely, restraining myself from showing the acclaim he really deserved. Mrs. Weavil-Scuttil took the horn from him and tried to straighten his shirt, but Gibbly pulled loose from her and went back to his seat.

"Fantastic," Bunny whispered in my ear. "I'm afraid none of Aahz's kids can compete with that!"

We were wrong. The little girl went out to the middle of the floor and snapped her fingers. I felt a rush of magik sweep in. When it cleared, she was surrounded by musical instruments. The rest of the children crawled or toddled to join her. The smallest boy clambered up on a stool behind the drum set. Another took up a guitar, the other a banjo. The girl took her place behind a keyboard just barely low enough for her to reach. The drummer beat his sticks together to set the beat, and they began to play. My eyebrows climbed all the way into my hairline.

They were good. In fact, they could have played club dates. I wondered if they did. The three elder children looked as if they were accustomed to taking their cue from the tiny drummer. Aahz had never shown much talent for music. It had to come from Rodna's side. Their expertise in playing as an ensemble impressed me enormously. The audience was enraptured.

Most of it. From the other side of the room, I heard yelling. I glanced up to see what was going on. Aahz was having a three-way argument with Emo and Wilmer.

"Are you or are you not saying that these are your children?" Wilmer demanded.

"Sure they are," Aahz said. "I bought them as a job lot."

Emo's voice climbed from tenor to soprano. "You *bought* them?"

"Well . . . maybe *bought*'s the wrong word."

"Then what *is* the right word?"

"*Acquired*?"

"*Acquired!*"

"What about your wife?" Wilmer asked.

"What about her?" Aahz countered.

"What did *she* have to say about this . . . this irregular arrangement?"

Aahz shrugged. "None of her business, is it?"

"Certainly it is! She has a say on what goes on in your house, doesn't she?"

"Why should she? They're not her kids."

"But . . . but she's your wife!" Emo exclaimed.

"Well, sort of," Aahz said, with a sly wink.

"You didn't marry her?" Wilmer asked. "Then what's she doing in this contest?"

Aahz got indignant. "You're asking me if I have a financial and domestic arrangement with this woman? Is that really any of your business?"

"Are you married?" Wilmer pressed.

Aahz waved a hand. "I've been married three times."

"Is *this* lady one of your wives?"

"Pervects are monogamous," Aahz said. "Anyone who knows anything about us knows that one Pervect woman is all that a man can handle at a time. Trust me."

"You didn't answer the question," Emo said.

"Good catch," Aahz said, slapping him on the back. He headed for the yellow table to get a refill for his drink.

Not surprisingly, the campaign managers descended on me and Bunny.

"You have to disqualify Aahz's family," Orlow demanded.

"Why?" I asked, innocently. To be honest, I had enjoyed the argument. As far as I was concerned, Emo and Wilmer were getting a taste of their own medicine.

"Because they're not his!" Carnelia exclaimed.

"Well, he says they are," I pointed out. "However, they became a family. I mean, if we have to accept Emo's extra daughter and Wilmer's substitute son, then if Aahz claims that this is his wife and children, you really have no reason to demand that we disqualify him. As far as I can tell, he hasn't lied once."

Orlow frowned. He was aware of the shaky status of his

request. "Well, you can't allow his so-called wife's cakes, then. She's probably a *professional* . . . er, baker, that is."

Bunny glared at him. "Are you saying that a woman can't have a career just because she's married to a politician?"

"No, of course not," Orlow said, fingering his collar.

"I am sure that is not what Orlow meant to say at all," Carnelia said hastily. "It's just that Aahz is making a mockery of our events!"

"Well, maybe if you weren't concentrating on window dressing instead of substantial issues," Bunny said. "How about more town hall meetings or debates?"

Orlow shook his head. "We just don't get enough turnout for them."

"Well, I couldn't say what Emo must be feeling, but I have to tell you, Mr. Skeeve and Miss Bunny, that Wilmer is on the edge with your Mr. Aahz," Carnelia confided.

"Do you think he might do something . . . extreme?" I asked, suddenly worried. "He just doesn't strike me as the kind to take physical action against someone else."

"Oh, don't let that white hair fool you," Carnelia said. "He was a champion swordsman in his day. His favorite weapon is twin flaming sabers."

Bunny and I exchanged concerned glances. With his thick, scaly skin, Aahz wasn't afraid of most edged weapons, but Pervects could be killed with fire. I had to prevent an outburst from any of the candidates that might result in injury or death.

"I'll see if we can tone Aahz down," I said. "Within the rules of the contest, of course."

"Of course," Carnelia said. "That'll relieve my mind enormously."

CHAPTER THIRTY-THREE

"I was only trying to make a point."

—A. BURR

As the others had surmised, Bunny and I had no choice but to call Aahz the winner of the Meet the Candidate's Family challenge. Whether or not he was married to Rodna or any of those children were his, they had charmed the audience more than the other families had. I had to give Aahz credit for creativity in taking advantage of the way Emo and Wilmer had bent the rules in the past. Whatever my feelings about what he was doing, he was the best. In my opinion, his opponents had no chance of winning.

Aahz knew it, too. Instead of letting the others lick their wounds in private, he had accepted the victory as his due.

"Thanks, everyone! I knew when I got here tonight that I had this contest knocked. So, with no hard feelings, I'm inviting the losers—oops, did I say that?—I mean, the runners-up and their families to my house for a celebration! Come on over! There'll be drinks, dancing, prizes, and plenty of great food!

Give me a one-minute head start, and I'll get everything going!"

The crowd cheered. In its midst, I could see Emo and Wilmer stewing. Aahz gathered his ad hoc family together and reached into his pocket.

BAMF!

The others couldn't not show up, of course. Bunny and I waited until the candidates and their families had cleared out of the room. I didn't want to be stuck next to them as we waited to board carriages.

I welcomed a chance to explore Aahz's new house. I knew exactly where it was. In fact, everyone in the main city knew. Aahz had paid to have cobblestones pried up from the road in the main street, leading all the way to his front door in the street above the town square, and replaced with stones in his campaign color. All you had to do to get there was follow the yellow-block road. Our carriage, drawn by a huge, lumbering beast with long, shaggy hair, pulled away from the Hotel Tippmore and made for the beginning of the stone path.

Traffic was heavy on the hairpin turn uphill, so Bunny and I left our cab. I flew us the rest of the way, joining a number of locals who had the same idea. Gleep slithered out of the carriage and ran up the road.

He caught up with us just before we alighted on the pavement outside.

"Gleep!" he said. He snaked his head up and aimed for my face with his long tongue.

"Gnaaah!" I said, wiping the slime off my cheek. "Come on, these are my best clothes!"

"Gleep!" he said reproachfully.

"Come on," I said, patting him on the head. "Stay close to Bunny, will you?"

"Oh, Skeeve," Bunny said. "There won't be any trouble."

A garden on the cliff side left a gap so you could see the façade of a grand, pillared home set into the rock. Twin, curving staircases led up to it from the street. Thousands of Fireflies were dancing in the garden between the staircases, drawing lines of colored light on the night sky. Four Tipps in muted-gold livery helped people out of their carriages, wagons, and taxis. A couple of little maids wearing frilly aprons handed a flower to each of the females. Two formal-coated butlers offered a drink even before the guests reached the front door.

I glanced down at the bonfire and did a shocked double-take.

"What's wrong?" Bunny asked.

"Look!"

I pointed. In the middle of the Firefly show, two Tipp-shaped dummies stood, waving hello to the arriving guests. I couldn't have been mistaken about who they were supposed to represent. One had a white wig and the other was dressed in clown-patterned fabrics. Each had a glassy-eyed, silly smile and one waving hand. Around the neck of each mannequin was a sign that read *LOSER*. Bunny was shocked.

"You'd better shut that down before Emo and Wilmer see it," she said. I rolled up my sleeves and prepared to smash the display into fragments.

"Too late," I groaned. At the bottom of the stairs, Emo had climbed out of his official carriage. He shouted at the Tipp valets, who turned up their palms helplessly. Wilmer, in the next car, piled out and added his booming voice to the argument.

"He *would* have to rub it in," she said.

"It's Aahz," I said. "We should have known he wouldn't bother to be subtle."

"Gleep!" my dragon added.

"That's it!" Wilmer said. He saw us and stormed up the stairs. He shook his fist in my face. Gleep lifted his head between us. The Tipp backed away a pace, but he did not calm down. "The gloves come off! Where is that Pervert?"

"I guess he's inside," I said. "Please don't overreact."

"Overreact?" Emo shrieked. He jabbed a finger toward the blazing scarecrows. "He's . . . he's saying he wants us publicly humiliated!"

I tried to explain. "No, that's not it. Those aren't really you. They're dummies that look like you . . . I mean, it's just a—a . . ."

". . . An insult." Bunny finished my sentence for me. "Elaborate presentation, admittedly, but nothing more, really. I thought politicians were always insulting one another."

"My dear lady, not like that!" Wilmer said, his eyes red with fury. "I am going to find him and demand satisfaction! Yes, I am! Don't try to stop me."

He bustled into the house, pushing past a butler with a tray of drinks. Emo followed him.

"Do you think he'll really challenge Aahz to a duel?" Bunny asked in horror.

"Flaming swords?" I asked.

I grabbed Bunny's hand and hurried into the house after them. Gleep snaked alongside.

Leave it to Aahz to treat himself to the very best. We entered a foyer lined with streaked white marble. Torches in pairs burned in golden sconces on each wall. The head butler, an austere Tipp with gray temples, came forward to greet us.

"Miss Bunny, Skeeve the Magnificent, and Gleep. Master Aahz has been awaiting your arrival. I'm Fardswarn."

"Uh, hi, Fardswarn," I said. "Do you know where he is? Those two, er, gentlemen who just went in are kind of mad at him. I want to warn him."

"They did seem a trifle heated, if you will permit the little joke," the butler said, a tiny smile bending the corners of his mouth. No wonder Aahz had hired him. "I don't believe they will find him until the hour of his speech, but he would be very glad of your company. If you wait here a moment, one of the valets will take you to him."

"We'd better not wait," I said. "I think they might do something we'll all regret later."

"As you wish, sir and madam." He bowed slightly and turned to greet the next guests.

Bunny and I plunged into the bustling crowd in the reception room. More white marble in the corners of the high ceiling had been carved into little fat Tipp babies in diapers with wings and harps. Another pair of twin staircases reached to a gallery on the second level lined with bookcases. I couldn't tell much about the rest of the décor. There were just too many people there. Servers glided from group to group, somehow not dropping the trays of canapés they carried on one hand. The rooms were full of people talking. Everyone seemed to consider that Aahz was absolutely going to be the next governor. A Tipp waitress in a very short skirt handed me a drink. I downed it. I had to find out what he was up to, but first we had to prevent him from fighting a duel with either of his angry opponents.

I made for Rodna, who was the tallest person in the room. She was beside the left-hand staircase chatting with a group of Tipp females. Bunny held on to my arm so we wouldn't lose one another.

". . . Well, that recipe is in my eighth cookbook," she said. "It's about to go into its twentieth printing. I'll get my publisher to send you copies."

"Oh, thank you!" the ladies gushed.

"Rodna," I gasped. "Have you seen Aahz?"

"Not for a while," she said. She regarded me with concern. "Is something wrong?"

"I hope not. Where was he when you saw him last?"

"In the dining room," she said, pointing between the staircases to a grand double doorway.

"Did anyone else ask where to find him, Rodna?" Bunny asked.

"Oh, yes," the Pervect replied. "Both of the other candidates. They looked mad!"

"They were," I said grimly. "Thanks."

A caterer setting up crystal glasses in the dining room told me to look in the library. A serving girl in the library offering drinks to guests told me to check the smoking room. Two hearty males enjoying cigars and liqueur in the smoking room sent me back down to the reception room.

Everywhere we went, Aahz seemed to have just been there, or was expected to arrive, but we couldn't find anyone who had seen him recently. Nor could we locate either of the two aggrieved candidates. Gleep stayed as close to Bunny as the fabric of her evening dress. No one even remotely suspicious approached us, but we hadn't seen the attack in the park coming, either. I was taking no chances.

"I can't believe that Aahz actually bought this place for cash," Bunny said, for the eleventh time, as we made our way down a paneled privy stair from the smoking room to the gallery. "He hates to turn loose a coin even for a drink."

"I know," I said. "I think he just really wants to be governor."

"Well, the Tipps could do worse," she said.

"Gleep!" my dragon said.

"There you are!" Shomitamoni stared up at us from the bottom of the grand staircase and stumped up to meet us. She looked around, then lowered her voice. "Where is Aahz?"

"We don't know," I said. "We've been looking for him. Emo and Wilmer want to challenge him to a duel."

"Pah!" Shomi said, waving away the notion. "A couple of cream puffs. Where I come from they would be found tied up in an alley, shaved and dressed in little girls' clothes."

"Really?" Bunny said. "I should tell my uncle about that one."

"Have you ever seen the Mixitulian Snake Charm gag?" Shomi asked her, an avid look in her round black eyes. "That's where you take their trousers, braid the legs, and pull them . . ."

"Just a minute," I said. "You can discuss ritual humiliation later on. We really need to find Aahz."

"*I* need to find him," Shomi said. "He was supposed to make a speech fifteen minutes ago about his excellent performance this evening. I cannot see that he would miss such an opportunity to drive home that point with the voters."

"Never," I agreed. Aahz loved to hold forth on his exploits

to a captive audience. "How long has it been since you saw him?"

"Not long after we returned here," Shomi said. She glanced at a crystal-and-gold clock on a green marble table. "Half an hour or more."

"Was there anyone in whom Aahz was, uh, showing a personal interest?" I asked. He was a great ladies' man, though I had seen him shot down as often as he succeeded.

"No, no popsies," Shomi said. "Of course he fancies that Rodna girl, but she has a stable of admirers back home."

"Well, if he's not eating, boozing, or chasing a girl," Bunny said, "I can't imagine what's holding him up."

"Unless Wilmer demanded he go through with the duel right away," I said. I turned to Shomi. "We'll help you look for him."

A word with Farnsward assured us that he hadn't left the house through the front door. The kitchen staff was certain he hadn't gone out the back way, either, and the small, enclosed yard was full of barrels of beer and crates of food.

"He's still in the house," I concluded.

"Then we will find him," Shomi said.

CHAPTER THIRTY-FOUR

"Now you see me, now you don't."

—C. CAT

We examined every possible space where a duel could be fought. Guests had wandered into most of the public rooms and a few of the private ones upstairs. No one had seen Aahz or the two other candidates. I began to worry.

After surprising a few amorous couples who had taken advantage of vacant bedrooms and parlors, Shomi led us to Aahz's bedroom at the top of the house.

I stopped her from opening the door.

"Aahz hates surprises," I said. I rapped on the door. "Aahz? Are you in there?" I waited for a moment, then knocked again.

"He is not answering," Shomi said. She reached for the latch.

"Wait!" I said. "Aahz likes to protect himself. There are probably a dozen traps in there."

Shomi put a hand forward, palm out. "Nothing," she said,

after a moment. She evaded my restraining arm and let herself in. Bunny and I followed.

Unsurprisingly, Aahz's bedroom was the nicest room apart from the reception chamber downstairs, and bigger than my parents' entire house in Klah. Warm, gold damask curtains hung on several long windows facing the street. The four-poster bed had matching quilts and hangings. I recognized the style of the plenitude of rugs on the floor as being from the Bazaar at Deva. All of them were silk dyed brilliant colors. Everything in the room was a display of taste and money. His room back in the Bazaar was far more spartan than this. He really had indulged himself. It looked as if he really was intending to live there for a long time.

I pointed at a black sphere next to the bed.

"Massha gave Aahz that." My former apprentice and current Court Magician in Possiltum was a mistress of gadget magik and sympathized with Aahz's lack of powers. The sphere was meant to go off when an intruder entered the room, tying him up in sticky webs while setting off a deafening alarm.

"Stand back!" Shomi said. She surrounded it in a thick globe of magik. The device went off with a POOF! The translucent globe filled with a mass of strands and the siren went off. I winced. Bunny clapped her hands to her ears. Shomi snapped her fingers. The globe, and the noise, vanished.

"It wasn't armed," I said.

I checked the wardrobe, a beautiful piece of furniture that looked as if it had been carved out of a single tree with honey-colored wood. A mirror hung on the inside of one door. The shelves were full of Aahz's clothes. It looked like he did stay there, at least once in a while.

As if I needed more evidence, I found a chest of his favorite books, a back scratcher, a huge silver goblet I had given him for his last birthday, and a padlocked and chained box of snacks that started shaking and rocking when I got near it.

In the bathroom, a vast chamber of warm-hued tiles with

a sunken alabaster bath large enough to hold a party in, I found a jar of an incredibly abrasive body wash called Perval Essence. Over the door was a spray jar that should have dumped sleeping potion on me.

"There are plenty of alarms and traps here," Bunny said, as we gathered in the bedroom to compare notes, "but everything is deactivated. And the left-hand window is open."

"Really?" Shomi said, disgustedly. "Really? They removed him through the window? How cliché."

"Removed him?" I asked. "Why do you say that?"

Shomi snorted. "Because I know a lot about your friend. Nothing short of abduction would prevent him from speaking."

"That's so true," said Bunny.

"But are we sure he didn't leave of his own free will?" I asked. "For all we know, he's back at the office in Deva."

"Gleep!" said my dragon. He held up a cylindrical device. Aahz's D-hopper. Aahz never went anywhere without it.

"You can't tell what happened?" Shomi asked, scornfully. "Some magician you are."

"I'm doing my best to learn," I said, defensively.

"Too late for that, wouldn't you say, when your friend has been abducted?"

Bunny descended on her and grabbed her by the wrist.

"Listen, Dustmop," Bunny said. "Cut out the insults right this minute. Skeeve is a good magician, and a more decent being than you will ever meet again in your life. You may be a professional irritant, but right now it's getting in the way of the facts."

"Okay, okay, missy!" Shomi said, freeing her wrist and clutching it. "Nice to see there's a backbone holding up all that pulchritude. My assessment is that Aahz was removed from here against his will. That is evidenced by the fact that nothing is broken except the window frame. It was executed by those who had magik powerful enough to defeat his security systems. That we could walk in here without being netted or locked up or having a giant weight dropped on us tells me that they did not bother to rearm the systems. That smacks not of carelessness but arrogance."

The word *executed* made chills go down my spine, but I did my best to analyze the situation.

"That makes sense," I said. "But was it the Syndication, or the other two candidates?"

We searched the house one more time. I noticed a couple of catering assistants coming up a set of stone steps.

"What's down there?" I asked.

"Just the cellar," said the taller of the two, who had a case of wine in his arms.

"Is anyone down there?"

"Yeah, a bunch of people," he said. "They're shouting at each other. I think they like the echo."

I didn't wait to hear any more. "Come on," I said.

The servers had been carrying their own lanterns. It was dark at the bottom of the stairs. I made a fire in the palm of my hand and led the way downward.

Gleep slithered down the steps into the gloom of the basement ahead of me. I heard voices yelling. I recognized those of Emo and Orlow. I sniffed the air and smelled smoke. Had they already fought the duel? I peered into the darkness. A small globe of light zipped around in irregular patterns, dipping in and out of shadow.

"Gleep!"

Gleep reappeared. He took my free hand in his jaws and pulled gently toward rows of bottle racks.

"Back there, boy?" I asked Gleep.

"Glmfh!" he exclaimed around my wrist.

I steeled myself. If there was bad news, I wanted to be prepared. I filled my mental batteries with magik. Whatever it took, I would avenge Aahz!

Gleep guided me past several dusty stands containing hundreds of wine bottles. At last, he stopped and let go of my arm.

I stepped around the rack. One lone torch burned in a sconce against the wall. Emo looked up at me a little goggle-eyed. He was seated on top of a large barrel. He hoisted a pottery cup in my direction, then drank deeply.

"To you, my friend!" he said.

"To Skeeve!" chorused three more voices. I directed my improvised torch to light the others' faces. Wilmer, Carnelia, and Orlow had propped themselves on other barrels or crates. All of them had full glasses. Four or five bottles lay on their sides, empty.

"Where's Aahz?" I asked.

"Aahz?" Wilmer asked. He looked very solemn. "No idea where Perverts go, you know, when they go."

"Why do you ask, Mr. Skeeve?" Carnelia inquired. She stifled a hiccup with a delicate hand. She waved a hand, and the globe of light came to hover over us. The four Tipps looked, well, tipsy.

"He's missing," I said. "And because the last time I saw you, you were bent on revenge against him, you're our best suspects."

"No!" Carnelia protested.

"No, never did anything," Emo muttered. "Nothing to do with us."

"Wilmer, what about you?" I pressed.

"Not me," he said. He harrumphed. "Confounded Pervert!"

"That's Per-*vect*," I said.

"That's right, defend him," Orlow said, accusingly. "Some impartial judge you're turning out to be."

That stung, but I had to admit it was probably true. "I'm sorry. I'll try to be more evenhanded in the future. But what about Aahz?"

"What about him?" Wilmer asked, turning his chin up. "I don't know where he is, and I don't care."

"He has to make a speech!" Shomi said.

"Are you sure you haven't seen him?" I asked. "You sure seemed intent on taking revenge on him. Do I have to go get some truth serum and ask again?"

"How's it taste?" Orlow asked, leering. He knocked back what was left in his cup and refilled it.

"No, I swear it!" Wilmer said. He seemed a trifle embarrassed. "I couldn't locate him, and I soon cooled down. We have been drowning our sorrows on Aahz's generous refreshments. I was about to pour the lady another drink. You say Aahz is missing?" He looked gleeful, but tried to hide it.

"Yes," I said.

"You'll forgive me, young man, if I say 'good riddance.'" Wilmer drained his glass and reached for some more wine.

"Hear, hear," said Carnelia, extending her cup to him. "To Aahz!"

"To Aahz?" Emo asked. He drew a deep breath.

He was about to start singing. I withdrew in haste toward the stairs, lighting the way for the others.

It was too late.

"Theyyyyyy're off to find the lizard / The ugly green lizard named Aahz . . . !"

"They're no help," Bunny said.

"Then if they are not responsible for his disappearance, where is the Syndication?" Shomi asked, as we emerged in the main hall.

"I don't know," I said. I noticed a knot of reporters clamoring around Rodna. "But I think I know who does. You keep the party going. I'll bring Aahz back!"

I plunged into the crowd and caught Ecstra by the arm. With Gleep's help, I cut her out of the herd and brought her into a side room that was empty at the moment.

"Why did you take me out of there?" she asked. "Do you know who that is? Aahz's wife is the most famous homemaking expert in all of Perv. A veritable Arthastuard!"

"How would you like to have the most exclusive story in all of Tipicanoo?" I asked.

She straightened her perky hat.

"Tell me more!" she said.

CHAPTER THIRTY-FIVE

"I wouldn't sign anything like that!"

—LUCIFER

We left Shomi keeping the party going. Bunny, Gleep, and I hurried Ecstra out into the night. In spite of the lateness of the hour, more guests were still arriving.

"And you say that Tolomi kidnapped you?" she said, jotting notes down as fast as her pencil could go.

"Not just him," I said. "All of the editors. They call themselves the Syndication, a secret cabal that is in charge of all news dissemination in this entire dimension."

"And they decided to suppress all the stories about the election," Ecstra said. "Whew! Well, it had to be a group decision, or someone would have broken ranks. I thought we journalists were supposed to be independent!"

"Of government, not of one another, I guess," I said.

"And you think that they have taken your friend," Ecstra followed up, flipping a page. "It could have been anyone. Aahz has irritated a lot of people. You should hear some of the stories I've been told! And Wilmer Weavil-Scuttil! He was *fuming* tonight!"

"It wasn't him," Bunny said, walking as fast as she could. Gleep hung close to her side. "And it wouldn't be because he simply offended someone. It has to be the Syndication."

"Why?"

"Because he's too interesting," I said. "He's tough and smart. He came into this race out of nowhere and it looks as if he can win. People are talking about him. He was making it too obvious that the election wasn't making the papers. They had to remove him. He is in danger. We have to save him!"

"So, where are we going?"

I stopped. We had walked about half a block from Aahz's townhouse. I glanced back. "I'm not sure. I tried to track him magikally from his room, but whoever took him was a better magician than I am."

"Do you think they brought him to the same place they brought you?"

"It would make sense," I said. "How many underground hideouts would a highly secret cabal that rules everything behind the scenes have?"

"Well, if they did rule everything, they could have as many as they want to," Ecstra said practically.

"Well, where were we?" Bunny asked. "It was pitch-dark. We entered and left it by magik, so we don't know anything about it."

"Yes, we do," I said, as a thought struck me. "Remember that sound? It was all around us, a rhythmic thumping sound."

"Like a printing press?" Ecstra asked.

"Yes!" Bunny exclaimed. "So we must have been in the cellar below a newspaper office!"

"Oh, this is going to make such a great story—if anyone ever printed it, that is," Ecstra said, wide-eyed. "But which newspaper? There are fifteen in the city."

"And we may not have much time. Aahz isn't going to go along with their demands to stop . . . being himself." Bunny looked grim. "They might just make him disappear."

"Only three of them did all the talking," I said. "It has to be one of their places. But I think Tolomi was in charge. We'll try the *Morning Gossip* first. We'll try to figure out what to do if and when we find them. I can't outmagik them, but maybe there'll be some way to negotiate for Aahz's safety. Do you know the way into the basement of the paper, Ecstra?"

"Can I have an exclusive on the story?" she asked. "And priority access on all upcoming electoral events?"

"Yes, anything you want!" I said impatiently.

"Then fly us near the office. I'll show you where to set down."

The street in front of the office was all but deserted that close to midnight, but I could still feel the rumbling of the printing press through the soles of my feet. It was funny, but I had not noticed it during the day. Too much else was going on. Ecstra stopped us before we walked in front of the glass door. Instead, she took a key out of her hatband and opened a door in the cliff face in between the pools of light from two streetlamps. It was so unobtrusive that I had ignored it completely. The lock opened silently. Ecstra beckoned us inside.

The passage beyond was narrow and slightly damp, but the walls were cut smooth. I made a small light and sent it on before Ecstra so she could see where she was going. She hardly needed it. She led us confidently as the passage intersected with other dark corridors, passing iron-bound doors and barred enclosures. She turned left, then right, then right again. All the time we were spiraling down into the heart of the mountain. Except for our footsteps and the occasional PLINK! of moisture dripping off the invisible ceiling, there was no sound.

After we had gone a long way down, I heard the murmur of voices ahead of us. We tiptoed more softly until Ecstra stopped

us at a huge wooden door. Beyond it I could hear the boom of
Tolomi's voice among others. He laughed uproariously at something. Bunny and I put our ears to the door. Then I heard a
familiar voice.

Aahz!

He protested something, then let out a wordless bellow.
Bunny gasped. I loaded up my internal batteries with magik and
made the tiny flame in my hand grow into a raging fire. Then,
when Tolomi laughed again, Aahz cried out.

"Come on, guys, you're killing me! Give me a break!"

That was it. I had no time to go back and get help. I nodded
to Gleep. The two of us took a few steps backward and lowered our shoulders.

We charged the door. It burst open. Gleep and I dashed
inside.

The brilliant light filling the domed chamber pierced my
dark-adapted eyes, but I spotted Aahz in a moment. I ran to
his side, putting myself between him and the others. As far as
I could tell, the entire Syndication was present. Fifteen Tipps
stared at me. I made the flames into a curtain and fed them
directly from the force line. They wouldn't be able to cross that,
not until we were long gone. Gleep sat in the middle of it and
hissed at the Syndication, his tongue licking in and out between
his fangs, daring any of them to take him on. The room was
filled with foul-smelling smoke. No doubt they had already
threatened him with fire.

"Come on, Aahz, we'll get you out of here!" I said over my
shoulder.

"Just what exactly are you doing, Skeeve?" Aahz asked.

"Are you all right?" I asked. "Have they hurt you?"

"I'm fine, except these crooks want to cheat me out of decent
royalty!"

I glanced back over my shoulder. Aahz wasn't being tortured.
He wasn't even tied up. In fact, he was lying back on a chaise
longue, his feet up on a pillow with a bucket-sized glass in his
hand. He winked at me. I looked from him to the Syndication,

who were hoisting similar yet smaller glasses. A table in the middle held dozens of bottles of wine, a tray of sandwiches, and bowls of snacks. This didn't look like a dungeon. It looked like a party.

I let my fire die out. Gleep whimpered in confusion and crept over to my side.

"Aahz, are you all right?" I asked.

Aahz leaned back and stretched, tapping the ash off the cigar in his hand.

"I'm fine, partner. Just finalizing a little business deal with my pals here . . . Now if you want me to autograph the special commemorative boxed edition, that's extra. I'll go flat fee per book or a percentage."

Tolomi shook his head. He took his own stogie out of his mouth. "No percentage! You're already killing us. Flat fee per copy. Standard rates, of course."

"Of course," Aahz said with a grin. I looked from one to the other.

"Aahz, what's all this about? These are the people who've been trying to throw us off for the better part of a month! They're the enemy!"

"Not at all, Skeeve. You never approached them with any kind of a deal that would interest them."

"A *deal*? What kind of a deal?"

"A profitable one," Aahz said, looking smug. "For both of us. I've just offered them full syndication and publication rights to my side of the election story. They're going to give me full coverage so they can make special collector's editions of the papers later on. In the meantime, I give them exclusive content. One month after the election, they get to bind the whole set and sell them."

"Clothbound and leather," Clea said, proudly. "And boxed sets."

"That's not fair," Ecstra said. "He's only one of the people running! What about Mr. Weavil and Mr. Weavil-Scuttil?"

"Miss Talkweather," Tolomi said heartily. "I wondered how these Klahds found their way. Have some wine!"

"No, sir," Ecstra said. "I'm on duty."

"We must cover the other candidates, as well," Romses put in. "We must be fair, or at least feign the semblance of impartiality."

"Sure!" Aahz said expansively. He held out his glass. Clea flicked a hand, and a bottle came to upend itself over it. Ruby-red wine poured out. "What's a story without antagonists? This could go big. We could see it on the Crystal Ethernet one day. It could make us all rich!"

"Hear, hear!" Tolomi said heartily.

"Aahz, why are you helping him?" I turned to accuse the Syndication. "You've been preventing this election from taking place for years!"

Tolomi shook his head at my denseness. "We have decided to let it go forward because we have now had it demonstrated that there's substantial profit to be made out of it, son. Aahz here showed us how we can increase our circulation for the short run, and then we'll have a product that can sell for years. And once he's elected, it's going to be a very interesting term of office, isn't it, Aahz?"

"You bet," Aahz said, glugging down the entire bottle of wine. "Hey, got another one of those?"

"Right here, my friend." Tolomi floated a bottle to him. The cork popped in midair. The sparkling wine foamed out. Not a drop splashed on the ground.

"Aahz, what about your speech? Shomi was looking everywhere for you!"

Aahz regarded me with impatience. "What about it? It'll wait. This is more important."

"No, it's not!"

"Well, you got what you wanted," Aahz said. "Voting Day is a lock for next week. Want a drink? Bunny? How about you?"

"No, thanks," I said. I doubted I could swallow anything.

"No, Aahz. I'm still on duty myself. I have to tell Shomi where you are."

"She'll see it in tomorrow's paper," Tolomi said. "Miss Talkweather, I admire your tenaciousness. You know, Aahz, she has tried for weeks to get me to reverse my stance, but business is business. You can have the exclusive on this article." He looked at his fellow editors. "Agreed?"

"Oh, yes, agreed," Clea said. "I can see her on our council one day."

"It's your story, Talkweather. Make it good. And"—he regarded her speculatively—"how would political editor on the *Gossip* sound to you? Think you can do it?"

"Yes, sir!" Ecstra saluted with her pencil to her forehead. She flipped open her notebook to a fresh page. "Sir, may I ask you some questions, for the record?"

"Go ahead," Tolomi said, taking a drag on his cigar. "Make sure you spell all the names right."

"First of all, when did you start controlling the timing of the election?"

Gleep, Bunny, and I left them there. I felt bemused and depressed.

"So he's really going to leave us," Bunny said, as we trudged out through the endless dark corridors. "I'm so sorry, Skeeve." She squeezed my arm.

I shrugged. "He's done a lot of things in his life. I guess it was time for him to find something else and move on. We don't have to like change, but it's a part of life."

"It's good you feel that way," Bunny said. "That makes it a little easier, I suppose."

I looked at her in surprise.

"Makes what easier?" I asked.

"Oh, nothing," she said, brightly. "At least we can stop worrying about the election."

CHAPTER THIRTY-SIX

"If a tool is appropriate to the situation,
I'd use it."

—A. LINCOLN

"Do you see?" Ecstra said, proudly, as we appeared in Tipicanoo the next morning. She pointed to the first column on page one of the *Morning Gossip*. The article was by *Ecstra Talkweather, Political Editor*. "I am so thrilled that I could toss a paper onto every doorstep on the island!"

"Congratulations on the promotion!" I said, spreading out the page so I could read it. The story covered the entire front page and continued on the following three, with links to features throughout the issue. It was sprinkled with photographs and boldfaced quotes. "How long were you there last night?"

"Hours!" Ecstra said. "I'm running on pure adrenaline. This is what I dreamed journalism would be like when I started out as a cub. And Tolomi said he was proud of me! He even gave me a new hatband. It's an editor's band. Black and white and red all over!" She showed us her fedora.

"Very nice," Bunny said admiringly.

"But I want you to read my article," she said. "I want your

immediate reaction to the facts as they were revealed to this reporter last night, in an exclusive interview."

I could see why Tolomi was pleased with her. Written in the top-down style of newspapers in most dimensions, information went from the most important to the least important, paragraph by paragraph and line by line. Her concise, crisp style didn't play favorites. She covered every part of the situation, even revealing in detail the ongoing subterfuge that had kept the candidates from selecting an election day for five years. I was surprised at the depth of detail. The plot went far deeper than I had dreamed. I knew Deveels who would drool with envy at the Syndication's machinations.

"Won't this make everyone on the island angry with the editors?" Bunny asked.

"Oh, no," Ecstra said, with an airy wave. "There's nothing people like more than a sensational story. This has it all! Intrigue! Deals made in smoke-filled rooms! An underdog pulling ahead of the favorites in spite of the odds against him! In the end, the people are the winners, because they get the very best candidate for the job! Your friend Aahz had lots of plans for the future. I was very impressed with him. He deserves the endorsement of the *Morning Gossip*!"

"Do you ever get dizzy spinning that much?" Bunny asked.

"All part of the job," Ecstra said. "I only stated the facts and quoted the people involved in the story. I did not editorialize at all."

We had to admit she was right. Her narration was straightforward. It was the quotes and pictures that gave the impression that Aahz was the only honest candidate in the field. In the middle of page one was a picture of Aahz shaking hands with Tolomi. Underneath was a quote from the Plague Party candidate, promising a clean, fair election with plenty of action and excitement, at bargain prices. "I won't extort every copper coin out of you, like my opponents have been doing for five years," Aahz was quoted as saying.

"That's not true," Bunny said.

"But it's what he said," Ecstra insisted.

"I'll talk to him about that," I said. Haranguing one's rivals was one thing; outright lies were another.

On page eight, I came across the image of the waving dummies in Aahz's front yard. I groaned.

"Why did you have to print that?" I asked.

"Sorry," Ecstra said. "Tolomi insisted that we use it. It happened, after all. He had a very clear description of it from one of the other reporters who was present, and the typesetter picked up on it right away. I am on my way to interview the other candidates and get their feedback on this issue."

Needless to say, Emo and Wilmer did not have such a positive reaction to the article. I went to the town square to deliver our daily briefing to Sid the She. Both the Friendship Party candidate and his Wisdom Party counterpart were there, pacing up and back until they saw me. Sid looked relieved. She hurried up the stairs into the gazebo as the candidates made for me.

"I have an announcement to make, and your lady there won't listen to me!" Wilmer said, storming over with a handful of newspapers. The whites of his eyes were red, from equal parts fury and hangover.

"Sid has orders to receive updates from me or Bunny only," I said. "That's to prevent anyone from giving her inaccurate information. It's worked so far."

"Well, this is accurate!" Wilmer thundered. He shook the newspapers at me until the figures in the images had to hold on to their frames to keep from falling off the page. "Did you read this outrageous nonsense?"

"I did," I said. "But you have to admit it's good to get the newspapers back in step with local events."

"Local balderdash!" Wilmer said. "He's soiling our public image! Outright fabrications! I was prepared to let things go after . . . after I went home last night, but that little reporter girl was on my doorstep while I was taking an asp—before I was ready to speak to her, and she thrust this in my face!"

It was page eight. In fact, the picture was worse the more I looked at it.

"I'm sorry about that," I said. "I didn't think they should have printed it, but I was told it was an editorial decision."

"Never mind whether they should have printed it!" Wilmer said, his voice ringing off the surrounding buildings. "Your friend shouldn't have done it!"

"And now it looks as if he has bribed his way into the heart of every newspaper in town," Emo said. "We were better off when they were ignoring us! This humiliation is going to be immortalized in leatherbound special editions!"

I winced, remembering the sweetheart deal Aahz had struck the night before. "Look, I spoke with all of the editors last night. They promised that they would cover all three of you equally. You'll have your chance to get your views into the papers. And we have several more events before Voting Day. The public will have plenty of opportunity to make an intelligent choice between the three of you."

Wilmer lowered his brows. "No, he won't! Soon there will be only two candidates again!"

"What?" I asked. "Are you leaving the race?"

"No," Wilmer said. He drew himself up and struck a statesmanlike pose. "I cannot take the abusive behavior of your friend any longer. I had a happy moment when I thought he was gone for good! But now he is back, and more trouble than he was before! I am going to challenge him to a duel! At least *one* of us won't have to put up with the other afterward."

"You can't do that!" I said in horror, remembering what Carnelia had said about his skills. Wilmer gave me a hard look.

"Can't I, son? Come with me and see!"

He turned on his heel and marched out of the square. Emo hurried to catch up with him.

Sid appeared beside me before I knew it. I caught a glimpse of her skeletal face out of the corner of my eye, and jumped.

"Sorry," she said. "What about it? Should I mention the duel? The hour is close when I make my announcements."

"No," I said. "I'm going to take care of this. Here." I felt in my belt pouch for the briefing that Bunny and I had prepared. "No changes, all right? I am going to stop it if I can."

"Good luck!" Sid called to me as I rushed after Emo and Wilmer.

"Wilmer, please," I said, all but running alongside them as they hiked up the hill. A herd of reporters had gotten word of something in the wind and pursued us, blocking traffic as we went around the hairpin bend toward Aahz's townhouse. "Violence isn't going to help."

Wilmer stopped and put a fatherly hand on my shoulder.

"Mr. Skeeve," he said. "There are times when you are going to have to decide if your honor is more or less precious than your life."

"I understand, sir, but it's not worth it! I mean, Aahz was only trying to make a fool of you—both of you."

"That part I understand very well."

He wouldn't listen to any more of my explanations. When we reached the door of the townhouse, he banged on it and pulled the bell rope. I heard clanging inside.

The door opened. Farnsward peered out at us.

"Yes, gentlemen?" he inquired.

"I want to see Aahz!" Wilmer demanded.

The butler looked sympathetic. "I am sorry, sir, but he wishes me to tell you, and I quote, that he 'ain't here.'"

"Well, he might be able to get away with that kind of bad grammar in Deva," Wilmer said, "but this is Tipicanoo! Step aside!"

"Of course, sir." Farnsward made way for us with a gracious bow.

Aahz didn't make us look for him. He was lounging in the library just off the main reception hall, with a Tipp beautician sitting on a stool by his side, filing his toenails.

He grinned as Wilmer strode in. "Hey, guys, how's it going? You see the papers? Biggest media event that this backwater burb has ever seen!"

"You had better believe I have seen them," Wilmer said. He stalked over to Aahz, brandished the sheaf of papers, and slapped him across the face with them, then back. "I demand satisfaction from you, sir."

Aahz waved the pedicurist aside and sprang to his feet. "I accept the challenge, pal."

"No, Aahz!" I pleaded.

He looked at me, his eyebrows raised. "You don't expect me to refuse, do you? I'm no coward. You want to finish this right here, Weavil-Scuttil?"

"No," Wilmer said, smacking the newspapers into his own palm. "We will do this is the correct and time-honored tradition."

"And if he doesn't finish you, then I will," Emo said. "Uh . . ." He took the papers from Wilmer and smacked Aahz on one cheek. He tried to hit the other side, but Aahz snatched the roll out of his hands.

"Don't push it, buddy," Aahz snarled, crumpling them into a ball and tossing them over his shoulder. "I accept yours, too. My second will call upon you this afternoon."

"Good," Wilmer said. "We will see you on the field of honor. Good day, sir!"

He spun on his heel and walked away. Emo hopped to get ahead of him and held the door for him. Wilmer strode through it, magnificent in his fury. Emo shot a reproachful look over his shoulder at Aahz, then slammed the door behind them.

Aahz slapped his hands together and rubbed them gleefully.

"I didn't think those guys had it in them!" Aahz chortled.

"Why aren't you upset?" I asked. "They want to kill you?"

"Will you act as my second, Skeeve?" Aahz asked. "You're the best friend I have."

"Sure I will," I said. "Look, Aahz, they're serious! Why are you so eager to get into a fight with these fellows?"

"I'm not," Aahz assured me.

"But Wilmer is an expert with flaming blades! He could cut you to pieces!"

"He won't get a chance."

He wasn't listening to me. "Carnelia said he used to be a champion. He's not soft, and he's not a coward. He wouldn't have issued the challenge if he didn't think he had at least a chance of winning. In any case, he could hurt you."

"But as the challenged party, the choice of weapons is mine," Aahz said, showing all his teeth. "Once you show them what they'll be fighting with, there won't be a duel. I promise you that."

He pulled out his D-hopper, pushed the button, and vanished.

BAMF!

"Wait a minute, Aahz!" I shouted.

"Sir?"

I jumped, for the second time that day. It was the butler. He seemed to be able to transport himself from place to place, only without a sound.

"What is it, Farnsward?"

"If you would like to wait, Mr. Aahz wanted you to enjoy some refreshments. Also, if you would care to avail yourself of the manicurist, she comes highly recommended."

The girl gave me a little wave.

"Uh, no, thanks," I said. "But I could use a drink."

Farnsward disappeared as if by magik and returned with a glass and a small carafe on a tray. He poured the wine for me. I drank half of it in one gulp.

"Please sit down, sir. Mr. Aahz assures you he will not be long." The small smile touched the corners of his mouth. "He says it will be worth your while."

"Farnsward?"

"Yes, sir?"

"Are butlers supposed to have a sense of humor?"

The Tipp drew himself up and gave me an austere stare. "Three years' intensive training, sir! I have certification from the Amusement Training Facility of Greater Tipicanoo. There are branches in every well-educated dimension, of course, sir."

Personally, I'd never had any dealings with the ATF, nor did I want to. "Thanks, Farnsward."

"At your service, sir."

As the butler promised, Aahz was gone only a short time. He was carrying three handsome red lacquered boxes.

"Take these to my wannabe adversaries," Aahz said. "I will bet you a thousand gold pieces that there will be no more talk about duels or honor or anything else."

I was shocked. Aahz never made a wager that might conceivably cost him money, let alone a fortune like that.

"What are they?" I asked.

He raised the lid on one of the chests. I looked inside.

"No bet," I said.

"No problem," Aahz said. "I didn't think you'd take it."

I accepted the boxes, preparing to leave, then hesitated. Aahz looked at me curiously.

"Something on your mind, kid?"

"Yes. Something's been bothering me for several days," I said.

"Yeah, Skeeve?"

I took a deep breath. Aahz hated to be told what to do, but I was the authority here. I didn't have a choice but to try.

"The others have a point, you know. You're waging an unfair campaign by bribing officials and buying votes with fancy gifts. It's completely uneven. They signed an agreement to run the campaign under certain strictures or face penalties. They can't spend more than a copper piece on gifts per person. Having you come in like a wild card and do whatever you want is leaving them in the dust. That's not fair. I'd appreciate it if you'd lay off. They can't compete with you. It's not life and death. You don't have to stomp them into the ground to win."

Aahz let a long, slow smile spread across his face. "Sure thing, Skeeve. No more gifts or bribes."

I raised my eyebrows. "Just like that?"

"All you had to do was ask, partner." Aahz grinned. "I know I can win without the window dressing. As long as you don't tell me I can't call them names anymore. Let me know what they say about the boxes."

I grinned back. "That will be my pleasure."

I had arranged to meet Wilmer and Emo in our office just before sunset. Wilmer wanted a public location, but I managed to convince him that it would be better to work out the details in private.

"Sir," I said, holding out the chest. "My friend's weapon of choice."

I whipped open the box. The smell, which could not be readily contained there or anywhere in the Bazaar where they were sold, filled the room. The Tipps looked inside at the small brown heap nestled in the green velvet interior.

"Is that Pervert serious?" Wilmer asked. I had arranged to meet him and Emo at our office. "What *is* it?"

"That's Per-*vect*, Mr. Weavil-Scuttil," I said, innocently. Bunny was behind me, hardly daring to breathe. If I met her eyes, she would have collapsed in hysterical giggles. "It's a Genuine Fake Doggie Doodle with the Realistic Smell That Really Sticks to Your Hands. It's a best-selling item in the Bazaar."

Emo and Wilmer exchanged horrified looks.

"I thought he would choose swords! Or knives! Or cannons! Or magik!" Wilmer exclaimed.

"He's good with all of those weapons," I said, "but this is really his style. What time tomorrow morning do you want to meet him? I have to let the newspapers know so they can send a reporter to cover the duel."

At the word *newspapers*, both their eyes grew wide.

"I . . . I . . . I . . . withdraw the challenge!" Wilmer sputtered.

"Me, too!" stammered Emo.

I was sympathetic. "If you really want to take him on, gentlemen, it would be safer, not to mention more effective, to beat
Aahz in the debate. I think you could really shine there. It's
two days to the election, you know, and anything goes."

"Anything?" Emo asked, his question ending on a high
note.

"Well, anything within reason," I said, concerned by the
sly look the two of them exchanged. They left our office, whispering together.

"I wondered if Aahz wouldn't have been better off with
swords at dawn," Bunny said.

CHAPTER THIRTY-SEVEN

*"You can always tell a politician is lying if
his mouth is moving."*

—CONVENTIONAL WISDOM

Bunny and I sat at a little table set on the right side of
the stage, watching the preparations being made for the
debate. I glanced at the sky. It was only a few minutes
before noon. The day was fine and dry. I had arranged with the
local weather wizards to hold off the storm that had been brewing
along the southwest coast of Bokromi. Once we were finished,
I didn't care what happened, but for an hour and a half, I wanted
as few variables as possible. Gleep lay behind us, snoozing with
his head tucked into his belly. I wanted him well rested in case
he was needed.

Since there were three candidates, we couldn't sit between
them, so we had the lecterns arranged in a line on stage left at
a slight angle so we could see the candidates' faces. Each desk
was painted the color of the appropriate party: purple, gold, or
green. I had to admit it was festive. The candidates took their
places: Wilmer on the left, Aahz in the middle, and Emo on the

right. Their campaign managers, magicians, and assistants bustled around them, making them look as gubernatorial as possible. Unfortunately, it looked as though the lecterns had been made all the same height, with adult male Tipps in mind.

"This is great," Aahz bellowed, waving an arm from behind his lectern, "if they only want to see the top of my head!"

"Are you kidding me?" Shomitamoni demanded, grabbing one of the carpenters by the arm. "This is ridiculous! Get Aahz a box to stand on, or something!"

"It just can't be helped if he is shorter than Wilmer," Carnelia said, looking as though she would gladly have supplied a box if she could have stuffed Shomi into it.

"They must start off on an equal footing!" Shomi said. "It is through their ideas they will set themselves apart!"

"No artificial elevation is going to help your candidate with that!" Orlow said.

"As if yours isn't spouting stale apothogems from half a decade ago!" Shomi retorted sourly.

No issue seemed too small to fight over. Tension filled the air. This was the final event before the polls opened in the morning for Voting Day, and everyone knew this was their last chance to make a good impression before the public went to the polls.

The Friendship Party and the Wisdom Party had canceled all joint appearances since the day Aahz accepted Wilmer's challenge. That pretty much left the field to Aahz, who had taken full advantage of it. He seemed to be everywhere at once in Bokromi. He handed out prizes at a children's track-and-field meet, opened a store, and held a fund-raiser at which Shomitamoni shook down everyone who got within a block of the event.

He made more than his share of headlines, too. Aahz never missed a chance to slam the opposition in print. Everywhere he went, he would stop suddenly and offer a stump speech on the issues, calling the sanity and intelligence of his opponents into question where they disagreed with him. Ecstra and the other reporters were always at his heels, shouting questions. Aahz never heard a question he didn't enjoy answering. I was annoyed that he was still telling outright lies about Emo and Wilmer. Bunny couldn't convince me that it was typical of politics.

He spent freely on parties every evening, shook hands and pinched cheeks. He became the darling of the reporters, always good for a sensational statement in time for the deadline.

I had to hand it to Emo and Wilmer. They showed amazing restraint in the face of Aahz's outrageous antics. When asked about his statements, they allowed themselves to be quoted in the *Morning Gossip* and other papers that they were holding out for the debate. "We want to give the best example of our character in an organized setting," Emo had said.

I wondered what we were in for.

My suspicions were raised further when Orlow came to lean over the backs of our chairs.

"Mr. Skeeve, Miss Bunny," he said in a low voice. "How are you all today?"

"Fine," I said, suddenly wary. "What can I do for you?"

He beamed at me. "Glad you asked. Nothing. I would hope you will do *absolutely* nothing. Don't interfere in anything you see. I promise that no one's gonna get hurt . . . who doesn't deserve to."

I frowned. "I can't make a promise like that."

Orlow leaned closer.

"Please, Mr. Skeeve, I think it would be safer for everyone if you do, a master magician like you. Things might get just a little . . . free-spirited."

Bunny put a hand on mine.

"It's fine," she told Orlow. "He won't interfere. Neither of us will."

"Thanks, ma'am. You won't regret it."

Bunny raised an eyebrow. "Yes, I will, but that's all right. By tomorrow night I intend to be neck deep in a bubble bath surrounded by scented candles with a book and a glass of wine, and Gleep will have orders to eat anyone who even *mentions* the word *politics* to me. Shall we get started?"

"Yes, ma'am," Orlow said with alacrity. He went over to Carnelia and whispered to her. They withdrew to the side of the stage, where chairs had been placed for all three campaign managers. I studied the candidates. My heart was in the pit of my stomach. If Aahz did well in the debate, it could propel him so far ahead that he couldn't help but be elected. I didn't want him to leave M.Y.T.H., Inc., though I'd never interfere with his ambitions. He was by far the most forthright and vocal of the candidates. Against him the other two seemed so . . . weak.

I noticed Mrs. Weavil Senior in the audience, clutching her handbag on her lap. Behind her were dozens of Emo supporters, each with a bag or some other container. To her left was Wilmer's nephew and chief rabble rouser, plus numerous Wilmer fans in purple, similarly furnished with hold-alls and lunch buckets. I knew none of the latter actually contained anything that had been edible for at least a week.

"Uh-oh," I said. I soaked up plenty of magik from the force lines and started to weave a barrier to protect the candidates from the audience.

"Don't," Bunny said.

I gestured at the crowd, now in the thousands. "But they've got mud! And vegetables!"

"Let it happen," Bunny said. "This is everyone's chance to get out everything that they've been holding in for a month. Goodness knows I feel like heaving a few turnips myself."

"All right," I said. I let my magik die away, but I felt power building up all around me.

Bunny stood up and tinkled her little silver bell. To my surprise, the entire audience quieted down so much that I could hear birdsong in the meadow beyond it.

Her voice rang out and was carried by the Echoes to the rear of the crowd. "Welcome to the final event in Bokromi's election circuit, the last debate between the candidates. On the left, please welcome the candidate for the Wisdom Party, Mr. Wilmer Weavil-Scuttil."

"Booo!" yelled an Emo supporter in the front row.

"Yay!" bellowed the entire purple contingent.

"On the right, Mr. Emo Weavil, from the Friendship Party."

"Booo!"

"Yay!"

"And finally, in the center, please welcome Aahz, candidate for the A Plague on Both Your Houses Party."

"Booooooooooo!" Both fan bases crowding the stage voiced their displeasure.

"Yaaaaaay!" came from hundreds, if not thousands, of Tipps ranged behind them.

"Let me just start by saying I shouldn't be on the same stage as these losers," Aahz said. "They might steal the wallet out of my pocket!"

The crowd roared with laughter.

"Now, just a minute!" Wilmer protested.

"I'm not a loser!" Emo said. "And I don't steal trash!"

"Hold it!" I said. "First of all, the debate hasn't started. Second, the public has let us know that they want honesty from you about your plans if you are elected governor."

Aahz produced a smile that showed all of his teeth. "Sure! I have all kinds of programs ready to go."

"As do I," Wilmer said.

"I have already been working on a project for my first hundred days in office," Emo said.

"Good," I said, rising. I reached into my belt pouch. From it I took three little Xs made of gold. "Then you won't mind putting these on."

Aahz recoiled. As an aficionado of Beliaz's Joke Shop in the Bazaar, he surely knew what they were.

"Now, wait just a minute, Skeeve. That's not fair!"

"What are they?" Emo asked.

"Honesty Monitors," Aahz said glumly. I pasted one to the middle of his chest.

"Do you swear to tell the truth throughout this entire debate, cross your heart and hope to die?" I asked. Aahz gave me a sly look.

"Well . . . I . . . Ow! All right, yes!" The little X dug its four tines into his skin. "You didn't have to resort to measures like this!"

"Yes, I did," I said. "I've been reading the papers for the last week."

Aahz wobbled a hand in the air.

"Maybe I did stretch the truth a little." We both saw the X rear up again. "Okay! I lied through my teeth!"

I swore in the other two and attached Honesty Monitors to them. When they were fixed in place, I stepped back.

"Okay," I said, dusting my hands together. "We can get started."

"Mr. Weavil-Scuttil, you're evading the question," Bunny said, not for the first time. The stage was littered with expired vegetables and a spreading mud puddle my father's pigs would have adored. The candidates had avoided many of the missiles, but plenty of them had struck home. Wilmer's beautiful white coat was dyed red and green from the tomatoes and melons that had hit him. Emo had huge gray mud polka dots all over his gaudy clothes. Aahz's face was encrusted with rotten garlic that no one but a Pervect could have tolerated. So far, our side of the stage was clear.

Wilmer ducked sideways to avoid a mudball thrown by Emo's mother. "Well, ma'am, it's hard to think with things being thrown at me while being pinched by this fiendish con-traption!"

"Not Fiendish," I pointed out. "Deveelish. Fiendish brooches don't distinguish between truth and lies. They just hurt the person wearing them."

"I stand corrected," Wilmer said. A stalk of celery, gray

with age, came hurtling out of the crowd and winged his shoulder. "Confound it!"

"Mr. Weavil-Scuttil, on what grounds do you call Aahz a ruthless profiteer?" Bunny asked again.

"No one can ever say that I have called my opponent a ruthless profiteer," Wilmer declared, hand high as if swearing an oath. "No, indeed! Nor have I referred to him as the scourge of all things decent. I leave my constituents to draw their own conclusions!"

"You're drawing things out pretty clearly for them," Aahz said. "All the money that has been collected by my able associate, Shomi, has been used for my campaign, and to enrich the good people of Bokromi. Not one copper piece has gone into my pocket for personal gain."

He didn't wince at all. The Honesty Monitor glowed. I was as surprised as anyone that what he said was true.

"What about you, Mr. Weavil?" Bunny asked.

Emo was just as forthright. He banged his fingertip down on his lectern. "I have *not* referred to my opposite number as an unscrupulous scalawag, a terror to society, and a blight on the landscape who causes drought just by looking at a field. No, I haven't! And anyone who says I have will have to show me in writing just where I did."

"What do we know about this Pervert?" Wilmer added, pointing at Aahz. "Just what he tells us. We can't check up on him. We don't know if he's bilked senior citizens out of their last coin. We don't know if he inveigles schoolchildren into robbing houses for him. We have just his say-so, and the reputation of his people!"

"I have a reputation for being completely honest and aboveboard in all my dealings," Aahz said. He winced as the Honesty Monitor dug in. That one had to hurt. "Calling my character into question is definitely two pots making personal remarks about the kettle."

That provoked a barrage from the audience. Clumps of sod

274 JODY LYNN NYE

sailed toward Aahz. He flicked a finger at the incoming missiles. Most of them went flying to either side, further dirtying his opponents. I knew Shomi was behind his defense. She scarcely moved a muscle. I admired her control.

"Both of them have held back giving straightforward reports to the press for weeks!" Aahz said. "Now, when I'm your governor, I will confer daily with the newspapers and other media. I want total transparency between the government and the people on the streets!"

"We weren't giving reports directly to the papers because they weren't *printing* them!" Wilmer bellowed.

"Do you deny you were holding back on them?"

"Well, no . . ." Wilmer said.

"Do you call *that* responsible campaigning?"

"I . . . uh . . . All necessary information was conveyed through outside contractors! We got the word out in *spite* of the papers!"

"So you decided to bypass the legitimate journals in favor of a scab performer and a bunch of messengers?" Aahz asked, rhetorically. "You might just as well have hired bloggers!"

"Hired what?" Emo asked. He glanced at Orlow for help. The campaign manager shrugged. "What does the timber industry have to do with the press?"

"Wood pulp is what they print on," Wilmer said, dismissively.

"I know that!"

"Then why ask?"

Bunny brought them back into line with a shake of her bell. They all turned to look at her.

"Can we get back to the *original* question?" she said, pointedly. "What are your plans to straighten out the finances of this island? They've been ignored for over five years. I'm sure the voters out there would like to hear your thoughts."

"Public safety is a chief concern," Wilmer said. "I plan to assess where funding is needed and where it is not, then apply capital as seems appropriate to me."

"Sounds like a stunning revelation," Aahz said. "If you like the obvious. Doesn't it make sense to do a comprehensive audit and see where fat can be trimmed before talking about adding revenue?"

"Fair enough, Mr. Aahz," Wilmer said, holding on to his lapels. They were not as white as they had been at the beginning of the debate. "What about *your* plans to increase spending in the fire and rescue department?"

"As far as I know, they're just like yours," Aahz said, nonchalantly. Wilmer's nephew sent a bucket of slop hurtling toward him. Aahz flipped a hand, and the pail upended in the middle of the stage with a juicy splash. "Only without the added ten percent for the special interests. I'm not from around here, so I can budget without my feelings getting involved."

Wilmer sputtered. "Now, wait just a minute, my plans aren't padded!"

"So you didn't leave any room for contingencies?" Aahz asked. "Tsk, tsk. I guess you saved all your planning to call me names. Would you say that was a pretty fair assessment?"

The audience broke into spontaneous applause.

"No! I . . . that's not . . . he's twisting my words!" Wilmer said.

Aahz grinned. "They're so eminently twistable."

Bamf!

"Hey, Bunny-honey!"

CHAPTER THIRTY-EIGHT

"A rose by any other name still has thorns."

—A. TITCHMARSH

Both Bunny and I turned in the direction of the voice. Cousin Sylvia appeared on the edge of the stage with Gascon the Deveel beside her. She wore a skin-tight green satin dress that rose about six inches above her knees. The tight skirt made it hard for her to climb the stairs, but she bustled up to us and leaned over to give me a kiss on the cheek. I tried hard not to look down her dress.

"Hey, Skeevie-pie," she said, fluffing up my hair with her long nails. "You're looking divine."

"Uh, thanks, Sylvia," I said, feeling my cheeks turn scarlet. "Look, we've got this debate going on . . ."

Bunny was more direct.

"Sylvia, we're busy. Not now."

Sylvia pouted.

"Yes, now. Uncle Bruce is in a sky-high snit, and your mother wants you there to help settle things. Skeeve can handle this silly little debate. Can't you, Skeeeeeevie-pie?"

I was all too aware that everything she said could be heard by thousands of people in the audience. The three candidates and their managers grinned at me.

"All right," Bunny said, resigned. She gave me an apologetic glance. "Do you mind?"

"No!" I said. "I hope it isn't trouble."

"I hope not," she said. "Thanks." She passed the bell to me and followed Sylvia down the steps. Gascon drew his magik circle, and the three of them vanished.

BAMF!

"Okay," I said, ringing the bell for order. "Let's get back to the debate, all right?"

"Sure, Skeeeeeve," Aahz said, drawing out the vowel in my name, though he didn't continue the jeer.

"Yes, sir!" Emo said. "To answer the question that my opponents have already covered, I say that it will be incumbent upon me as governor to make public inquiries, comprehensive ones, to see what the people are thinking! I want to know what they need as well as what they want!"

"Are you kidding?" Aahz said. "Given a chance, the public will always vote itself a raise. Now, I have no intention of asking anyone what I should be spending. They'll find out when the bill hits the legislature. They're electing me to make the hard decisions for them, and I will."

Emo frowned at him. "I thought you just said you favored transparency in government."

Aahz looked taken aback. "That's not exactly what I said!"

"But you did! It was just a few minutes ago."

Aahz leaned over the lectern and grinned at the audience as if taking them into his confidence. "You must have heard me wrong."

The crowd wearing yellow *Vote for Aahz* ribbons laughed.

"No, I'm sure that's exactly what you said!"

Aahz's fans threw water bladders at Emo. The Friendship Party candidate went wide-eyed when he saw them coming. He ducked underneath his lectern.

SPLASH!

When he came up again, his fur was plastered to his skull. At least the water had washed some of the mud off.

"Not only that," Aahz added, "I favor restricting information when it might be unnecessarily embarrassing to my administration."

"Okay, Aahz," I said, holding up a hand. "I heard you, too. You're contradicting yourself."

"With this thing doing an outpatient coronary bypass on me?" Aahz asked, pointing at the Honesty Monitor. "You've got to be kidding."

"I don't know how you're scamming it, but stop it."

Aahz turned to his fans. "Do you think that sounds fair and impartial? It doesn't sound impartial to me."

"Boooo, Skeeve! Boooo, Skeeve!" the crowd chanted.

Suddenly, bushels of leaking tomatoes came hurtling in *my* direction. I threw up the biggest magik shield I could make. Just before they hit it, I felt it dissipate. I was left openmouthed as the tomatoes struck and exploded, covering my hair, my face, and my clothes with acid juice. I fell backward to the stage. The tomatoes were followed by soggy grapes, mushy peaches, and wilting lettuce. I scrambled to my feet and grabbed for my chair. My shoes slid in the ankle-deep mound of sludge. I wiped my face and glared at Aahz.

"Don't look at me," Aahz said, his face blank with innocence. "You know I couldn't have done that."

I felt my temper rising.

"Well, if you—?"

Another would-be compost heap catapulted toward me. I fell to my knees. I pictured a steel umbrella over my head and pushed all the power I had into it.

TWACK TWACK TWACK TWACK TWACK!

SPLUSH!

My umbrella gave out unexpectedly. The rain of rotting vegetation covered me like a shower of manure. I squeezed my eyes closed until the pelting stopped. I spat out sweet, mealy pulp. I smelled like the back room of a tavern. My feet slipping with every step, I stood up and confronted the candidates.

"Who did that?" I demanded. I looked at Emo and Wilmer. Both Tipps were grinning like idiots. "Which one of you was responsible for that?"

They pointed at each other.

"I promise you, sir," Wilmer said, his lips twitching, "I did not deprive you of your protective spell, nor did I heave a single piece of produce in your direction."

"It wasn't me," Emo said, fluttering his false eyelashes. "You're our judge! I treat you with respect! Ooch!" He clutched his chest, and held up a hand in surrender. "Perhaps I encouraged my fans a little. I'm sorry! I won't do it again!"

"All right," I said, fighting down my ire. Bunny would be angry with me if I lost my temper again. "That's a point against you. Let's get started again."

I brushed bunches of sagging grapes off my chair and slid into it. The silver bell was nowhere to be seen. Clearing my throat, I addressed the candidates.

"Would each one of you give a brief statement of your vision for the future of Bokromi, say ten years down the road?"

Emo held up a finger.

"Yes, Mr. Weavil? You can go first."

"I think everybody is just tired of the politics as usual. We want to set up trade with some of the provinces that are near us, but frankly, they don't trust us. We have to show them we will be easy to deal with. That we're open for business!"

"That's only half the story," Wilmer said, leaning back and holding on to his right-hand lapel. "They want us to have strong leadership in place. It doesn't mean a thing to have us say we're friendly if all they find is chaos!"

"Neither of you clowns is the whole package," Aahz said. "I am. In me, Bokromi will have a successful businessman who knows how to identify commodities as well as open markets. I'll welcome businesses who want to set up shop here and show them the best way to appeal to the Tipp population."

"If they don't turn tail and run when they see you!" Wilmer said, bobbing back and forth. The Wisdom Party hooted and laughed.

"So you're only going to trade with other Tipps?" Aahz asked. "That'll take you further on the road to poverty."

"No! But we will choose our trading partners based on trust."

"The only real criterion for trade is common interest in making a profit," Aahz said. "How you protect yourself from getting cheated is up to you. If it isn't already too late for that."

"Ooooh!" Aahz's supporters loved that. They waved their pictures of him.

"Well, you *are* the expert on cheating," Emo said.

I swiped banana peels off the table and found the scorepad. I should have known better. After promising that they would stay clean and straightforward, they'd gone straight to dirty and sordid.

"Another point, Mr. Weavil," I warned him.

"Boooo!" howled the Friendship Party.

Mrs. Weavil Senior led the attack that time. She smacked me right in the chest with a well-aimed mudball.

"Stop it!" I said.

"Oh, Mom," Emo said, mildly.

"Her aim's deteriorating," Wilmer said, pointing.

"No, it isn't!"

Wilmer shook his head. "Are you joking? Last year that would have hit him in the face! Why, I remember my speech on Harbor Day when she caught me with my mouth open. That was some throwing."

"Well, your nephew tosses a mean tomato," Emo said.

I waved my hands. "No one is going to hit me in the face with anything!"

SMACK! SMACK!

From two directions at once, mushy handfuls slapped me on each cheek. I wiped tomato *and* mud out of my eyes.

"Cut it out," I warned the candidates. "You're encouraging them!"

"Who, us?" Aahz asked, innocently.

Everyone in the audience laughed loudly. The candidates tried to look solemn and dignified, but they couldn't stop grinning.

"As your moderator, I expect a certain amount of respect," I said.

I got my answer as a veritable storm of rotting produce came hurtling out of the audience at me. I repelled some of it, but I couldn't keep it all off. Slime poured down my shirt and into my pants and boots. I started plucking missiles out of midair and tossing them back. Was there a single vegetable left anywhere else in Bokromi?

"Haw haw haw!"

Aahz was laughing. So were Emo and Wilmer.

I looked down at the mess around my feet. Reaching down into the force line that ran beneath the stage, I sucked in so much magik that it felt as if it were leaking out of my ears. I pictured gigantic brooms sweeping the bushels of spoiled fruit and vegetables until it made one horrible, unsavory blob the size of a swimming pool. I rolled up my sleeves and stretched out my fingers. The blob rose from the stage, quivering and roiling.

"Oh, no, Mr. Skeeve," Wilmer said in alarm. "You can't throw all that at us! That would be unethical!"

"After all," Emo said, nervously, "you are our moderator."

"C'mon, Skeeve, it's just a joke," Aahz added.

"I won't," I said, sounding calm, though the ire in my belly blazed like a volcano. I set the mass down on the stage. "I absolutely won't throw a single vegetable at you."

"Good," Aahz said. "You—"

Instead, I took all the magik at my disposal, picked up all three candidates from behind their lecterns, and dropped them into the soup.

SPLAT!

I dusted my hands together and sat down.

The audience was shocked silent for a moment, then broke into wild applause or jeers, depending on who was a supporter of whom. The reporters, Ecstra included, made copious notes. The Shutterbugs flew around our heads, snapping their wings, capturing the moment. I didn't know how the rainbow-colored carnage would look in a newspaper, but I knew I was going to find out.

Aahz, Emo, and Wilmer stumbled to their feet. Fur, scales, and clothes were completely covered with thick goo. I could smell rot on them where I sat. I was a little ashamed of myself, lowering myself to their level, but I had gotten all my anger out of my system. I was at peace.

"Shall we finish this?" I asked, pleasantly.

"Oh, my goodness!"

Bunny was back. I stood up, brushing at the sludge on my tunic. The others did their best to make themselves a little more presentable. She stepped up on the dais, picking her way gingerly between the burst vegetables. I hoisted up another bucket of magik and cleaned off her chair. It occurred to me that maybe I should do the same to myself. She gawked at the mess.

"What happened?" she demanded, planting her hands on her hips.

"Well . . ." I began.

"It's not really his fault, Miss Bunny," Wilmer said.

"We all got just a little playful," Emo added.

"It's nothing," Aahz said.

"Just Skeeve," Bunny said, firmly. "Well?"

I hemmed and hawed a little, but I had to come clean, in every sense of the word. Bunny listened, her huge blue eyes on my face. I noticed her cheeks beginning to twitch. Then her lips. Then her nose.

"And that was all you could think to do."

"Gee, I suppose so," I said, with a shrug.

Bunny gasped in her breath and let out a loud snort. She began laughing uproariously, not at all the measured and contained Bunny I had come to know. She pounded on the desk, slid out of her chair onto the floor, and kept laughing underneath it. The hollow sound echoed down the field. She waved a hand at me. I reached down to help her up.

"So you're not mad?" I asked.

Bunny's eyes twinkled. "Mad! I'm surprised it took you so long! They probably couldn't believe it, either."

"Truthfully, ma'am, there was nothing else he could do," Wilmer said, with a courtly bow.

Emo nodded. "I think we can safely say Mr. Skeeve proved that he has hidden depths that it is not wise to plumb very often."

"I was pretty impressed," Aahz said. "You have to applaud that kind of creative mayhem."

"Okay," Bunny said, taking a deep breath. "In that case, shall we get the rest of this over with? On the subject of education . . . ?"

"**. . . And that's my plan to reorganize the local councils. The** guilds and special-interest groups get a seat on the panel, but everybody will have a voice." Aahz cracked a section of dried sludge off one ear and ate it. His voice was as strong as ever, but half the audience had started to sway and nod off during the final half hour of his exposition. "I hope that answers your question."

Emo nodded, trying not to yawn openly. Aahz had bested him, in both length and argument. He couldn't outtalk him. I had never met the living creature who could. I was impressed. He had really thought about the topic and researched it to the smallest detail. He would make a great governor. And I would miss him.

Orlow cleared his throat. "May we have a moment?"

Bunny sighed. "Just one moment," she said. Our hopes of having the debate over in an hour and a half were long shattered. As long as the weather and the candidates held out, we had no choice but to let them continue. With Voting Day imminent, they were making use of every moment before their supporters.

Shomitamoni floated a half keg of beer to Aahz and cleaned him off while he drank it. Orlow and Carnelia had called their clients into a mutual huddle. I wondered what they were up to. I tried to listen in, but Carnelia had blocked out eavesdroppers. With reporters present, I couldn't blame them for wanting secrecy as they talked strategy.

With gleeful looks on their faces, they broke apart. The campaign managers retired to their seats. Carnelia gave Wilmer a thumbs-up.

"Mr. Aahz," Wilmer said, leaning back from his lectern and holding one of his filth-encrusted lapels, "you're making a lot of promises to people. You'll forgive me if they sound a little . . . outrageous in their scope?"

"What's wrong with thinking big?" Aahz asked.

"Will you keep those promises after you are elected?"

Aahz smiled at them, his four-inch teeth gleaming. "I'm a politician running for office. Of course you can believe me—as much as you believe any other candidate."

"But you, sir, are not any other candidate. In fact, you're a Pervert, sir, are you not?"

"We of the dimension of Perv prefer the term *Pervect*," Aahz said. He lowered his brows.

Wilmer grasped one of his food-spattered lapels and rocked back on his heels. "Well, we here on Tipicanoo like to call it like we see it, and what I see is a Per-*vert*. A squat, ugly Pervert. We have heard plenty of stories about people of your dimension. I figure this many stories get out, at least some of them have a chance of being true."

"Possibly. Possibly they're urban legends," Aahz said. His eyes were beginning to glow. I knew from long experience that meant trouble. He clenched his claws on his lectern. I knew Wilmer could see it. So could Emo.

"And maybe they're not. After all, if more people believe something than disbelieve it, it's probably true, isn't it?"

"For a long time everyone believed that thunder was caused by gods bowling," Aahz said. "That's only true in two dimensions I know, hardly a majority."

"What about the Perverts in Perv? What do they believe?"

I sat up straighter. So did Bunny. Gleep snaked his head up, his eyes wide and wary. We all expected Aahz to explode. I had never seen him swallow that particular insult. Normally he would have bellowed like a wounded dragon. I was impressed. He must really want to win the election. His eyes were bright yellow with ocher veins almost bursting off the surface of the orbs. He blinked twice and smiled gently at the audience, who were waiting with burning anticipation for his reaction.

When he spoke, his voice was calm and measured.

"You see, ladies and gentlemen, why I am the *only* viable candidate for this office? Because the opposition, who have wasted your time for five long years, can't resist making ethnic jokes at my expense." He looked at the audience, and his face turned tragic. "They're picking on me because of my origin. Now, I'm the last person who would play the race card, but if I did, wouldn't you say that I was justified?"

"You poor man!" a woman's voice cried from the audience.

Emo and Wilmer gasped. I was just as astonished. They'd been had. Aahz smiled. The audience's mood had turned against the local candidates. The reporters crowed with glee.

"Now, that's going too far!" Bunny said, recovering her wits. "Mr. Weavil and Mr. Weavil-Scuttil, that's a point against each of you. The rules say you can comment upon an opponent's behavior, but no personal remarks are allowed. Especially not icky nastiness like that! I'm surprised at you!"

I looked at them severely. I remembered why I had disliked both of them on sight a month ago.

"I wouldn't call that wise *or* friendly," I said. "If you really want to make points, you're going to have to start thinking differently."

"Yes, sir," Wilmer said, with a little bow. "I am very sorry. Please allow me to offer my apologies to you, Mr. Aahz."

"Me, too," Emo said.

"Don't let it happen again!" Bunny added.

"No, ma'am!" they chorused.

They both looked thoughtful. I hoped I had gotten through to them.

Aahz looked so pleased with himself that he went easy on them through the last few questions. He was also mercifully brief in his closing remarks.

". . . And all I ask is that when you go to the polls tomorrow, you vote for the candidate that you know in your heart has the will and talent to take Bokromi forward into a glorious destiny! Thank you."

Emo and Wilmer made their final speeches, but I could tell that the heart had gone out of them. They had been counting on Aahz overreacting and showing his true colors to the crowd, but it had backfired on them.

They retired from their lecterns to the bosom of their campaign committees. Carnelia ministered to both of them with tea and sandwiches. Shomi buzzed around Aahz like a bee, humming with delight. The result was a foregone conclusion. They all knew it.

At last, Bunny looked up from her tally sheet.

"It is my pleasure to name the winner of this debate. The winner is . . . Aahz."

Aahz raised his joined hands over his head in a victory pose. "Thank you! I look forward to being your next governor!"

"That's all, folks," Bunny said. "We're done here."

"Hold on!" Orlow said. He walked up, his hand in the air. "My client has an announcement to make."

"Both of our clients do," Carnelia corrected him, coming up beside him.

"That's right," Orlow agreed.

Wilmer stepped forward, his coat restored to shimmering whiteness. He held out a hand to Emo, who came forward and took it.

"Friends, after a great deal of discussion and thought, the Wisdom and Friendship Parties—"

"Friendship and Wisdom," Emo put in.

"—have decided to join forces. It would seem that we do indeed lack the talents that the other possesses. Therefore, we are becoming one party, in defense against a common enemy—I mean, honorable opponent."

"What?" Shomi shouted. "You can't change parties the night before the election!"

"Sure they can," Aahz said.

"Really?" Bunny asked. "You don't mind?"

"No problem," Aahz said. "I expected something like that." He grinned at the audience, who were hanging on his every word. "It won't make any difference, will it?"

CHAPTER THIRTY-NINE

"The trouble with a win-win situation is that the other guy wins, too."

—W. GATES

For the rest of the day, Wilmer and Emo were the talk of the town. They went everywhere together, deferring to one another like a newly engaged couple. They were so chummy that it made me feel a little sick. Bunny and I fled back to our office and closed the door. Unfortunately, not before one intrepid reporter slipped inside.

"What do you think of this development, Skeeve?" Ecstra asked, brandishing her notebook at me.

"Off the record?" I asked wearily. I had poured my one drink for the day. I felt I deserved it.

She looked at me, surprised, but put her pencil away. "Sure."

"I don't think it'll help. The polls in every paper show both of them so far behind that even their combined votes are fewer than half of Aahz's."

"That's what I thought. We've got the front page for the day after tomorrow ready to go—two of them." She straightened her jaunty hat. "Well, I've got to go get quotes from someone who *will* speak on the record. See you on Voting Day! I'm going to be taking exit polls!"

Security was tight around the voting booths arranged in long rows in the town square. A line of voters led down the street and looped back and forth on itself five times. I had dozens of volunteers working in pairs to guide voters in and give them ballots, then show them out the other side, where Bunny and I were waiting with dozens of newspaper reporters. Guido and Nunzio patrolled the perimeter to make sure there was no electioneering within fifty paces. Shomitamoni had had her minions out before dawn planting *Vote for Aahz* signs in the grass around the gazebo. I had to brave her screaming protest to get them pulled up again. Orlow had sent Pixies flying overhead with *Friendship and Wisdom* banners and pretended innocence when I complained. Bunny sent Gleep to stop Carnelia from sidling up to voters waiting their turn and chatting with them. The Tipp female kept up her protests all the way out of the square.

"I swear I am not trying to make anyone do anything against their will!"

"Gleep!" my dragon said, pushing her with his head any time she hesitated.

"One more day," I muttered to myself, and I'd never have to listen to her or any of the other campaign managers again. I busied myself with my clipboard and tried not to hear their voices receding in the distance.

"How's it goin', boss?" Guido asked, coming up beside me.

"Not at all what I expected," I said. I heard a clink in the enforcer's pocket. I gave him a curious look. With a glance around to make sure no one saw, he pulled the flap of his neatly pressed suit jacket aside to show me a bandolier of quarrels for his miniature crossbow. "Guido, I doubt you're going to need any of that!"

"Can't be too careful, boss," Guido said. "So, what's the beef?"

"No beef," I said. "Excuse me, ma'am?" I stopped a Tipp matron in a flowered dress as she left the cordoned enclosure. "May I ask whom you voted for?"

She smiled at me. "I voted for Wilmer Weavil-Scuttil."

"Really?" I asked, ticking off another mark in the Wisdom-Friendship column. "You voted for Wilmer? May I ask why?"

"He's so dignified. I think he'll make a great governor."

That was the opinion of the great majority of the voters leaving the polls. I stopped a male whom I knew had been one of Aahz's volunteers.

"What about you, sir?"

"I want Emo Weavil as lieutenant governor. He's great. A really decent guy."

"What about Aahz?"

The male shrugged. "Well, he's fun, but boy, he got nasty, didn't he? I kinda prefer someone who's gonna treat his opponents with respect. And that Wilmer guy, he knows stuff."

The next woman in line agreed with him. "They have it all! Wisdom and charisma!"

So did the teenager coming out humming one of Sid the She's haunting melodies.

"Mr. Aahz is a smart guy, but compared with Emo, he seems . . . well, crude. I don't want to use the *P* word."

"You mean *Pervect*?" I asked, my face innocent.

"Uh, yeah," the youth said, hurrying away.

It was the same throughout the entire afternoon. When the polls closed, my informal inquiry showed that the combined Emo-Wilmer party had gained about seventy percent of the votes, compared with ten percent undecided and twenty percent for Aahz. I was shocked.

"Funny how no one remembers how Wilmer and Emo treated each other before Aahz arrived, isn't it?" Bunny asked.

"I know," I said. "I guess it's true that people remember the last thing they heard."

Rumors of the outcome spread long before the Gnomes from Zoorik retired with the ballots to make the final count.

The square filled with Tipps whispering to one another. When the candidates arrived, the crowd broke into applause and cheers. Aahz climbed the stairs into the gazebo and waved to the wedge of yellow-wearing Tipps, but they were far fewer in number than they had been the day before. Shomi tried whipping them into louder cheers, but they were vastly outnumbered by the Tipps wearing ribbons of purple and green twisted together. Wilmer and Emo took the stage together to deafening acclaim.

I felt a poke in the ribs. Bunny and I looked down to see a pair of large-nosed fellows with blue skin and ruffled ears who stood no higher than my waist, Hass and Gotz, the accountants. Gotz held a tightly rolled scroll.

"Ve haf it," Hass said, peering at me over green-rimmed glasses. "Do you vish to see the numbers?"

"Bring it up to the stage," she said. "I don't want any accusations of tampering."

"Hah!" Gotz said. "Our papers iss tamperproof."

Every eye was on us as Bunny broke the seal on the parchment and unrolled it.

"In the race for governor of the island of Bokromi in the dimension of Tipicanoo, the Wisdom-Friendship Party, eighty-seven percent; the A Plague on Both Your Houses Party, thirteen percent. These results are certified by the firm of Hass and Gotz of Zoorik." Bunny waved a hand toward the Gnomes. "That's it. Wilmer and Emo are the winners!"

Orlow thrust his hand out, and Emo took it, grinning widely enough to swallow his ears. Carnelia hugged Wilmer, who patted her on the shoulder. Behind them, the two wives hugged one another. Confetti fell from the skies, and the Pixies on the roof lit off a deafening firework display.

Cheers echoed from one side of the town square to the other. The Tipps, now governor-elect and lieutenant governor–elect, were mobbed by reporters from all fifteen papers. The crowd rushed past us.

At the side of the gazebo, Aahz was standing alone. I touched

Bunny's arm to show her where I was going, and went over to him. He glared at me.

"Gee, I'm sorry, Aahz," I said.

"I don't need your pity!" he snarled.

I didn't back away.

"I'm not pitying you," I said. "You taught me you don't get everything you go for. No one went broke. No one got killed. If you really wanted it, I'm just sorry you didn't get it."

"I'll live, kid," Aahz growled.

Shomitamoni came over and slapped Aahz on the back. She stuck out her tiny hand.

"Aahz, it's been a stitch. Call me again if you are ever *serious* about running for office."

"Thanks, Shomi," he said, shaking it. "Send me your bill."

"Don't worry, I will." She turned to me, took both my hands in hers, and bowed deeply. "And you, Skeeve the Magnificent, don't ever go into politics. It's not your scene. Now, that Miss Bunny, *she* would be a great candidate. She has a knack for running things."

"Uh, thanks," I said. With a wink, Shomi folded her hands into her voluminous sleeves and vanished. I turned to Aahz. He looked a little sheepish. I became suspicious.

"Didn't you want to be governor?" I asked him.

Aahz gave a casual shrug. "Nah. Public service isn't for me. I prefer the private sector. The salaries are higher and the perks are a lot better. I did it for the team. You were stuck. I was just there to help. It didn't cost me anything, and I had fun. People making a fuss of me. Parties every night. Pretty girls. Endless booze." At last, a twinkle appeared in his eye. "Who doesn't like a little attention?"

I had to gather my wits.

"You mean, you entered so you could lose deliberately?"

"If they'd voted for me, I would have served," he said, "but I stacked the deck pretty heavily so I'd lose."

"I'll say," I said, thinking back on his intense campaign.

"You made fools of the other candidates, you bent the rules, you bribed officials and were openly corrupt in public."

Aahz waved a hand. "I had to force Emo and Wilmer to work together. Otherwise, they were splitting the vote. I would have gotten in by default."

I studied him in disbelief. "You did all that on purpose? Why?"

"What the heck," he said, slapping me on the back. "We're a team, aren't we? You needed my help."

My gratitude was heartfelt, and so was my relief.

"Thanks, Aahz," I said.

"No problem, kid. Come on." He let out a theatrical sigh. "I suppose I have to let the winners think they pulled one over on me."

Aahz made his concession speech in record time, for him—about half an hour. The candidates accepted his concession gracefully, and the election was certified and entered in the island's archives.

My delight at having Aahz not elected was only a fraction of the joy shared by the candidates who were. Then Bunny and I went over to congratulate them. We shook hands, and their wives kissed us. Orlow and Carnelia couldn't stop grinning.

"Are you satisfied?" I asked Emo. "I mean, you hired us to get you elected."

"No," Emo said, looking happy. "I asked you to run a *fair* election. I did mean it. I believe that this was the fairest of them all, to coin a phrase."

"I can't believe that it's over," Bolla said, hanging on his arm. "And I am so glad! I can get rid of all those dowdy dresses!"

"Well, send us your bill," Wilmer said. "We'll pay it, and gladly. We both signed contracts with Tolomi, and we're getting a piece of the publishing contract, so we're looking at a little extra income. Not a bad day's work, I'd say!"

"How about you two?" I asked Orlow. "Will you keep managing campaigns in Bokromi?"

"I doubt it," Carnelia said, with a fond smile at her opposite

number. "We're not thinking too far ahead just now. We've
got a little announcement of our own."

Orlow cleared his throat. I noticed that he had a firm grip
on Carnelia's hand.

"I asked the lady to marry me, and she accepted," he said.
"We're going to work together from now on. After we come back
from our honeymoon, we're going to get into a simpler line of
work, like managing professional sports teams."

"No more politics, ever again," Bunny promised us, as we
gathered in our small office to go back to Deva.

"You don't have to prove yourself to us that badly," Aahz said.
"We already acknowledged you as president of M.Y.T.H., Inc."

"Yeah," Guido agreed. "You're the boss, boss." Nunzio
nodded.

"Gleep!" said my dragon.

"Maybe you just needed to prove it to yourself," I said.

Bunny gave us all a quizzical look. "Maybe that's what I
was doing. Thanks."

"No problem," Aahz said. "By the way, here." He handed
Bunny a huge stack of small slips of paper. "My expenses for
this job. Put it on their bill."

Bunny thumbed through the papers. "Marching band,
transportation for the parade from Satchmo, even the bill for
the townhouse. You want us to make them pay for your *house*?
How can we do that?"

Aahz waved a hand. "They've got plenty of money in their
war chests. They can handle it. Without me, neither one of them
would have been elected for maybe another five years."

"I think he's right, Bunny," I said, whipping up my spell.
"Believe me, for not having Aahz as their governor, it's a small
price to pay. And you can quote me on that."

ROBERT LYNN ASPRIN

Robert (Lynn) Asprin, born in 1946, is best known for the Myth Adventures and Phule series. He also edited the groundbreaking Thieves' World anthologies with Lynn Abbey. He died at his home in New Orleans in May 2008.

JODY LYNN NYE

Jody Lynn Nye lists her main career activity as "spoiling cats." She has published forty-two books, including *Advanced Mythology*, fourth in her Mythology fantasy series (no relation); six science fiction novels; and four novels in collaboration with Anne McCaffrey, including *The Ship Who Won*. She has also edited a humorous anthology about mothers, *Don't Forget Your Spacesuit, Dear*, and published more than a hundred and ten short stories. Her latest books are *Dragons Deal*, third in the series begun by Robert Asprin, and *View from the Imperium*, first in the Thomas Kinago series. She lives northwest of Chicago with her husband, author and packager Bill Fawcett, and their cat, Jeremy. Visit her on the Web at www.sff.net/people/jodynye.